BAILEIGH HIGGINS

Last Another Day

Book 1 Dangerous Days

First edition

This book was professionally typeset on Reedsy.
Find out more at reedsy.com

Contents

Acknowledgments

Many thanks to my family and friends for their tireless support and dedication to me during good times and bad. Also, a quick shout-out to Angie from Pro_ebookcovers for the lovely book covers she designed for this series.

I love and appreciate you all!

Dedication

Special dedication to my mother, Linda. I know you would have been proud of me, Mom. Wish you were here, and I'll always love you. Forever and ever.

Chapter 1 - Morgan

The steady thudding of his fists on the door had become a part of her. Like the beating of her heart, she relied on the sound to keep her sane. It prevented her from screaming, reminding her she was still alive. For the moment, at least.

For what seemed like an eternity, Morgan huddled in the shower. With her arms wrapped around her knees, she listened to the constant crashes interspersed with frustrated hisses. An occasional drop of cold water from the shower head dripped onto her back. She might have sat there forever if a new sound hadn't joined the first.

"No! No, no, no," she cried, jumping to her feet.

The wood was splintering around the lock at a rapid rate. It wouldn't last much longer. Raging adrenaline triggered a desperate need for survival. She scanned the small bathroom for a weapon. Her eyes landed on the shower rail.

Morgan grabbed it and shook off the curtain, ripping the plastic stoppers from the ends. She barely had time to ready herself before the door burst inwards with a shuddering crash.

Immediately, Brian was upon her, moving fast with hands outstretched and teeth bared in a vicious grin. Growls sawed through his throat, and his eyes were bloodshot and crazed. She gripped the rail and thrust it into his chest. He staggered, regained his balance and lunged again.

Morgan gasped, stumbling backward. Her mind slipped into pure terror. It was a scene from her worst nightmares. Again, she stabbed him with the pipe, but the blow skimmed off his shoulder. He grabbed her, digging his fingers into her arms with brutal strength while snapping at her face.

She pushed against his chest with the pipe held in both hands as a shield, trying to keep those teeth at a distance. He slammed her up against the wall. Pain exploded through her head as it smashed against the tiles. He had her in a death grip, bloody lips a mere breath from her face.

"What's wrong with you?" she screamed. "Please stop! It's me, Morgan."

Time slowed as she stared into his eyes, searching for a sign that he was still human, still the man she loved, but his eyes were empty. Brian was gone.

Fear and determination lent her strength. With a great shove, Morgan pushed him away, kicking him in the stomach to gain distance. She lifted the rail and used it as a spear, aiming for his throat.

The metal end tore into the soft flesh, impaling him. Clotted, black blood spurted from the wound and splashed onto her chest. She pinned him against the opposite wall and slid him around like a dog on a leash until she stood with her back to the broken bathroom door.

Her newfound strength waned. With no idea what to do, Morgan bolted. Her bare feet slapped a staccato beat on the floor, echoed by Brian's heavier tread. She slid around a corner and headed for the front door, silk pajamas billowing behind her. She slammed up against it and tore at the deadbolt with frantic fingers. With seconds to spare, she unlocked it and stumbled through, pulling the door shut as his body connected with a crash.

Morgan stumbled back on legs turned to water and stared at the peeling paint on the wood. Brian growled with anger, and she flinched as the now familiar beat of his fists filled the air. However, the bathroom door had been locked while the front door was not. The seconds ticked by as she waited.

Waited for him to open the door.

Waited for him to find another way out.

Waited for death.

Her husband had turned into a monster, and nothing made sense anymore. After a while, however, it became evident he didn't know how to turn the knob. Nor did he have the intelligence left to look for another way out.

In the fresh air, Morgan fought to gain control of her body. Her heartbeat slowed, and she noticed her surroundings for the first time. Standing there on the front patio in her pajamas, she shivered and folded her arms across her body. *What the hell is going on? What happened to Brian?*

Until today, Morgan would never have believed him capable of harm. With searching fingers, she touched the marks his hands had left. It hurt, the flesh bruised. The back of her head was tender and swollen.

Morgan turned and stared out into the street. It was chaos. The whole neighborhood was going to hell. She stumbled across the lawn to get a closer look. Were there more people as sick as her husband? Was this a disease? Something that drove them crazy? It was the only explanation her frozen mind would accept.

Whatever it was, it was spreading with the ferocity of wildfire. A car sped around the corner, tires screeching. The driver never spared her a glance, and she was too numb to care.

To her left, a trio of sick people cornered a woman and ripped away at her flesh. The agonizing screams tore at Morgan's heart before they were abruptly cut off. More bodies lay scattered around on the immaculate green lawns of their front yards.

A corpse stirred and rose to its feet. A man. He stood there, strips of flesh hanging off of limbs covered in blood. His intestines dragged on the ground as he staggered around. Morgan reeled, vertigo making her sway. *It can't be. He can't still be alive!*

Dogs barked at the monsters that used to be their owners until they too died in a welter of howls. Wincing at the distressing sounds, she realized anything and everything that moved would fall victim to these things. Further up the street, shots rang out. Through her fence, she glimpsed a man herding his family into a car.

Morgan knew she should move, but her limbs remained frozen to the spot until something caught her eye. One of the walking dead clawed at the palisades bordering her lawn. It rasped through a ruined throat and reached out a bloody hand as if in supplication. Behind it, two more had noticed and followed. *I'm being surrounded!*

This thought galvanized Morgan into action, and she sprinted around the house to the backyard. Brian's truck was the only realistic means of escape. She ran to it and reached for the handle, crying out in frustration when she realized it was locked.

"Shit, where are the keys?" They hung on a board in the kitchen. "I can't go back in there."

She had no choice, though. Maybe if she moved fast enough,

she could grab them and get out while Brian still hammered on the front door. Luckily, the back door was unlocked owing to her clandestine smoking habits. She had snuck out for a quick cigarette that morning while he still slept.

Before her nerves could fail, she rushed into the kitchen and ran to the board, searching for the keys. From the front of the house, she heard Brian's growls pause before they resumed in heightened pitch as they headed her way.

Morgan ran trembling fingertips over the keys, and heart hammered in her chest until she found the right ones. Grabbing them, she turned to run but fumbled her grip. They clattered to the floor.

"Fuck," she cried, scrambling around on all fours.

The slap of Brian's feet on the kitchen tiles caused her heart to stutter. She snatched up the keys and lunged outside. A brief glimpse of his pale, inhuman visage tore at her as she shut the door in his face. Morgan crumpled to her knees with a cry. "I can't do this. I can't."

She reached up and laid a hand on the wood. It shivered beneath her palm from the force of his blows. "Brian, please come back. What am I supposed to do now?"

She was ready to give up and slumped down, but a voice from within nagged at her. *Get up. Run.*

"I can't," she whispered.

Do it. You can't give up now. What about your family? Your friends?

"Oh, my God. Mom. Dad."

Morgan bolted for the truck, barely noticing the gravel cutting into her bare feet. She pushed the remote button to unlock it and jumped in. After a deep breath, she turned the key in the ignition and shifted into gear.

At the gate, a mob of infected had gathered. They clawed through the gaps with creepy yearning. She hesitated. They were people, after all, but they also blocked the exit. This left her no choice. She had to go through.

"Here goes," she said and pushed the remote button.

The gate opened, and they flooded inside, swamping the car. They beat on the windows and climbed onto the hood, crawling over each other like insects. She shuddered in disgust as one licked the window next to her face, leaving a smear of bloody spittle behind. For once, she was grateful she'd never gotten to know her neighbors.

When the gate was finally open, she floored the gas and roared through, biting her lower lip when she ran over a few of them. The metallic taste of blood filled her mouth.

A glance at the clock read twenty past eleven. She'd hidden in the shower for far too long. For all she knew, her parents, her sister, everyone she loved, could be one of those *things*. "I'm coming. Please be okay. I need you to be okay."

The trip through town gave her a clear view of the chaos breaking out everywhere. It was horrific. People tried to escape, loading possessions, kids, and pets into cars. Most didn't make it. Infected swarmed through the neighborhoods and descended on the healthy with rabid hunger. They left the dead in their wake, only to have them rise minutes later to join the hunt. Screams rang through the air and confronted her at every turn.

A young mother ran out of her house, dragging a little boy by the arm. She spotted Morgan and rushed out into the street. "Help us! Please, help!"

Behind her, a man burst through the door and sprinted towards them. Morgan slammed on the brakes and leaned over to unlock the passenger door. "Get in. Hurry!"

The woman ran towards her, feet slapping on the tar road as she closed the distance. The child cried, his mother half-carrying and half-dragging him. Morgan stared at the unfolding scene, and her heart sank when she realized the truth. "They're not going to make it."

The infected man reached them and latched onto the boy first, ripping him out of his mother's hands.

"No," the woman cried, stumbling to a halt. "He's your son."

He ignored her and buried his face in the boy's neck. Blood, bright red and arterial, spurted through the air. The woman screamed, her desperate wails stabbing into Morgan's heart.

She wanted to close her eyes, wanted to look away, but couldn't. Instead, she watched as the woman grappled with the man that used to be her husband, fighting for the life of her child. It was no use.

Like a rag doll, the boy was tossed aside to bleed out on the asphalt. His eyes glazed over in death while his mother was savaged beside him.

The spell broke, and at last, Morgan looked away. She leaned over and locked the passenger door, the click loud in her ears. With an iron grip on the wheel, she steered the truck around the family and drove away. The entire time, she whispered, "I'm sorry, I'm sorry, I'm sorry," until the words were branded into her psyche. That was the last stop she made.

Morgan headed for the suburb where her parents lived. It lay on the edge of town. If they were lucky, the infection hadn't reached there yet. As she drove, the streets became quieter, and her hope grew apace. A hope dashed once she reached her destination.

A knot of a dozen infected crawled on the front lawn of a neighbor's house. They were feeding. As the group shifted, a bloody arm flopped out. Morgan swallowed as a flood of bile pushed up her throat. She recognized the next-door neighbors, the Robertson's, in the pack. Mrs. Robertson still wore a robe with curlers in her hair which prompted a hysterical laugh from Morgan, one she quickly swallowed.

There was no time for weakness now. Not with her parents and little sister waiting, possibly alive. It was a hope she couldn't let go of just yet. Morgan stared at the infected and tried to come up with a plan. There was no way she could run past them. Barefoot and unarmed, they'd pull her down and rip her to shreds. However, she sat inside a solid mass of driven metal.

She rammed into the front runners with a crunch. Bodies bounced off the hood while others disappeared beneath the wheels. The truck plowed through them effortlessly, up onto the lawn into the knot. She shifted into reverse and rolled back, clipping a straggler to the left, then she repeated the whole procedure again, and again.

It was sickening, but a small part of her felt pride at overcoming such an obstacle. The rest of her was horrified at the slaughter of innocents, no matter how dangerous they might be.

Afterward, she sat, staring at the carnage. It brought to mind a medieval battlefield with torn and crushed body parts strewn about. A few still tried to move despite their gruesome injuries. That single horrific detail confirmed one crucial fact—they were neither sick nor crazy. They were dead. *Zombies.*

Morgan reversed into the driveway with the nose pointed

towards the gate for a quick escape. She unlocked the doors and left the keys in the ignition. Behind the seats, she found a tire iron.

With one last look around, she slid out of the truck and closed the door with a soft click. She felt vulnerable, standing there in the open air while imagining what those things could do to her exposed flesh.

With a deep breath for courage, Morgan gripped the tire iron and walked up the driveway. She ignored the few broken corpses that groaned as she passed. They were no threat to her anymore.

The concrete felt cold and rough beneath her feet, grounding her in the present. She tested the front door and found it locked. With a muttered curse, she walked around to the back. Her nerves jangled. She kept hearing sinister sounds behind her, and only the thought of her family kept her going.

Morgan turned a corner and screamed as she spotted the remains of her parents' domestic worker. The woman was barely recognizable. Bloodstained bandages covered her arms, but the cause of death was apparent: A gunshot to the head.

Hope for her family's safety faded as she stepped around the body. The back door stood open, and she inched forward to peer inside the kitchen. Her eyes flew to puddles of blood on the floor. The drops formed a trail into the hallway and bedrooms.

She crossed the kitchen and dared a peek into the hall, then the living and dining rooms. Nothing. It was empty. No signs of a struggle. No sign of her family, either.

Morgan swallowed, her mouth dry, and moved onward. The silence was eerie. A subtle threat hung in the air. She quailed at the thought of being confronted by the sight of her parents turned into monsters, or even worse, her baby sister.

The passage promised terror with sticky patches of smeared blood that led past Meghan's bedroom. Inside, everything was just as she remembered. The stuffed animals on the bed and posters of ponies on the walls made her heart flutter. "Please, God. Let her be okay."

After that came the spare bedroom and the hallway bathroom. Both were closed, and she crept past on silent feet. The main bedroom beckoned—a yawning gateway to a mysterious horror. With a growing sense of dread, she moved through the doorway.

Morgan stopped abruptly, one hand flying to her mouth. On the bed lay her father, stretched out on his back. He was torn up, and she guessed he was attacked. Blood pooled beneath his body and stained the duvet cover.

She stared, unable to utter a word. First her husband and now her father. How many more people would she lose today? Tears pricked at the corners of her eyes, and her knees threatened to buckle. *Why? Why did this happen?*

A part of her remained alert, though, and after a moment, she dragged a hand across her eyes. No more tears. She needed to find her mother and Meghan. Before it was too late.

Morgan was about to leave when the smallest of sounds echoed from behind her. The hair on the back of her neck rose. She whirled around, swinging up the tire iron.

Chapter 2 - Julianne

At the age of forty-eight, Julianne should have had a quiet and restful Sunday to look forward to, but since she'd welcomed a late little lamb into the family fold, that was a foregone luxury. Sure enough, the sun had barely come up when little Meghan jumped onto the bed with her dog, Princess.

"Morning, Mommy," she cried, giggling as she rocked back and forth.

Julianne lay still and waited until Meghan got close. With a mock roar, she pounced on her daughter and yelled, "Watch out for the Tickle Monster!"

Meghan shrieked with delight, and pandemonium broke out. They rolled around, joined by Princess who let loose a barrage of ear-splitting yaps. Next to them, John groaned and crushed the pillow over his head. Princess took up the challenge and tried to dig him out, much to his chagrin.

Since sleep was out of the question, Julianne got up to shower and dress instead. She brushed her hair back into a ponytail and frowned at the fine lines adorning her eyes, smoothing anti-wrinkle cream onto the delicate skin.

"You're still as lovely as ever, sweetheart. Stop frowning; you're just making it worse," John said, emerging from the steaming shower cubicle. He smacked her on the bum and laughed when she shrieked.

An hour later, after a breakfast of eggs, bacon, and coffee, John headed outside to the garage to tinker with his latest project. With Meghan ensconced in front of the TV to watch her favorite shows, Julianne tidied up the house and fed Princess.

She watched in amusement as the little Jack Russel wolfed down its food then ran back to Meghan, licking her face. The little girl collapsed in a fit of laughter, and for the next few minutes, the two went at it. *Princess Sophia. What a ridiculous name for a dog. But that's what you get when you leave it to an eight-year-old to name a pet.*

Julianne supposed she shouldn't be so hard on Princess. She was only a puppy, after all. An excellent playmate for Meghan even though she was as naughty as hell.

Thoughts of the busy week ahead distracted her, and she decided to finish up the ironing. Meghan went through clothes at the rate only kids were capable of doing. With her around, Julianne was forever busy with piles of laundry.

She was on her way to the washroom when she heard John scream. The agony in his voice kept her frozen for a second before her protective instinct thawed out her muscles. She darted for the door.

Julianne stopped short when she saw John struggling on the lawn with their maid, Sarah. The woman was off on weekends but stayed in a flat at the back of the property.

"Sarah?" she cried. "What are you doing?"

She stared in disbelief as Sarah snapped at John with her teeth much like a rabid dog, making odd clicking sounds. Blood stained his front, dripping from his arms, and Julianne realized this was no joke. He tried to fend her off, but the woman kept attacking with insane fury.

12

"John!" she cried as Sarah bit down again and tore a chunk of flesh from his forearm. "No!"

A girlish scream scared her out of her wits, and she looked down to see Meghan standing next to her with her eyes fixed on the scene. "Daddy!"

Next to Meghan, Princess Sophia barked, her small body quivering with excitement. Sarah's head snapped towards them. Baring bloodied incisors, she growled. She abandoned John and sprinted across the lawn, a terrifying caricature of a human being.

Julianne shoved Meghan behind her, prepared to fight for her daughter. Before she could act, though, John tackled Sarah from behind, pinning her to the ground. "Run, Julianne. Phone the police!"

Julianne paused, torn between her child and her husband, before reacting. She snatched Meghan into her arms and ran to the house, driven ahead by the sounds of the struggle behind her. Princess followed, claws skittering on the concrete. Julianne slammed the door shut and raced to the bathroom.

Inside, she put Meghan down and shoved Princess into her arms. "Stay here, and keep quiet. I'll be right back, but first, I have to help Daddy, okay? Do you understand?"

When the little girl nodded, she rushed outside and closed the door behind her. Julianne staggered to the bedroom and scrambled for the keys to the safe. Every second counted. She struggled with the lock until the safe opened with a click then pulled out her gun, a small .38 Rossi John had bought her years ago. After checking it was loaded, she ran outside, her breath thin and ragged.

John and Sarah rolled on the ground, grappling for dominance. John was weakening as blood streamed from his many wounds. At the sight of Julianne hope kindled in his eyes, and he lost concentration. Taking full advantage of his distraction, Sarah clamped down on his exposed throat and shook her head like a beast.

John screamed, and blood spurted from the wound. Julianne aimed for Sarah's head. The pistol kicked as the shot rang out. At such short range, she couldn't miss. The woman slumped, drained of life. She lay with her limbs splayed, and Julianne had the fleeting thought that she looked like a rag doll, flung down by a giant's hand onto the concrete.

Her husband moaned in pain; his hands were clamped around his neck as red liquid oozed out between the web of his fingers. There was more blood than she'd ever seen before in her life. "Oh, my God."

Julianne grabbed him by the arm and lifted him off the ground. Staggering beneath his weight, she helped him to the bedroom where she tried to staunch the bleeding with towels. "Just hold on, John. Don't give up. I'm calling an ambulance."

She snatched her cell, and with trembling fingers dialed emergency services only to be met by busy tones. "What's going on?"

Trading her cell for the house phone, she punched in the numbers, hands shaking. This time, she got a dialing tone, but calling for help proved pointless. A harassed operator responded to her pleas with vague promises. "Ma'am, we will send an ambulance as soon as we can, but we currently have no units available to respond."

"What? That's crazy. My husband is dying!"

"Ma'am, I'm sorry but—" The line died.

"Damn it." She rushed back to the bedroom, determined to

take John to the emergency room herself. All such thoughts drained away when she returned to him. He lay still, eyes closed, his features slack. For a moment, she stood still, fighting against the knowledge that welled up inside her mind. He was dead.

Julianne couldn't recall a time without him, the faint memories of her childhood obscured by the life he'd given her. Now snatched away by a crazy person. Anger blossomed in her chest, only to be replaced by sorrow. "Oh, John. What did she do to you?"

For a moment, she wanted to collapse, to wail in grief and despair, but the thought of Meghan sustained her. She closed his eyes and kissed him on the forehead.

With what felt like unnatural calm, she walked toward the bathroom, but sounds from outside drew her attention. She opened the front door and stared out into the street. Two people ran past, terror glued to their faces as several more gave chase. The pursuers looked like Sarah had. Crazy. The two runners had only a small lead. One, a senior man, was far slower than the other and ran with a pronounced limp.

It didn't take long for the crazed people to overtake the straggler. He went down with a weak cry. She looked on, sickened, as he disappeared beneath a heaving mass of bodies.

Julianne had no illusions about trying to help. There were far more of them than she had bullets for, and she had Meghan to think of too. She closed the front door and locked it before closing all the curtains and switching off the TV.

Without a sound, she went to the bathroom and slipped inside, closing the door behind her. At the sight of Meghan's frightened face, her calm deserted her, and tears welled up unbidden.

Meghan looked from her mother's pale and tearful face to the blood stains on her clothes. Her face crumpled, and she blubbered something about her Daddy.

Julianne gathered her into her arms and squeezed her tightly. "Come here, baby. It's okay. It'll be all right."

She whispered meaningless words into Meghan's ear and sang old lullabies, rocking back and forth. Princess crawled onto her lap, whining, and they sat like that, seeking comfort from each other's arms.

***

The sound of an intruder roused Julianne from her cocoon of grief. She whispered to Meghan to be quiet. Getting up, she pulled the gun from the back of her jeans. She opened the door and gasped in shock. Morgan, her middle daughter, stood holding a tire iron in the air as if she was about to bash in her skull.

"Morgan!" she said.

They stared at each other for a second. A mixture of relief and joy flooded Julianne's veins. Her eyes fell on the large blood stain on the front of Morgan's pajamas. Alarmed, she said. "Are you hurt?"

Confused, Morgan stared down at her clothes. "Huh? Oh, no, it's not mine."

Julianne lowered her gun and started towards her daughter, a happy smile on her face, but from the bed rose a bloody specter of death. *John.*

He looked different, wild and crazed. With his eyes fixed on Morgan's unprotected back, he charged with arms outstretched. Before Julianne could process what was happening, she raised the gun and aimed it at his head.

At the outer edge of her consciousness, she was shocked by her actions, but her hands were steady as she squeezed the trigger. Three steps from his daughter's back, John's head snapped back, and he collapsed in a heap on the carpet. Her need to protect her child had won out over her love for her husband.

For a second, nobody moved, nobody even breathed. The gunshot faded away, leaving a gaping emptiness. Julianne broke the silence first by grabbing Morgan and hugging her with fierce intensity. "Are you okay?"

Morgan nodded, her eyes as large as saucers.

"Are you sure?"

"I'm all right." Morgan turned back to look at the body on the floor. "But Dad..."

"I don't know what's going on," Julianne cried. "What's happening? Do you know?"

Morgan shook her head, unable to reply.

Julianne rushed into the bathroom and gathered Meghan into her arms. With one hand shielding the child's eyes, she said, "Morgan. I hate to ask this, but we can't let her see him. Please..."

Morgan blinked, shifting her eyes from Julianne to her father's corpse. "Okay...I'll...I'll do it."

While Morgan wrapped up the body in a sheet and dragged it outside, Julianne took the time to calm herself and Meghan down. She settled the little girl in her room once she stopped crying and put on her favorite movie. Afterward, she headed to the kitchen and made two strong coffees laced with whiskey.

"What happened to Brian?" she asked once Morgan returned. "Where is he?"

"He went out last night to buy bread at the shop. When he came back, he said some crazy guy had attacked him and bit him on the arm."

Morgan shook her head, tears welling up. "I did what I could, cleaned the bite, bandaged it, but I never expected…" A sob escaped her lips. "I should have taken him to the hospital."

Julianne pulled her daughter into her arms, smoothing a hand over her hair. "It's okay, sweetie. You didn't know. It's not your fault."

Once Morgan stopped shaking, she carried on. "During the night, he became ill, complained of a headache. He developed a fever."

Morgan paced back and forth, her face anguished. "I wanted him to go to the emergency room, but he refused. Said he didn't want to ruin my night. My night!" She laughed brokenly. "The next morning he attacked me out of the blue. I managed to lock myself in the bathroom at first, but he broke in." Morgan told her mother how she'd escaped, and what she'd seen since. "So, here we are."

"Sarah was attacked by someone at a taxi rank. He bit her too. I treated the wounds, but this morning she changed. I can't explain it."

Morgan winced. "It's more than that. I've seen people rise from the dead."

"That's impossible," Julianne said.

"Maybe, but you saw what Dad did."

"I don't know what I saw."

"He was dead, mom. They die from their injuries and rise again as monsters."

"Don't you think we'd have been told if dead people were

walking around eating other people?"

"Would we? Can you imagine the panic? Besides, who'd believe it? Zombies?"

With trepidation, they switched on the television. Reports from all over the country of extreme violence and cannibalism perpetrated by infected individuals flooded the channels. Things were worse overseas where the virus had broken out days before.

A desperate effort seemed to be underway in their own home, South Africa, with the army being deployed to all the principal cities. The word "zombie" was bandied about, but at this stage, the official name was infected. Nobody was willing to admit that actual corpses were killing people.

How could this happen? Why didn't they warn us? Julianne wondered.

It felt surreal to sit and watch the world burn. They had already lost loved ones. Millions more were dead or dying. What were the odds of them surviving? Two women and a little girl?

"Well, we can't stay here. The streets are overrun with those things," Morgan said.

"Where would we go?"

"I don't know. Somewhere outside of town. A guest house or a farm, maybe?"

With the decision to leave made, they attempted to call the rest of their family and friends. It was no use.

They even tried contacting Morgan's younger brother, Max. He was stationed in Upington with the military, but they couldn't reach him and left a note stuck to the fridge, instead.

Julianne's eldest daughter Lilian lived in Johannesburg with her husband and two children. Although Julianne said nothing to Morgan, she feared for them, living as they did in the center of a metropolitan city. *I can only imagine what the cities must look like.*

She dressed Meghan in jeans, t-shirt, and tackies, tying her hair back in a ponytail. Small and delicate with blue-gray eyes and blond hair that curled, she took after her mother. *Lillian took after me too.*

A knot formed in her throat which she swallowed with difficulty. Taking out a pink backpack, she stuffed it with Meghan's favorite toys and handed it to the little girl. "Be brave, sweetheart. No more tears."

"Okay."

After kissing the top of Meghan's head, Julianne got up and continued. She packed as many clothes as possible, focusing on the practical and sturdy. Towels and toiletries filled another bag, and she dusted off her old first aid kit, filling it up with all the medicine she had in the house.

Morgan posed a problem in her pajamas. Although they were both slim, Morgan was taller and more muscular. Finally, in the spare bedroom, she found old horse riding clothes of Morgan's which still fit.

Kitted out in black tights, knee-high boots, and a navy t-shirt, Morgan looked beautiful. She took after John with her thick brown locks, tanned skin, and large greenish-gold eyes. Her mouth was set in a determined line, and for once, she looked like the confident, strong woman Julianne knew her to be.

"I'm proud of you, you know? You showed a lot of guts today," she murmured.

"You think so? I don't know." Morgan shrugged and averted her eyes. "At least, you gave Dad peace. I left Brian like that.

He wouldn't have wanted that."

"Don't be too hard on yourself. You did the best you could, sweetheart."

"Maybe."

They packed food, water, batteries, flashlights, and bedding, then they loaded their supplies into the back of the truck, keeping a careful eye out for infected.

The crushed and broken bodies on the front lawn were a grotesque sight, one that convinced Julianne they were indeed zombies. Their mouths moved, and their fingers twitched even though there was almost nothing left of them. More than once, she had to stop to vomit into the bushes.

To Julianne, it felt like a part of her life was ending. Watching John die and then killing his re-animated corpse was the stuff of nightmares. She could tell Morgan was struggling too, but they both tried to hold it together for Meghan's sake.

She pulled on a pair of beige cargo pants and a white t-shirt. With her hair pulled back into a ponytail, she gazed at her reflection in the mirror. No traces of the earlier tragedy showed in her eyes which surprised her. *I should look different.*

She went to the safe and found a small holster which she attached to her belt. After reloading, she tucked away her pistol. John's 9mm and holster she handed to Morgan. At least they were better equipped to face danger now.

"Time to say goodbye," Morgan said, leading the way. John and Sarah lay side by side on the grass where she had left them, covered in sheets. The sun shone with hateful cheer while birds chirped in the branches overhead.

Julianne stared at the bodies, struck by the unfairness of it all. Tears welled up, and she let them flow, allowing herself the luxury of grief. Meghan cried as well while Princess whined at their feet. "This is so hard."

Morgan placed an arm around her shoulders and squeezed. "I'm sorry, Mom."

"I miss him already," Julianne added. "Why did this happen? Why him?"

"I don't know."

"And Sarah...what about her family? She had children."

Morgan sighed. After a few seconds, she cleared her throat. "We've got to go now, Mom. It's not safe here."

Julianne nodded. After one last look around the house, she walked away, leaving a lifetime of memories behind. Locking the door, she tucked the key under the mat and strode along the path, brushing her fingers over the tops of the rosebushes she'd spent years cultivating. *It's only temporary.*

Silent tears trickled down her cheeks as they reversed out of the driveway. She watched her house getting smaller and smaller in the mirror until it faded from view.

Julianne navigated the outskirts of Riebeeckstad, taking in the sights of horror that met her eyes everywhere. Meghan crouched inside the footwell with Princess, trying her best to ignore the sounds outside. "Don't worry, baby. Mommy won't let anything happen to you."

Morgan suggested they drive past the homes of friends, but they saw no one they knew, neither dead nor alive. They also didn't dare stop anywhere for long. The first time they tried, a mob of infected swamped the car. They beat on the windows with their fists, growling and screeching, frantic to get to the warm, living flesh inside.

Julianne panicked and jammed her foot on the accelerator. The truck swerved toward the curb, and she slammed on the brakes. They stopped just short of a signpost. Meghan screamed shrilly while Morgan clutched at the dash, her knuckles white. "Careful, Mom!"

Julianne reversed, rolling over an infected with a sickening crunch, and raced up the street away from danger. "Let's not do that again."

Morgan bobbed her head up and down. "Agreed."

Only when they approached the house of Brian's mother did they get their first break. Brian's dad had passed away three years before, but his mother, Joanna, still lived. They inspected the yard and blew the hooter.

Much to their surprise, the curtains in the main bedroom's window swept aside, and the frightened face of Joanna peeked out. After a careful look, Morgan slid out of the car, holding her gun. She ran over, and they exchanged a hurried conversation.

"She's coming. I told her to pack a bag with the essentials," Morgan explained as she slid back into her seat. "Let's keep an eye out for danger."

"I hope she hurries," Julianne replied.

The minutes ticked by, and their impatience grew. Julianne's head swiveled, paranoia consuming her every thought. *This is too dangerous.*

Meghan whimpered in the footwell, and Princess barked for the hundredth time.

"Shut up, Princess," Julianne hissed, nerves making her short-tempered. Meghan's face crumpled. "Oh, God. I'm sorry, baby. Please, be quiet," she whispered before rounding on Morgan. "What the hell is taking her so long?"

Morgan shrugged. "No idea. She always does this. She'll be late for her own funeral one day."

"Well, this might be the day, because if the zombies don't

kill her, I will."

After what seemed an eternity, Joanna appeared around the corner dragging a colossal suitcase far too heavy for her slender arms. She was dressed in her best, done up with perfectly coiffed hair and high heels.

"Oh, for goodness sake. Does she have feathers for brains?" Morgan swore, sliding out to help. She grabbed the suitcase and an indignant Joanna, heaving both into the back of the truck. A cloud of perfume wafted into the cabin.

Out of the corner of her eye, Julianne saw an infected race across the lawn, heading straight for Morgan. The woman's mouth gaped, and fresh blood covered the front of her clothes. "Get in now!"

Morgan dove inside, and Julianne pulled out the driveway with a screech of burning rubber. This time, they didn't stop for anything.

Chapter 3 - Logan

Logan fumbled in the Land Rover's cubbyhole for his sunglasses, squinting into the glare of the rising sun. He'd been driving throughout most of the night and was worn out. A glance at the rearview mirror revealed haggard eyes and stress lines around the mouth.

In front of him, the road stretched as straight as an arrow in the monotonous tedium of the flat, dry landscape, offering nothing to distract the eye. Even this early, the sun scorched all it touched. He'd never liked the Free State and escaped from both it and his parents the moment he finished school. Now he was back.

In the distance, a man walked beside the road, carrying a military duffel bag. Logan slowed. The man was a soldier, dressed in field gear and carrying a sidearm and rifle.

He sighed. Should he pull over or not? He wasn't in the mood for company, but it couldn't be fun walking in this heat either. The Land Rover rolled to a stop, drawing level with the soldier who turned to face the open window with a look of wary caution.

"Do you need a lift?" Logan asked.

"Yeah, I could use one. Where are you headed?"

"Welkom."

"That's where I'm going too. I'm Max."

"Logan."

Max got in, and they settled into an awkward silence as Logan pulled away. Max looked to be in his late twenties, with dark blond hair and green eyes. He was big, tall with broad shoulders and an earnest, clean-cut face. *Typical soldier boy.*

Logan had been too much of a free spirit and rebel to tolerate the rigidity of the army. Instead, he'd found a job as a game ranger, spending most of his time roaming the bushveld with his rifle and a bushman tracker as his only company.

Max coughed. "Have you watched the news lately? Lots of strange stuff going on with this viral outbreak, don't you think?"

"I've seen a little, not much. It's all over the radio, though. Bullshit, if you ask me. People are panicking over nothing."

Max was silent for a while as if weighing his next words. "It's real, and it's worse than it looks on TV. A lot worse. That's why I'm headed home."

"Where'd you hear that?" Logan asked.

"I've got contacts in HQ."

"So it's not just the latest case of the flu?"

"Not by a long shot." Max shook his head. "We're in real trouble, I tell you."

Logan digested this bit of info. "And the army let you go? If things are as bad as you say, wouldn't they need you?"

"I pulled strings for a three-day leave to check on my family. After that, I'm heading back."

Logan looked at Max askance, wondering how honest he was about his 'three-day furlough.' Logan doubted the army would let him go in a time of National crisis, but it was none of his business. He made a point of not meddling in other people's affairs.

"Besides, I've got a feeling not even the army can turn the tide on this one," Max continued.

"Really?" Logan asked, his voice laced with skepticism. "What are you saying, exactly?"

"What I'm saying is, it might be too late already. This disease is extremely contagious. It kills you and brings you back to life as a cannibal."

"Brings you back to life?" Logan snorted. "That's impossible."

Max shrugged. "Believe what you want."

"You're talking zombies here."

Max nodded.

"That's crazy." Logan shot a disbelieving look at Max, noting the latter's grave expression.

"That's what everybody else thought too until it was too late. Have you even watched the news overseas?"

"I'm not much of a person for television," Logan said, wondering if he'd made a mistake picking up a stranger. The guy sounded utterly nuts. The whole story was ludicrous. Still, he *had* heard a few things on the radio, things that had bothered him enough to make this trip. *Maybe it's like the Ebola or something. A new form of rabies, perhaps.*

Max turned toward the window, leaving Logan to his thoughts, and his mind drifted back to his childhood. None of it had been pleasant, but at least, the intervening fifteen years had done much to blur the worst of it. His father was an alcoholic and a wife beater. Once Logan became old enough to take a punch, his father became a child abuser too. Logan's mother always made excuses for the man, saying they deserved it by angering him. As a young boy, Logan had believed her at first, trying ever harder to please his father.

As time passed, he came to recognize the man for what he was—a bully and a coward. Logan grew to resent his mother for failing to protect him. After school, he packed his bags and left, never looking back. Now, with reports of a mysterious disease spreading, he found himself heading back home. Why?

A sense of loyalty?

Loneliness?

He had no idea.

The small town of Bultfontein loomed in the distance. A small community, it served the farmers in the area and boasted a tiny population. Logan checked his fuel gauge, frowning when he spotted the needle heading towards empty.

The town seemed quiet, even for a Sunday. Nothing stirred when he arrived. He pulled into the nearest garage and waited for a petrol attendant, but no one appeared. It was like a ghost town. Deserted.

He glanced at Max. "This is weird."

"You're telling me."

"I'll check inside. There has to be somebody around."

Max nodded. "Be careful."

Logan got out and walked toward the shop, noting the unnatural silence that hung over the place. There was not a soul in sight, a fact that disturbed him deeply. Where was everybody?

A lone plastic bag fluttered past in the breeze, and the hair on the back of his neck prickled. He had a strong instinct for danger, honed by years spent among predators, and right now his internal alarm was going crazy. *Something is wrong. Could the soldier boy be right, after all?*

With his eyes peeled for trouble, he continued to the tiny

store. They needed fuel, or they wouldn't get much further. He peered through the glass into the dim interior. It was empty. Placing a hand on the handle, he pushed. The door creaked open.

Logan paused, listening. The radio was playing a love song. The woman's voice wailed in the background, grating on his nerves. The shop was deserted. The till stood open and abandoned, picked clean. On the counter, a jar of toffees had overturned, spilling its contents onto the floor.

"Looks like the place was robbed." He turned in a circle. "Hello?"

Nobody answered, the place as empty as the lot outside. Once again he wondered if there was some truth to Max's story. Surely, there should be someone around. If the place had been robbed, the police should've been there already.

On top of the counter lay one of the petrol attendant's cards. Deciding to take a chance, he picked up the card and backtracked out of the shop, leaving cash in the till. *Let's just get out of here.*

Outside, Logan shielded his eyes from the glare. Before he could take a step, an unearthly snarl sounded from beside him. He whirled and spotted an employee in uniform coming around the corner, but the man wasn't ordinary.

Fleshy pink bite marks marred the smooth, dark skin of his face, and a hole in his neck gaped obscenely. Dried blood stained his clothes, and his movements were jerky.

Logan took a step in the opposite direction, disconcerted. "What the hell happened to you?"

The attendant's head swung toward him, and his gaze locked onto Logan's. The look in his eyes reminded Logan of a rabid jackal he'd shot a few years before. Absolutely crazed

29

The employee lurched forward and tried to grab hold of Logan. He skipped backward, stumbling when a stone rolled beneath his foot. He went down on one knee and held his hands out to ward off the incoming attack. Fetid breath washed central his face. The man's fingers were like hooks, stretching out to catch him.

Suddenly, a shot rang out. The thing that used to be a man collapsed in front of Logan, half his head blown away. Logan blinked, shocked into immobility.

A spray of dark red blood stained the rough stones, and something about it drew his interest. He looked closer. It had a thick, clotted appearance which struck him as odd.

Old blood.

The blood of a dead man.

"No fucking way," he said, staring at the corpse. So Max was right after all. The sound of Max's voice calling to him pulled him out of his daze, and everything snapped back into focus.

"Move your ass, Logan!" Max cried. "We've got to go. They'll be drawn to the gunshot."

He jumped to his feet and raced toward the truck. Sliding the petrol card through the pump's slot, he thrust the nozzle into the tank. The air hummed as fuel pumped into the Landie.

Logan looked around, still shocked by what he'd seen. A dead man, a corpse, had just attacked him. It seemed unreal except…it was real. No use denying it.

Movement in a nearby shop window drew his gaze. A flash of white. Stumbling figures emerged from doorways and side streets, their feet carrying them toward Logan and Max. They all moved as the petrol attendant had. Jerkily and off balance.

"Shit, there's more of them," Logan said.

"I told you," Max replied in a terse tone. "Just fill the tank as fast as you can."

Logan eyed the meter, willing the numbers to move faster. He didn't want to think about what had just happened, or about what was coming their way. *Is the whole town dead?*

The meter ticked with excruciating slowness. "Come on, come on."

"Logan. We gotta go," Max warned. "Now."

A growing tide of groans reached Logan's ears, carried on the wind. A whiff of rot filled his nostrils. "It's not enough. We need more."

"Logan, there's no time." Max's R4 let loose a barrage of bullets. He'd set it to full-automatic, his arms braced against the door frame. Meaty thuds told Logan the shots found their mark.

"Almost there," he said, nervous tension causing his muscles to twitch.

"Hurry!" Max screamed. "They're coming. Get in, get in!"

Logan glanced up the street, and his stomach clenched. The stumbling figures had become a tidal wave of crazy that rolled towards them in astonishing numbers. The front-runners were fast, their attention fixed on the truck and its two occupants. "Fuck, fuck, fuck. Where did they all come from?"

He slammed the petrol cap shut, sprinted around the car and jumped in with mere seconds to spare. They roared out of the lot as bodies slammed into the Land Rover, monstrous faces obscuring the windows. They growled, screeched, and rasped until the noise rose to an ear-splitting crescendo.

Logan raced up the street, swerving to avoid stationary cars.

The Landie shook and shuddered as it powered through the throng, loud thuds echoing through the interior.

Max clutched the dash with both hands. "Shit!"

"Almost there," Logan answered, swerving to take advantage of a small gap. They shot through, one man bouncing off the bonnet to disappear from view. Blood and gore splattered the windows.

At last, the buildings thinned, and the town's population fell back. When Bultfontein and its undead were left behind, Logan let out a deep breath and slumped back in his the seat. "Man, that was close."

Max was pale, his lips pressed into a thin line. "It's spreading faster than I anticipated. We might be too late."

"I can't believe it," Logan said, shaking his head. "Real zombies."

"Told you," Max said, though he sounded anything but happy about it.

Half an hour later, Welkom showed on the horizon, its buildings beckoning to them. They decided to come up with a strategy first and got out to stretch their legs. Logan pulled two beers out of a cooler box in the back and handed one to Max.

"If the infection has reached this far, we'll be facing a horde of hostile people. We need to prepare," Max said.

While Logan watched, he reached into his duffel bag and pulled out an R4 rifle, standard issue for the army, and a tactical load-bearing vest, or 'battle jacket.' Strapping on the vest over his short-sleeved camouflage shirt, Max loaded it with magazines for the R4 and a few hand grenades.

There was space for eight magazines on each side and nine grenades in the front. That much Logan remembered from his brief stint in the army. At thirty-five rounds per magazine, Max packed quite a punch.

Logan looked into the bag and whistled. "You aiming to fight a war?"

"You never know," Max replied. He turned to Logan. "I've got extra guns and ammo for you."

"That's all right. I've got my own."

Logan scratched around in a toolbox until he found a small ax with a sturdy handle which he thrust it through his belt. From behind the seat of the truck, he removed a hunting rifle, a .308 Winchester that looked like it'd seen some use.

"I would prefer to use old trusty here. She and I go back many happy years." He smiled, running a loving hand over the oiled stock.

"Suit yourself, but at least carry a sidearm for backup." Max presented him with a 9mm Parabellum in a holster with extra cartridges. "If you get swarmed that rifle won't be of much use to you."

"Thanks," Logan slid the holster onto his belt and tucked away the spare ammo.

They climbed back into the Land Rover and took off, leaving a cloud of dust in their wake. When they reached the town, they turned onto the main road running through the heart of it.

At first, it was quiet, the double lanes empty of traffic with rows of houses flashing by on either side. Max and Logan were silent as they studied their surroundings, wary after their brush with the infected earlier that day.

A streamer of smoke warned of trouble, and Logan slowed as they approached the first crossing. It was jam-packed with cars, and the main problem was an overturned truck. Debris littered the road, and shards of glass glinted on the tar like diamonds in the sun. A bunch of infected people wandered between the numerous wrecks, their heads turning as one when they spotted the Land Rover.

"We need to get through," Max said, craning his head for a viable route.

"Piece of cake," Logan replied with more confidence than he felt.

He gripped the wheel and drove up onto the pavement beside the road. With extreme concentration, he wove between the lamp poles and signposts, jostling over dips and hollows.

Infected people streamed in from the road, seeking to surround their vehicle, but he ignored them and forged ahead. They scratched at the windows and screeched their rage, not caring when he hit them. In the rearview mirror, he saw them getting back on their feet despite broken bones and debilitating injuries. That more than anything convinced him of the truth. "They really are zombies, aren't they?"

"Who'd have believed it possible?" Max replied with a sad shake of his head. "All these people, dead. Just like that."

Logan sighed and focused on the road ahead, speeding up and leaving the zombies in their wake. He didn't get very far before a shrill scream grabbed his attention, though. He twisted in his seat. "What's that?"

Behind them, a teenage boy came tearing up the road, followed by a pack of infected. He yelled as he ran, his skinny arms and legs pumping like mad to stay ahead of the running corpses on his trail.

"What now?" Logan asked.

"We help him," Max said.

"All right." Logan stopped the truck but left the engine running. He grabbed his rifle and got out, his movements mimicked by Max.

Bracing himself against the door, he raised his rifle and sighted on the infected closest to catching the boy. He pulled the trigger, and the slug tore a hole through the zombie's chest. It fell to the ground but got back up, snarling as bloody spit drooled from its lips. *What the fuck?*

"Aim for the head!" Max shouted.

"What?"

"The head. It's the only way to kill them." A spray of bullets from the R4 proved Max's point as several infected fell, their heads exploding like overripe melons.

"Good to know," Logan shouted back, taking the next one down with a headshot. A gap opened between the infected and the boy, and he reached them unscathed and out of breath.

"Get in the back, and keep your head down," Logan cried, waiting until the boy was safe before he ducked back inside. With a screech of tires, he pulled away, forging deeper into the heart of town.

It was clear a battle had raged for its survival, a fight lost as the dead took over. Overrun police barricades and crashed anti-riot vehicles littered vital points throughout the central business district. Infected roamed the streets with few living people to be seen. Those they spotted were either barricaded inside their homes or fleeing in their cars. Columns of smoke rose from burning buildings, the fires spreading with no one to stop them.

"Where to now?" Max asked, his voice subdued.

"I need to check on my mom," Logan replied, not bothering to swerve for a zombie in pajamas. It bounced over the hood, leaving a spray of blood on the window.

He wondered why he even cared, why he'd come here in the first place. It wasn't like he missed or loved her. She'd failed him all his life, and when he left, she'd spurned his offer to escape with him. *She chose him. She always chose him.*

He left the shopping centers behind and headed for a suburban area on the edge of town. It was one of the poorer districts, the houses old and dilapidated, the streets rutted and full of holes.

Logan was ruthless, leaving a wake of destruction behind him. A black-haired girl without a jaw passed by his window as he plowed over a rose garden, leaving muddy tracks on the lawn. He clipped a sedan reversing out of its driveway, ignoring the string of expletives the driver flung at him.

A police car raced past them with sirens blaring only to collide with another oncoming vehicle. With a hard right, Logan swerved around the crash. In the mirror, he spotted a bruised and bloody officer staggering from his car before he was pulled down by two infected.

Another wreck blocked the road ahead, and once more, Logan plowed over gardens, driveways, and infected, crunching over the odd garden gnome and bird bath. A chuckle escaped his lips. It grew into a laughing fit which prompted a glare from Max. "What? Didn't you see the pink flamingo? It flew!"

Max returned his smile with reluctance before bursting into laughter as well. "Yeah, okay. That was funny. Did you see the gnome?"

Their hysterical mirth relieved the tension, but it returned full force when they reached their destination. At the sight of his old house, Logan was abruptly thrown back to his unhappy childhood. Once again he played in the dusty yard under the blazing sun. There'd be nary a breeze, and sweat would trickle down his back, staining his threadbare clothes. It was better than being inside the house, though.

On the rare occasion the ice cream truck made a pass, his mother would sneak him a bit of money behind his father's back, even though she'd get in trouble for it later. He'd race against the heat, lapping up the chocolaty goodness as it melted over his fingers before crunching into the sugar cone. Pure bliss.

Logan blinked, taken aback by the memory. He suddenly knew why he'd come back. *I still love her, my mother, despite everything. I'm here to save her...from him.*

"Ready?" Max asked.

"Yes."

"We've got to move fast. More infected will come."

"I know." Logan got out, not at all sure if he wanted to do this. He sighed, remembering his mother's haunted eyes and work-roughened hands. *What if she's one of them?*

"Let's go," he told Max before turning to the back window. "Hey, boy. Stay down and keep quiet. We won't be long."

He jogged up the garden path and stepped through the open front door, followed by Max. The familiar walls of his childhood home closed in around him, and his heart thumped in his ears. The faded carpets brought back memories of the hours his mother spent on her knees scrubbing the rough fibers because his father refused to replace them.

Everything was quiet except for a ticking clock on the wall. The furniture gleamed, the air rich with the mixed odors of wood polish and fried bacon. Logan walked through the living room and past the dining room where he spotted a half-empty plate of food on the table. The kitchen was empty, the oven still warm to the touch.

He moved toward the other side of the house, and the hair on the back of his neck prickled. He stepped into the hallway, glancing back to make sure Max was still behind him. Much as he hated to admit it, he needed the reassurance.

With careful steps, he made his way to the end, checking each room as they went. All was clean; all was as he remembered it. Nothing had changed.

They reached the bathroom, and Logan paused when he saw a trail of blood leading to his parent's bedroom. He swallowed and pointed it out to Max before rounding the corner on silent feet, with the 9mm held ready to fire.

He jerked to a stop, and his eyes fixed on his mother's kneeling form. She wore a bathrobe, pink and fluffy, now torn and stained. She was chewing on his father's intestines, her fingers digging into the open cavity with wanton abandon.

The old guy was still alive, his mouth working as his eyes rolled around in their sockets. His limbs twitched every time she pulled a piece of meat free, fresh blood gushing from his lips.

So, she got the old bastard, after all, Logan thought, the errant thought buzzing around in his brain while shock and horror held him immobile.

Max nudged him, and he looked away long enough to collect himself. He had no choice. Raising his gun, he aimed at his father's head. At the last moment, his dad saw him and reached out a trembling hand. Disturbed, his mother looked up with empty eyes before she snarled, her fingers wrapped around a rope of bulging innards.

Logan pulled the trigger...twice.

Two shots and he lost the only family he ever had.

With the gunfire ringing in his ears, he turned and stumbled outside in a daze. At Max's insistence, he handed over the keys and allowed himself to be driven. Not once did he notice his surroundings or ask where they were going. None of that mattered now.

All he could see when he closed his eyes was his mother's dead gaze, any sign of the gentle soul that once inhabited her body gone. Despite everything, he'd always loved her, and now he'd never get the chance to tell her that.

Chapter 4 - Max

As he approached the turnoff to Riebeeckstad, Max closed his window. Wind edged through a small gap at the top, and the atmosphere was stifling. Sweat pooled under his armpits, staining his uniform with salty patches. Up ahead, the crossing materialized. Once again, disaster had struck.

Cars choked the road with broken, bloodstained windows while infected wandered about aimlessly. He glanced at Logan who stared into the distance, showing no signs of interest. "You okay, Logan?"

Seconds ticked by before Logan responded. "I will be. Just get us to wherever we're going."

Max took the hint.

Using Logan's tactics from earlier, he steered onto the shoulder of the road and forced the Land Rover around the crossing, driving through ditches, over rocks, and termite mounds. Infected tried to cut him off, but he ignored them, gritting his teeth whenever he clipped one.

They're not people anymore, he reminded himself when guilt threatened to set in. *They're dead; their souls are long gone.*

He glanced into the back where the boy they'd rescued earlier still waited. Happily, the kid had enough sense to keep his head down. He'd been lucky to escape, and Max guessed his family was gone.

He'd heard enough at the army base to know what was really happening. The virus had broken out several weeks before in Europe. Due to a combination of disbelief, denial, and incompetence it could not be contained and spread throughout the unsuspecting population. Like everyone else, the South African government ignored the signs. They didn't believe the reports streaming in until it was too late. The virus snuck in, and from there on, it was all downhill.

A family returning from holiday unwittingly brought it with them. A ferocious little girl bit their twelve-year-old son on the beach. After a visit to the clinic and a tetanus shot, the incident was forgotten. They went home the next day.

At OR Tambo airport in Johannesburg, a businessman returning from Tokyo neglected to mention injuries incurred that morning when he was attacked on the street. A day later he became violently ill and died in hospital. Unfortunately for the medical staff at the morgue, he failed to remain dead.

Elsewhere, an illegal immigrant crossed the border. He settled into a hostel with fellow illegals and turned during the night. It was a bloodbath.

The virus took South Africa by storm when these incidents culminated that fateful week, reaching the more sparsely populated Free State countryside by Saturday morning and exploding into a full-blown catastrophe by the next day.

Max had not reckoned on the virus moving so fast. Earlier that week the bulk of the army had been dispatched to all the main cities. They believed the situation could still be resolved as they scrambled to put quarantine measures in place. News reports from the media about virus related violence was suppressed to keep order, and the government reassured people everything was under control.

This prevented a widespread panic but also left people unprepared and vulnerable to attack. Max applied for leave then went AWOL when his request was denied. Though loyal to the uniform, his family came first. He snuck out of the base with all the equipment and guns he could carry. It cost him a boatload in bribes but was worth it in the end.

He glanced at Logan, wondering what kind of man he was. He was older than Max, mid-thirties and tough looking. Tall and lean, with the air of a troublemaker, stubble lined his jaws, and his dark hair stuck up at all angles. Max hoped the two of them would get along as he had the distinct feeling they were stuck together for a while.

The drive through the streets of his hometown proved challenging, but not as tricky as Welkom with its much larger population. When they reached the home of his sister Morgan, however, they faced a problem. Several zombies wandered about, and more had followed them from the previous block.

"Are you prepared to back me up? I need to check if my sister's here," Max asked.

Logan nodded, his face cold and remote. He pushed open his door, jumped out, and swung up his rifle. His every move spoke of intense and uncontrolled violence. It was evident he wasn't thinking straight.

"Logan, wait!" Max cried in alarm.

Logan ignored him, taking down the nearest infected with a quick headshot. Max jumped out, scrambling to catch up before Logan could get himself killed.

His feet barely touched the ground when an infected raced for him at full speed. Startled, he fumbled with his gun, all training deserting him in an instant. His first shot missed by a mile. Before he could shoot again, she pounced on him, and they rolled on the asphalt together.

He grabbed her by the throat and pushed back. He couldn't keep his grip, however, and his hand slipped down to her collarbone. Like a snake, she slithered from his grasp and bit him on his chest. Shock reverberated through his body like an earthquake. Instinct kicked in, and he lashed out, knocking her to the side.

Grabbing his pistol, he shoved the gun into her mouth and pulled the trigger. Blood and brains exploded onto the pavement, splattering the right side of his body.

Max got one foot underneath him before another zombie fell onto his legs. He kicked it in the chest before planting a bullet in its forehead. Adrenaline pumped through his veins, and his nerves steadied. Two more of the monsters were almost upon him.

Taking a deep breath, he aimed and killed one after the other, still crouched on the ground. He jumped up, trying to get his bearings. Another hissed as it crawled towards him, its face twisted in a mask of bloody death. The gun bucked in Max's hand, and its head exploded in a fine spray of red and gray. The ruby drops glittered in the sun as an uneasy silence fell.

Max gazed around, his muscles tense as he readied for another attack, but the infected were all down. Logan nodded at him, his eyes remote and deadly. A circle of the undead surrounded him, a silent testament to his deadly aim.

In a moment of clarity, Max remembered being bitten and grabbed his chest. There, on his tactical vest, bloomed a sticky wet patch with deep teeth indentations. Despite her best efforts, the zombie had failed to bite through the thick material.

"Oh, thank God." Max slumped in relief. "That was close."

Relief made way for anger. Furious, he rounded on Logan. "What the fuck were you thinking? We're supposed to work together."

"I work alone," Logan said.

"Then you can die alone too."

A muscle ticked in Logan's jaw, and his eyes were as hard as stone. His knuckles whitened as his fists clenched.

Tensed for a blow, Max waited.

After a long moment, Logan relaxed and blew a breath out of his nose. "Fine. We'll work together. For now."

With a terse nod, Max pointed to the house and said, "Let's go before the gunshots attract more of those things. We don't have a lot of time."

He clapped the back of the Land Rover. "We'll be right back, okay? Stay down and keep quiet."

The boy's head popped up, eyes wide and frightened, but he nodded and ducked out of sight again.

The gate stood open, and judging by the bloody tire tracks, someone had made a run for it. After a quick check revealed no zombies and no car in the yard, Logan said, "Seems like they got away."

"I hope so," Max replied as he opened the kitchen door and stepped inside. "This is probably a waste of time, but—"

Brian leaped at him, howling in fury. Surprise froze Max to the spot, and he was helpless to defend himself. Logan yanked him back by his collar, hauling him out the door and onto his ass. Swinging his rifle like a cricket bat, Logan nearly decapitated Brian. With a thunk, the gun connected with his temple, crushing the bone and brains into mush. A second hit put him down for good.

After a second, Logan nodded at the corpse, "Who was that?"

"That...that was my brother-in-law, Brian," Max said, shaky after his second near brush with death. He climbed to his feet, brushing off his pants with trembling hands. *At this rate, I'll be dead by sundown.*

He bent down and examined the corpse with a sense of grief and remorse even though he'd never known Brian very well. "Rest in peace, brother."

Logan took the lead as they searched the house. They found the bathroom with the bloodied railing and broken door, but no Morgan.

"Well, looks like she put up a fight and got away. Any idea where she'd run to?" Logan asked.

"My parents. That's all I can think of. It's the only family we have here. Our other sister lives in Johannesburg."

"We'd better hurry then."

They rushed back to the Land Rover and drove off without delay. Fifteen minutes later, they pulled to a stop in front of the house and sat there, surveying the scene. It looked like a war zone. Somebody had taken down a sizable group of zombies on the front lawn with what they guessed to be a truck.

"I'm impressed. Your sister's quite resourceful," Logan said, a tinge of admiration lacing his voice.

"That she is," Max agreed.

It didn't take long to find the bodies. The sight of his father's face, bloodied and still, shook Max to the heels of his feet. The horrific wounds and the gunshot told its own story. He didn't even need to read the explanation in the note stuck on the fridge to know what had happened.

He was relieved to learn everyone else was safe until he

realized one crucial fact. He had no idea where they'd gone and had no means of finding them.

"Shit." Max scratched his head.

"Now what?"

"We have to find a place to fort up and survive. A base from which I can search for them."

"Any idea where that might be?"

Max thought about it. "What about the riot police quarters? It has a sturdy fence, and it's outside of town."

"It might still be occupied."

"Even better. We can team up with them."

"Worth checking out, I suppose."

A few minutes' drive was all it took before they faced the entrance. Everything appeared quiet, and the gates stood wide open. There were no people and precious few vehicles left on the premises. No infected either.

Being placed on the edge of town like it was, there weren't that many people around, and those that were got an early warning from the riot police. Rolling through the gates, they kept watch but saw no movement.

Half an hour later, after a quick and thorough search, they confirmed their suspicions. Whoever had been there had responded to the emergency situation and never returned. It was deserted.

With relief, Max rapped his knuckles on the Land Rover's back window. "You can come out now. It's safe."

With some hesitation, the boy emerged, apparently unconvinced by this statement.

"Thanks for saving me," he whispered, ducking his head.

"I'm glad we could help," Max said. "What's your name?"

"Thembiso."

"How old are you?"

"Sixteen."

Max sucked in a breath. "Your family?"

Thembiso shook his head, his eyes fixed on the ground. "They're gone." Fat teardrops slid down his cheeks, dripping onto his torn t-shirt.

"Did you get bitten? Scratched? Got blood in your mouth or eyes?" Logan probed.

The boy shook his head.

"Will you let me have a look?" Max asked.

"Okay."

After a brief search, Max declared him clean, and they headed inside.

"We should secure the place as best we can for the night. Close all the windows and curtains and shut off any lights as you go. Look for the keys too while you're at it," Max said. "Oh, and shut off anything that can make noise. Phones, alarms, anything that could draw those things here."

"Good thinking," Logan replied.

They each headed off in their own direction.

Thembiso stuck to Max like a shadow, and no wonder after everything he'd been through. The secretary's office yielded a set of keys to the building and a stash of chocolate. Another office offered up half a bottle of Jack Daniels.

In the equipment and storerooms, they found a bounty of uniforms, batons, shields, rubber bullets and stun grenades. Max wasn't sure if the bullets and grenades would have much effect on the undead, but he wasn't about to complain. Logan found the keys to the gate and the two Nyala anti-riot vehicles left behind in the parking lot.

"These will come in handy," Max said, dangling the keys.

Though the army didn't use them, Max knew that Nyala's were uber tough.

Together they searched the lockers and bathrooms, finding a wealth of personal items. It was sad to see all those people's stuff, knowing that most of them were probably dead.

While Logan slipped out to go lock up, Max set about making coffee in the small kitchen. In a cupboard, he found bread; the fridge yielded butter, an overripe tomato, cheese, and some leftover chicken. Somebody's lunch.

After a rough supper in the small sitting room just off the kitchen, Logan fetched the last beers from his Land Rover. Max posted Thembiso off to sleep with a stiff shot of Jack Daniels.

"Poor boy needs it," he said with a shake of his head.

They had no bedding, but it wasn't cold, not with summer in full swing. Seating themselves in the central office with the beer, Max tried to raise someone on the radio but with no success. They tested all the phones again.

Nothing.

"I hate feeling so damn isolated," Logan said.

"Yeah, it sucks. Not knowing what's going on out there. Let's try the Internet."

To their surprise, the Internet still worked.

"Must be because it's an ADSL line. The land lines are still going for now," Max explained.

They found one horror story after the other, flooding the web like viruses. It was apparent the world was in chaos, and billions of people had died.

"Please, if anyone can help me, I'm trapped in my apartment. They're at the door, and I don't know how long it will hold. Please, can someone help me?" a young girl begged on her

Facebook page. She wasn't the only one.

Some governments were telling people to fort up and survive while others, including their own, told people to go to their nearest hospital or community center.

"Big mistake," Max muttered. Too many individuals in a confined space spelled disaster if the infection got in. Some sites offered advice to survivors: aim for the head, watch out for fresh ones because they're fast, stick together.

The list went on and on.

There was more. Too much to take in.

Max sighed, rubbing his stiff neck. He glanced at his watch. "It's late. Let's bed down for the night. Tomorrow will be a long day."

The last thought he had as he tried to stuff his tall body onto a couch was of Lilian. *Are you still alive, Sis?*

Chapter 5 - Breytenbach

The night air was cold with just the barest hint of a breeze. It rustled through the leaves on the trees, granting a whisper of sound to the quiet surroundings. With complete confidence, the group moved through the shadows. They operated as a unit, running in concert to hand signals passed between them.

They passed through the wealthiest suburb in Johannesburg with as little sound as possible, heading towards their target. Only once, as they flowed around a car parked on the sidewalk with the passenger door open, did a sound disturb them. A low growl shivered through the night as a zombie lurched out.

With quiet efficiency, one dark figure dispatched the corpse with a powerful thrust from a fearful looking knife. He stabbed up into the brain through the soft tissue beneath the chin. Without a sound, it crumpled to the ground.

A gleam of white teeth showed in the faint glow of the moon, all the more startling against ebony skin. The owner of the knife cleaned it on his trouser leg and thrust it back into its sheath. His massive frame moved with the grace of a cat as he took up his position at the back of the group again.

One, two, three more blocks they walked, well on the way to their target, until they heard it. A dark, low thrum that issued from the throats of countless undead to form one collective groan. The source of this unearthly sound soon became evident. Not far to the left, a horde of infected pushed against the fence of a kindergarten school.

Inside, lights shined, and the cries and screams of children could be heard if the group listened hard enough. The fence bowed beneath the horde's onslaught. It wouldn't last. Even as they watched, it buckled under the combined weight of so many bodies.

Captain Breytenbach could only shake his head at the blatant stupidity of the people inside the school. With all the lights and noise, they'd put up a virtual sign saying: Attention all Zombies. Fresh food!

It was a miracle they'd lasted this long already. Then again, people never thought straight in a crisis, and panic usually overcame common sense. Either way, it was none of his business. He was on a mission to rescue a billionaire's son hiding in his family mansion not far away, a job he'd been paid handsomely for.

Ex-military, Breytenbach and two other members of his team used to be part of the South African Army's special forces. Having fought and trained together for years, they were happy to sign up when Breytenbach opened his own security company, one that catered to the super-rich. Over the years, other professionals had joined the team. Mercenaries one and all, they lived for the action and the money.

Now he weighed their options, considering the risk to his team. The simplest thing would be to slip past the zombies and carry on with their mission. That's what they were paid to do, but the thought of children being torn apart while he did nothing didn't sit well with him. Mercenary he might be, but he still had honor. He looked at each of his team and asked a silent question. *Detour?*

One by one they nodded. With a faint smile of approval, he motioned Lenka to the right flank. With his knife skills and incredible strength, he was a fearsome adversary. Johan, his right-hand man, took the left, while he and Ronnie took the lead. Kirstin and Mike stayed in the back, providing cover fire to the rest.

Shots fired through silencers filled the night with muffled pops as they picked off the undead. They fell by the dozen, thinning the crowd as Breytenbach's group advanced. A few stragglers caught on, charging them only to be intercepted by the flankers.

At the front, the throng finally pushed over the fence, trampling each other in their rush to get to the school. Glass shattered, the bell-like tinkling followed by hysterical screams as the infected broke through the windows. Urgency descended on the group. They sped up their efforts and closed in on the building.

The doors dangled on their hinges, granting easy access. They slipped inside. The foyer was empty, and a pot plant had toppled over; the only sign of disturbance. The screams were coming from the left.

The Captain placed Ronnie and Mike at strategic points in the foyer to cover their rear while the rest advanced. They moved down a corridor and passed two offices. The first was deserted, while the second revealed a trio of undead feeding on a woman. Her vacant stare burned into Breytenbach's mind as he put a bullet between her eyes, preventing her corpse from rising while Lenka took care of the infected.

Breytenbach pushed aside all feelings of horror and pity, to be taken out and examined at a later date. For now, his entire focus was on the sounds issuing from a set of double doors, smashed open. It led to a large hall, likely used for functions and concerts. Now it played host to a macabre scene of pain and suffering.

Screams ripped through the air as harsh to the ears as nails on a chalkboard. The bodies of tiny children were strewn about. Broken porcelain dolls stained with the dark red of arterial blood. A few were still alive, trying to crawl away from the monsters tearing at their flesh. Others lay silent, their sightless eyes staring up at the ceiling as their bodies jerked in concert with the feeding mouths.

It was a traumatic scene that burned itself into the mind forever, flashing to the forefront with all the shock and brilliance of a lightning strike at times. Breytenbach lifted his gun and pulled the trigger. Beside him, Lenka, Kirstin, and Johan stepped up, their shots joining the swirling chaos.

The infected dropped like fat, bloated ticks off a hide, their thick, black blood draining out to mingle with the fresh, crimson blood of the living. The smell of it hung in the air and coated his tongue with a coppery tang.

In a corner, three teachers were fending off attacks with an assortment of makeshift weapons. A small knot of children cowered behind them. They were the last left standing. With controlled haste, Breytenbach moved his squad closer.

The undead continued to fall until the last dropped to the ground with a loud groan, protesting the injustice of its final death. The thundering of Breytenbach's heart slowed to a murmur. He lowered his gun, surveying the scene.

"Fucking hell," Johan said, staring.

Dozens of bodies were thrown about, the walls and floor coated in blood. Breytenbach looked at the remaining women, settling on one. "Miss, can you move everyone to the foyer, please?"

She wielded an umbrella like a cricket bat, eyes so large they almost popped out of her head.

"Miss? I need you to take these children to the foyer. You'll be safe there." She gaped at him before managing a shaky nod.

"Johan, go with them. Make sure they're all right. Check them for bites," he ordered.

With the survivors out of the way, Breytenbach turned to the grim task ahead. "Kirstin, Lenka, move out. We need to take care of the injured and the dead. You know what to do."

With curt nods, they fanned out in different directions. The nearest body he found was that of a little girl, maybe two, her face smeared with blood. She was already dead, and a quick stab through the temple ensured she'd never reawaken.

The next, another little girl. Her rosebud lips moved without sound, and tears leaked from her eyes. The infected that had attacked her lay to the side, its fingers still buried in her stomach. Bile rose to Breytenbach's lips. This was too much. Never in all his life...

But there was no time. Or choice. He knelt down and ended her misery. Brushing her eyes closed, he got up and moved on. This had to be done quickly, or not at all. After that, it all became a blur of faces. Dead children, teachers, and parents.

He found three more still living. A young father clutched his dead child to his chest as he bled out from a torn artery. A boy was drowning in his own blood. A baby mewled as its last breath left its tiny body.

Never had Breytenbach seen so much human suffering, or come so close to losing his mind. To the left and right, Kirstin and Lenka went about the same horrific task, their faces pale and drawn. The dead had to be prevented from rising and the dying...the dying had to be granted peace.

Breytenbach found her towards the end. The woman. She was hunched over in a fetal position, holding something close to her chest. From the looks of things, she had tried to roll into a defensive ball.

The flesh on her back and shoulders were torn to shreds with bits of rib and spine showing through in places. He positioned himself for a swift stab but paused when she shivered and moaned. "Help me."

He nerved himself to do it, to end her suffering. He lifted the knife, pressing the point to her temple. *Just do it.*

A bead of blood welled up beneath the sharp edge, and his muscles tensed for the thrust. A mewling sound alerted him, and he stopped. Gently, he rolled the woman over onto her side and gasped. Clutched in her arms was a baby, swaddled in a soft pink blanket.

The woman tried to speak. Blood bubbled from her lips, and her eyes swam with pain. "Please, take my baby. She's all that's left. I couldn't save...her brother."

Breytenbach looked at the little bundle, surprised to find the baby unharmed. She was crying through the pacifier in her mouth, her little face scrunched up in a ball.

"They took him from me," the mother whispered, stretching an arm to a crumpled body lying in a pool of blood. It was a boy of about four or five, his eyes glazed over in death, flung down like a rag doll.

With trembling hands, the woman fumbled for a handbag lying on the floor. "Take... my diary. She must know who she is. Promise me she'll be safe."

He rummaged through the bag and found a black diary,

pocketing it before reaching for the pink bundle.

"I promise," he said, locking his gaze with hers to show his sincerity.

She nodded, satisfied.

He took the baby in his arms and rocked her back and forth. Her crying ceased, and he glanced back at the mother. Her eyes stared unseeingly towards the little boy, one hand stretched out toward him.

With a heavy heart, he performed his duties, ensuring they'd both rest forever before spinning around and leaving the hall of horrors behind.

In the foyer, he handed the baby to one of the remaining women to care for. He didn't want to let go of the warm little body, her eyes gazing up into his with complete trust. "Here, can you take her, please? For now?"

"Of course."

He turned back to his squad and cleared his throat. *Back to business.*

"Right, let's get going. Same positions as before, survivors in the middle," he ordered. "Make for the mansion."

With the women and children bunched together, they moved out as fast as they could. It took longer than Breytenbach would have liked, and they had a few encounters with infected, but thirty minutes later they reached the mansion's gates.

A three-man team scouted the grounds and buildings for danger. They found only the billionaire's son hiding in his room, to the immense relief of Breytenbach. *At least, I can still fulfill my mission.*

A bigger problem faced him, however. How to get everyone to safety. Johannesburg was a hot zone, and there was little hope of survival there. Walking out was not possible.

They had only one option. Hole up at the mansion and radio for an airlift. The walls were sturdy and the gates made of thick steel. They'd be safe for the time being as long as they didn't advertise their presence.

With Ronnie and Kirstin on guard duty, he headed inside. It had been a long night, and exhaustion dragged at his shoulders. He longed for a hot shower and a comfortable bed.

Inside the house, he was surprised to find a scene of ordered chaos. Two of the women busied themselves in the kitchen while the third watched the kids. The aroma of coffee drifted through the air, intermingled with the smells of frying steak and eggs. The young blond with the umbrella shot him a shy smile and asked, "Can I dish up food for your team, er..."

"Captain Breytenbach," he finished. "And yes, I'm sure they'd be grateful."

The kids sat in a corner, spooked and deathly quiet. He felt sorry for them. No amount of therapy could take away the sights they had seen, but at least, they were alive.

A middle-aged brunette approached him, holding the baby he'd rescued earlier in her arms. "Hi, I'm Zelda. I used to be principal of the school."

"Captain Breytenbach."

"That's Linda," she continued, pointing to the umbrella-wielding blonde before introducing the third. "And that's Mannuru. They're both teachers."

"Glad to meet all of you."

"No, thank you, Captain." She smiled, but her eyes were vacant, empty. He recognized the signs of trauma. "We would've died tonight if it wasn't for you."

He shrugged, casting around in his mind for something to

say. "It was nothing."

"What will happen to us now?"

For a moment, he hesitated. "To tell you the truth, I'm not a hundred percent sure. I'm here for the boy." He nodded toward the teenager, huddled in a corner with his head between his knees.

"As far as I can tell, most people are being evacuated to quarantine zones in Natal, the Drakensberg, and Robben Island. You'll be taken to one of those, most likely."

She shifted the child in her arms. "What about this little one? I don't know her or her parents. I'm not even sure how she ended up at the school."

He pulled the diary out of his pocket. "She's an orphan now. I'll find a place for her once we get out of here."

"All right. Thank you," she answered, rejoining the kids.

Breytenbach looked down at the diary in his hand. It wasn't much, meant more for telephone numbers and accounts, but there was enough information for him to glean a few basic facts.

The family lived in a middle-class suburb some distance away. How the mother and her children ended up at the school was a mystery. The boy, Michael, was five, his birthday penciled in for a month from then. The baby girl, Samantha, was the sole survivor of her family. Other family members lived in Riebeeckstad, wherever the hell that was. He wasn't willing to bet they were still alive.

Linda interrupted his thoughts by handing him a plate of food, "Here you go, Captain."

He accepted the dish, and his mouth watered as the aroma hit his nose. "Have my team eaten?"

"Yes, Captain," she nodded. "I made sure of it."

"Thank you."

The plate was heaped high with steak, eggs, and buttered bread, and he dug in with alacrity. One thing he'd learned in the army was to eat when you can and sleep when you can because tomorrow you might not get the chance.

He ate fast, sopping up the last of the juices with his bread and swallowing the bitter coffee in one gulp. It settled in his stomach, a pleasant warmth radiating throughout his limbs.

He handed the cup and plate back to Linda. "That was good food. Thank you."

"My pleasure, Captain. It's the least I could do."

"Please, can you gather up supplies?" he asked. "The helicopter should be here in about fifteen minutes, and I don't know what the quarantine camps look like. Extra supplies might be welcome."

"Of course."

He left her to the task and stepped outside, glancing at his watch. He watched as Mike let off a flare, the light bright against the inky backdrop of the sky. Who could have thought it would come to this?

Zombies.

He'd seen and done so much in his lifetime; he'd thought there was nothing left that could shock him. How wrong that assumption had been. The world was burning, and it was their own dead that struck the match. He felt far older than his forty-nine years at that moment.

He took out the diary once more and leafed through the pages. In the back, he found a photograph of the family. The husband seemed ordinary enough, sporting a suit and tie.

Breytenbach recognized Samantha's mother with ease. She was pretty, with blond hair and blue-gray eyes, unclouded by the suffering he'd witnessed earlier. She smiled at the camera with genuine warmth. In her arms, she held her daughter and clinging to her legs with a shy smile was little Michael.

From a distance, he heard the helicopter approach as it spotted the flare, and he put the diary away to oversee the evacuation. Fifteen minutes later, everybody was loaded and on their way. The last to leave, he jumped in and settled back in his seat, staring down at the now ruined city.

Like ants, the dead swarmed through the streets, illuminated by the coming of dawn. Fires had broken out, and he could spot the overrun police and military barricades. As they left the once thriving City of Gold, the name of the woman who'd entrusted the safety of her daughter to him lingered in his mind. Lilian.

Chapter 6 - Morgan

Morgan stared out the window as the scenery rolled past. The urban landscape had been replaced by the Free State veldt, a mixture of browns and yellows with just a hint of green. But her eyes were unseeing, her chest a hollow void.

Her mind flashed back to the last time she saw Brian. The image of his inhuman eyes caused her to flinch, and a sob welled up. One she stifled by biting down on her clenched fist. *I can't believe he's dead. Or...undead. What does that even mean? Will he slowly rot away to nothing, or just stay like that forever?*

Already she missed him, missed his steady presence beside her, always warm and reassuring. To others, he might have appeared dull, but to her, he was home. *My safety net.*

Then there was her father. Morgan chanced a look at her mother's face and regretted it immediately. Silent tears streamed down Julianne's cheeks. Her lips were pressed together and as white as her knuckles which gripped the steering wheel. Morgan reached over and squeezed her arm. "I'm sorry, Mom."

"It's...it's okay. I'll be fine."

"Are you sure? Should I drive?"

"No. Just...how's Meghan?"

A swift glance told Morgan that Meghan had dozed off,

huddled next to Joanna on the backseat with Princess in her arms. "She's sleeping."

"Good. I don't know what to tell her. This is bad enough for us, but how do I explain what's happened to a child?"

"We'll think of something."

Morgan looked back again, and Joanna's faded blue eyes met hers. The pain in them was so real it felt like a physical blow to her stomach. Brian's death had come as a shock to the old lady, one she refused to believe at first. Morgan didn't blame her. The whole situation was surreal. Like something out of the twilight zone. "Joanna, I...I'm so sorry about Brian."

"Is he really gone? Turned into one of those things?"

"Yes, I don't know what this is...this virus that takes people over, but he got it last night when that man attacked him."

"Why didn't you take him to a doctor? Why did you leave it?" Joanna's eyes hardened, turning to chips of ice. "You could have saved him!"

Morgan gasped, the accusation stabbing deep into her heart. It hurt all the more because she believed it to be true. If she'd listened to her gut and forced him to go to the emergency room, Brian might have gotten treatment in time.

"I...I didn't know. How could I know?" she asked, but the words rang hollow in her ears.

"You should have done something. Anything."

"It's not her fault, Joanna. None of us saw this coming. I know you lost your son, and it hurts, but we all lost someone today." Julianne's face was unyielding as she glared at Joanna in the rearview mirror. "Do not place that burden on my daughter's shoulders."

"It's okay, Mom. She's right. It's my fault."

Julianne turned angry eyes on Morgan, her voice rising in

pitch. "Don't you dare say that."

"But…"

"Now listen to me, both of you. This is a tragedy. A horrible, senseless tragedy. But it's nobody's fault. Neither of you caused this. If you want to blame someone, blame the people who made this sickness or whatever it is. They're the ones you hate."

"You think someone engineered this?" Joanna asked.

"I do. This has bioterrorism written all over it. Or maybe it was a lab accident. Who knows? But fighting among each other is not the answer," Julianne said.

Joanna didn't reply, but she nodded and looked away. One trembling hand rested on Meghan's head. She seemed to draw comfort from the child's presence, an emotion Morgan did not share.

She stared at the road ahead, and pain flooded her veins like acid. The thought that someone let loose a virus like this on purpose, or even worse, that it was an accident, defied belief. Her chest constricted to the size of a golf ball, and her lungs refused to expand enough to let in oxygen. Black spots danced in front of her eyes, and sound faded away, replaced by blood rushing through her ears.

"Morgan? Morgan!"

Julianne's voice came from a distance, and she placed both hands on her temples, squeezing her eyes shut. For a moment, she was taken back to her teen years. Years filled with fear and the belief that nothing would be okay, that everything was doomed to disaster. She sucked in a deep breath. *Focus!*

A loud bang tore her from the panic-induced attack, and she snapped to attention. The truck swerved off the road as Julianne lost control of the steering. Meghan screamed, and

Princess yelped as she flew to the side. The tires bounced over tussocks of grass. With a cry, Julianne yanked the wheel, forcing the vehicle back onto the road before slamming on the brakes.

Morgan groaned, cupping her forehead where she'd hit the dashboard. An egg was forming, swelling at a rapid rate. There was no time to worry about it, though. Julianne was trying to calm down a hysterical Meghan, helped by a shaken but otherwise unharmed Joanna. That left Morgan as the only one wondering what had caused the accident.

Blinking, she looked out the window and scanned the area. It seemed clear in the immediate vicinity, but she couldn't be sure. Reaching down, she felt the gun at her side. She pulled it out and flicked off the safety.

The truck's door creaked as it swung open, and she paused. The sun felt hot on her skin after the air-conditioned cab, and her cheeks flushed with blood. She raised a hand, shielding her eyes from the glare.

"Morgan? What are you doing? Get back inside." Julianne's voice held a sharp note of fear, overlaid by Meghan's shrill cries.

"It's okay, Mom. I'm just making sure everything's okay."

"But..."

"I'll be right back, don't worry."

Morgan slid out of the truck and placed her booted feet on the ground. Tiny pebbles crunched beneath the soles. With the gun pointed at a half angle, she swiveled, looking for danger. It was clear, but the fine hairs on her arms rose to echo the tension within her breast. With slow steps, she walked around the vehicle, searching for what the cause of the near accident. Her eyes fell on a dark shadow on the road.

It was some distance away, and she squinted, trying to make out what it was. Morgan walked closer, and her confusion gave way to understanding. "A pothole. It's just a dumb pothole."

Shaking her head, Morgan turned back, but her relief quickly turned to dismay when her eyes fell on the front right tire. It was flat. "Shit!"

She hurried to the truck to examine it. The rim was bent, and the wheel had a deep cut through the rubber. *It must have burst on impact.* "This is just perfect. Fucking perfect."

"What's wrong, honey?" Julianne's face popped out of the window above Morgan's head.

"We've got a flat."

"What?"

"Yup. You hit a pothole back there, and the wheel must have popped."

Julianne got out of the cab, her face twisted in worry. "What do we do now?"

Morgan shrugged. "Guess, I'll have to change it."

"Do you know how?"

"No, but I'm sure I can figure it out. I've watched Brian do it before." Morgan rummaged in the back for the spare, heaving it out with a grunt. After locating the jack, she positioned it under the car and put the wheel spanner nearby.

Julianne hustled everyone out of the truck, and they stood huddled to the side. Morgan glanced around, her unease at being out in the open not lessening at the apparent lack of life. "Mom? I think you should keep watch. You know..."

Julianne's eyes widened. "You think they'd be out here?"

"Better safe than sorry." Morgan turned to the task at hand. *The sooner I get this tire changed, the sooner we can get out of here.*

65

Pumping the handle, she jacked up the truck and watched with satisfaction as the wheel lifted off the road. With a light push, she tested its stability. *Seems okay.*

Locking the spanner over a wheel nut, she began the tedious task of loosening them. It was hard, but she managed, her arm muscles bulging with the effort. Her job as a personal trainer now seemed to bear fruit in ways she'd never have thought of before. *Thank God I work out a lot.*

Even so, one of the nuts proved particularly tough. After straining for several minutes, she rocked back on her heels. Beads of sweat had risen across her forehead and trickled down her face. The salt stung her eyes, and her head ached from her earlier injury.

"Are you okay?" Joanna asked, placing a soft hand on her shoulder.

Morgan glanced up, surprised. "Yeah, I'm all right."

Her mother-in-law handed her a bottle of water. "Here. You must be thirsty."

"Just a little." Morgan took the proffered drink and swallowed a few sips. She recognized the gesture for what it was, one of reconciliation. It was Joanna's way of saying sorry. She handed back the bottle. "Thanks."

"Sure thing."

Joanna turned away, returning to the group. Meghan had stopped crying at last and was sitting on the ground munching on a packet of potato chips. Princess wandered from bush to tussock, peeing on everything in sight while Julianne kept watch.

With a smile, Morgan turned back to the stubborn wheel nut, pushing down with all her weight. It groaned then came loose with a rush. "Yes!"

Working faster, she pulled off the flat tire and picked up the spare. The thing was heavy, and she grunted as she propped it up and tried to slide it on. Her arms shook, the muscles burning. "Come on, fuck it!"

"Morgan!" her mother scolded. "Not in front of Meghan."

Morgan rolled her eyes but muttered a quick reply just as the wheel settled into place. "Sorry."

One by one, she tightened the wheel nuts, vaguely aware of Meghan telling her mother she needed to go to the bathroom. With the spare locked in place, she bent down to drop the jack. The truck settled back onto the road.

With swift movements, she began packing up until a shrill scream froze her in place. Her head whipped up, and she spotted Meghan running through the brush at breakneck speed. Princess barked like crazy, bouncing along on her heels.

Behind them, Julianne stood with her back to Morgan. She pointed her gun at something that crashed through the dry bushes. The pistol bucked, the report loud in the still afternoon air. Julianne turned and ran toward Morgan. "Hurry! Get in the truck. There's more coming."

"Oh, shit." Morgan opened the back door and tossed in the jack and flat tire before turning to the others. "Come on, come on!"

Meghan ran to her, and Morgan swung her inside while Princess took a flying leap, sailing in after her. They were followed by Joanna who slammed the door shut. Julianne had reached the truck by now and was running to the driver's side. A freshly infected man, fast and vigorous, was almost upon her. His outstretched fingers brushed her collar, and Morgan scrambled to pick up the spanner.

She swung the tool at his head, connecting with his snarling mouth. A few teeth cracked, one flying free as his head snapped back. Another blow put him off balance. With a quick shove, Morgan pushed him to the ground and sprinted to her open door. She jumped inside, shrieking when he smashed into her window. Julianne started the truck and pulled away, leaving the infected man in their dusty wake.

Morgan watched him in the rearview mirror. He ran after them, legs uncoordinated but fast. His figure grew smaller, but he never stopped. She wondered if he'd just keep going until he collapsed. *Do they get ever tired?*

They passed a stationary car. It was empty with the doors wide open. *Is that where they came from? Those infected?*

She pressed trembling fingers to her lips, breathing out through her nose. Her heart bounced in her chest, but the panic from before was missing. Instead, she rode high on the buzz of adrenaline.

The moment when she'd hit the infected with the spanned played over and over in her head. The swing of the tool, the way it connected with a dull thud, the crunch of broken teeth. It was sickening.

That man used to be a person, a father, a brother, a son. Albeit a dead one. Still, Morgan couldn't suppress the feeling that rose within her being. It was an emotion she never expected to feel at that moment, yet she did.

Victory.

Chapter 7 - Logan

Logan woke up with a start. He blinked at the bland surroundings, confusion clouding his mind. "Where in hell's name am I?"

A snore pulled his attention to the figures of Max and Thembiso, and the events of the previous day rushed back.

He'd spent the night in the riot police quarters in Riebeeckstad. On a couch to be exact, and judging from his stiff, sore muscles, a very uncomfortable couch.

Logan sat up, massaging the crick in his neck as he straightened his spine. An early riser by nature, he got up to fetch his luggage from the Land Rover. Luckily, the bathrooms had showers. After a wash and a shave, he felt like a new man.

Memories of the day before lay like a dead weight on his mind, but he pushed it aside for the moment. He had never been one to dwell on emotional angst, preferring instead to pretend everything was okay. Not the best way to cope, perhaps, but the only way he knew how. He stumbled across a bleary-eyed Max in the hallway. "I'm making coffee. Want some?"

"Sure, I could use a cup," Max replied.

Logan prepared a pot of the brew strong enough to take the paint off a wall before waking up Thembiso. "Time to get up, kid. We've got a lot to do today."

He handed the boy his cup and chuckled when Thembiso's nose scrunched up as he took a sip. Evidently, they didn't serve real coffee where he was from.

Max sauntered in a few minutes later, running his hands through his damp hair before taking a seat.

Logan sat down opposite him. "So what's the plan?"

"Fort up and survive." Max gave Logan a long look. "I'll understand if you want to leave. I'd be glad of the help if you stayed, though."

Logan was silent for a beat, then replied, "I'll stay. For now."

"Thanks." Max blew out a breath and leaned forward. "I thought we could start by searching the houses in the vicinity. If there are any problems we need to know about, we should find out now. Plus we need supplies."

"It's a start," Logan said, stretching out his long legs.

While sipping his coffee, Max filled Thembiso in on the current situation. It was an ugly picture he painted, but Logan didn't object. He figured the boy needed to know what the score was.

"We're in this for the long haul. There's no telling when things will get back to normal, if ever," Max said.

"I understand," Thembiso replied.

"Are you okay? Do you need to talk? You know, about your family?" Max trailed off.

Thembiso shook his head, blinking back sudden tears. "No, I'm all right."

"Are you sure?" Max asked, reaching out a hand. "Don't you—"

"Leave the boy alone. If he wants to talk, he'll talk," Logan interrupted, his tone brusque. In his opinion, nothing sucked more than people trying to get you to talk about your feelings.

"Let's get going. We've got work to do."

Max shrugged. "Sure, just trying to help."

Logan fixed Thembiso with a hard look. "You stay here. Lie low, keep quiet, and keep busy. You can sort out the storeroom next to the kitchen for a start. Get it ready for the supplies we bring in."

"Why? Can't I come with you? I can help."

Logan had to give it to the little guy. He was barely sixteen, as skinny as a rake and had just lost his entire family to a zombie plague, but he had guts.

"No, you'll only be a liability," Logan replied, mouth set in a stern line.

Thembiso stared at the floor, dejection written on his face.

"Maybe next time, once you've learned how to use a gun."

The boy's face brightened. "You'll teach me?"

"Sure. If you want." Logan shrugged, feeling strangely warm inside. *Nice kid.*

He walked away, slinging his rifle over his shoulder. Outside, he was greeted by a beautiful day, one at complete odds with their desperate situation. For a moment, he missed being in the bush, alone and independent, surrounded by nature.

"Soon," he muttered, slipping behind the wheel. Despite what he'd said to Max, he wasn't planning on staying. Just long enough to help the two settle in.

As he gripped the familiar wheel of the Landie, his melancholic thoughts vanished. He was ready to go and eager to put the tragedies of yesterday behind him. Action was what he knew best.

After Max got into the seat beside him, he reversed and drove to the gate. There was still no sign of any zombies as Max unlocked the gate, and Logan wondered how long their luck would hold.

They approached the first house with caution. It was situated across the street from their new home. A single row of houses stretched down with another row behind that, most of it surrounded by open veldt. To the left, about two hundred meters up the road, the small town of Riebeeckstad began, with them right at the edge.

He parked in front of the first house. Garbage bags lay uncollected on the sidewalk while a gentle breeze stirred the tops of the daisy bushes lining the pre-con. No signs of life could be seen.

"Well, time to find out if the neighborhood is as deserted as it looks," Logan said.

They got out and walked to the front door. Logan held his ax at the ready while Max carried a hammer he'd borrowed from Logan's toolbox. Neither wanted to attract infected with the sound of gunshots. That was a lesson learned the previous day.

The house was the type Logan hated. Bland and boring. To him, it represented the white picket fence scenario. The same situation he'd run from his entire life.

The front door stood wide open, leading to a stuffy looking living room. Porcelain figurines stared at them from shelves on the wall while an antique clock ticked away the time in age-old fashion.

Max took the lead as they searched the house, room by room. Nothing had been disturbed. It was empty. Either the owners had run at the first sign of trouble, taking nothing with them or they never came home.

After making sure the house was secure, they split up to search for supplies. Logan spotted the fridge, and his stomach rumbled, reminding him he hadn't had breakfast yet. He opened the door, and his mouth watered. "Jackpot."

Logan unpacked margarine, cheese, ham, pickles, and mustard before he raided the bread bin and made a monster sandwich. It was bigger than his head, just the way he liked it.

"That's better," he mumbled through a huge mouthful.

"I see you've got the food supplies well in hand," Max said when he walked into the kitchen with a first aid kit under his arm. He shook his head. "Just leave something for the rest of us."

"Yeah, yeah, relax." Washing down his breakfast with a glass of orange juice, Logan scrounged around for plastic bags and packed up the rest of the food.

They stripped the house of anything useful, taking care not to let their guard down or to make too much noise. With the Land Rover loaded, they dropped the supplies off with Thembiso and went on to the second house.

"We should get furniture," Max mused.

"What for?"

Max shrugged. "You know, make it homey."

Logan looked at Max with raised eyebrows. "*Homey?*"

"Hey, we'll be staying there for a while. Might as well get comfortable."

"If you say so."

"A few beds would be nice. There aren't any at our base, and those couches are shitty to sleep on," Max added.

Logan thought about that for a moment. *He has a point.* "True. We could load it on the roof rack. We should get fridges too for the meat and stuff."

"It's all about the food for you, isn't it?" Max laughed.

"Funny, but I'd like to see how long you keep cracking jokes on an empty stomach." Logan shook his head. "I've spent many hungry nights in the bush. You won't believe some of the things I've eaten."

"I can imagine," Max shuddered. "But seriously, how long do you think the power will last?"

"Around a week. Two if we're lucky. We'll need generators and fuel to keep us going."

"Mm. This is gonna be more problematic than I thought." Max frowned. He fiddled with the radio but found nothing but static.

"Electricity, water, guns and ammunition, food, medicine. All the more reason to get moving," Logan said.

The second house didn't look as peaceful as the first. Blood spatters marred the walls, and the flower beds were trampled.

"Looks like trouble," Logan said.

"Agreed."

"You first."

"Chicken."

Together they searched the yard and the rooms, finding nothing but emptiness. Whatever had happened, it was over now. In the hallway, Max turned to Logan and spoke in a normal tone of voice. "It looks clear enough."

In the next moment, a woman burst out of a door behind him, bowling him over. As small as she was, Max went down with her on top of him. She snapped at his face with her teeth, wriggling like a worm on a hook.

Logan jumped forward and lodged his ax into her temple before she could bite. Her body sagged, and she slumped to the side.

It was an old lady, dressed in a pink cardigan with court shoes and permed hair. She looked like just she got home from church. Logan gently pulled her to the side and closed her eyes. She reminded him of his grandmother, and he tore his gaze away, staring at the wall instead.

Max got to his feet, his face pale with his lips compressed. Thick, black blood covered the front of his jacket. He went to the bathroom to clean himself, shouting over his shoulder. "How did we miss her? We checked everywhere."

Logan shrugged. "Not well enough it seems. We skipped the walk-in closet. How she wound up there, I don't know, but let this be a lesson to us." He turned away. "I'll recheck the house."

That close call set the tone for the rest of the day. Having learned from their mistake, they checked every corner of the houses they visited, never assuming it was safe. It was hard, dangerous work and unpleasant too. Each zombie they dispatched used to be a person, and seeing them in their homes brought that to the forefront of their minds.

The worst was the children.

Logan ran his fingers over a row of plush toys sitting on a shelf. Their button eyes stared at him, cold and empty. The flowery bedding beside him emitted a faint baby powder smell, and from a framed picture, a young girl smiled.

His eyes flicked to a pair of red shoes that peeked out from underneath a blanket on the floor. It reminded him of Dorothy from the Wizard of Oz. Never one of his favorites, he now loathed the story.

Unable to stop himself, he stared at the pretty shoes. From underneath the cloth, a growing pool of black blood spread outward like tentacles of death. He fled the room and slammed the door shut behind him.

Max emerged from the room next to his, his face paper-white. He clutched a bag of teenage boy clothes in his left hand, and Logan spotted the crumpled form of the former owner on the floor behind him.

"Thembiso could use these," Max said.

"One more for the day and we call it quits?" Logan asked.

"Best idea I've heard so far."

They loaded up and moved on to the next house. It was a beautiful place that spoke of loving care. The lush gardens beckoned to the weary Logan, promising rest and reprieve amidst the green foliage. A pang of longing for the wild hit him again and had to be repressed with an effort.

He fixed his eyes on the goal and approached the side door to the garage, pushing it open. It creaked, and an answering raspy growl alerted him to infected.

From the gloom, a middle-aged man wearing nothing but shorts appeared. He lifted a hand and shuffled closer, dragging an injured leg behind him. Logan split his skull, marveling at how easy the deed had become. He pulled aside the body, gagging as he caught sight of the mangled leg.

"Some zombie really did a number on you." On a happier note, Logan discovered an Amarok, almost brand new, parked inside the garage. "Now this will come in handy."

"Let's look for the keys," Max said.

Inside the house, an eeriness dwelt. A half-eaten, dried-out sandwich stood on the counter next to a cold cup of coffee. The Disney channel played on the TV, and a box of cookies lay discarded on the carpet, crawling with ants.

Logan's heart sank. More children. There were no signs of a struggle, no blood, but he knew better than to take that as a good sign. They searched room after room. All empty.

Finally, they reached the main bedroom. It was closed, and

Logan wondered what waited on the other side. The hair on the back of his neck rose in anticipation.

"Ladies first," Max whispered.

Logan rolled his eyes, but the joke soothed his nerves as he cracked open the door. Stale air wafted out, and he waited for possible infected to attack. When nothing happened, he eased open the door. It was dark inside, and the curtains were drawn.

"Hello?" he called.

The seconds ticked by as he waited.

He glanced back at Max.

Max nodded and lifted his hammer. "Go on."

Logan stepped inside, waiting for his eyes to adjust to the gloom. *There!*

A shadowy figure flitted across the room to the bed, barely visible in the gloom.

"There's something there," he whispered to Max.

"Infected?"

"Don't know. It's not attacking."

"Maybe it's a person. A living one."

Logan paused as that possibility sunk in. Could it be?

"Hello? Is there anyone in here? We mean no harm," he said.

A hesitant face popped up beside the bed. It was a woman.

"Who are you?" she asked, blond hair flopping over her eyes.

"I'm Logan, and this is Max. We're survivors, looking for supplies. We're not here to hurt you."

"Well, I sure hope not, or I'd have to shoot you." She showed him a pistol as proof of her intentions.

Logan blinked, taken aback. "Uh, well I can assure you we're not."

She studied him. "All right." She rose to her feet. "Come

children. Greet our guests."

Two faces appeared next to her, a boy of about fifteen and a girl of ten or so. "Hello," they chorused.

"I'm Elise. This is Peter and Anne. Have you seen my husband? In the garage?" she asked. A tense look flitted across her features.

Logan remembered the infected man he'd killed earlier and hesitated, not sure what to say.

Elise eyed him. "I locked him in there for our safety. Is he gone now?"

"Yes, ma'am. He's gone," Max said, stepping forward and saving Logan from having to answer.

"I thought so." For a moment, her shoulders slumped, but her kids were looking at her, and she straightened. "Are you here to rescue us? You're with the army, aren't you?"

Max glanced down at his uniform. "Well, ma'am. I'm not with the army anymore, and this is not a rescue mission. We're just survivors, like yourself."

Her shoulders drooped with disappointment. "So what do we do now?"

"You can come with us. We're setting up a base in the riot police headquarters up the street," Max offered.

"Is it safe?"

"I can't guarantee your safety, ma'am, but it's better than staying here. We'll do our best to protect you," he replied.

"Well, I suppose that's all I can ask for at the moment." She clapped her hands. "Come on, kids. Let's pack our things."

She took charge of the house while Logan disposed of her dead husband's body. After loading the two vehicles with as much as they could salvage, they headed back. It was just after three in the afternoon, and after unloading, they collapsed into chairs.

"I'm beat," Logan said, rubbing his face. "And hungry."

"Me too." Max's shoulders drooped.

"Why don't you boys relax? I'll make something to eat and sort out all this stuff."

"Thank you, ma'am," Logan said, looking forward to a decent meal.

"Call me Elise."

Chapter 8 - Julianne

Half an hour passed while Julianne drove, searching the side of the road for a sign. Anything or place that offered safety. She found none. The needle of the fuel tank dipped steadily, inching its way from three-quarters to less than half.

Her fear grew with each passing second. They needed to find something soon, somewhere to spend the night or...the alternative didn't bear thinking of. *Maybe leaving the house wasn't such a good idea, after all.*

The roadside swept passed in a blur of nondescript browns. She missed the vibrant colors of her rose garden. The vivid reds, pinks, oranges, and yellows were a delight to the senses. Her memory conjured up the heady scent of the blooms, and the buzzing of bees gathering nectar until their legs were fat with the yellow powder.

"Mom! Turn back."

"What? Why?"

"There's a sign back there. Like a farm sign or something." Morgan twisted in her seat, bouncing with excitement.

"Are you sure?"

"Positive."

Julianne made a U-turn. She saw the sign Morgan had spotted and turned onto the rutted dirt track. For several minutes, they bounced and jostled along until they saw a building.

Hope rose in Julianne's chest and bolstered her waning strength. She guided the vehicle to the entrance and drew to a stop in front of the place, idling the engine. Her eyes took in the details of what looked like an old farmhouse. "Oh, no."

Peeling paint and a collapsed front porch dashed her hopes. It was abandoned, the windows shattered and all useful materials stripped away.

Morgan slumped back into her seat. "I'm sorry Mom. I thought..."

"It's okay, sweetie. It's not your fault."

She reversed out and returned to the tarred road, fighting back the hysteria that threatened to overwhelm her. *We'll find a place. We have to.*

They continued on their way, each passing moment lowering their spirits to match the dropping needle of the fuel indicator. Even the typically exuberant Princess was quiet and sat huddled next to Meghan. She sensed the fear they all felt.

"What's that?" Joanna asked.

Julianne looked at the object she pointed to. A garage. "We need to stop and refuel."

"We can ask for help too. There must be someone here," Morgan replied. "Maybe they'll know of a place we can stay."

They rolled to a stop next to a petrol pump and looked for any signs of life. There was none. It was deathly quiet, and the windows of the single shop were dark, grimy with long-accumulated dirt.

"Doesn't look like there's anyone here," Joanna said, echoing what Julianne already suspected.

"I'll look," Morgan volunteered.

"No, it's too dangerous," Julianne protested, but Morgan was already gone.

With her heart in her throat, she watched helplessly as her daughter walked across the cracked concrete floor, one hand on her gun holster.

Princess whined, adding to the tension while Julianne scanned their surroundings with paranoid intensity. The place had an abandoned feel, the bulk of a rusting car in a patch of brush reinforcing that perception. A dove took flight, and a single feather drifted down. *Maybe it will be okay. There's no one here.*

Morgan reached the small building and knocked on the shop's front door, calling out. "Anyone there?"

Nothing happened.

She knocked again, louder this time.

Still nothing.

Morgan turned back to them and shrugged. "I think it's desert..."

A body slammed into the glass behind her. Morgan screamed and threw up her hands in an instinctive reaction. The thing that used to be a person threw itself against the door, pushing it open.

Julianne gasped as Morgan flung herself against the frame, preventing the infected from getting out. She strained as she held on, her booted feet scraping across the gravel.

The zombie went berserk, smashing its head into the glass until it shattered. It thrust a hand through, ignoring the jagged shards that cut into its flesh. Its grasping fingers hooked onto Morgan's ponytail and pulled her head toward its gaping maw.

"Mom, help me!"

"I'm coming! Hold on!"

Ignoring the cries of Meghan, Julianne jumped out of the truck and raced across the gap. She reached the struggling duo, pistol in hand. The zombie had thrust its head through the opening, and its teeth gnashed at the air mere centimeters from Morgan's face. Spit drooled from its grinning lips, and the broken glass had peeled back the skin from its cheeks in a gruesome display.

Fury flooded Julianne's veins. "Let go of my daughter!"

She pushed the gun to its forehead and pulled the trigger. The bullet entered the skull, mangling the brains which exploded out of the exit wound in a spray of rotting gunk. The zombie slumped, releasing its hold on Morgan who slid to her knees, gasping.

"Are you okay? Did it hurt you?" Julianne grabbed Morgan's shoulder, pulling her upright and into a tight hug. "Oh, my God. I don't know what I'd do if I lost you. Don't scare me like that ever again."

Morgan's chest heaved as she fought for air. After a moment, she gulped and stepped back. Her trembling hands examined her scalp and face, checking for possible injuries. "I'm okay, Mom. It's all right."

It took a few more moments before they'd calmed down enough to return to the truck. Julianne gathered the hysterical Meghan into her arms and soothed her while Princess caused a ruckus.

"Are you two all right?" a concerned Joanna asked. She fussed over Morgan, wiping the blood spatters off her face with a tissue.

"We're okay, but what do we do now?" Morgan said.

"I guess we get what we came for. We need supplies and petrol," Julianne replied.

"What about him?" Morgan pointed to the shop.

"He's dead, and anyway, it looks like he was alone."

Morgan nodded. "Okay, but we better make sure first. I don't fancy any more nasty surprises."

"This time, I'm coming with you," Julianne said.

Together, they searched the building. It consisted of the shop front, a single bathroom, and a tiny storeroom. Out back, they found a parked car, probably belonging to the infected man Julianne had shot.

Once they determined it was safe, Julianne dragged the corpse out of the way and stashed it behind the counter. She covered it with an old towel before examining the contents of the shelves. Outside, the afternoon had flown, and the sun dropped toward the horizon. A thought occurred to her, and she turned to Morgan. "It's getting late. Why don't we stay here for the night?"

"Really?"

"Why not?" Julianne shrugged. "There's a toilet, food, and water."

"It's not safe." Morgan gestured to the shattered door.

"We can sleep in the car." Julianne looked around. "It's better than spending the night beside the road."

"I suppose."

"Why don't you get Joanna and Meghan? We can all use a bathroom break and have something to eat." Julianne paused. "One of us has to keep watch, though."

"Okay."

Julianne returned to the task of scrounging up a meal from the shop's limited supplies. When Meghan appeared, her eyes still swollen from crying, she smoothed a hand over her child's hair and steered her to the bathroom. "Let's wash up, sweetie."

A meal of questionable nutritional value followed: Sandwiches cobbled together from stale bread, processed cheese slices, and margarine, served with potato chips, cold drinks, and chocolate bars. At least, it filled them, but Julianne longed for a hot meal.

Meghan giggled as she fed Princess bits of bread and cheese, hiding the pieces in her shirt for the dog's quivering nose to sniff out. Julianne was glad to see her smile again.

They took turns to attend to their ablutions, including the dog, and Morgan loaded up the truck with more supplies. The card for the petrol pump they found in the till and used it to top up the tank plus a few jerry cans as well.

Night approached, the light fading inside a murky soup. Clapping her hands together, Julianne called, "Into the truck everyone. It's getting dark."

Nobody needed to be told twice.

***

It was close to midnight, and try as she might, Julianne could not sleep. In the passenger seat next to her, Morgan shifted. Her breath hitched in her throat, and a whimper escaped her lips. On the back seat, Meghan and Joanna were in similar states of distress. Julianne could only imagine what nightmares plagued them.

It was these same dark dreams that kept her awake, preventing her mind from escaping their current situation. *What are we going to do? Where do we go tomorrow?*

It was hot inside the airless cab without the air conditioner, the heat of the day slow to dissipate. Sweat dampened her clothes, while mosquitoes took advantage of the opportunity to prey on her skin leaving a trail of red bumps in their wake.

The events of the day played over and over in her mind, threatening to derail the delicate equilibrium she'd balanced all day. John, Max, Lilian, Ronald, and their children...all lost. She could only pray that some of them still lived.

Julianne pressed her cheek to the cool glass and stared into the night. Tears trickled down her cheeks, a sob lodging in her throat. *I miss you, John.*

Finally, she nodded off, exhausted by her emotions. The next morning she awoke in the pre-dawn hours with the sun yet to put in an appearance. She pushed herself upright and groaned at the ache in her back and shoulders. When she noticed the empty seat beside her, she gasped. "Morgan!"

Julianne twisted around, reassured to find Joanna and Meghan still fast asleep. Casting about, she searched for her other daughter and spotted her figure a short distance away from the car. A cigarette glowed in Morgan's hand, the red tip burning brightly in the gloom.

With a muttered curse, Julianne jumped out and hissed, "What the hell do you think you're doing? You scared me half to death."

"I'm sorry. I needed space to think."

Julianne prepared to let loose a barrage of fury until she saw the silent tears that streamed down Morgan's face. She sighed and shook her head. "I understand, just warn me next time. I can't lose you too."

Morgan nodded. "Okay, Mom."

Julianne let her be, preparing instead for their departure. Meghan woke up soon after that followed by Joanna. In silence, they had breakfast and freshened up in the bathroom.

"Time to go," Julianne said at last.

"Where to?" Morgan asked.

"I don't know. Guess we'll find out."

Julianne drove off, silent worry haunting her every thought. The road stretched ahead, and she scanned the sides for signs of life. *Come on, come on. There has to be something.*

After forty minutes of fruitless searching, she saw a sight that caused her to cry out. "Look!"

Morgan sat upright. "What is it?"

"Over there," Julianne replied, pointing at a battered truck parked behind a gate. A fence stretched to either side, and a dirt road led to a sign that welcomed visitors to Sweet Water Valley Farm. A man of small and wiry build stood beside the tall metal gate, evidently on his way out.

Julianne jerked the car off the tar and onto the dirt before slamming on the brakes. Amidst a cloud of dust, she got out. "Wait here, guys."

The farmer watched with a perplexed frown as she strode over, lifting her hand in a wave. He doffed his faded khaki hat in a gesture reminiscent of the old days and smiled. "Good morning, ma'am. Can I help you, perhaps? Are you lost?"

Julianne shook her head. "No, we're not lost, but we do need your help."

"Yes?" he asked with infinite patience.

A sudden sob lodged in Julianne's throat, causing her to choke on her words. "You have no idea how good it is to see you, to see another person alive and uninfected."

"Uninfected?" Surprise flitted across his weather-worn features. "What do you mean?"

"You don't know what's going on?" Tears blurred her vision, and the farmer took a step closer. "We've been so scared."

With a concerned look, he patted her on the back. "Why

don't I take you back to the house? You can tell me all about it over a cup of coffee."

"Yes!" Julianne cried. "Thank you, thank you so much, Mr..."

"Henri. Just call me Henri."

Chapter 9 - Breytenbach

"Captain," Mike shouted, his voice faint above the helicopter's rotors. "We're being diverted."

"What?"

"We're being diverted to a quarantine camp outside Pretoria and Johannesburg."

"What for?" Breytenbach frowned, leaning forward.

"Just got a message from the base, Captain. We can't land."

"That's crazy! Why? Do we even have enough fuel?"

"We should make it, Captain. Just." Mike glanced over his shoulder, shaking his head. "Thaba Tshwane has fallen. It's a hot zone now."

Breytenbach sat back with a thump, his mind a blank. *Fallen? The military base in Pretoria has fallen? Impossible.*

Thaba Tshwane was a massive joint operation military base, home to the South African Army College, the Military Police School and Hospital, a Parachute Battalion, and much more. It even boasted the Pretoria Regiment, tanks. That it had fallen was beyond belief. If that was true, they were in even worse trouble than he'd thought.

Samantha, who'd fallen asleep in Zelda's arms awoke. She bawled, her face red and contorted. He stared at her tiny, scrunched up features and waving fists, and his heart stuttered as he remembered his promise. *I'll take care of you, little girl. I swear it.*

A short while later, they reached their destination, and the chopper landed. Breytenbach hustled the survivors out while Mike cut the engine. The noise and wind died away, leaving an eerie calm in its wake.

He looked around, curious to see where they found themselves. A flat expanse of dusty ground surrounded by barbed wire greeted his eyes. Military vehicles littered a square concrete lot, and soldiers in field gear patrolled the fence. A sea of tents covered the packed earth, and hundreds of people swarmed between the lines.

"Captain Breytenbach?" A young voice interrupted his study, and he turned. The owner of the voice turned out to be a young Lieutenant with light blue eyes and an earnest expression. His uniform was new, too new to have seen any action, and he looked what he was: As green as grass.

"Former Captain Breytenbach," he corrected.

"Lieutenant Nathan. At your service." The soldier shook his hand before looking at the small knot of women and children. He gestured toward another soldier hovering nearby. "You can accompany Second Lieutenant Smith here. He'll take you to your new lodgings."

The women hesitated and looked at Breytenbach for guidance.

"Where's that?" he asked.

"We've set aside a tent for orphaned kids. They'll be well-taken care of, I assure you."

Breytenbach nodded at Zelda. "Go with him. I'll check on you later and make sure everything's okay."

"Okay." With faltering steps, they gathered up their few belongings and left.

90

Breytenbach turned back to the Lieutenant. "Who's in command here?"

Lieutenant Nathan hesitated. "I am. Major Smart was in command, but he died a few days ago."

"Infected?"

"Yes, we had a breach."

"Breach?" Breytenbach looked around, his unease intensifying. "How are the defenses?"

"Piss poor, Captain."

This straight-forward admission took Breytenbach off guard, and he sucked in a breath. "That bad?"

"Let me show you."

It was far worse than Breytenbach had initially thought. Three thousand souls were squeezed into the quarantine camp, stuffed into canvas tents with few supplies and even less water. No ablutions, either. A latrine trench had been dug, and already the stench was unbearable.

The site was indefensible, manned by a handful of soldiers with very little in the way of munitions. Twice already, the fence had failed with infected forcing their way inside. A small burial site hosted the dead, growing larger by the day.

As they walked, formality gave way to the reality of the situation. "Who in God's name chose this piece of land for a quarantine camp? I'd like to strangle the piece of shit."

"A politician who thought he was clever. Personally, I hope the zombies ate him alive."

"What about Command?"

"We've been receiving conflicting reports and orders all day." Lieutenant Nathan shook his head, his lip curled in disgust. "The President and his cronies have fled the coop. They're holed up in the hills with half the army and a boatload of supplies. They don't give a crap about us."

"Do you know what happened at Thaba Tshwane?"

"Overrun."

Breytenbach swore. "So it's true. If they fell..."

"Then we don't stand a chance," Lieutenant Nathan finished.

***

Hours later, Breytenbach was exhausted and ready to crash. He'd been assigned a one-man tent and stretcher and very much looked forward to some rest.

All day long he'd been occupied with Lieutenant Nathan, checking the supplies and defenses. The young man, thrown into the deep end after his commander died, was eager to pick Breytenbach's brain. At least, he recognized experience when he saw it.

Breytenbach had toured the medical tent and been introduced to Jonathan, the resident doctor. The poor guy was hopelessly overworked and ill-equipped, besieged by countless sick people. The entire situation was depressing.

The promise he'd made to Lieutenant Nathan to stay and help, weighed heavily on him. It was a huge responsibility. Yet, where else would they go? Thaba Tshwane was gone, and the chopper didn't have sufficient fuel to reach any of the other bases.

His initial reservations about staying fell away when he saw the plight of the people. The hungry faces, the sunken eyes, and the crying children. How could he say no to that? So he'd agreed to stay, as had his team. *I just hope to God we can make a difference.*

Before he could sleep, he had one last job to do. His weary

legs carried him to the tent set aside for the orphaned children. He pushed the flap open and stepped inside.

Ordered chaos met his eyes. Cots and cribs lined the walls while playpens and toys dotted the floor. Babies cried, toddlers screamed, and children complained while their caretakers did their best to soothe them. The air was warm, carrying the scents of baby powder underlined with poop, and he wrinkled his nose at the weird combination.

He made his way through the tent, searching for a familiar face but found none. He saw neither Zelda nor Linda and was about to give up when a voice called out.

"Captain! Over here."

He craned his head and saw a slim hand waving at him. It was Mannuru, calling him over to Samantha's crib. She wore a clean babygrow and sucked on a bottle, one hand fisted in a soft blanket. He felt an involuntary smile grow on his face and said, "She looks well. Happy."

"Yes," Mannuru replied, brushing a soft hand over Sam's head. "She's strong."

"Just like her mother," Breytenbach whispered.

"Would you like to hold her?"

"Yes, yes I would." Breytenbach was surprised to find it was true and held out his hands eagerly. Little Samantha had latched onto his heart with all her might, and he felt more and more like her adoptive father.

Mannuru picked the baby up and handed her to Breytenbach. "Here."

He took her with care, scared he might hurt her. Mannuru helped him, and after a time, he got the hang of it. As he cradled her to his chest, he inhaled her scent. That wonderful warm, milky smell unique to all infants. Warmth blossomed

93

in his chest and his resolve hardened. *I will never let anything hurt you. I promise.*

Chapter 10 - Logan

What followed the rescue of Elise and her children turned out to be a strangely peaceful period, one that passed in a blur of hard work interspersed with constant raids.

Elise took over the running of their home base. Under her enterprising hand, the dining and sitting rooms expanded to become a common area where everyone gathered to have their meals. She also cataloged and stored the incoming supplies, turned the offices into bedrooms, and expanded the kitchen.

The children appeared to be adjusting. Anne was a sweet child and often helped her mother with the chores, while the two boys became very close. They tried hard to act like adults and took it upon themselves to patrol the fence and keep watch.

As for Logan and Max, they went out each day, raiding the shops and houses in the area and eradicating any infected in the vicinity. After a week had passed, they convened in the dining room to discuss their progress.

Elise was putting the final touches on supper, and Logan's stomach rumbled as the delicious smells drifted through the room. "God, I'm starving."

"You're always hungry, Logan. What's new?" Max said.

"Do you blame me with Elise's cooking?"

"Nope. Can't say I do."

"Right. So where are we sitting at?" Logan asked.

"Well, we've cleared the houses in the vicinity. We've erected roadblocks to discourage wandering infected, strung barbed wire all around the fence, and built up a small stockpile of guns and ammunition. What am I missing here?"

"We've gathered a fair amount of supplies too. Food, blankets, clothes, that sort of thing," Logan added.

"We need more medicine, though, and guns," Max replied.

"That will have to wait. We have a more pressing problem."

"What's that?"

"The fence. It's not strong enough. If a horde of those things comes through, they'll plow right through it. They don't feel a thing."

"That's true, but what happens if a breach occurs? We should reinforce the doors and windows too," Max suggested.

"Don't forget the electricity. It's bound to go out any day now. We need a generator and a lot of fuel."

Max sighed, looking down at his chest, and Logan took the opportunity to study him. His uniform wasn't quite so pristine anymore, sporting stains and tears in several places. His face boasted the beginnings of a wiry beard, and his hands were cut and blistered from stringing the barbed wire.

At first, Logan had thought little of the clean-cut soldier boy Max represented, but after a week of brutal labor and the threat of constant death, his respect for the man had grown. It was one reason he hadn't left yet. That, and the fact that with Elise and the kids there, Max needed him.

"Okay, first things first, where can we get a generator and lots of fuel?" Logan asked.

"The industrial area," Max said. "It's not far from here."

"Can we risk it?"

"I think we can. The virus hit this town on a weekend while the industrial shops were closed. It should be safe enough."

"We might find other supplies too," Logan mused.

"Such as?"

"A truck would be nice, some tools, building material, a tank to store water in."

"Sounds like we've got a plan. First thing tomorrow?"

"Yup."

"Do you think we—"

"That's enough talk, boys," Elise interrupted. "Time for dinner."

She placed plates heaped high with mashed potatoes, gravy, fried mushrooms, and steaks in front of each.

"Have you washed your hands?" she asked.

"Yes, ma'am," they answered in concert.

"Good. I don't want zombie blood at the dinner table."

"Where are the kids?" Logan asked.

"I sent them off to bed with an early supper. I wanted to talk to you two in private." She placed a large salad in the middle of the table before seating herself.

"About what?" Logan crammed a huge forkful of potatoes into his mouth.

"I want to know what the situation is."

"Max, that's your department," Logan said. "You're the leader here."

Max raised an eyebrow at that but didn't protest, turning instead to Elise. "What do you want to know, exactly?"

"First, how's it looking out there?"

"We haven't gone out far enough to know. We're sticking close to home, clearing the area and gathering supplies."

"Speaking of which, we're running out of fresh vegetables."

She indicated the salad. "That's the last of the lettuce. I'm preserving and freezing as much as I can, but I need more Consol bottles, vinegar, and salt."

"All right," Max nodded. "Think we could hit a store soon, Logan?"

"Maybe. If we're real careful." Logan jammed another forkful into his mouth. His plate was emptying at a rapid pace, so he scooped up a double helping of salad.

"You could look for seeds too. Then I can start a garden out back," Elise added.

"All right, but tomorrow we're hitting the industrial area first. We need generators and fuel. The electricity's not gonna last," Max said.

"What about water? Once the power goes out, the water will stop too," Elise said.

"I didn't even think of that," Max replied, looking sheepish.

"It's a problem," Logan agreed. "A big one."

"Elise, get the boys to fill up every available container we've got with water tomorrow. Meantime, Logan and I will get a generator and fuel and building material for the fence," Max said.

"The fence? What's wrong with the fence?"

"It's not strong enough, but I don't know how we're going to fortify it with just the two of us," Max leaned back in his chair. "There's too much to do."

"Why don't you use cars?" Elise asked.

Max and Logan stared at her, unsure what she meant.

"You know, take abandoned cars and park them along the inside of the fence."

"That might work," Max said.

"It could. It would strengthen the fence and obstruct the

view of the inside of the grounds," Logan added.

They spent another hour hashing over the challenges they faced before seeking their beds.

The next morning, fortified with a solid breakfast, Logan and Max left. They drove in one of the Nyalas—not taking any chances. With its armored plating and bulletproof windows, there wasn't much that could stop a Nyala. Nothing undead anyway. They pulled to a stop in front of an auto repair shop.

"Want to try it?" Logan asked.

"Sure, why not," Max answered as he got out.

It was a chilly morning with a stiff breeze that cut through their clothes. Lifting his head, Logan sniffed the wind. "It's going to rain."

"You can smell rain?"

"No, but I can see the storm clouds on the horizon over there," Logan pointed, and Max grinned at this rare joke from him.

They moved fast and without making a sound. After a week of working together, they'd built up a rapport and were quite efficient. They'd walk forward in stages, clearing room after room. At times, they'd pause and make a noise, a knock or a shout, to see if any infected responded. It lessened the chances of being surprised and gave them a fighting chance. One they sorely needed.

The auto repair shop proved to have a lot of useful tools, car spares, and oil, but no fuel or generator so Logan pointed at an engineering shop across the street. "Let's try over there."

The doors were locked. Logan tried to pry open the security gates with a crowbar, but they were impossible to break into. Eyeing the fence, he said, "Give me a boost?"

Balancing on Max's back, he peered over and studied

the yard. In the far corner, he spotted movement. "I see something."

After a moment more, Max eased him to the ground. "There's one infected in the yard, probably a security guard."

"Let's go then."

They climbed over and approached the lone zombie. The ex-security guard stood with his back to them, moaning plaintively at something on the other side of the fence. Creeping up, Logan dispatched him with a swift blow.

He bent down to wrench free his ax and search for the shop keys when Max whistled. "Would you look at that."

Logan looked up, through the chain-link fence and into the next yard. A large warehouse dominated the grounds, surrounded by scraggly grass and patches of gravel. Attached by a chain to a tree, lay a large dog. Or at least, it used to be big. Now it was a mere shadow of its former self.

"Ah, shit," Logan swore. At the sound of their voices, the dog moved its head, gazing at them with glazed eyes. It was still alive.

"That's what he was after," Max said, nudging the dead security guard with his foot. "What do we do now?"

"We try to save it," Logan replied.

They used the guard's keys to get inside and search the premises. They found a small truck, big enough to load everything they needed, a generator, a tank of fuel, and bolt cutters.

Filling a bowl with water, they headed back to the fence. After making a hole, Logan slipped through while Max stood guard. The dog was emaciated, but it had enough strength left to drink the water. Empty bowls next to the dog explained how it had managed to last so long. *Probably drank rainwater too.*

Logan rubbed its head, "There you go, boy. Drink up. We're taking you home." He looked at Max. "Let's load him into the truck with the rest of the stuff and go back. We've got what we need."

"Yeah, let's not push our luck. The next place might not be so easy to hit," Max cautioned. "We can always come back."

An hour later, they returned home to an astonished Elise and three excited kids.

"Can we keep him?" Thembiso begged with his dark brown eyes fixed on the dog.

"Yes, we can keep him. If he lives," Logan replied.

"Oh, he'll live. I'll make sure of that," Elise replied. "What he needs is good nourishing food. Thembiso, warm up a bowl of leftover soup. Peter, get him more water. Anne, why don't you make him a nice, warm bed?"

Satisfied that the dog was in good hands, Logan and Max returned to their work. They unloaded their booty and spent the next few hours setting up the generator.

"We should get a backup generator," Max said. "And more fuel. Water too."

"We're in trouble, aren't we?" Logan asked with a sigh, thinking of all the stuff they still needed while there was only the two of them to do the work.

"I didn't want to say anything, but yes, we are." Max sighed. "What if a horde of those things attack? None of the others can fight, and scavenging is pretty dangerous. How long before one of us gets killed?"

"I know. It's depressing."

They trudged back inside and sat down at a table. The kids chattered, excited by the new addition to their home while

Elise dished up their food. As he ate, Logan looked around at the smiling faces that surrounded him. It was warm and comforting. Like home.

While the atmosphere helped to lift his spirits, it also drove home the fact that he was needed. Despite his natural inclinations to go it alone, he couldn't leave. Not while so many lives depended on him.

The days passed, filled with ceaseless activity and hard work. The dog survived, his ribs filling out under Elise's care. They reinforced the doors and windows while Max taught Elise and the boys how to shoot. He tried to show Anne too, but she cried every time he put a gun in her hands. Then, on the morning of the fifteenth day, something unexpected happened.

Logan woke up with a start, ears pricked for danger. He was certain he'd heard a noise. Getting up, he got dressed and looked out the window through a slit in the wooden boards. It was still dark, but the promise of dawn glimmered on the horizon. A hoarse cry drew his attention once more, and he was sure it was that which had woken him up earlier. He spotted movement at the gate. *People.*

Logan moved fast, waking up both Max and Elise. "Elise, stay here and guard the children."

She nodded, her eyes wide in her pale face.

Together, Max and Logan approached the gate, theirs guns at the ready. A small group of people huddled in front of it, and they slowed, approaching with caution.

Logan nodded to Max. "Go ahead."

"Who's there?" Max cried, taking the lead.

A shadow detached itself from the group. "Are you sur-vivors?" The voice belonged to an older man with iron-gray hair. "Please, let us in. I'm begging you."

"Who are you?" Max asked while Logan scanned the group for any signs of danger.

"Just people. Survivors running from those things."

Max didn't reply, a look of uncertainty chasing across his face.

To Logan, they looked like a pitiful bunch. Hardly a threat. He looked at Max and shrugged. "Your call. They look okay to me."

"Please, we mean no harm. We've got a pregnant lady here and a girl who's wounded. If we stay out here, we'll die," the older man added, desperation lacing his voice.

Max bobbed his head. "All right. Let's give them a chance."

Chapter 11 - Elise

Elise watched the sad little group troop into her home with a mixture of apprehension and fear. Who were they? What were they doing here? More importantly, what did they want?

These questions and more milled through her mind as she struggled to keep the two boys and the over-excited Buzz under control. She needn't worry about Anne, though. Her daughter stood behind her with both hands latched onto her shirt-tail.

Elise's eyes traveled over the members of the group. An older man with a lined face and husky build was in charge, hustling everyone inside like a mother hen with chicks.

Two young men, brothers by the looks of it, half-carried a red-headed girl. Sweat beaded her forehead, and her skin had a waxen sheen to it that boded ill. Elise spotted a wound on her arm, seeping blood. *That'll need attention.*

A dark-haired girl stuck to them like a shadow, looking around her with a deep mistrust which Elise put down to fear. Lastly came another man, middle-aged, tall and slim, supporting a pregnant woman, probably his wife. Her bulging belly spoke of an advanced pregnancy, and it was here that Elise's attention fixated. The poor woman was in labor, arousing her motherly instincts.

"Peter, put water on to boil. Thembiso, fetch clean towels,"

Elise ordered. She turned to Anne, prying her fingers loose. "Anne, sweetie. Take Buzz to your room and keep him busy. I need to help these people."

With eyes as large as saucers, Anne nodded and coaxed the dog away. Buzz wasn't keen on going, his protective instincts coming to the fore. "Go on, Buzz. Shoo!"

With a whine, he followed Anne, helped along by Peter who dragged him by the collar.

"What do we do with them, Elise?" Max asked.

She found it amusing that he'd turn to her for direction when he was the leader. His consternation became apparent, though, when the pregnant woman cried out, causing him to flinch.

"We need to get the rest of them settled while I see to her, Max. She's in labor."

"Oh, shit," he muttered, turning pale.

"Why don't you help them to one of the spare bedrooms? I'll be along shortly."

"Okay," he replied.

Elise was grateful she'd prepared extra rooms in case they found more survivors. Not that she'd been expecting an entire group to show up on their doorstep. She turned to Logan. "Why don't you check them for bites?"

"She's been bitten," he replied, pointing to the red-haired girl, his eyes cold and remote. "She's a danger to us all."

In an instant, the atmosphere in the room changed. The older man in charge of the motley group placed himself in front of the sick girl. "No one is harming her."

The rest of them likewise clustered around, forming a barrier and lending their silent support. It was an explosive situation. They were all armed, and Logan did not inspire confidence with the stony expression on his face. The two brothers, in particular, watched him with wary caution.

Max stepped to the forefront, raising a placating hand. "No one will hurt her, but we need to check the rest of you for infection, and we'll have to take precautions."

"What kind of precautions?" their leader asked.

"She has to be guarded at all times. We cannot put anyone here at risk."

The older man considered this. "That's fair."

Elise stepped forward. "Logan put her in the bedroom furthest from the rest. I'll bring a first aid kit to treat her wound."

He nodded, and they trooped away.

Once everyone left, Elise rushed to the storeroom, grabbing supplies as she went. Her mind surged along, considering all the possibilities. She did not foresee the night ending well for either the girl or the pregnant woman.

Max had led the couple to the nearest spare room, and Elise thrust a first aid kit into his arms. "Here, go check on the wounded girl."

"Okay," he replied, rushing out.

Elise got to work and piled several large cushions onto the bed to form a backrest. Afterward, she laid out her bundle of supplies on the side table and turned to the woman. "Ma'am, I need to make sure you weren't bitten. Will you let me take a look before you lie down?"

The woman glanced up at her husband, fear in her eyes. After a few seconds, he nodded, and Elise shut the door.

Together they undressed her, and Elise scanned her smooth dark skin for bites. She was clean. They dressed her in a clean nightgown and helped her to lie down, propping her up until she was comfortable.

Elise turned to the husband. "Sir, if I may, I'd like to help your wife with the birth."

He scanned her face with sober eyes and must have been comforted by what he saw because he nodded. "Her name is Tumi, and I'm Joseph. Joseph Masakale."

Elise smiled, relieved. "My name is Elise." She glanced at Tumi who lay moaning on the bed. "How far along is she?"

His brow knitted in confusion, and Tumi answered instead. "Seven months."

Elise's stomach knotted at the words. *Seven months. It's not enough. Not without a hospital.*

She gave Tumi a broad smile, though. "Don't worry. We'll take good care of you."

Tumi nodded, some of the tension leaving her face. A knock on the door announced Thembiso with a stack of towels, followed by Peter carrying a kettle.

"Put it over here," Elise indicated a spot before waving them away. "Look after your sister, Peter. You know how scared she gets."

"Okay, Mom."

They left, and Elise turned back to Tumi, examining her. The news wasn't good. There was no way to halt the contractions. She was fully dilated.

Elise turned to Joseph and led him aside. "The baby is coming, and it's too soon. Do you understand?"

His eyes darkened, the lines around his mouth deepening.

"I'll do what I can, but you need to be prepared. The baby may not survive."

After a moment of silence, he turned away, his mouth compressed. She let him be, focusing on Tumi instead who

107

writhed as another contraction gripped her. Minutes later it passed, and Elise turned to Max who'd appeared in the doorway.

"How are the others?" she asked.

"I've treated the girl's wound and given her painkillers," he replied. "She's all right for the moment, but the virus is progressing fast. It won't be long."

"Poor thing. What will happen once she turns?"

"Their leader, Ben, has assured me he'll take care of it when the time comes, but I've left Logan to guard the door."

Elise closed her eyes for a moment. *So young to die.*

"They're all clear? The rest of them? No bites?"

"They're clean." He pointed at Joseph. "But I still need to check him."

Joseph, who'd been listening, stepped forward. "I am not infected, but you can examine me if you want to."

Elise left them to it and returned to Tumi. Once Max finished his inspection, he went to organize food and drink for the newcomers while Joseph paced up and down, worry furrowing his brow.

Elise briefly left to check on Anne and the boys. They were in the common room, playing board games while Buzz hovered around them. Once she was sure the kids were okay, she checked on the others.

They were all sitting on the red-headed girl's bed when she entered, their faces drawn. Max must have given the girl strong stuff because she was pretty out of it, staring at the ceiling with glazed eyes.

The man she now knew as Ben rose when she entered, extending his hand to her. "Thank you for helping us, Ma'am."

"Elise," she answered. "And you're welcome."

"I'm Ben or Big Ben as most like to call me. This is Jacques and Armand." He pointed to the brothers. "And that's Angie."

Angie nodded, her dark eyes showing no expression while the brothers each shook her hand.

"What's her name?" Elise asked, gesturing toward the stricken girl.

"Susan," Big Ben answered.

"What happened?"

"Our shelter was overrun. In the chaos, one of them got Susan." His shoulders sagged. "I should have protected her."

"It's not your fault, Ben," Armand answered.

Ben did not seem comforted by the words, and Elise felt her insides tighten with sorrow. "Your daughter?"

"No." He shook his head. "But as good as."

"I'm sorry." Elise's eyes traveled to Susan. Her freckles stood out against the pallor of her skin, light blue eyes swimming with the knowledge that death was coming for her. Even the drugs could not ease that.

Elise swallowed hard, thinking of Anne. *That could be her on the bed.*

"You've had something to eat? Drink?" she asked, trying to distract herself.

"Yes, thank you." Ben looked at her. "How is Tumi? We're worried about her."

Elise decided the group needed no more bad news and plastered on a smile. "She's fine for now. I'm helping her to deliver the baby. In fact, I'd better get back there right away."

He nodded. "Well, thank you again."

She left the room, noting Logan who kept watch like a stone statue. A hard man, she was nonetheless grateful he was there. He'd make sure Susan did not turn and hurt anyone else.

Elise returned to Tumi's side, focusing all her attention on delivering the baby. Long hours passed during which Tumi writhed and cried. Elise sponged her brow, gave her water and juice to drink and helped her to the bathroom. There wasn't much else she could do.

At one point, Joseph left the room, preferring to stand outside away from his wife's screams. Elise understood. Witnessing a loved one in pain was hard.

A little while later, Max reported that Susan had passed. A muffled shot confirmed that someone had taken care of it. Elise didn't know whether to be sad or relieved and pushed her feelings aside for the moment.

It was mid-afternoon before the head of the baby crowned. Elise crouched between Tumi's legs, helping the baby out of the birth canal. The umbilical cord was wrapped around its neck, and one look at the grayish pallor of the skin was enough to confirm her worst fears. That, and the silence.

The baby was stillborn.

Small enough to fit into her cupped hands but perfectly formed, Elise cried silent tears as she handed the tiny form to Tumi. The poor woman burst into heart-rending sobs.

"I'm so sorry," Elise said to Joseph when he entered.

He stood beside the bed with a stricken expression, reaching out a hesitant hand toward his wife. She gripped his fingers in hers, clinging to him. Their pain was hard to watch, private and intense. Elise excused herself, brushing away her tears. It would have been a perfect little boy.

Chapter 12 - Morgan

The dull thunk of an ax blade echoed through the humid air. Two pieces of wood landed in the grass on either side of an old stump. In the distance, dark clouds promised rain, but the heat was unrelenting.

Morgan wiped the sweat from her brow and lifted the ax high again, bringing it down in a smooth arc. For half an hour, she split logs until there was enough to last them a few days.

She groaned, straightening up to ease the nagging ache that nestled in the small of her back. Her skin prickled with heat, and she longed for an ice cold drink.

Morgan loaded the split logs into a wheelbarrow and headed towards the house. She added the firewood to the small stack next to the kitchen door before going inside.

Weathered by sun, wind, and rain, the battered old farm-house welcomed her into its shadowed confines. She pulled off her work gloves, tossing them on the table before slumping into a chair.

Hannelie stood by the counter, chopping tomatoes and onions while Joanna stirred a boiling pot. Flames flickered in the old coal stove Henri had dug out of storage. If it weren't so hot, it would be homey.

"Finished, my dear?" Hannelie asked.

"For now," Morgan replied. "I still have to check the fences with Henri. Where is he?"

"In the barn, but have a drink first before you go." Hannelie pressed a tepid glass of water into her hands, and Morgan swallowed it gratefully. These past few weeks, she'd learned not to complain.

Her thoughts wandered back to the first day of the outbreak. It all seemed like a bad dream now. Brian, her father, all of it. A nightmare they had yet to awaken from. The first few nights, she'd cried herself to sleep, mourning everything she'd lost, but by now a certain numbness had set in.

"Are you all right, dear?" Hannelie's concerned voice broke into her thoughts.

Morgan shook off her depression. "I'm all right."

Hannelie had welcomed them into her home without any reservations. One night turned into two and before they knew it, a week had passed. She never complained, taking them in like the lost orphans they were.

The farm workers disappeared one by one, leaving to be with their families. The oldest, Daniel, who would have brought his family back to the farm, promised to see them within a day or two. He never returned either.

Being young and active, Morgan had volunteered to help with the farm work, while Joanna and Julianne helped around the house. At night, they watched the news on TV to keep abreast with events. When all broadcasts ceased, they listened to the radio. Eventually, that stopped too.

The cellphone networks never came back on, and none of them knew what had happened to friends and family. Perhaps, it was better that way.

After two weeks the electricity went off, and the water followed soon after. Morgan reckoned it had been around six weeks now and things weren't looking good. Then there was her little sister.

"How's Meghan doing?"

"Still the same," Joanna replied.

That was bad news. A few days ago, Meghan had developed a hacking cough which soon escalated. Last Morgan saw she was running a fever, a fiery red blush coloring her cheeks. Julianne never left her side, sponging her forehead ceaselessly.

Morgan sighed and put down the empty glass, wishing for more. She would not ask, though. *Time to get back to work.*

Henri was busy mucking out the barn when she found him. As small as his wife was large, he possessed copious amounts of energy. The gleaming tack on the walls and carefully arranged equipment testified to that.

Lola, the milk cow, lowed at her when she walked in, and Morgan scratched her forehead while the chickens clucked around her feet.

"Need help?" she asked.

"Not with this," Henri replied. "But you can put the buckets out for when it rains."

"You think it will?"

"I'm hoping so. We need the water."

That they did. Once a day, Henri switched on the generator to power the borehole, pumping just enough water for their most pressing needs. More he could not do as they were fast running out of fuel.

Morgan set the buckets down outside, glancing at the clouds on the horizon. "Please let it rain."

Afterward, she saddled Pete, an old draft horse, and set off to check the fences. It was an essential task every day. They could not afford for any infected to get through. That barrier was all that stood between them and death.

It was also the one task she looked forward to every day. Riding on Pete's broad back gave her a taste of precious freedom. A freedom lost now that they were confined to the farm.

Every day she wished she could head out, explore, find out what was going on in the outside world. The old folks wouldn't hear of it, though, insisting it wasn't safe. Perhaps it wasn't, but the uncertainty was killing her.

The ride also gave her a chance to process the feelings of guilt and grief she harbored. At first, it had been all she could think of. Now it wasn't so bad anymore, perhaps because she was too busy trying to survive.

Today, like most days, the ride was uneventful, free from intruding zombies. Within an hour, she was on her way back. Only twice in the past weeks had she come across an infected. Both times they were stuck in the fence, entangled in the wire. The memory of their empty eyes caused a shudder to ripple through her. Still, she had done what needed to be done.

When she reached the farmyard, a cool breeze stirred her ponytail, bringing blessed relief from the heat. The clouds had moved closer, and once more she prayed for rain.

She spent the rest of the afternoon weeding the vegetable patch, noting with displeasure the wilted stalks and leaves. If it didn't rain soon, they'd have to pump more water.

Supper was a quiet affair, notable only by the absence of Julianne and Meghan. It was also bland beyond belief. Since the electricity gave out, all the refrigerated goods had spoiled. They were left with the pantry and what the animals and garden could provide. Tonight, it was maize porridge with tomato and onion gravy. No meat. *What I wouldn't give for a nice juicy steak.*

But food was food, and Morgan scraped her plate clean until it shone before putting it in the sink. "Thanks for supper, Hannelie. Joanna. I'll just go check in on Mom and Meghan."

"Take them something to eat while you're at it, dear," Hannelie replied, pointing to two plates on the stove.

Morgan obeyed, making her way to the small room Julianne shared with Meghan. As expected, Julianne sat hunched over on a stool next to the bed where Meghan lay, tossing and turning. Every few seconds her small body spasmed, wracking coughs tearing through her chest. It was painful to hear.

"Here, Mom. Have something to eat."

Julianne looked at the plate like it crawled with insects. "I'm not hungry, thanks."

"Come on. Try to eat, please. You've had hardly anything all day."

Julianne took it from her with reluctance, picking at a tomato without enthusiasm while Morgan tried to coax a few bites into Meghan. Hannelie had used some of their precious sugar and milk for the little girl's porridge, knowing it was her favorite.

"Do you think she'll get better?" Morgan asked.

"I don't know." Julianne shook her head, looking defeated. "Her fever is so high. If only I had medicine to give her. Antibiotics."

Afterward, Morgan went to the kitchen where Hannelie was preparing a pot of tea. The older woman eyed the two plates and pursed her mouth. "You might as well eat that, dear. It will only go to waste if you don't."

"Are you sure?"

115

"I'm sure. You need it anyway, working as hard as you do."

This was true, or so Morgan's screaming stomach tried to convince her. Before she could feel too bad about it, she gulped down the leftovers, groaning with satisfaction when the cramping in her abdomen eased.

"Have some tea."

Hannelie thrust a steaming mug into Morgan's hands which she accepted with muttered thanks. Henri lit his pipe, sucking on the aromatic tobacco while Joanna read out of the battered Mills and Boon book she always carried around with her.

She must have read that thing a thousand times by now, Morgan thought.

She said nothing, though, not mentioning that the smell of tobacco was torture to her either. It was nobody's fault she was a smoker. One who now had to do without her usual fix. Still, it was hard to contain the irritation boiling up within. *God, I'm so tired of this, I could scream!*

Moments later, Julianne joined them for a rare cup of tea. "Meghan is sleeping," she explained.

Silence descended over the room, disturbed only by Morgan's fidgeting. She couldn't stand to sit there, and she couldn't understand how they could do it either. Every bone in her body itched for action. The world was dying around them, day after day, yet here they were: spectators.

She watched the others through lidded eyes, wondering how they would react to what she was about to say. "I'm going to town."

The words dropped into the silence like a stone. She kept her face straight, lips firm in an attempt to look decisive. *This time, they won't talk me out of it.*

"You can't," Julianne cried.

Hannelie gasped while Joanna dropped her book, fixing shocked eyes on her face. Only Henri said nothing, watching her with a shrewd expression.

"My mind's made up."

"No," Julianne replied.

"We need food. We need fuel. We need water."

"It's too dangerous," Julianne protested. "I've already lost Lilian and Max. I can't lose you too."

"We have no choice. If we do nothing, we'll starve or die of thirst." Morgan fixed her mother with a determined look. "Besides, how do you know you've lost either Lilian or Max? We know nothing!"

"I can't take that chance," Julianne whispered.

"If you don't, you might lose Meghan for real. She needs medicine." Silence fell as Morgan delivered this, the killing blow. It was the one thing guaranteed to sway her mother.

"She's right," Henri said, surprising Morgan. "Let her go."

Julianne shook her head but uttered no further objections. After a few seconds, she got up and left the room, not saying a word. Morgan knew she had won, but the price had been high.

"Well, dear. If you're going into the lion's den, you'll need your sleep," Hannelie said, ever practical.

Morgan agreed, excused herself and went to bed. As she changed from her work clothes into pajamas, she studied her body, noting the changes six weeks had wrought.

Her limbs were lean and muscular, every muscle showing while her shoulders had broadened, packing on the width that came with swinging an ax. Always athletic, she now moved like a well-oiled machine.

I can do this, she thought with fresh determination. *I'm strong enough.*

The next morning, Morgan awoke to a hearty breakfast of fried eggs and potatoes.

"You'll need your strength, child. Eat up," Hannelie admonished as she dished up a second helping.

"Thanks," Morgan mumbled through a mouthful.

She kept eyeing the doorway, hoping her mom would come to say goodbye but in the end, had to acknowledge that Julianne wasn't coming.

"Give her time, dear. She's distraught, but she loves you something awful."

"I know. Tell her I said goodbye."

Morgan walked outside, tears pricking her eyes. Furious, she brushed them away. Time to be brave. She climbed into Brian's truck and drove away while Joanna and Henri waved to her in the rearview mirror.

Still no sign of Julianne.

Morgan sighed and fixed her eyes on the road. Next to her on the seat, lay an ax and a bottle of water while her dad's gun rode in its customary place on her hip. She felt as prepared as it was possible to be.

The road was quiet, and she saw neither people nor cars the entire way. That was eerie. Only as she neared town did she spot the first signs of human activity.

Crashed cars clogged the crossing, forcing her to find a way around. She drove over the island and onto the sidewalk, circling the site.

A lone figure aimlessly wandered along the road until she neared it. Its head whipped up, and it honed in on her, stumbling after the car on faltering legs. It was impossible to ignore the gaping wounds in the abdomen that trailed intestine, or the monstrous face leering at her.

Morgan's breath came in short gasps as the sight took her back to the first day of the outbreak, reminding her of Brian. "Oh, God. I was wrong. I don't think I can do this."

Once she left the creature behind, Morgan pulled over and leaned her forehead against the steering wheel. "Come on. Pull yourself together."

After a few minutes, she calmed down and drove further. More infected showed up, their numbers increasing as she went deeper into town. It was disturbing to drive amongst them, seeing the ruined faces of people who used to be fathers, mothers, brothers, and sisters.

They ran, tripped, and fell over themselves to reach her, and she realized they would continue to follow her no matter where she went.

Some were faster than others, agile too. This rang true of the last broadcasts they'd heard about the infected. The fresher and more intact the zombie, the more dangerous they were, retaining their previous speed and strength for a time.

Using a circuitous route on less inhabited roads, she lost most of them until she faced her destination, the pharmacy. In the distance, three infected still hobbled along. They were slow, the old and decayed type. She was sure she could make it in and out in time. "Now or never."

Despite her determination, her voice sounded shrill to her ears. Fear was an ever-present obstacle.

Morgan ran to the shop, holding the ax at the ready. The glass front had been shattered leaving the inside wide open and well-lit.

"That's a plus," she muttered before yelling, "Hello?"

Nothing moved. Tightening her grip, she gathered the

nerve to walk inside, her feet crunching over glass and debris. But it soon became apparent that the place was ransacked, and her enthusiasm waned. Would she find what she was looking for? The only good thing about the situation was that a raided shop meant other survivors. *Perhaps even the army.*

The knowledge that three infected were heading her way spurred her on, and Morgan grabbed a basket. She walked through the aisles, scanning the shelves and floor for anything useful.

Petroleum jelly, vapor rub, tampons, soap, shampoo, and toothpaste all found their way into the basket. Energy bars and drinks followed. Morgan loaded with haste, the hair on the back of her neck prickling.

At the back, the shelves were empty of medicine, and Morgan ground her teeth in frustration. A few bottles were strewn on the floor, though. She scrabbled around, pushing aside papers and files. *There. Amoxicillin. That's an antibiotic, right?*

Morgan grabbed the bottle along with another of anti-inflammatories. Sure that her time was up, she got up and ran to the exit. The light was bright after the dim interior, forcing her to pause while her eyes adjusted.

A wild feeling of relief flooded her when she noticed that the three infected were still a little way off. She rushed to the truck, tossed the supplies in with the basket and all, and made a return trip. This time, she scored cough syrup, wet-wipes, batteries, and plasters.

By now, the infected were too close to ignore. She either had to kill them or leave. Next to the pharmacy, a convenience store beckoned with the promise of precious food and water, everything they needed. Morgan hesitated, torn between the desire to flee and the urge to get more supplies.

With a deep, fortifying breath, she squared her shoulders and took a firm, two-handed grip on the ax. She'd have to learn to face the infected at some point. *Might as well be now.*

She set her sights on the closest one and sprinted forward until she was within reach. It snarled at her through torn lips, and the smell made her want to gag. Before she could overthink it, she brought the blade down onto its skull, splitting it the same way she'd been cutting logs for weeks.

Brain matter and black blood sprayed out, and she danced back to avoid it. The ax stuck in the bone, pulling the zombie with it. It toppled over, nearly falling onto her legs. With one foot planted on the shoulder, she wrenched her weapon free with barely enough time to get ready for the next one. *Don't get it stuck in the bone again!*

A short choppy blow to the temple put the second infected down, and she readied herself to face the third. From this close up the actual horror of the virus revealed itself in minute detail.

Milky eyes, putrid flesh, and a death head's grin combined with tattered clothes and stringy hair to conjure up a person's worst nightmare. Morgan forced herself to look, to study and if possible, get used to it.

A sideways blow to the neck struck it to the ground where a second strike caused the head to roll free, teeth gnashing at the air. With a shudder, Morgan turned away, her stomach heaving, but overlaying it was triumph. She *was* strong enough to do this.

With newfound determination, Morgan turned in a slow circle to study her surrounds. It was clear. For now, at least. A quick jog took her to the shop front, the doors propped open by strewn trolleys and baskets.

The interior looked far spookier than the pharmacy had. Precious little light found its way inside, and Morgan paused, daunted by the gloomy sight.

"Hello," she called, waiting.

When nothing happened, she cast a last glance around and stepped inside. She cleared a path and grabbed a trolley, heading for the nearest rack. It didn't take long to determine that raiders had been here too, and most of the items on the shelves had been carried off.

The sweet smell of rot hung in the air, and she studiously avoided the refrigerated section. Scavenging among the empty aisles, she found a few forgotten items. It was not anywhere near enough for their needs, though. *Guess I'll have to look somewhere else.*

Morgan headed outside, eager to leave the dank, stinky shop behind. Tossing caution aside, she quickened her pace and ran smack into a zombie coming around the corner.

Acting on instinct, Morgan shoved hard with the trolley and bowled it over. A quick glance up the street caused her heart to drop. Infected were trickling down from all sides, converging on her location.

Abandoning her meager supplies, Morgan ran for the truck, not prepared to lose her life over a can of baked beans. Behind her, the surprisingly limber zombie got back to its feet and followed, its snarls spurring her on.

She sprinted around the back of the truck but stopped short at the sight of two more zombies waiting at the driver's side. She groped for the ax then remembered she'd left it in the trolley.

In one smooth motion, she pulled the gun from its holster

and fired, hitting the closest infected in the face. Her expertise was mainly due to an insistent Henri who'd forced her to practice every day for weeks now.

Morgan shifted her aim, ready to pull the trigger again, but grasping fingers hooked onto her ponytail. A sickly stench washed over her face as the zombie leaned in for the kill, its raspy growl raising goosebumps on her flesh.

Morgan wrenched her head free and stepped out of reach. Its other hand flailed, brushing across her chest. The sound of tearing cloth barely registered as she twisted free and dashed up the street.

With infected closing in on all sides and the way to her truck blocked, she was left with only one option: run. She tore up the street, arms, and legs pumping as she ducked and weaved between the limbs reaching for her with bloodthirsty eagerness.

Panic lent speed to her feet while all rational thought fled beneath the onslaught of fear that pulsed through her veins with each step. She no longer cared about supplies. No longer cared about anything other than escape with the specter of being eaten alive looming large in her mind.

Once she'd outdistanced the infected, a semblance of clarity returned, and she stumbled to a halt, heaving for breath. Her truck now lay far behind her while her panicked flight had carried her into the heart of town. From the corner of her eye, she spotted more zombies heading her way. To make matters worse, they were fresh which meant fast. "Oh, God."

She broke into a run again, pulling on reserves of strength she didn't know she had. Over the next hour, she evaded groups of infected until her body came close to collapse.

Ducking behind a small wall, Morgan pressed her back

against the cool concrete and tried to catch her breath. It came in deep, ragged gasps that shuddered through her ribs. The stitch in her side made her wince every time she moved. She slid down to her haunches and huddled in the shade as she listened for the sounds of pursuit.

Morgan snuck a quick peek around the corner of her barricade. She had to get back to her truck. There was no way to get out of town alive without it. Breathing deeply to calm her panicking heart, she reflected that it felt like forever now since she'd arrived that morning. *It sucks to be at the bottom of the food chain.*

She peered around the corner again. No sign of zombies yet, but she knew they were coming. It was only a matter of time.

"Dear God, please let me make it out of this alive," she pleaded, wiping her forehead with a trembling hand. "And I don't mean by becoming a zombie!"

Judging by the sun, it was around noon, and it was blisteringly hot. Sweat trickled down her back, and her ponytail drooped. Her mouth was parched.

In the distance, she heard the sounds that heralded the arrival of another group of infected. Upon looking around the corner, she saw a big crowd moving up the street in her direction. They were aimless for now, but they'd spot her soon enough.

Closing her eyes, she marshaled all her strength. It was make or break now. Throughout the chase, she'd been tracing a large circle back to her vehicle. Now she was finally close enough to reach it in one last push.

"C'mon, Morgan. You can do this."

Taking a deep breath, she plunged forward and took off at a

flat run. Behind her, she heard the moment they spotted her and gave chase. Adrenaline coursed through her veins. Sweat streamed down her face, but she ignored it and focused on her footing. To fall now would be the end of her.

The stitch in her side was back, and her lungs burned like fire. She could hear them gaining. In the distance, Morgan made out the shop where she'd parked that morning and kept going through sheer force of will.

A quick glance over her shoulder nearly proved her undoing when she saw how close the infected were. She could almost smell the decay, could practically feel the teeth sinking into her flesh. Not far in front of her, a second group ran out of a side street, seeking to cut her off. *Shit!*

Redoubling her efforts, Morgan closed the distance, and a kernel of hope blossomed inside. *I'm going to make it!*

With only a hundred meters to go, she spotted a zombie beside her truck. Biting back a curse, she forged ahead. There could be no stopping now.

She pulled out her gun and shot at the zombie as she ran. Most of her shots went wild, but one bullet hit got in the shoulder and spun it around with enough force to make it fall. Vaulting over it, she hit the door of her truck and jumped in with seconds to spare.

The first zombie slammed into the side with enough force to make her cry out, and within seconds she was surrounded. Morgan fumbled for the keys in the ignition and froze. Her fingers grasped at air. *Where are the damn keys?*

With her brain in overdrive, Morgan tried to remember where they were, what could have happened. She'd last gotten out and...her pocket! She patted the small breast pocket on the front of her shirt and came up empty.

The material flapped loosely, and the memory of tearing cloth returned to her. Craning her head, she stared at the spot outside the truck where the zombie had hooked its fingers into her shirt. Sure enough, a glint of silver shone in the sun.

It was only a few meters away, but it might as well have been the breadth of the ocean. The swarm was upon her, and there was no escaping this time.

She was trapped.

In a sudden fit of rage, Morgan smashed her hands against the steering wheel, pouring out her anger in a torrent of abuse. Then she burst into tears. Sobs wracked her body as she stared at the monstrous faces leering at her through the glass. *I don't want to die.*

At that moment, she realized that no matter how bad things were or how much she missed Brian, she wanted to live. More than anything.

The infected beat on the windows, and she wondered how long the glass would hold. The seconds ticked by as the tears on her cheeks dried up. The beating fists retreated to a distant thrum, and a hollow space opened up inside her.

A few of the infected crawled onto the hood and slammed on the windscreen. A crack appeared in front of her eyes. She watched it run across like a line being drawn with an invisible pen. Little starbursts punctuated it, and with trembling hands, she pulled her gun from its holster.

Morgan pressed the barrel to her temple and squeezed her eyes shut, filling her mind with images of happier days. "I'm sorry, Mom, Meghan."

A distant sound penetrated her thoughts, and her finger froze on the trigger. It sounded like gunshots. Wild hope suffused her body with a tingling rush. For several seconds, nothing happened. Then the throng surrounding her thinned out as their attention shifted. The crowd rippled before it rolled away from the truck toward the new arrivals.

One by one, the infected dropped to the tar, black blood puddling around their wounds. When the last one fell, a muted shout reached her ears, and she craned her head to see. In the distance, a man waved at her. "Anyone in there?"

Tentatively, Morgan cracked the door open, checking for lurkers. She waved a trembling hand at her rescuer. "I'm here!"

He slung his rifle over his shoulder and jogged over.

As he neared, her heart jumped.

No.

Impossible.

That gait, those shoulders.

Can it be?

She jumped out and screamed, "Max? Is that you?"

He faltered. "Morgan?"

"Oh my God. It *is* you," she cried, sprinting towards him. How many nights had she tossed and turned, wondering if he was still alive?

He met her halfway and swept her off the ground. She cried as his familiar arms enveloped her, his voice booming with laughter. A year younger, they'd been close as siblings, always getting into trouble together. He dwarfed her at six foot three, and she always felt safe around him.

"Max, I can't believe it's you. I've missed you so much. I thought you were dead," she said, alternating between crying and laughing.

He whooped, swinging her in a circle, "I'm here. It takes more than a few zombies to get rid of me." He set her down

127

and inspected her at arms-length, "Are you okay? Where's Mom and Meghan?"

"I'm fine, and they're safe for now, but if you had shown up two seconds later, I'd have been a goner." She stared at the bodies littering the parking lot in the ugly aftermath of death. "Speaking of which, we'd better get out of here. The shots are going to draw more of them."

Max nodded, "Let's go. You've got a ride?"

She walked over to where the keys lay and picked them up. Dangling them between thumb and forefinger, she grimaced. "Now I've got these, I'm ready to go. Go ahead, I'll follow."

Max shook his head, herding her to the passenger side. "I'm driving."

He jogged back to the Nyala and had a brief conversation with the driver. Next moment he was back, sliding in next to her.

Although they followed a circuitous route, she recognized the riot police's quarters when they got there. It didn't look at all the same. The walls were reinforced with barbed wire and sheet metal on the outside and an assortment of vehicles on the inside. The gate was heavily fortified, a barrier extending out from the sides on top of which two young men stood guard. They each had an R4 rifle slung across their backs and carried long metal spears.

As Max drove inside the barriers, the men scanned their vehicles and the surroundings before giving the all clear. Only then did the gate open, swinging inwards on its hinges.

Once inside, Max cut the engine. "Can you get out for a moment, sis?"

Hesitating, she stared at the unfamiliar faces surrounding her.

"Don't worry. It's just procedure. Anybody who's gone outside has to be checked for bites."

The driver from the Nyala jumped out when she did. Morgan looked on in silent appreciation as he walked over to join them. Tall and well built, he was handsome with black hair and steely gray eyes.

"Logan, this is my sister, Morgan."

"Nice to meet you." She smiled and stuck out her hand, feeling awkward beneath his intent stare. *Have I got something on my face?*

He shook her hand, and his touch sent a tingle up her spine. "The pleasure is all mine."

Morgan could feel a blush creeping up her cheeks and stepped back. *How embarrassing.*

Max carried on with the introductions, and Morgan took the opportunity to get away from Logan. The man was dangerous. She could sense it. She also didn't like her reaction to him. It felt like a betrayal to Brian.

The two men on the wall gave her a wave as Max introduced them. "That's Armand and Jacques," he indicated, "and this is Angie."

A petite, young woman with dark eyes and hair stepped forward to shake her hand. "Hi, if you don't mind, I'd like to check you for bites."

With a nod, Morgan allowed her.

Makes sense, she thought. The last thing anybody needed was for the infection to hitch a ride inside.

Her amazement increased as they got back into their vehicles and drove around the back. The cars parked alongside the fence had been formed into a makeshift walkway with an assortment of material, and little guard towers dotted it at intervals.

Max explained it all to her on the way. "We have at least two people guarding the walls at all times. The zombies stumble across us often and have to be dealt with swiftly before they draw more of their kind. We've found the spears are a good way to kill them from a height."

"When did you get here? How did you do all this?"

"I arrived here the day of the outbreak. I must have missed you and Mom by a matter of hours. As for the rest, I'll explain inside."

"All right, but we have to hurry. Meghan is sick and needs medicine. I have to get back."

He turned to her, face sober. "She's sick? How bad is it?"

"We don't know. She's got a cough and a fever, and it's getting worse. She needs antibiotics."

He nodded. "Right, let's hurry then."

She followed Max inside, surprised to find it so cozy. A little girl sat at a table coloring in pictures. An Alsatian lay at her feet, while a blond woman prepared sandwiches in the kitchen. The smell of fresh bread filled her nostrils, and her mouth watered.

"You've got electricity?"

"Yes. Courtesy of a generator. The fuel won't last forever, but for now, we're comfortable enough. Water is the main problem here."

"Elise, this is my sister, Morgan."

The blond smiled from ear to ear. "Your sister? You found her! So nice to finally meet you." She shook Morgan's hand. "Where's your mom and the little one?"

"They're on a farm. I came to town for food and medicine. Meghan's ill."

"We're going there now," Max interjected.

"Have you got food?" Elise asked.

"Not much," Morgan admitted, sniffing the air. "You're baking bread?"

"I've got a lot of flour, and Joseph rigged up a wood oven for me, so yes. Give me a moment, and I'll pack some to take with you. How many people?"

"Five and the little one, including me."

Elise sat them down at the table with a sandwich and a cold drink each before leaving to pack a hamper.

Morgan crammed the bread into her mouth, nearly fainting at the taste of ham and pickled onions. *Where did they get all this food?*

After a moment of silence, Max asked, "What happened to you? And Brian?"

She swallowed, tears rising unbidden. "I don't know what happened. He went to the shop and got bitten the night before. The next morning he tried to kill me. Lucky for me, I snuck out to grab a smoke. If I hadn't, he'd have attacked me while I slept."

"How did you escape?"

She shrugged. "Luck and a shower rail."

"I went to your house, you know."

Startled, she stared at him. "Did you see Brian?"

He nodded, unable to meet her eyes. "He attacked us and...I had to kill him...or more accurately, Logan did to save me. I'm sorry."

"He did? Brian's dead?"

"Yes."

"I'm glad. I didn't want him to be like that forever. Now he can be at peace." She sniffed and looked away. "You know about Dad?"

"I saw. I can't believe he's gone."

"I have a hard time believing it myself." Morgan swallowed the last of her sandwich and took a sip of her cold drink.

"All of this," she waved a hand around, "is surreal. I can't believe what's happened. It's like a nightmare you can't wake up from."

"At least, we're together again. We'll survive. We have to." Max smiled at her, determination shining in his eyes.

Morgan could feel her tension recede. It was true. They would survive.

"Here's your food, love. Now hurry over there and bring back your family," Elise said, handing Max a large basket.

"Thank you, Elise. You're one of a kind," Max said, grinning. "Ready to go, sis?"

She jumped up, wincing as her legs cramped. "Let's go." She turned to Elise. "Thanks for everything."

"Oh, it's no bother. Just make sure you all get back here safely, okay?" She pointed to the little girl and dog. "Anne could use a friend, and so could Buzz."

"Buzz?" Morgan asked, perplexed.

Elise shrugged. "They named him after Buzz Lightyear."

As they walked out, Morgan thought about that. Perhaps, there was still hope for the future.

Kids, dogs.

An ordinary world.

Chapter 13 - Julianne

Julianne's back was sore and cramped from sitting on the little chair next to Meghan's bed. Smoothing a hand over the sleeping child's forehead, she chewed her lip in worry at the fever blazing there. Meghan's breath whistled in and out of her lungs through the phlegm. Julianne felt tears well up in her eyes. *What will happen to my little girl? And what happened to Morgan? It's been hours.*

She knew deep down inside that Lilian was gone even though she still clung to hope. That was a tragedy she could neither admit nor ignore. Her eldest daughter, the children...it was too much.

At least Max was in the army, so he might still be alive. But John...at times she missed him so much, it physically hurt. And now both Morgan and Meghan were in danger.

To Julianne, nothing mattered more than family. It was what she lived for. When she lay alone in her bed at night, stifling her sobs, it felt like broken glass was grinding into her heart. She missed her home. She missed her rose garden and her kitchen. But most of all, she longed for her family.

Princess Sophia lay at the foot of the bed, looking sad and lost as she stared at Meghan.

"Don't worry, Princess. She'll be fine." Julianne smiled as she rubbed the dog's head, not sure if she believed a single word, but it felt good to say it anyway.

"Oh, my dear. You shouldn't wear yourself out so much. Let me sit with Meghan for a bit," Hannelie exclaimed, bustling into the room. "Why don't you have a bite to eat?"

Hannelie was warm and caring but took no nonsense. Resisting her was futile, and Julianne obeyed out of sheer exhaustion. Joanna, Morgan's mother-in-law, was already there, seated at the table with a pot of tea.

Miserably she sat down and poured herself a cup too. She wasn't a tea person, but they had run out of coffee days ago. That was something else to add to their long list of worries. The supplies were running low, and she knew Henri was worried about the fuel. She understood why Morgan had gone, especially when Meghan needed medicine. At the same time, she wished her daughter hadn't left.

Rubbing her throbbing temples with her fingertips, she hardly noticed the bowl of soup and crackers Joanna placed in front of her.

"Eat something, Julianne. You need to keep your strength up."

Julianne picked up a cracker and ate mechanically without tasting a crumb. She kept glancing at the clock on the wall. Each second seemed like an eternity. At ten minutes past four, Morgan still hadn't returned.

Perhaps, she was dead already, eaten alive by a mob of monsters. Graphic images filled her head, and she almost choked.

She finished her food and sat back with her hands wrapped around her tea to bring warmth to her frayed nerves.

"You shouldn't be so worried. Morgan will be fine. That's one tough girl you've got there even if she doesn't realize it herself yet," Joanna reassured.

Julianne couldn't help but smile a little. It was true. Morgan was as tough as nails and had overcome many obstacles in her life. She was beautiful and smart yet never seemed to believe in herself. She lacked confidence in her abilities, but Julianne was sure that would come in time. *She's still young after all.*

"I know, but I can't help worrying about her and Meghan. They're all I have left, and I don't think I could carry on without them." Then she blushed in shame, realizing how insensitive she was being.

Six weeks ago, Joanna lost her son Brian. She'd heard nothing from her other son Neil since the outbreak began either, and Julianne guessed she empathized quite well. How many other people had she lost? Friends, perhaps? Yet, the old lady never complained.

As if Joanna could read her thoughts, she smiled sadly and said, "It's a terrible thing to outlive your children, and these are terrible times. We have to be strong if we hope to survive."

"You're right. May the Good Lord have mercy on us all." Julianne got up from the table. She needed fresh air.

Outside, she shaded her face from the sun with her hands and looked around. Henri was puttering around in the yard as usual.

Julianne stepped off the porch and walked with no idea where she wanted to go or why. She needed to move and clear her head. As she reached the fence, a sudden noise startled her. It came from beyond the wire, but trees and shrubs obscured her view.

With her heart in her throat, Julianne stood immobile as she tried to decide what to do until she heard it again. Wet, tearing sounds punctuated by snarls and growls. She knew those snarls. Remembered them clear as day. *No!*

Everything inside her screamed to run back to the house, but she had to know if they were inside the fence. Lives depended on it.

Creeping forward on rigid limbs, Julianne tried to get closer without making a sound. A bead of sweat ran down the side of her face, and a fly buzzed around her head, but she didn't dare shoo it away.

It was well into November if she guessed correctly, and so far it had been a hot and dry summer. Despite the earlier promise of rain, nary a drop of it had fallen to relieve them of the stifling heat or nourish the earth.

The grass and leaves were brown and parched, crackling with the slightest movement, so she had to be extra careful when she moved. She spotted a gap in the brush. It allowed her a clear view to the front.

Just beyond the fence, two infected crouched in the grass. They were decayed to the point where it was hard to know what they once were. The stench was overwhelming, hanging in the air until she could almost taste the rot.

They were feeding on something, and she prayed it was an animal. Revulsion filled her, and Julianne retreated the same way she came. Once she was satisfied enough distance separated them, she jogged back to the house at a rapid pace, heart pounding.

"Henri," she whispered. "There's infected on the other side of the fence."

He straightened up. "How far away?"

"Right over there," she pointed. "Not far."

"Well, I don't think they can get through the fence. We should be okay," he chewed on his lip and seemed to think it over. "Let's stick close to the house and keep quiet, just to be safe."

Julianne wasn't so sure. Who knew what those things were capable of? Yet, Henri had a point. The fence was high and sturdy. *Morgan checked it yesterday.*

"Warn the others, would you?"

Julianne nodded and rushed inside. After telling Joanna and Hannelie, she scrounged around until she found a cricket bat and laid it down next to Meghan's bed. *I'm not leaving her side with those things around.*

At least, Meghan's room had small windows situated too high up for an infected to climb through.

Meghan smiled when she walked in before breaking into another fit of coughing. Julianne tipped her onto her side and rubbed her back while holding a tissue in front of her mouth.

After a while, she subsided and fell back onto her pillow. She was hot to the touch, and Julianne didn't like the glassy look in her eyes. Taking a wet cloth, she pressed it to Meghan's forehead, wishing she could do more.

An hour after dark, Julianne stared at Meghan in the light of a flickering candle. *Am I going to lose her? Have I lost Morgan?*

The sound of a car penetrated her sad thoughts. Wild hope filled her, and she shot to her feet, racing to the kitchen door where the others soon joined her. Two sets of headlights shone in the night, blinding her. Julianne wavered. Had Morgan found other survivors? Or had strangers come to their door?

A door slammed shut, and footsteps crunched around a large truck. Then a figure appeared silhouetted in the light. "Hey, Mom, it's me."

"Morgan?"

With a cry of relief, Julianne rushed forward, clutching her daughter to her breast. Joy filled her heart as she crushed Morgan against her, sending up a silent prayer of thanks to heaven.

Another prayer was answered when Max stepped into the light. With a gasp, Julianne released of Morgan and rushed forward. "Max! Is it really you?"

Max swept her up into his embrace, laughing with abandon as she sobbed with happiness. "It's okay, Mom. It's just me."

"But how? Where have you been?"

"It's a long story," he grinned, setting her back on her feet.

Little Princess was going ballistic, her body quivering with excitement. Julianne scooped her up, soothing her with a calming hand. Remembering Morgan's original purpose, Julianne gripped her by the arm. "Did you get the medicine? Meghan's not doing well at all, and I'm worried sick."

"I got it, along with food and other things. Sorry it took so long to get back, but we couldn't risk luring infected here," Morgan explained. "Go ahead. We'll bring the stuff inside."

Behind Max, two more figures appeared from a second vehicle and were introduced as Logan and Angie. They were armed and moved with a certain wariness that foretold of previous brushes with death.

Hannelie seemed ready to burst out of her skin at the thought of having guests, while Henri watched her rush about with dry amusement. He winked at Julianne, "Go to your little one. We'll take care of the rest."

Feeling that everything was in hand once more, Julianne took herself and Princess back to Meghan's room. "Hey, guess what, sweetie? Morgan's back."

Meghan's eyes brightened. "She is?"

"She brought you medicine. Now you'll feel much better soon." She smoothed a blond curl away from Meghan's forehead. "But I've got an even bigger surprise for you. Max is here too."

"Really?" Meghan struggled upright in the bed. "I want to see him."

"Now, now. Relax," Julianne soothed. "He'll be here any moment."

A minute later, Morgan walked in with a bag full of medicine, followed by Max carrying a teddy bear.

"Max!" Meghan squealed, launching herself at him despite her illness.

Max laughed, swinging her up into the air as she giggled. Julianne got a lump in her throat, watching them. *My family.*

The reunion didn't last long before Meghan broke into a fit of coughing. Max set her down on the bed, bringing Julianne back to the present.

Julianne scratched in the medicine bag and came up with antibiotics, cough syrup, something for pain and fever, and a nasal spray. With the expertise learned through years of motherhood, she dosed Meghan with each, then wiped her hot, sticky body with the wet wipes. Laying her back in bed, she rubbed vapor rub on her chest.

"There we go, sweetie. Go to sleep now, and when you wake up, you'll feel much better." She covered Meghan with a thin sheet and sat back. "I'll be right beside you."

Meghan smiled and reached for her new teddy. "Can Max and Morgan stay too?"

"Of course they can. We'll all stay."

Meghan smiled with content, one hand on the teddy and the other on Princess who lay next to her. Morgan fiddled

139

with a small battery operated fan Elise had given her, getting it going in the corner. It wasn't much but relieved the stifling heat in the cramped room.

For a while, everything felt right in the world. Weeks of grief and worry seemed to fall off Julianne's shoulders, and she relaxed for the first time in days.

A gentle knock on the door announced Hannelie with a glass of juice and a sandwich for Meghan. "I thought she might try to eat something."

"Thank you, Hannelie. I don't know what we'd do without you."

"Don't thank me. This is courtesy of your son." Hannelie flashed Max a grateful smile. "Thanks to him and a lady called Elise, we'll be dining like royalty tonight."

Julianne shot Max a questioning look as Hannelie left, retreating to her kitchen and guests.

"I'll tell you everything once Meghan is asleep," Max said. "Let's just talk about...better things for now."

"Agreed," Julianne replied. For the next half hour, they chatted about anything and everything except zombies. Meghan's eyes drooped as the medicine kicked in and after a while, she fell asleep.

By tacit agreement, the adults left the room, joining the others in the kitchen where they discovered everyone relaxed around the table. Julianne sat down and accepted a mug of sweet coffee. She took a sip and savored the aroma. *It's been a while.*

Hannelie distributed plates, and everyone dug in. The first bite transported Julianne to heaven. The bread was fresh, topped with ham, pickles, and cheese. She could even detect mustard.

"Oh my God. This is the best sandwich I've ever had," she mumbled around a bite. "Who baked the bread?"

"Elise did. She's our resident cook slash house mother," Max laughed.

The rest agreed. With nods and murmured gratitude, the food disappeared. Swallowing the last bite with a big swig of coffee, Julianne sighed and picked at the crumbs on her plate wondering when she'd get to have a meal like that again.

"You must have a ton of questions," Max said.

"Of course. Where have you been these past weeks? What have you been doing?"

Everyone gave their attention to Max. He cleared his throat and began at the beginning, the day he met Logan. The minutes passed as he told their story, and Julianne's amazement grew.

"You've got electricity?" she asked. "That explains the bread. This Elise, she baked it?"

"Yup. She manages the kitchen. The ham, pickles, and cheese, it's all frozen or preserved."

"I see. Well, thank her for me, please. For all of us. That was the best meal I've had in weeks."

"You can thank her yourself, Mom. You're coming back with me, aren't you?"

"I suppose so, yes. Is it safe?"

"As safe as it's possible to be. We've got a high fence, barricades in the streets, and guards twenty-four hours of the day."

"Have you been attacked yet?" Henri asked.

"We have. Lone infected and small groups find us from time to time," Max replied.

"But there's so many of those things in town. Why haven't

they attacked you in mass yet?" Morgan asked with a puzzled frown.

With a shrug, Max said, "I guess it's because they don't know we're there. We keep quiet and lie low. That's not to say a horde won't find us eventually."

"Could you fight off a horde?" Henri asked.

"We could, but we'd need more firepower."

"You don't have enough guns and ammunition?" Henri asked, his bushy eyebrows drawn into a frown.

"We've got a stash. Mostly what Max brought from the army and private stock we found in houses. The riot police had little, just rubber bullets and stun grenades which won't work on zombies," Logan explained.

"Why stay so close to town? Why not move to a place like this, for instance?" Henri asked.

"It's an idea. We need a permanent water source. We're operating on bottled water for now which won't last. The fuel for the generators won't last either. We need a more permanent solution to our problems."

"Solar power. That's what you need. And a farm where you can raise animals and grow crops," Henri interjected.

"We'd need to find a place that fits the bill and move all our people over. It'll be dangerous," Logan said.

"I'd say your most pressing problem right now is finding more guns and ammunition," Henri said.

"I agree. In the meantime, you should all join us," Max said.

"Thank you for the offer, but Hannelie and I will stay. This is our home. I'll be sorry to see the rest of you go, though. Especially the little one."

"We'll miss you too, Henri. You and Hannelie have been so kind to us," Julianne said.

"Well, the offer stands. You can join us anytime you want. We'll leave you some food and water before we go," Max said.

"Oh, I'm going to miss you all so much, my dears!" Hannelie cried, struggling to hold back her tears. "But enough of that. Let's get you settled in for the night. I should have enough spare bedding." As ever, her cure for any distress was to keep busy.

That night, Julianne struggled to fall asleep. The silence seemed deafening after the lively bustle of before. Even Meghan slept peacefully due to all the medicine.

Her mind raced with possibilities in the quiet. If Max had survived, couldn't Lilian still be alive? It was possible.

Her mind spun in circles. Was it safe to move so close to town even with everything Max and the others had done to safeguard it? Was she making a mistake? Meghan's life depended on this decision.

Around midnight, fatigue overcame her, and she drifted off to sleep, at last. The sound of breaking glass snapped her eyes open. She struggled upright, disoriented.

"John," she cried. "What's happening?"

Julianne realized she was calling to a ghost when reality flooded back, and she blinked. Meghan came awake more slowly next to her, mewling as she clutched her teddy bear.

Princess was going crazy, scratching at the door and barking herself hoarse. A loud scream cut through the dark and jolted Julianne out of her stupor. *Hannelie!*

Julianne vaulted out of bed, scooping Meghan into her arms and rushed towards the small walk-in closet.

"Sweetie, you must listen and do as I say," she whispered, holding Meghan's face and staring into her confused eyes. "I need you to be as quiet as a mouse, okay? I'm going out, but

143

I'll be right back."

Meghan's face scrunched up, and tears flowed down her cheeks.

"Shh, baby, don't cry. *Quiet as a mouse.* Understand?"

Meghan nodded, sniffling. "I'm fetching your brother and sister. I'll be right back. Don't move, and don't make a sound."

She crushed Meghan to her chest then closed the closet. Grabbing the cricket bat, she ran to the door. Several gunshots punctuated the night, making her jump. With her heart in her throat, she slipped out. Princess vanished, leaving her alone in the long dark hallway.

Faint moonlight streamed into the corridor through open doors ahead, but it was hard to see anything. Gulping, she raised the bat with shaking hands, her stomach coiled with fear. Frantic shouts and footsteps came from the main bedroom. She quickened her pace.

A figure lurched out of the darkness, and Julianne stopped. An awful stench hit her nostrils, and she swung the bat. It connected with a solid thunk, and she jumped back as the zombie collapsed at her feet.

Julianne hit it several more times, panic taking over. When it stopped moving, she stepped over it, shuddering when her bare feet landed in a sticky puddle of blood. *Yuck.*

Morgan burst out of a doorway and staggered, struggling with another infected. Before Julianne could even think to help, a shot rang out. It fell backward as the muzzle flashed in the dark. Breathing in ragged gasps, Morgan rose and swung the gun towards Julianne.

"Stop! It's me," Julianne cried.

Morgan's shoulders slumped in relief. "Come on, Mom, we've got to help the others."

144

They hurried onward and found Joanna hiding underneath her bed, scared out of her wits. With her in tow, they reached the main bedroom where the sight of Max confronted them, standing still with his gun hanging by his side.

On the bed, Henri sat with Hannelie clutched in his arms. There was blood everywhere. Three infected bodies lay on the floor. Princess gnawed at the trouser leg of one before Julianne scooped her up.

"No, Princess," she scolded before turning to Henri.

He rocked back and forth, mouth working with unintelligible pleas. His eyes were glassy and distant. Hannelie was no longer there. Her eyes were sightless, rolled back into her head. Blood covered the front of her nightdress, seeping out of a bloody wound in her torn throat.

"What happened?" Julianne asked. This situation reminded her of John. Painful memories resurfaced to haunt her once more.

"A group of infected broke in through the windows. They attacked Hannelie, and I was too late to save her," Max said. His voice was flat, his face bleak.

"Where's Logan and Angie?"

"They're outside, patrolling the area."

There wasn't much more to say. Henri refused to let go of Hannelie and wouldn't speak to any of them, even when Max warned she would turn. They dragged out the bodies and mopped up the blood. Grim silence hung over the household. They all knew what would happen next.

Julianne put Meghan back to bed with Princess after giving her another round of medicine, then made coffee. None of them could sleep further that night. For Julianne, the warm, comforting house had turned into a nightmare. Without

Hannelie, it would never be the same.

Julianne was sipping her coffee when a gunshot caused her to spill all over her shirt. Max walked in, his shoulders stooped.

"Hannelie?" she asked.

"Yes, she turned. Henri shot her."

Although she'd known it would happen, Julianne still felt stunned and bereft. "So what now?"

"We're loading up. I'd like to leave within the hour. It's not safe here. Can you be ready?"

"Yes, I'm just finishing up."

"See you outside then." Max squeezed her shoulder.

Moving fast, Julianne went back inside the room and packed. She dressed in a soft forest green blouse, black pants, and ballet pumps then gathered up their stuff. *Time to go.*

She scooped Meghan up in a blanket, her head resting on her shoulder. The sleeping child never even woke up.

Joanna sat at the kitchen table, nursing a cup of tea. Always groomed with her hair and makeup done, she usually looked a great deal younger than her seventy-four years. Except for today. Today she looked her age.

"They're waiting outside," Joanna said, a quaver in her voice. Hannelie's death had hit her hard. They'd been fast friends toward the end.

They walked out into the misty gray of early dawn, dragging their suitcases. Max and Logan took their luggage and loaded it into the vehicles while Julianne looked around her. Henri was nowhere to be seen. "Where's Henri?"

"He's not coming," Morgan replied. "He says he won't leave Hannelie."

"We buried her under the apple tree at the back of the barn,"

Max added.

"Let's pay our respects before we leave," Julianne said.

Henri stood next to the grave, shoulders hunched. His face was drawn and pale, but no tears were in sight. His grief shone as brightly as the sun, and Julianne approached him with hesitation.

"Won't you come with us, Henri? We need you," she begged, reaching out a hand.

Wordlessly, he shook his head. She dropped her hand back to her side. In silence, they held vigil over Hannelie's grave, each saying goodbye in their own way. After a few minutes, Henri left, striding off into the veldt with a mere nod and a wave.

"We need to go now, Mom. I know it's hard, but we can't force him to join us," Max said, putting an arm around her shoulders.

"I know. It's not easy, though." With a heavy heart, Julianne turned and left.

As the farm that had been their home for the past six weeks receded into the background, Julianne bit back tears. This was a new beginning. *Then why does it feel so much like the end?*

Chapter 14 - Max

The sun beat down on the earth with relentless force as it scorched away the greenery, evaporating all traces of moisture. It roasted any bit of unprotected skin without mercy and sapped a person's will to live. Summers in the Free State were always hot, but this was unusual. Speculations of drought were rife, and morale flagged as everyone suffered from the high temperatures.

Climbing up the makeshift ladder to the top of their improvised fence, Max surveyed the surrounding area with a pair of binoculars. Everything seemed quiet for the moment. He walked over to one of the ramshackle guard towers.

It wasn't much, but it provided shelter from the sun and boasted two lawn chairs. Morgan was there before him. They always patrolled the walls in pairs for backup. Max and Morgan had this shift. Sitting down, he studied her unnoticed.

She seemed different. The sister he'd always known was strong but also insecure. In her teens, she'd gone through a phase, struggling with depression and eating disorders. But after a few years, she picked herself up, studying fitness and nutrition. Even then, she still questioned her self-worth.

Now the uncertainty that always shadowed her actions was gone. She was proving to be a lot tougher than he'd ever thought possible. When they returned from the farm four days ago, she'd wasted no time equipping herself and taking an active role.

Her standard uniform was a pair of black shorts, tank top, and her old knee-high leather riding boots. The belt slung around her hips sported their dad's 9mm Parabellum on one side and a serrated hunting knife on the other. She was in great shape too, due to her former job. He couldn't help but notice the way the guys looked at her, especially Logan. He wasn't sure how he felt about that.

"What's with the frown, Max?"

"Nothing, sis. Just thinking."

"Suit yourself." Her lips quirked, suppressing a smile.

He sighed. She could always tell when he wasn't honest. As kids, they were very close and became even closer once they reached adulthood. They both took after their dad in athleticism, sharing a love for nature, and possessing a daring spirit. As kids, they got into endless trouble. Lilian, on the other hand, took after their mother. Petite and delicate, she was every bit the lady and always acted with restraint.

Feeling restless, he got up and patrolled the fence. There were no zombies in sight, but he'd learned that you couldn't take anything for granted in this new world and lingered. It gave him a chance to think about their situation.

The time to leave was approaching fast. There wasn't enough space for all of them, and they were too close to several densely populated areas like Welkom and Thabong. Then there was the water situation.

Max stared down at the grounds inside the fence, studying its occupants. Big Ben, with his broad frame and benign face, was teaching boxing. In his younger days, he used to be a professional, but injuries cut his career short. He settled down and opened a studio in Bloemfontein.

Peter and Thembiso were two of his most eager pupils. Max chuckled as he watched them practice the moves. Angie also joined in. Short and petite, she was an unlikely but fierce fighter. A former student at the University of Bloemfontein, she and her friend Susan escaped campus during the outbreak, joining up with Ben.

On the road, they met up with Jacques and Armand, two brothers fleeing the family farm after zombies overran it. Things had gone badly for the group from there. On the run, they moved from place to place until they came upon Joseph and his wife, Tumi, who was seven months pregnant. They headed for the nearest town, Riebeeckstad, hoping to find more survivors.

A mob of infected discovered their shelter, and they fled. Susan was bitten during their escape, while shock sent Tumi into premature labor. Somehow, they all ended up on Max's doorstep.

With nowhere else to go, the survivors had opted to stay. This turned out to be a bonus as each brought something valuable to the group. With the extra hands, their little fort improved over the weeks that followed. Max knew, however, that it was time to move on.

Morgan joined him on the wall, and he turned to her. "I think we should have a meeting tonight. Discuss our options."

"Good idea," Morgan replied.

Max thought for a moment. "What do you think of our chances? Honestly?"

"Honestly?" she shrugged. "I think we're living on borrowed time."

"Why do you say that?" Max asked, surprised at Morgan's

fatalistic outlook. "You don't think we stand any chance at all?"

"No, I don't. There are millions of infected and just a few of us. The army's gone, and there's no cure or vaccine. We're screwed."

"Wow. Thanks for the pep talk."

"However, we've got a solid group and a great leader. If we fight for tomorrow, we just might get to see it. Or we might not," Morgan added, grinning.

"You're enjoying this?"

"Not enjoying. How can I enjoy something that killed billions of innocent people? My father, my husband, and probably my sister and her family?" Morgan sighed. "But I find myself rising to the challenge, and I'm determined to see it through, even if we lose."

Max was silent, not sure what to say. This side of his sister was one he'd never seen before.

"Having lost so much, I now realize how precious life is and that we should savor every moment," she continued.

"On that, we can agree."

"Come on. We can talk later, discuss the great mysteries of life and all that, but right now we've got work to do." She punched him on the arm and pointed.

Max turned to look and saw a trio of zombies making their way to the fence. Thank God, they were slow ones. The fast ones always creeped him out, reminding him of The Exorcist.

They didn't understand the virus or its progression, but they all knew that freshly turned corpses were fast, only slowing down once decay set in. Max supposed it made sense they'd slow as their muscles and tendons rotted away. What none of them could figure out, was why they waste away. Weeks after the outbreak, the infected were still going, though slow.

When the zombies came within reach, Max stabbed downwards into the nearest one's skull, killing it. It wasn't a foolproof method. You had to get a solid shot and aim right. It was effective, though.

The shit part was disposing of the bodies, dumping them in an open field chosen for the purpose. The stench was incredible and the sight even worse, but it had to be done.

"Toss a coin on who gets to dispose of the bodies?" he asked.

"Forget it. It's your turn!" Morgan laughed.

"Since when are you a shrinking violet?"

"Do I look dumb to you?" She shook her head, folding her arms across her chest.

Grumbling, Max finished the job, wrinkling his nose in disgust. An hour later, Armand and Jacques, relieved them, and he set out to arrange the meeting. After supper, the kids were put to bed, and the group convened to discuss the problems facing them.

Clearing his throat, Max began, "I think the time has come for us to move."

Murmurs broke out among the group.

"Why? We've got it pretty good here," Ben said.

"We're too close to town. What if the infected find us? We can't fight off hundreds, or even thousands of zombies at once." Max replied. "We also have to consider the long-term implications of this plague. What happens when the food and water run out? How do we live? We can't scavenge forever."

Silence descended as the group absorbed this information.

"We need a farm," Jacques said. "We need to live off the land. Like the Voortrekkers. That's something Armand, and I know how to do."

Angie snorted, "Like the Voortrekkers? That would be like going back to the stone age."

Jacques blushed. "That's not true. They were pioneers, survivors. Our forefathers."

"They might be your forefathers, but they're not mine. I don't have a drop of Afrikaner blood. I'm a hundred percent Greek," she shot back.

"Don't be rude, Angie," Ben said. "What Jacques says is the truth. What will you eat once the shops are empty? Do you think the ancient Greeks had canned food?"

Max took up the reins again, trying to regain control of the meeting. "Jacques makes an excellent point, and I'm sure their farming expertise will prove invaluable." He shot Jacques a smile, and the boy blushed again, this time with pleasure. "As for the rest, we need to work together, regardless of our heritage, if we hope to survive."

Angie opened her mouth to protest, but a pointed look from Ben made her sink back into her chair with a frown.

"Well said, Max. Any ideas?" Ben asked.

"Our best chance of survival lies somewhere isolated. It must be well fortified with a clean water source and space for livestock and crops."

"There's a place about twenty-five kilometers from here, on the way to Kroonstad. It's far enough from town to be safe yet close enough to make supply runs when needed. It's fenced, stocked with game, and there's water too. We could get what we need in the surrounding farms," Morgan said.

"Sounds good. Can you show us on a map? Maybe make a drawing?" Max said.

"Hold on; we should scout it out first. It could be occupied or overrun with infected," Logan interjected.

153

"Good idea," Morgan agreed. "I volunteer."

"I'll go with you," Logan said, staring at her intently.

Morgan shot him a glance then looked away, cheeks stained with hot blood.

Max picked up on the exchange and interrupted, "Actually, I have a different job in mind for you, Logan."

"What?"

"We're in urgent need of more guns and ammunition. I'd like to raid the police station in Welkom. It'll be a dangerous mission, and I need you to back me up. You're an excellent shot. The best we have."

Logan stared at him, not at all happy with the change of plans but unable to fault Max's logic. "Fine. Armand can join us. He's a crack shot too."

Nodding in agreement, Max opened his mouth but was interrupted by Jacques.

"I should go with Morgan. I can tell if the place is suitable for farming or not."

"Excellent idea," Ben agreed, smiling like a benevolent father who'd just found a way to end an argument between squabbling children. "Why don't you take Angie with you? I'm sure you two can learn to work together."

Jacques grumbled, and Angie looked pissed, while Morgan's mouth twitched in silent amusement.

"This will be an exciting trip," Morgan said, standing up. "We'll meet here at dawn. Agreed?"

"Agreed," everyone involved chorused.

"I'll make breakfast," Elise said.

"I'll help," Joanna said.

"Well, time to turn in. My old bones need their rest," Ben added, effectively ending the meeting.

Max was left behind with the distinct feeling he'd been had. In seeking to keep Logan away from his sister, he'd also lost all control of the meeting. "Hey!"

"Don't take it personally, dear," Julianne said, patting him on the back. "The best leaders know when to step back and let people get on with it."

With that parting bit of wisdom in his ears, Max took himself off to bed. He awoke before dawn and lay still, thinking of the day ahead. He didn't look forward to it at all. Besides a new home, the thing they needed most was weaponry.

He rose and dressed in his full army uniform with boots, battle jacket, and webbing. He'd cleaned and repaired it to almost its former glory, even shining the shoes. Then he slung his R4 over his shoulder and loaded up with ammo and grenades. Tucking his customary hammer into its spot and slipping on his sidearm, he felt ready. Max walked to the common room with a confident stride.

It seemed almost everybody was awake, and the air buzzed with anticipation. The kids giggled at his gear and uniform, and he couldn't help but feel a little macho as he took a chair.

That feeling faded when he spotted Logan. Dressed in jeans and a tight t-shirt with a five o'clock shadow, he cut a dangerous looking figure. His lean body moved with predatory grace matched by his intense stare.

Armand hovered nearby, looking nervous but determined. Robust and fit from his active lifestyle on the farm, he was also an excellent shot due to frequent hunting expeditions. A solid addition to the group.

Morgan walked in, followed by her group. She looked Amazonian with her hair pulled back and a steely look in her eyes. Angie cut a fierce figure with her dark eyes, olive skin, and black hair, while Jacques seemed out of his depth and a little lost.

Max ground his teeth in chagrin when Logan made a bee-line for Morgan, claiming the seat next to her. The first few days, she'd acted cool towards him and kept her distance, but he persisted, and her manner was warming fast.

Elise exited the kitchen balancing plates like a pro, followed by Anne, Meghan, and Joanna. Breakfast was served, consisting of a solid helping of bacon, beans, and corn fritters.

Silence descended as everyone settled down to the serious business of eating. Julianne sat at Max's table along with Anne and Meghan. The two girls had become fast friends, and Max smiled to see them whispering and giggling together.

"Hey! Keep your hands off my plate," Morgan cried, drawing his attention.

Logan shoved the corn fritter in question into his mouth, chewing with gusto. "I'll trade you," he said. "Two fritters for a kiss."

He reached for her plate, and she stabbed him with her fork, eliciting a yelp. "Please, like I'd want a kiss from you."

"Just admit it," Logan teased. "You want me."

"Yeah, right," she replied, but her face was beet red.

Elise walked over and plonked a large lunch box in front of Logan. "So you don't eat your friends on the road," she said, referring to Logan's legendary appetite.

This earned her a rare and dazzling smile. "You're the best, Elise."

Logan turned his attention back to Morgan and resumed his shameless flirting. Max shook his head. *If she wants him, she'll have to learn how to cook, because the way to his heart is through his stomach.*

Julianne noticed his displeasure. "What's wrong? Don't you like Logan?"

"It's not that, Mom. He's a good guy. A loner and unpredictable, but good. It's Morgan."

"What about her?"

"Don't you think it's too soon? Brian's only been gone for a few weeks."

Julianne was silent for a while. "What's too soon, Max? Six weeks might not seem like a lot, but so much has happened."

"I don't know," Max shrugged. "I thought she loved Brian, that's all."

"She did love him," Julianne replied, "but he wasn't the love of her life."

"What does that mean?"

"She settled, Max. She chose security and loyalty over passion. That's not a bad thing, and if Brian had lived, they'd probably have been very happy together. Now he's dead, and real passion is staring her in the face. Should she deny it?"

"That's not what I'm saying. I just think she should wait," he replied, wondering if he knew anything about his sister at all. *Settled? Did she setlle for Brian?*

Max kept quiet after that, feeling chastened. Perhaps, Julianne was right. Life was short. Even more so now. Could he blame Morgan for moving on? Maybe not. That started him thinking along different lines. *What about me? What do I want? What am I waiting for?*

***

After breakfast, they loaded the Nyalas with their gear, and the two groups set off, each on their mission. The going was slow as Max tried to sneak into town without attracting too much attention.

Several times he was forced to take a detour due to road-blocks and car crashes, but after two hours they arrived at their destination. He parked across the street and scouted the area.

The police station squatted next to the road like a toad, staring at them from shattered windows. The parking lot was blocked off and impassable to vehicles. It looked like a war zone. Blood encrusted the ground while wrecks and burn marks decorated the tar.

The police had created a perimeter, setting up barricades in a half moon around the doors. It hadn't worked, and they'd been overwhelmed.

To Max, the aftermath was apparent, the scene playing out in front of his eyes like a ghostly theater. The officers were crouching behind their flimsy shelters, shooting at the oncoming dead, taking some down but unable to stem the tide. Perhaps one of their own had been bitten earlier, and now turned on his colleagues, killing and infecting. Or maybe there were just too many to shoot, and the dead flooded over the barricades like water.

Now, infected wandered around between the abandoned barricades. They were aimless, lifeless. That would change if Max and the rest tried to enter the lot.

"Shit," Armand said. "What now?"

"We need a diversion," Logan replied. "Something to draw them off. There's too many to kill."

Max chewed on this. Logan was right, of course. A diversion was the only way. *And that means bait. I can't ask it*

158

of them. I'm the leader.

"I'll do it," he said. "I'll draw them away on foot while you two go in."

"That's crazy, Armand said. "You can't run forever."

"I'm not planning to. I'll get them to chase me for a block or so and circle around." He fixed them with an earnest look. "Just hurry. When I come back, it will be with a horde of hungry fuckers on my heels, and you'd better not still be in there."

"Are you sure about this?" Logan asked. "The chances of you making it are slim. We can always come back with more fighters.

"I know, but a shootout here? In the middle of town? We'd be overrun within seconds. More would die, Logan."

"We can come up with a different plan."

"It's okay, Logan. I'll be fine. I'm fast, fit, and armed. We need those guns, so let's get them."

"Fine, but be careful," Logan replied. He reached out and shook Max's hand. "Don't die on me. I'd never be able to tell Morgan or your mom. They'd kill me."

Max laughed. "I'll try."

He opened the door and slipped his legs out. His boots hit the asphalt with a dull thud. A shiver ran through his spine. *This had better be worth it.*

"Hey, assholes! Come and get it! Fresh meat!" A dozen sets of diseased eyes fixed on him.

He backed away from the Nyala and broke into a sprint when the spell broke. The infected in the lot ran, shuffled, and crawled after him, each according to their capabilities. More emerged from the shadows and alleys. The trickle of bodies became a stream, then a river.

The hunt was on.

Chapter 15 - Logan

Logan and Armand waited until Max disappeared around a corner before heading to the station in a low run. The doors stood wide open, and the entrance was well lit, illuminating the streaks of blood on the walls. Time was of the essence, and Logan knew they had to move quickly.

He dashed through the lobby, checking rooms as he went. Armand, nervous and pale, stuck close to his heels. They came upon the body of a policeman stripped to the bone. Despite that, it still stretched out skeletal fingers and gnashed its teeth in hunger. Logan hacked into its skull with his ax.

Further down the hall, they came to an office barricaded from the outside. He leaned his ear against the door. Faint rustles could be heard from the inside, and he shook his head. With a finger to his lips, Logan motioned to Armand, and the two snuck past without a sound.

They continued down the hall, painfully aware of every second that passed. Max couldn't run forever and would make his way back soon. *If he makes it back at all.*

It was a thought Logan didn't want to entertain for long. Despite his natural loner inclinations, Max was his friend.

They pressed deeper into the building. Hair prickled on the back of his neck. He hated being cooped up inside strange buildings, loathed the sense of entrapment. Visibility decreased as the windows dwindled. The atmosphere grew creepy, the silence pressing down on them and crushing the breath from their lungs.

Another door loomed ahead, cracked half-way open. Logan peeked around the corner. Confronted by three infected, he backtracked but was too slow.

With a raspy growl, the first threw itself at him. Gripping it by the throat, he lifted his ax, but the second zombie was almost on him. With a wild flail, he sunk the blade into its face.

Holding the one by the throat and the other by the ax handle, he braced for the third. Armand appeared, shoving it away before stabbing it through the temple with his sharpened crowbar. He wrenched out the crowbar and reversed his aim, catching another zombie through the back of the skull. It too crumpled to the ground.

Logan focused on his remaining attacker. With a kick he knocked it to the ground, pulling the ax out of its face. A swift hack finished it off. Silence fell.

"Man, that was close," Armand said.

"Too close," Logan agreed, wiping spatters of blood from his face with his shirt tail. "Come on. We have to hurry."

A set of bathroom doors once more halted their progress. Logan approached with caution. The ladies' bathroom was locked from the inside, and Logan decided he didn't want to know what awaited within.

The men's bathroom door gave without a struggle, creaking open on unoiled hinges. A hand shot through and grabbed his ankle, followed by a hideous face.

"Fuck!" Logan screamed as teeth sunk into the toe of his boot. Shaking his leg, he tried to dislodge the corpse attached to his foot. "Fuck, fuck, fuck!"

Armand jumped in and bashed the zombie on the head until it resembled ground meat. Even then it wouldn't let go, hanging on like a dog with a bone.

Shuddering with disgust, Logan pried loose its jaws and examined his shoe, relieved to find it intact.

"Did he get you?"

"No, I was lucky."

Armand snickered, and Logan looked up with a frown. "What?"

"You should have seen your face!"

"Shut up," Logan muttered, embarrassment turning the tips of his ears red.

"Wait till Max hears about this," Armand said, unfazed by the scowl Logan bestowed upon him.

"Let's go." Logan shoved past with a sour look, but his ill humor soon faded when they reached the rec room and cafeteria. The door stuck when they tried to open it, only moving a finger width. "We need to go through here. Help me push, and be ready for anything."

With grunts of effort, they shoved the double doors until they moved in with a harsh grating of wood on tile. No infected came rushing out through the gap to attack, so Logan stuck his head through.

It stank—a peculiar mixture of sewage, rotten food, and disease hung in the air—but he couldn't see any zombies.

"Clear," he called to Armand. He squeezed through the gap then stopped short, stunned by what he saw. "We've got a problem."

"What's wrong?" Armand stepped inside, then froze as he spotted what Logan already had. "Holy shit."

A man was propped up against the wall, staring at them with glassy eyes. He was emaciated to the point of death, the bones threatening to burst through skin strung as tightly as a drum. The only sign that he was still alive was the faint rise and fall of his chest.

About a meter away from him, lay a woman, curled on her side. She was dead, her eyes glazed and unseeing.

"Please," the man croaked through cracked and bleeding lips.

Logan kneeled on the floor and examined the stranger. "He's close to death." Looking up at Armand, he added, "We don't have time for this. We need to get those guns."

Armand was shocked. "Let's make time."

Logan debated then shook his head. "No. We leave him."

"We can't. I can't." Armand squared his shoulders and looked Logan in the eye. "I'll take him back on my own if I have to."

Logan sighed. "He won't make it."

"We have to try."

With a final shake of the head, Logan gave in. "Fine. Let's carry him out, but you better hope we make it in time."

"Thank you," the man whispered before closing his eyes, worn out by the effort of speaking.

They each took an arm and lifted the stranger off the floor. He weighed almost nothing so was hardly a burden, but the smell that wafted off his body was enough to make anyone hurl.

"He's been here all this time. Hiding. Living off the cafeteria food until it ran out," Armand said as they walked out, shock evident in every word.

"Yes. Too scared to come out."

Armand swallowed. "The girl. What an awful way to die."

"We'll all die if we don't move faster."

They hurried along, their sense of urgency causing them to drop their guard. They rounded a corner and stepped right into the middle of a crowd of infected.

With a guttural growl, the nearest flailed a hand at Logan. He threw up an arm, backpedaling to gain distance. "Get back!"

Too late.

Several hands latched onto the stranger. For the briefest of moments, Logan resisted their pull. He let go when a hand closed on his shoulder and jerked. Armand was shoved aside by the weight of two infected, fighting fiercely.

The zombies wrenched the stranger into the center of the group. With a cry, he fell, one hand outstretched. They shredded his flesh like a school of piranhas. Warm blood spurted out, coating Logan's face in a red mist.

He fought, swinging his ax with lethal precision. The undead fell, but it was the stranger's death that saved their lives. It distracted the mob and gave them enough time to kill a few, evening out the odds.

The last one fell, and Logan stared down at a heap of bone and innards, all that remained of the stranger. *Whether he knew it or not, he saved our lives.*

Armand pointed at the previously barricaded door they'd passed earlier, standing wide open. "They must have heard us."

"Yes." Logan turned back the way they came. "Now, let's go."

Armand stared at him, shell-shocked. "What?"

"We need to go," Logan repeated, enunciating each word with care. "We need to get the guns."

165

Armand stared at him, mouth working.

Logan sighed. Why was it always up to him to be the hard ass?

"If we don't go now, Max will get back with a horde of zombies on his ass, and we'll all die. If we don't get the guns, the people back home might very well die. Understand?"

With that, he spun on his heels and made his way back, trusting that Armand would follow.

He did.

They skirted around the woman's corpse in the cafeteria, and five mercifully uneventful minutes later, they reached their goal.

The armory turned out to be a gold mine. Whistling, Logan eyed all the guns lined up on the walls. "Let's get cracking. There's not much time left."

They unslung two duffel bags from their backs and loaded up. Guns in the one, ammo in the other. When both were full, Logan nodded. "Let's go."

They ran back, pausing outside to let their eyes adjust. It was still clear. No sign of Max. *Come on, buddy. Where are you?*

They ran to the Nyala, slinging both bags into the back. "Get in. We've got to be ready to go."

Slamming the door shut behind Armand, Logan scanned the streets. He jogged to the driver's side and waited beside the open door. The seconds ticked by. He itched to move, shifting from one foot to the other. Just when he was about to go, a distant yell resounded. Max rounded a corner with a horde of infected on his tail.

There were quite a few of the fast variations in the crowd, and they were hot on Max's heels. Red-faced and stumbling, it was evident he was spent. Logan doubted he'd make it on his own. With icy calm, he swung his rifle off his shoulder and rested the muzzle on the frame of his door.

In quick succession, he dropped three of the infected closest to Max. His next two shots went wide, and Logan took a moment to center himself before dropping two more. Always a good shooter, he'd never needed his aim to prove true more than then.

The fallen zombies tripped up some of their comrades, and Max gained a small lead. From inside the Nyala, Armand's rifle boomed. *Good boy. He's firing through the loopholes.*

More zombies dropped.

The gap between man and horde widened.

"That should do it." Logan slung the rifle back onto his shoulder and climbed into the vehicle.

He watched as Max shot around the front to the passenger door and jumped in with seconds to spare. The front-runners thudded into the doors and bonnet, howling in frustration as their meal disappeared behind solid steel.

Logan pulled away with a roar of the engine and crunched over anything in his path. They made a clean getaway. After a few minutes, Logan stopped and turned to Max. "You okay?"

"I'm all right," Max gasped, still breathless from his exertions. Sweat dripped down his face and ran in runnels onto his shirt, pooling underneath his arms.

"Really? Cause you look like shit." Logan reached behind the seat and pulled out a bottle of water. "Here."

"Thanks." Max chugged it down in one long swig. "Now I know what Morgan felt like. Running for your life from a pack of rabid wolves is not fun."

"Must run in the family," Logan agreed, grinning. "Home?"

"Home," Max agreed, closing his eyes as he leaned back in his seat.

Logan steered back onto the road, glad his friend was okay. *I've never had a friend before. Then again, I've never experienced a zombie apocalypse or been in love before either.*

An image of Morgan's brilliant smile and mischievous eyes rose in his mind. He knew she was the one. She just needed to realize it too.

Max dozed off while Logan drove until he spotted activity to the left. He shook Max, rousing him from his nap.

"What? What's happening?" Max asked, struggling upright.

"Survivors."

Fully alert now, Max looked around. "Where?"

"Over there." Logan pointed to a row of shops. They were deserted, standing forlorn and forgotten. Except one. The pharmacy.

A small crowd of infected were gathered in the front, moaning as they banged on the doors. "There's something in there they want. That means people."

"You're right. Up for a rescue mission?"

"Sure. Why not?"

They filled Armand in on the plan and left him behind to provide cover with his rifle. Limbering up, Max and Logan pulled out their weapons. The zombies didn't even notice the two men approach so intent were they on the shop.

With the advantage of surprise on their side, it only took a minute to get rid of the infected. It was a dance now so familiar it might as well have been choreographed.

"We make a good team," Max grinned afterward.

"We've had plenty of practice," Logan replied.

He hung back as Max peered inside and yelled, "Hello!

Anyone there?"

A pale face appeared in the gloom, staring at them with wide-eyed surprise. It disappeared and was followed by rattling and scraping. The door swung open to reveal a man. He was short with a pot belly, salt-and-pepper hair, coupled with spectacles perched on the end of his nose. Logan guessed him to be in his late fifties.

"Thank you, thank you. You don't know how glad we are to see you. We thought we would die," the man gushed. "Oh, I'm David, David Nelson."

"We?" Logan asked.

"Well, there's four of us." Behind him in the gloom, three more faces popped up wearing similar looks of surprise and relief.

"Have you been here all this time?" Logan asked.

"Yes, we were trapped from the start. Luckily we had plenty of meal replacements, vitamins, protein bars, bottled water and so on, but it hasn't been pleasant."

David talked fast, a nervous tick in his right eye. Logan decided they needed to get him out of there before he had a nervous breakdown.

"Max? We need to move."

"You want to come with us?" Max offered. "We've got a safe place."

"What about our families?" David asked. "We must go to them."

Max sighed, "Look, I'm sorry to say this but your families are likely dead, or they've fled town. If you come with us, we can offer a safe place to stay and maybe later we can look for them."

David nodded, struck dumb at the news.

From the back, a girl asked, "Is everybody dead?"

"Most everyone," Logan answered. "Listen, we can talk on the way, but right now we've got to go before more infected arrive."

After a brief whispered conference, the group agreed. Everyone piled into the Nyala after grabbing bags of medical supplies. Logan was happy to learn that David was a pharmacist and Hannah, a middle-aged woman, was a nurse working in the clinic. This added valuable medical personnel to their group.

Liezel, a young girl, used to be David's assistant and Rosa, a student, was trapped with them during the outbreak.

As they drove off, Logan reflected that it had been a terrifying but prosperous day. *I just hope Morgan's trip proved equally fortunate.*

Chapter 16 - Morgan

Bare thorn trees and brittle, dry grass flashed past the window. Morgan stared at the landscape, lost in thought. Jacques drove with Angie squeezed in between them. They bickered back and forth, and she'd long since tuned out.

That day she'd been trapped in the shower was still burned into her mind with ferocious intensity. Her life had been safe and predictable until that moment, although she'd struggled with silent depression.

After her teenage years, she'd taken great care to hide her feelings from everyone, including her husband. Her often unpredictable mood swings and insecurity had strained their marriage at times, especially because Brian didn't know where the real problem lay. Despite that, it had been a happy union, warm and loving.

That day in the shower changed everything. The one person she'd never feared, became the being that tried to murder her. Not only did she lose Brian, but also any certainty in the status quo. Now, she felt challenged to rise above herself and become a stronger person, one able to overcome adversity, not just live with it.

Morgan found herself excited at the prospect. The depression was fading, her mind responding to their situation by becoming tougher. Though she missed Brian, he was receding into the background, becoming part of a life she once had but now couldn't even visualize.

Morgan scrutinized their surroundings while absentmindedly rubbing the stock of her handgun. *It can't be far now.*

A kilometer further, she saw the sign signaling the turnoff. The next few minutes were spent jostling and bumping along on a rocky dirt road. A tall iron link fence ran along their right, and soon they reached the gates.

It was closed. Keeping a wary eye out for trouble, Morgan jumped out and opened it. She noticed a padlock and chain lying to the side. They'd been cut through, and she frowned as she considered the implications. *We're not the first ones here.*

She jumped back inside the vehicle and showed Angie and Jacques the cut chains. "The place could be occupied. Either way, expect trouble."

They drove through the gate, leaving it open for a quick getaway and trundled further up the dirt track. When the tops of the buildings showed through a screen of trees, she called a halt.

"Listen, guys. We've got no idea what's waiting up ahead. I propose we leave the Nyala here and sneak in, make sure the coast is clear."

Agreeing, they got out and approached the tree line, keeping quiet. A faint breeze stirred the grass stalks, creating the sense of a rolling beige ocean. The ground rose, sloping upwards into a long ridge. The grass petered out, and the pines soared overhead, the wind susurrating through the needles. No other sounds could be heard. It was eerie.

Morgan crouched down, studying the clearing ahead. She had an excellent view, afforded by the high ground. A long, flat structure that served as the restaurant, hall, and bar area, lay to the left. A patio ran along its length, decorated with lawn furniture. It edged onto a big, square swimming pool.

She remembered a distant weekend spent at the reserve with Brian. It had been summer, the days hot and lazy. They'd had breakfast on the patio, followed by a swim in the cool, blue pool. Cottages dotted the lawns, interspersed with a play park. It looked very different now. The grass was overgrown, and the kids equipment broken down. The pool resembled a swamp, thick with algae and sludge.

The dirt road wound past the base of the ridge and through a gate set in a low wall surrounding the buildings. Past that, it led to a camping site with stands and ablution blocks.

Even further along lay a dam stocked with fish and an inner reserve, fenced off and filled with wildlife, mostly buck. The place was perfect for their needs but also occupied. Trucks were parked next to the bungalows, and rubbish lay strewn across the ground. Her shoulders slumped. *Someone beat us to it.*

"No go," she mouthed, jerking a thumb back toward the Nyala.

Angie and Jacques nodded, inching back the way they came. Morgan's heart was heavy, but approaching the strangers was out of the question. That was a decision for the group to make.

Easing back, a strong gust of wind swept through the trees. It carried the taint of death, and Morgan paused. Her senses kicked into high-alert, and her hand hovered over her gun. Movement caught her eye. Toward the end of the tree line, closest to the cottages, a body swung from a rope. Morgan frowned and looked closer. *What the...?*

It was the corpse of a young woman, swinging slowly

back and forth. She was naked, long dark hair covering her face. Purple bruises adorned her body. Morgan smothered a gasp, her mind skittering like a frightened mouse at the implications. *Who did that?*

Jacques noticed her reaction. He followed her gaze. The color leached from his ruddy skin until it matched his ash blond hair. Angie looked at them, a question mark on her face.

Movement below the dead girl's feet drew Morgan's attention. She moved closer, making out the shape of two women huddled against the tree trunk. Curiosity stirred, and she turned to the others. "Wait here. I'm going over."

"You can't," Angie hissed. "What if it's zombies?"

"They're not acting like infected."

"So? You don't know that. Leave them," Angie insisted, her dark eyes flashing.

"No." Morgan's eyes narrowed, surprised at Angie's reaction. "Maybe they need help, and I'm going to find out."

"We can come back later with more people."

"They could be dead by then," Morgan replied, her eyes going back to the hanged girl.

"She's right, Angie. We have to try," Jacques argued.

Angie shot them both a glare but gave in. "Fine, I'll cover you from here, but if something happens, I'm getting out of here."

Ignoring her, Morgan and Jacques moved closer to the girls. On closer inspection, it appeared they too were naked and in bad shape. Both were chained to the tree. *What's going on here?*

In a soft voice, she called out to them. The nearest girl turned her head. She appeared dazed. Then her eyes lit

174

up, and she scrambled upright, rising out of the nest of pine needles she'd burrowed into.

Morgan gasped at the purple bruises covering her thin frame, fading to mottled yellow in places. Her lips were split and bleeding, and a gash festered above her cheekbone.

Morgan's gaze shifted to the dead girl's toes swinging not far from her face, and her shock hardened into resolve. *Whatever's going on here, we've got to save them.*

"I'm here to help," she whispered.

The girl nodded, a look of hope flashing across her face. She turned to her companion, shaking her awake. Shooting upright, the second girl stared wildly at Morgan and Jacques before bursting into tears.

"Shh, be quiet," Morgan pleaded. After frantic hand gestures and pleading, the girl stopped crying though she still hid behind her friend. *They're both so young.*

Morgan examined the chains binding them to the tree. "Jacques, get the ax and tell Angie to bring the Nyala closer. Be quiet."

He slipped away, and she turned back to the girls. "I'll cut your bonds, then you run to our vehicle, okay?"

"Okay."

"What're your names?"

"I'm Lisa. This is Michelle."

"Is it just you two?"

Lisa shook her head, pointing a trembling finger to the cottages. "No, Jackie's down there."

"Shit." Morgan thought for a moment. "How many of them are there? Are they armed?"

"There's eight of them, and they've got guns."

With regret, Morgan let go of the idea of trying to rescue

the unfortunate Jackie. "I'm sorry, but there's only three of us. We can't take on eight armed men."

"Please," Lisa pleaded. "She's my friend. You've no idea what those men did to us...what they'll do to her. We have to save her."

Michelle began to sob while Lisa spoke, small broken gasps that shook her tiny frame.

Tears burned Morgan's eyes, but she shook her head. "I can't. I'm sorry. I have to think of my friends too."

Lisa swallowed, looking down. "I understand, but..."

"We can come back for her with reinforcements," Morgan offered.

"Would you?"

"We'll try," Morgan promised. The thought of leaving Jackie behind sickened her, but there was no choice. *We'll be back, but right now we have to get out of here.*

Jacques returned with the ax, and Morgan explained the situation to him. "You cover me while I chop through the chain. The girls will run to the truck with me protecting the rear."

"And Angie?" he asked.

"She can drive. Have her ready to go as soon as we get there."

"All right, I'll tell her." He snorted. "She'll bitch like she always does, but she'll do it."

Morgan waited until he took up his position and fingered the ax, examining the chain. It wasn't very thick, and she thought a solid blow would do the trick.

"Pull back on the chain. Hold it tight against the trunk." She pointed in the direction of the Nyala. "Once it's done, run. Don't stop and don't look back. I'll cover you."

Not willing to waste any more time, Morgan positioned herself for the blow and swung. The blade cut through the chain, reverberating like a thunderclap.

"Go! Hurry!" Morgan cried, helping the girls to their feet.

Lisa took the lead, supporting the more fragile Michelle while urging her on. Morgan's heart thumped in her chest while she stared anxiously at the cottages.

A door burst open, and a shirtless man stumbled out. He paused, fumbling for the gun at his belt. He spotted the fleeing girls and shouted, "Hey! Where do you think you're going?"

Morgan pulled out her gun and took a shot at him. She missed, the bullet going wide. The girls were moving way to slow for her liking, their bodies weakened and malnourished.

The shirtless man got his gun to bear, aiming the muzzle in their direction. A rifle report boomed, and a red flower blossomed on his chest. He fell with a cry, and Morgan took the opportunity to run.

More men tumbled out of the huts. A bullet clipped the bark next to her face, showering her with splinters. She ducked as another shot struck the ground, sending up a spray of dirt. "Shit."

Whirling, she took a knee and pulled the trigger. Her shots went wild. Grabbing hold of the gun with both hands, she steadied her aim. A knee stuck out from behind a wall, and she took a chance at hitting the small target. The limb exploded in a shower of blood and bone before disappearing from view. "Gotcha."

Jacques laid down a blanket of fire. One shooter fell back, hit in the chest while Morgan ran, scrambling over tree roots. The rolling edge of the ridge was near. She saw Lisa and Michelle drop out of sight, running toward the Nyala.

A sharp blow from behind sent her flying forward. She hit the ground, scraping her chin and eating dirt. Her leg felt numb, refusing her commands to move. *I've been shot.*

"Morgan, move!" Jacques screamed.

Bullets pattered around her like rain. She crawled forward on her elbows, snaking through the trees. Jacques scrambled over, yanking her to her feet. "Let's go!"

Holding onto him, she ran as fast as she could, limping on her bad leg. The rumble of the Nyala's engine reached them as Angie fired it up, spurring her on.

They tumbled into the back, yelling. Angie floored the gas, and Morgan nearly rolled out again. Jacques grabbed her with one hand, leaning over to slam the door shut. He fell back as a bullet hit the glass in front of his face. He screamed, and for some reason, Morgan found that funny. "Relax. It's bulletproof."

He shot her an annoyed look before his eyes dropped to her leg. "You've been shot."

"No shit." She glanced down at the wound for the first time and blanched. A small hole in the back of her thigh ballooned to a ragged exit wound in the front. Blood pumped out in a steady stream, and she felt nauseated.

"We need to stop the bleeding," Jacques said.

He pulled off his shirt and ripped the belt from his pants. Folding the material into a pad, he strapped it over the bullet holes with the belt, cinching it tight.

The bleeding slowed to a trickle. After a moment, Morgan lay back, closing her eyes as she tried to ride out the pain. It radiated through her leg in a red-hot blaze. She registered the moment they reached the tar road as the ride smoothed out, and the truck sped up.

"The girls?" she asked.

"In front, with Angie."

"Thank God. I was scared they wouldn't make it."

"They're all right."

"No signs of pursuit?"

"None yet."

"Good," she replied.

"Does it hurt?" he asked after a minute.

"Fuck, yes," she answered, not mincing words.

"You're nothing like your mom, you know that?"

"I know. She's a lady, and that's something I'll never be."

He laughed, "Try to rest. We'll be home soon."

She didn't bother to answer, saving her strength instead. The blood loss and heat combined to make her drowsy, and she drifted off. What felt like hours later, she blinked when Jacques shook her arm. "We're here."

With his help, she struggled upright and scooted out through the door. A small crowd had gathered, eager for news. When they saw the girls and Morgan's leg, a collective gasp went up.

"Morgan!" her mother cried, rushing forward.

Her knees buckled as her feet hit the ground. A pair of arms caught her, scooping her up, and gray eyes stared down into hers. Their intense regard sent a bolt of electricity through her spine. *Logan.*

A new voice, one she was unfamiliar with, joined the rest. "Make way, people. Let me help her. I'm a nurse."

Nurse? When did we get a nurse?

Warm blood flowed down her leg, the makeshift pad soaked through. Her head spun, and she grinned at Logan. "My hero."

She had the vague thought she was being silly but didn't

179

care. *Everything feels so strange.*

"She's losing a lot of blood."

"Bring her in. We need to get her stitched up. Do you have a first aid kit? Sutures?"

"I'll get it."

The disembodied voices floated around her while she clung to Logan. To her, they were meaningless, sparking only vague interest. Her feet swung as he carried her inside to lay her down on a bed. A sharp prick in her arm burned for a moment, then it all went black.

She came back to the light after a time, once more listening to voices discuss her and the girls they'd saved. That reminded her, and she managed to say, "Lisa, Michelle."

Her mother's warm voice washed over her. "They're fine, sweetheart. Don't worry; we're taking good care of them."

"Okay." She sank back into the cushions, relieved. "My leg?"

"It's fine," Julianne assured. "Hannah patched you up like a pro."

Morgan blinked, staring at the small crowd surrounding her bed. It gratified her to see so many worried faces. She wondered briefly who Hannah was, but the thought faded.

"Jacques told us what happened," Max said.

"Did he tell you about Jackie?"

"Who's Jackie?"

"We have to go back," she said. "There's another girl."

"Another one?" Max asked.

"Ask Lisa. She'll tell you."

"That poor girl. We have to get her, Max," Julianne said.

A grim silence fell as looks were exchanged. Finally, Max replied. "Get some rest, sis. I'll speak to Lisa, and we'll discuss it later."

"But..."

"Hush, sweetheart. Sleep. We'll take care of it, I promise."

Morgan allowed her mother's reassurances to soothe her, and she slipped away, falling into a deep sleep.

Chapter 17 - Logan

The meeting was convened two days later. Everyone gathered in the common room, summoned by Max. The atmosphere buzzed with tension. By now, everyone had heard what happened.

Logan studied the crowd through lidded eyes. It was a social gathering, with people forming groups much like herds of animals did. Unlike animals, though, he struggled to make sense of their motivations. He'd never been a people person.

Some were easy to figure out. Like the newcomers from the pharmacy: Dave, intelligent but fussy; Hannah, the matronly type; Liezel, shy and bookish; Rosa, bubbly and outgoing. They sat together in a corner, sticking together in an environment they knew little about. This he understood.

There were the two rescued girls, Lisa and Michelle. They had chosen not to attend the meeting at all, and this too, he understood.

Then there was Max and his family, the nucleus around which the camp revolved. They stuck like glue, supporting each other without fail, their collected strength outweighing any weaknesses apart. It was Julianne who kept them together, the matriarch of the clan.

Admiration stirred in his breast, increasing when his eyes fell on the alluring form of Morgan. She sat in the corner, her bad leg propped up on a chair. Hannah's surgery had been successful, and after two days, she was walking around on crutches.

What stumped him utterly, though, was the way Armand buzzed around Morgan like an insect. She didn't return his slavish adoration, treating him like a younger brother. At the same time, the boy was too stupid to see what was right in front of his eyes. Angie. *That girl is smitten. Why won't he give her a chance?*

Max cleared his throat. "You all know why we're here. Morgan's team rescued two girls from captivity. According to them, there's another girl still being held captive. We're here to decide whether or not to go back for her. Any thoughts?"

"We have to go back," Jacques said.

"I agree," Julianne said.

"So do I," Morgan added.

"You understand what will happen if we go back," Max warned. "It'll be a fight to the death."

"We can't let them get away with what they've done," Jacques protested.

"Those could be our sisters, daughters or wives," Joseph agreed, looking at his wife, Tumi.

"I understand how you feel, but I want to make sure you fully understand the consequences," Max insisted. "We've killed, yes. Infected, zombies, the undead. Not living people."

"We have no choice, Max. People like that can't be reasoned with. If we don't stop them now, they'll do worse," Julianne said. "Can you live with yourself knowing there are more girls out there being raped and tortured?"

"No, I can't," Max said. "But we all have to agree on this,"

"We can't just kill them," Rosa protested, shocked.

183

"What do you propose?" Max asked. "Leave them?"

"I don't know. Killing them just seems so barbaric."

"People like that are barbaric," Elise said, "and the police no longer exist to punish them. It's up to us now."

Rosa shook her head, uncertainty warring with disgust, "I suppose."

"This is stupid," Angie interjected. "Not that I give a flying fuck, but why must we go back? Leave them."

"What about the other girl?" Jacques asked. "The one we left behind?"

"What about her?" Angie shrugged. "She's not one of us. I say we look out for ourselves."

"How can you say that?" Jacques asked, outraged.

Pandemonium broke out as people fought, each shouting out their own opinion.

Logan shook his head. This was why he preferred to live alone. People were so stupid, and all this fighting was a waste of time. He decided to do something before the argument could escalate and stood up. "The time for convention and niceties has gone. These people are a threat. They live in our territory, and who's to say they won't come after us next?"

Silence fell.

"If we don't deal with them now, we'll have to deal with them later, and then it might be on their terms. It's kill or be killed."

"He's right. This could become a real problem for us later on," Max said.

After another lengthy discussion, everyone reached a consensus. The enemy group had to be removed, even if it meant killing. Some, like Rosa, did not wholeheartedly agree but understood the necessity, at least.

Max, Joseph, Jacques, and Big Ben were chosen to go. According to Jacques, there were only six left in the enemy group, one of whom had been shot in the knee and incapacitated. Max was confident it could be done with no losses on their side if they were smart. The rest would stay, guarding their home base.

After the meeting, people drifted off one by one, either to their beds or their duties. Slinging his rifle over his shoulder, Logan headed outside to take up his shift. Morgan was there ahead of him, determined to do her share despite being injured.

"Hey there," she greeted. "Up for some guard duty?"

"With you? Always."

"Don't joke."

He climbed up the ladder on the wall then reached down a hand and hauled her up. She gave a little squeak of surprise as her feet left the air. By the time he set her down, she was blushing furiously.

"It's no joke," he said. "You know how I feel."

Mumbling something unintelligible, she hobbled off to the nearest tower. She flopped down on a chair and stretched her leg out with a muffled groan. He offered no sympathy. She wouldn't want it.

Deciding to give her time to think over his words, he made a slow circuit of the walls. The night air was fresh, and the silence was soothing as he enjoyed the break away from humanity. Most of his adult years had been spent out in the bush, hunting, foraging, and game ranging. A loner by nature, he found people tiresome. All except one.

Spying Morgan's silhouette, he grinned. Being around people had its perks. She stood guard like a sentinel, her bad leg balanced on the toes and a spear gripped in her right hand. Her hair waved in the breeze like a flag.

He came to a stop next to her, and together they surveyed the terrain. After a few minutes, she turned those beguiling eyes on him and smiled. "You know, I never thought it would take the end of the world to make me feel truly alive again."

"I know what you mean."

"There's something about being in danger and living on the edge that makes me excited, eager to meet the challenge," she added.

"I'm familiar with the feeling," he replied. "Out in the bush, the game changes in a second. A lion can charge, a snake can strike. Life hangs in the balance. It makes a person aware."

"I get that."

Logan took her hand in his, entangling their fingers. "Morgan," he said, waiting.

Her lips quivered as she looked down at their hands. "I don't know if I can do this, Logan. It's too soon."

"It's not too soon."

"Will this last?" She looked down, lashes sweeping her cheeks. "I need to know this will last."

"It will, but once you do this, there's no going back. This is it, Morgan. There won't ever be another for me. Or you."

She shuddered, understanding dawning in her eyes.

Logan knew what he was asking. He'd found his woman, and once he had her, he had no intention of letting her go. She either had to go all in, surrender her soul, or walk away. It would be an all-consuming relationship, one of passion and possession.

Morgan hesitated, then stood on tip-toe, offering her lips. Logan lowered his head and claimed what she gave. He was neither gentle nor hesitant. He kissed her roughly, with all the fervor he possessed. When the kiss ended, she swayed. He pulled her close, nestled into his body. It felt right.

Together they stood, neither of them speaking, and watched the moon rise higher in the cobalt sky. It was a moment Logan would remember forever. "Happy?"

"Happy," she replied.

The minutes passed, and he relaxed as he breathed in her scent. A whiff of a different scent interfered with his happy moment, though. The smell of rot and decay. Death had arrived.

In his arms, Morgan stiffened as she noticed them too. "Duty calls."

Gripping her spear, she hobbled over to the corner. A group of zombies clawed at the fence, pushing at the barrier with insistent groans.

"Be careful," Logan said, eyeing her leg.

She shrugged and flashed him a grin. "I'll be fine."

Her spear flashed down with unerring accuracy. The point buried itself deep in the eye socket. With a twist to scramble the brains and a yank, she ripped it free, her victim collapsing in a heap. "See? Piece of cake."

Logan joined her, and the next few seconds passed in a blur of blood, bone, and brain matter. It was going so well, what happened next came as a complete surprise.

Morgan's spear flashed down and embedded itself in the cheek instead of penetrating the eye socket. Despite her best efforts, she could not pull it free. Her wounded leg didn't allow for a firm foothold. The zombie dragged its head back with a growl. Teetering on the edge, Morgan screamed, "Logan!"

Logan raced to her side, reaching out a hand just as she

187

tumbled over. "No!"

Morgan landed with a thump on her back, grunting as the breath left her lungs in a rush. She held on to the spear, keeping the impaled zombie at bay. Two more closed in.

Without thinking, Logan threw himself off the wall and onto the nearest. Its spine crackled, the brittle bone breaking with an audible snap. Logan smashed its face into the dirt and scrambled over, trying to head off the second zombie aiming for Morgan.

He dove forward, tackling it around the waist. They crashed to the ground. The zombie thrashed wildly as it snapped at Logan. It was a lot fresher than the others, intact and possessing herculean strength.

Logan grappled with it, rage fueling his actions. He pushed the infected back by the neck and swung his rifle up, bashing it on the temple. The blow glanced off. He didn't stop, hitting it over and over until a muffled pop told him the skull had collapsed.

Logan turned his head away just in time to avoid a spray of blood and brains in the face. Beneath him, the zombie stilled, 'unlife' leaving its body at last.

Morgan cried out in pain, grabbing his attention. His insides froze. He rushed over, too scared to look. Somehow she had kept hold of the spear with the zombie on the other end, but the crippled zombie had gone after her. She kicked at it with her good leg, but it had a death grip on her foot. It levered itself higher up, biting down on her shin.

Logan delivered a stunning kick to its head that would have made his old rugby coach proud and sent it flying. He ended its existence with a few decisive hits with the but of his rifle before turning back to Morgan.

She got up, red-faced with anger. She kicked the legs out from underneath the remaining zombie. Wrenching the spear free, she delivered the killing blow. Staggering back, she let her weapon clatter to the ground. "Crap!"

"Your leg," Logan said, his voice devoid of emotion.

Morgan bent down and examined her shin. Her hand came away shiny with saliva, and Logan's heart dropped.

"Yuck," she shuddered, wiping her hand on the ground. She looked up at him with a half-smile. "I'll be okay. The boots. There's a reason I wear them all the time."

"Oh, thank God. Don't ever do that again." He slumped with relief and pointed at the wall. "Let's get back before more arrive. We can dispose of the bodies in the morning."

She nodded, gulping in air. "Agreed."

They climbed up. Logan helped Morgan to the nearest chair where she remained for the rest of their watch. Logan patrolled the walls, left alone with his churning thoughts. If he had lost her...

From the beginning, he'd planned on leaving, only staying long enough to help Max build a secure base. Their unexpected friendship had caused him to hesitate. When Big Ben and his group arrived, Logan told himself he'd stay another week at the most. Until that day—the day they saved Morgan. The moment he laid eyes on her, he knew she was the one. She just had to realize it too.

When Armand and Angie showed up to take over the next watch, Logan was more than ready to go. He helped her off the wall, and she leaned on him while they walked. She collapsed on her bed with a gasp, and he frowned. "Should I call Hannah?"

"No," she said. "I'm fine. I just need to relax."

"Let me have a look."

"It's no big deal, Logan. Come on, don't fuss over me."

He fixed her with a glare. She shut her mouth, and she stuck out her leg with a huff.

He unwound the bandage and examined the wounds. The stitches had survived the fight. It was swollen and bruised but otherwise okay. He disinfected the area before wrapping it with a clean bandage and gave her the medication Hannah had prescribed. Antibiotics and painkillers.

"I'm so tired," she moaned, flopping back onto the bed.

"Let me tuck you in," he teased.

She cocked an eyebrow at him, and he laughed. "Relax, I'm just gonna take your boots off."

He eased them off her calves followed by the socks but stopped when he saw the crescent-shaped bruises covering her shin. "That must hurt."

"Not anymore," she giggled, winking at him.

"I see the drugs are kicking in," he replied with wry amusement. "You've got no head for meds, you know? It makes you loopy."

She giggled again and hooked a finger in his collar. "You make me loopy."

He let her pull him up onto the bed, unable to resist her charms. She kissed him with abandon, curling her fingers in his hair. He could feel his restraint slipping and gripped her ass, pulling her tight against him. She moaned, swinging her leg over his hip as her fingers traveled down to his belt and fumbled with the buckle.

Logan sighed and broke off the kiss. "I'm going to hate myself for this later but..." He pushed her away, gently but firmly. "I can't let you do this."

She pouted. "Why?"

"Because you're all drugged up. I won't take advantage of you."

"But I want you to."

"I can't."

"You're not making this easy, are you?" She pulled a face and rolled away. "Fine, be the gentleman."

"I'm sorry, love," he said, planting a kiss on her brow. "See you in the morning."

He got up to leave, but she grabbed his hand. "Wait. At least stay the night."

Logan hesitated.

"Just hold me, okay? I can't blame you tomorrow for having a cuddle, now can I?"

"I suppose not," he conceded.

He shuffled into bed next to her. Morgan curled her body into his, pulling his arms tight around her. Her breathing slowed as she drifted off. Logan tried to relax, tried to think of anything except the warm body pressed to his and the pulsing need in his crotch.

"You've got no idea what you're doing to me," he whispered, resigning himself to a long, sleepless night.

Morning came far too soon. Morgan wanted to say goodbye to her brother and the rest before they left. Everyone else had the same idea, and the dining room was packed. Delicious smells wafted through the air as Elise prepared a proper send-off for the heroes, and Logan's stomach growled.

It was evident to everyone in the room that things between Morgan and Logan had changed. Whenever Logan looked at her, she blushed a deep, beetroot red. This caused much amusement among the observers.

"Guess the cat's out of the bag," Morgan said with a sheepish smile.

"Not like it was ever a state secret," Julianne teased.

The only tense moment occurred when Joanna arrived. Morgan stiffened, and Logan removed his arm from around her shoulders.

Joanna forestalled Morgan's stuttered explanation with a raised hand. "Morgan, dear, don't apologize. It'sIt's your life and your decision."

She turned and made a dignified exit, leaving Morgan red-faced and guilty-looking.

"That went well," Logan said.

Morgan swallowed, chewing on her bottom lip.

"It must be hard for her, losing her son, and seeing you with someone else." He studied her stricken face. "How do you feel about it?"

"I feel bad. How can I not?"

"Are you sorry?"

"No, I'm not. I could die tomorrow and then what? Besides, this doesn't change the fact that I loved him. He was a good man."

"I'm sure he was," Logan said.

"Thank you for understanding." She kissed him on the cheek. "I'll help Elise wash up. See you later."

Slinging his rifle to its customary spot, he walked out into the chilly pre-dawn air. He nodded to Armand and Angie who stood off to the side. Max and the others were preparing to leave, and he ambled over to see them off. He could not help but notice the hostile look Armand shot him, though.

Angie whispered to him, but the boy ignored her, glaring at Logan instead. She tugged at his arm. With a violent pull, he shrugged her off. Tears shimmered in her eyes as she turned away. *Stupid. Too caught up in his damn fantasies to see what's staring him right in the face.*

Logan shrugged. The boy would learn or not. It was no business of his what Armand did. *As long as he stays away from Morgan. She's mine, and I don't intend to share.*

Chapter 18 - Big Ben

It was well before dawn, and the road was dark and quiet, the only signs of life being the odd startled meerkat or guinea fowl caught in the headlights. Ben sighed and rubbed his eyes, tired from all the peering into the dark. His eyesight wasn't quite what it used to be anymore, and a trip to the optometrist was out of the question now.

I'm getting too old for this. He shifted in his seat, trying to get comfortable. *Strange how life takes the most unexpected turns.*

When he was younger, he was a boxer. A good one too. But the injuries took their toll, and he retired early to open a gymnasium. He met and married a good woman and hoped for a family. It wasn't meant to be. Mariana was diagnosed with cervical cancer a year after their marriage, and all dreams of children died with that discovery. Thankfully, Mariana recovered from the illness after treatment, and they spent many happy years together. Now he was glad they'd never had children. Losing his wife was bad enough. He still had nightmares of those first few days of the apocalypse.

He had gone to the studio at ten that morning. After class, he was perplexed to notice several missed calls from Mariana which was unusual since she didn't like to bother him at work. He called back, but she didn't answer.

Dismissing the next class, he jumped into his car and raced

home, a feeling of foreboding gnawing at his gut. He found the streets in chaos and traffic jammed to a suffocating degree. The sense of wrongness intensified.

When he reached home, his worst fears were confirmed. Someone had broken into the house. The dining-room windows were smashed into pieces.

He followed a blood trail to the bedroom, finding the door open. More blood than he had ever seen before in his life obscured the room. It was splashed onto the walls, the ceiling, the bed, and soaked into the carpet.

He found his wife on the floor on the other side of the bed. He could barely identify her there was so little left. Only the blond hair and wedding ring confirmed his worst fears. Luckily or unluckily, depending on the point of view, her skull had been cracked open and her brain eaten, preventing her from turning and coming back as a monster.

Shocked and confused, it took some time to figure out what was happening and make a run for it. He picked up Angie and Susan along the way. They barely made it out of Bloemfontein alive.

On the road, they met up with the others and were chased from one place to the next. During that time, he grew fond of the girls, along with Armand and Jacques, coming to see them as his adopted children.

The night they ended up at Max's place, they were attacked. Susan got bitten. He blamed himself for that. He should have been there for her and protected her just as he should have protected his wife. At least Angie was still alive, and he would make damn sure she stayed that way.

Up ahead, the other vehicle slowed down and pulled over to the side of the road. Max had briefed them all beforehand,

and they'd decided to launch a surprise attack at dawn.

Joseph shot Ben a smile, his teeth gleaming pearly white against his ebony skin. Ben had grown to trust him after the many near misses they'd faced together in the past, and the two men were as close as brothers.

"Today, my friend, we might die," Joseph said.

"Comforting," Ben replied.

Joseph laughed, "Don't look so sad. We've faced many dangers together, and if we die today, we go to meet our ancestors."

Ben snorted, "Forgive me if that prospect does not excite me."

Joseph clapped him on the back and walked ahead, joining the rest. Ben stretched out his stiff limbs, hoping to get the blood flowing again. He did not look forward to what awaited them. The idea of killing repulsed him, but he realized the necessity. What bothered him the most was the thought of the remaining girl. He hoped they weren't rescuing a corpse.

They huddled together as Max dispensed last-minute instructions. Then they were off, jogging along the dirt track spaced loosely apart, each keeping a wary eye out for trouble.

The sun was rising which relieved Ben. It enabled him to see better. A light sweat broke out on his forehead, but his body moved with ease, and he enjoyed the activity. The gate appeared, the silver metal gleaming with dewdrops. They fanned out to the sides, hunkering down with their rifles ready.

Max cleared the area as they slipped through the gate in single file. Fanning out again, they approached the tree line, keeping low in the grass. They each chose a sheltered spot with a wide field of fire while Max reconnoitered to make sure there weren't any surprises in store for them, either guards or infected.

Lisa had told them much about both the men they faced and the layout. She'd also told them the group sometimes captured infected, using them for sport.

Ben admired the girl for being so clear-headed despite what she'd been through. Her companion Michelle was both younger and more traumatized. They had not questioned her.

After a tense few minutes, Max gave the all clear and took up his position. Max exchanged a glance with each of them and mouthed, "Ready?"

They nodded. Max pulled the pin on a grenade and tossed it into the center of the buildings. It detonated with a terrific bang, sending up a shower of dirt and dust to leave behind a crater. Doors burst open, and figures spilled out, firing shots at random. The bright morning sun blinded them, and their bullets went wild.

"What a bunch of dumbasses," Ben muttered. Clearly, intelligence wasn't their strong suit.

He lined up his sights and squeezed the trigger, putting a bullet between the eyes of the nearest, a burly man with a bushy beard worthy of Grizzly Adams. He went down, twitched once and lay still. Joseph, Max, and Jacques each picked their targets, and two more fell while the third ducked behind a car, wounded in the shoulder.

That's three down, Ben thought, *with the fourth wounded. That leaves two, of which one is nowhere in sight, and the other is minus a knee thanks to Morgan.*

Silence fell, overwhelming after the wild gunfire and grenade blast. It was broken only by the hoarse cries of the wounded man.

After a few seconds, Max spoke. "Drop your gun and come out with your hands in the air." Silence met his demand. "If you don't, I'm tossing a grenade over there."

"No way. If I come out, you'll shoot me."

"He's got that right," Jacques muttered under his breath.

Joseph snorted.

Max silenced them both with a glance. "We won't shoot you if you come out, but if you don't, I'll blow you to pieces. How's that?"

A moment's silence. "Fine! I'm coming out. Please don't shoot." He tossed his rifle away and crawled out from behind the vehicle.

Max motioned to the others to stand down. "Where's the rest of you?"

"The rest?"

"We know there's at least two more of you. Don't play dumb with me unless you want a bullet between the eyes."

"Okay, okay." He raised his hands in surrender. "Gary's dead. That bitch did him in with that shot to the knee. Cried for hours before he died."

"The other one?"

The guy swallowed. "There isn't anyone else."

"Don't talk shit. Do you want to die?"

"No." He looked over his shoulder, his eyes straying to a cottage not far from him. "I swear I'm the only one that's left."

"You're lying."

"Okay, fine, he's over—" A shot rang out, and he fell, red blooming on his chest.

Max looked around. "Who shot him?"

Ben shrugged, "Not me."

The other two also shook their heads. Max looked back,

scanning the grounds. "Must be his partner. He doesn't want to be found."

"Smoke him out," Ben suggested. "Put those grenades to use."

"Good idea." Max tossed a grenade, followed closely by two more. Explosions rocked the ground, and the percussive sounds made Ben's ears ring.

When the noise faded, Max shouted, "We know you're in there. You might as well come out, or I'll blow you into so many pieces there won't be enough left for the ants to carry away."

Silence.

Max looked at the others. "What now? If I keep throwing grenades, I risk killing the girl."

"We hunt him down," Joseph said, "like the animal he is."

"It's too dangerous. There's no cover," Max said, shaking his head.

"We don't have a choi—" Joseph replied before being interrupted.

"All right. I'm coming out, but if you try anything, I'll shoot the girl," a strange voice shouted. They all looked down, trying to pinpoint its location.

Max narrowed his eyes. "Come on out. We won't shoot."

In the doorway of a cottage, the struggling figure of a girl appeared followed by a slender frame.

Ben blinked, surprised at what he saw. "It's just a boy!" he exclaimed, exchanging incredulous looks with the others.

The last remaining survivor of the enemy group was still in his teens, seventeen maybe eighteen. Wide eyes and freckles dominated his features, lending him an innocent air; his red hair gleamed in the sunlight.

"What the fuck?" Max muttered.

The boy pushed the girl along in front of him. Ben focused on her. She wore a torn red dress. Her brown hair was unwashed and limp and shrouded her face. Duct tape covered her mouth. She wouldn't stand still and fought against her bonds, utterly ignoring the gun trained to the back of her head.

"Let the girl go," Max shouted.

"No," the boy yelled back, defiant. "I'm taking her and getting out of here. If you shoot me, she dies."

"No deal. Let the girl go, and..." Max hesitated, "and you walk."

Ben shot Max a look. "Max, we can't let him go. He's a monster."

"What choice do we have? We have to rescue her," Max protested.

"I can take him," Jacques said. "He won't know what hit him."

"It's too risky. She's struggling too much." Max shook his head and turned back.

"I give you my word. Let her go, and you can walk free. No consequences."

The boy thought about it, emotions flickering across his face in rapid succession. Ben found it hard to read him. The innocent looks threw him off. There was something there, though, something cruel and hard but most of all, devious. *He can't be trusted.*

After a tense moment, the boy nodded, "I agree. If you give your word."

"I give you my word and the word of my men."

"You'll have to come fetch her," the boy smirked. "She might need some...assistance."

Ben's blood boiled, enraged at the thought of what the poor girl had been through. *Fucker.*

Debating briefly, Max stood. "I'm coming."

Jacques jumped up with the eagerness of youth, "No, let me, Max."

He started down the ridge without waiting for permission, and Max had no choice but to let him go.

Ben's instincts screamed at him. Something was wrong. He looked at the girl again. She was still struggling, refusing to back down. As he focused on her, he noticed something off. A crescent bite mark peeped out from underneath the long hair over her shoulders.

"Max, stop him!"

"What's wrong?"

"She's a fucking zombie!" Ben shouted, raising his rifle."Jacques, come back!"

Things happened so fast, it all became a blur. Jacques stopped a short distance away from the girl and looked back at Ben, confusion written on his face. The enemy boy reached over her shoulder and ripped off the duct tape, revealing torn and bloody lips pulled back into a snarl. He cut her bonds with a swift stroke and shoved her forward. She growled and reached for Jacques, her hands latching onto his shirt. His eyes widened in horror, and he batted at her face.

Ben aimed his rifle at her head, squeezing off a shot. It missed. She latched onto Jacques' throat and tore out a meaty chunk. The boy screamed as blood spurted from the wound. Ben fired off another round, but shock and horror seized his muscles. He missed again.

Jacques tumbled to the ground with the girl on top of him.

Hoarse cries bubbled from his lips. She tore out another chunk and reared up, throwing her head back. Red blood flowed down her milky white skin, blending in with her dress. Someone else took the shot, and her head exploded into a fine spray of red mist. She was flung backward and lay splayed, her eyes staring at the blue sky unseeingly.

Shots continued to fly back and forth. Joseph had pinned the enemy boy down behind a small wall. He appeared not to care about his life, having just screwed up his one chance to walk away. A final bullet fired from Max's rifle shattered his skull, and the fight ended as quickly as it began. It was over, and the grass lay strewn with bodies, but Ben saw none of that.

Jacques had rolled over on the grass, choking on the blood that gurgled up his throat. His hands reached to Ben, and his fingers clawed at the ground. Ben dropped his gun and ran to him. "Jacques!"

He dropped to his knees and gripped Jacques by the shoulder. The boy's eyes were glassy. His mouth worked, forming a word he couldn't say: Armand.

Ben worked to stem the flow of blood even though he knew it was pointless. When the light left Jacques' eyes, he grabbed the boy's shoulders, shaking him back and forth. "Fight damn it. Don't die on me. Fight!"

Joseph gripped his shoulder. "Ben. He's gone."

Sobbing bitter tears, Ben slumped to the ground. "No. God, please, no," he cried, tears rolling down his cheeks, mingling with the blood on his hands. "It's my fault."

"It's not your fault, Ben," Joseph said, but Ben knew the truth. He'd missed. He'd missed his shot. A shot that could have killed the girl and saved the boy. *His boy.* Ben cried out as agony gripped his heart with vice-like intensity.

Max and Joseph searched the cottages and cleared the grounds, leaving him to his grief. They found no more people, either dead, living, or undead. They did find a burnt clearing filled with the remains of corpses, though.

A field of death, Ben thought with bitter rage as he fixated on the dead gang members.

"Burn them," he said, his voice hoarse.

"What?" Max asked.

"Burn them," Ben repeated. "They don't deserve a burial."

Max complied without argument, fetching a jerry can of fuel and lighting the bodies with a match. Together, they watched the corpses burn, acrid smoke stinging their eyes. The smell of burning flesh permeated their clothes.

The girl, Jackie, they also cremated. It was the accepted way to deal with infected as they did not want to bury the bodies and possibly contaminate the environment, but they did so with respect and a murmured prayer.

To Ben, it felt like the world had stopped turning. Not only had they failed to rescue the girl, but he'd also failed to protect his boy. *I'm sorry, Jacques. So sorry.*

They wrapped Jacques' body in a sheet scavenged from one of the cottages and loaded him into the back of a vehicle, but only after they ensured he would not reanimate.

The sad little cavalcade drove through the gates, stopping only to secure it with a thick chain brought along for that purpose. The gunfire and grenade blasts would draw in any undead in the vicinity, and nobody wanted their new home to be overrun.

Ben was in a haze, his mind a mess of conflicting emotions. Scenes from the past kept flashing before his eyes. His wife, smiling at him on their wedding day, then the gruesome discovery of her body. Susan lost and scared until he found her, then the life leaving her eyes as she died from the virus. Jacques, so young and eager, then choking on his own blood. He had failed them all. Tears coursed down his weathered skin unheeded, and he ignored Joseph's concerned looks. What was there to say?

All too soon, they arrived home. Ben's heart sunk as he saw the waiting crowd. He got out, flanked on either side by Joseph and Max. It felt like he was in a lineup facing a firing squad.

The smiling faces of the crowd sobered at the grim looks on the trio's faces, and eyes danced around for the whereabouts of Jacques. It was Julianne who broke the silence. "Max? What happened? Where's Jacques?"

The question hung in the air, resonating through the expectant hush that had descended. From the back, Armand pushed his way through the people. His eyes searched, growing wilder by the second. "Where's Jacques?"

When no-one replied, Armand stepped forward and grabbed Ben's arm. "Ben? Where's Jacques?"

Ben swallowed, his mouth gone dry and his hands trembling. "I...he..."

"Where is he?" Armand roared.

Ben shook his head and pointed to the back of the truck. Armand stormed over and ripped the door open. He froze, confronted by the blood-soaked sheet covering his brother's body. He tore it off and swayed when he saw the terrible wounds.

"No, not him. Not my brother." A shudder tore through his body, and his shoulders heaved. He turned and glared at Max.

"I trusted you. I placed his life in your hands. I believed you would keep him safe."

He snapped off a punch, hitting Max in the nose. Gasps of shock went around as blood spurted, and the cartilage crunched. Armand followed it up with a second blow that split Max's lip before Ben grabbed him and wrestled him away.

"It's not his fault!" he said, strong-arming Armand. "It's mine."

Armand stilled, and shock and disbelief chased each other across his face. "What do you mean?"

"I could have saved him," Ben admitted. "I had the shot, but I missed."

"Tell me what happened to my brother."

Ben glanced over his shoulder and saw Elise herding the children away as the group backed up to give them privacy. He focused on Armand's icy blue gaze. In a guilt-stricken voice, he related what happened, leaving nothing out. When the last words died away, he waited, waited for the hatred and condemnation that was sure to follow.

Armand stared at him, his face a blank slate. In an emotionless voice, he said, "You were like a father to him, to us. We trusted you with our lives."

He turned and walked away with Angie close on his heels. Ben's knees buckled, unable to hold him up any longer. He fell to his knees in the dust and stared at his hands. His shoulders shook as dry, wracking sobs tore through his body.

Joseph and Max gripped him by the arms and guided him inside, speaking softly in his ears. It was nothing but noise to Ben as he faced the reality that his whole world was collapsing.

Chapter 19 - Lisa

Lisa sat on the wall, basking in the early sunlight. She fingered the metal spear on her lap. It felt good to hold a weapon again, to be able to defend herself. It was something she needed after her ordeal.

It was quiet. She liked it that way. The usual hustle and bustle were gone. It was just her and the sun and the birds. Peaceful.

Michelle was inside, helping in the kitchens. Most of the others had left to prepare their new home for the big move. Only a few remained. She shuddered, thinking about that place. *I don't want to go back there.*

Her memories of that place tortured her. How could it not? The thought of living there was enough to make her scream, but she had no choice.

A flashback caught her off guard, throwing her back to the moment when she was captured. She was walking along the highway, a rucksack on her back. In her hands, she carried a steel pipe. Her eyes searched for movement, either the living or the undead kind.

She was tired and thirsty but dared not stop. She might never get going again. The sun beat down on her with relentless force, burning her skin to a dark ruddy red despite the sunscreen she'd slathered on.

The sound of a car caused her to stumble. People! Living people! Maybe they could help her. She'd been alone for a week now. Alone and frightened to death.

A truck appeared, dirty white in color. It slowed, the window drawing even. She smiled, a greeting hovering on her lips. Only to fade when she saw the muzzle of a gun pointed at her.

Despite her protests, she was tied up and tossed into the back with cruel indifference. Whimpers met her ears. The back was filled with others like herself, all young and female except for two teenage boys. They were taken to a place, the place where Morgan found them. That night they dragged her to the fire and used her. Over and over and over again.

Lisa fought against the memory, but it was too vivid. It intensified until she could taste the blood in her mouth. She could hear them, taunting and cheering; smell the odor of sweat and alcohol; feel them violating her inner being. *They took everything from me.*

Hot tears streamed down her cheeks and burned fiery paths across her skin. Her chest constricted. Her hands fisted, nails cutting into her palms. She closed her eyes and found that place inside her. The one she ran to whenever things got hard. Her breath flowed through her nose. In, out, in, out.

She stilled, mind becoming blank. The clouds drifted past overhead; a pigeon flew by; the breeze picked up. She felt nothing, heard nothing. Her heartbeat slowed, becoming regular once more. The panic passed.

Opening her eyes, Lisa stood up. She did a slow circuit of the walls and thought about the people among whom she now found herself. She liked Morgan, admired her gutsy approach to life. Hannah and Elise as well. They were both warm and motherly, caring for her and Michelle with a sensitivity that she appreciated.

Angie was a different story. Lisa's lips thinned at the thought of the other girl's callous demeanor. She made no secret of the fact that she resented Lisa and Michelle for the attention they got. If Lisa had to guess, she'd say Angie was spoiled, used to being the center of attention.

"At least, she's gone for the next few days." Angie had moved to the new base to help with the preparations. It was a welcome reprieve from the girl's cutting remarks.

As to the rest, Julianne and Joanna were a little more aloof but pleasant, as was Liezel and Rosa. Tumi didn't talk much. Shy and reclusive, Lisa had heard that she still mourned the loss of her child.

She had yet to get to know them all, and the men kept their distance. That was a blessing. Especially for Michelle who struggled to cope. Of all the captives she'd been the youngest at sixteen. *It's a miracle she survived.*

Once more, Lisa's memories betrayed her, and she was swept along on the tide of remembrance. A week had passed. The girls slept outside, chained to a tree, stripped of both their clothes and their dignity. Their captors fed them when they remembered, which wasn't often, and used them whenever they felt like it, which was often.

Their ablutions consisted of two buckets. One with drinking water and the other for bodily functions. At night, the mosquitoes drove them mad, and they scratched their tender skin until it bled. They bonded quickly. It was only natural that they'd turn to each other for comfort in their hellish circumstances.

The teenage boys, Tommy and Errol, were a different story.

Their purpose at camp was to provide free labor. They performed the chores their captors would not. They were grunts, but they got treated a lot better in return, a fact that made the girls jealous. There existed a state of animosity between the two groups.

Then one night, everything changed. It was warm, and the men were drunk. They'd gotten hold of a few infected and had chained them to the tailgate of a truck. The zombies snarled, desperate to reach the flesh that tantalized them.

It was terrifying to have the things so close at hand. Michelle sobbed softly into Mpho's arms while Lisa prepared herself for the worst. Who knew what their captors had planned? And she was right.

Tommy and Errol, who had thus far escaped the worst, now ran out of luck. Bored and jaded, their captors decided they were in need of entertainment. The boys were forced into a makeshift ring with the infected and given sharpened sticks for weapons.

Errol fought, grappling with the nearest zombie, trying to keep its teeth out of his flesh. He forced it backward and stabbed it through the eye. It fell, but a second was already on him. He kicked it and broke the thing's kneecap before he delivered another killing blow. The watchers cheered.

In the meantime, Tommy sidled out of reach. Slim and agile, he danced around the stumbling bodies while his shrewd eyes looked for an escape route. He found it in Errol. Performing a few quick maneuvers worthy of a fox, he led the infected straight to his fellow captive. They fell upon the hapless boy, defying his attempts to defend himself.

While they ripped into his flesh, Tommy used the opportunity to pick off the zombies, one by one. Lisa could still hear

Errol's screams when she closed her eyes, and see the look of triumph on Tommy's face.

Impressed by his ingenuity, their captors released him and made him one of their own. He turned out to be an apt pupil, the worst of them all, cruel and sadistic.

Tommy was the one responsible for Becky being hung. He wanted to see what it looked like in real life. He was also the one who drove Mpho to suicide. She slit her wrists one night with a pair of stolen scissors.

Perhaps, Lisa should have known better than to hope that Jackie would make it out alive, but hope is hard to kill. It burned inside her, the thought of what Tommy must have done to Jackie. Infecting her, hurting her, and who knows what else?

Lisa crumpled to the ground. Sobs tore from her breast, cutting through her chest like a knife. *They were my friends! Why did this happen? Why?*

She buried her face in her arms, hoping no one would hear her. Hannah hadn't wanted her to stand guard, arguing that she needed more time to recover, but Lisa had insisted. She could not sit around anymore. She needed to keep busy.

A soft hand on her shoulder startled her. It was Morgan.

Lisa wiped away the tears, composing her face as best as she could. She did not want Morgan to think her weak. Nor did she want pity. She hated pity more than anything in the world.

"Can I sit?" Morgan asked.

Lisa nodded, unable to speak.

Morgan sat down, folding her legs. "I want you to know something, Lisa."

"Yeah? What's that?"

"You're the bravest person I've ever met."

"What?" Lisa stared at her in shock. "You've got to be joking. I'm not brave!"

"Yes, you are."

"Back there, when I found you, you kept it together. You got Michelle out of there. It could have turned out very differently if you'd panicked."

Lisa shook her head. She studied her clenched hands and picked at a broken nail. "I'm not strong, I..."

"You are. More than you know." Morgan reached out and squeezed her arm. "This camp needs you, so just promise me one thing."

"What?"

"Don't let what they did to you, break you. Don't let them win." Morgan got up and dusted off her shorts. "I've got to go. Logan and I need to deliver material to the new base."

"Okay."

"Just remember. You'll always have a friend in me."

Lisa watched Morgan leave, her throat thick with emotion. Morgan was right. She couldn't let them win. She wouldn't.

Chapter 20 - Angie

Angie's lower back ached as she scrubbed at the inside of the freezer. The smell of disinfectant made her eyes water. It only barely overlaid the smell of rotting food. It was a nauseating mixture of spoiled fruit, vegetables, meat, and sour milk. It was now a week since they'd taken over the game farm, and the work that needed to be done was monumental.

Armand and Joseph were installing a solar panel system on the main building complete with wiring, charge controllers, inverters, and battery banks. There was no running water yet. The borehole needed electricity to function, so they fetched it from the dam in buckets.

Elise swore like a trooper. "Didn't these people know what oven cleaner was?"

The fumes emanating from her region was enough to put them all on a high. Joanna laughed at Elise and soon they were all giggling like schoolgirls. In the dining room, Liezel and Rosa looked over the breakfast counter at the three women and joined in after a moment.

Childish laughter drifted through the windows. Anne and Meghan were playing on the lawn with Princess and Buzz. The little terrier bounced around on the grass like a jackrabbit, chasing a ball while Buzz chased her.

Julianne sat in the shade, keeping watch with a rifle on her knees. She had pulled a muscle moving furniture and had been reassigned to babysitting duties. Ben also kept an eye on them as he cleaned up the yard and swimming pool. Angie didn't envy him the task. She wouldn't be surprised if he found crocodiles in there. She supposed they wouldn't be keeping the pool—too much water. *It would have been nice, though.*

Angie eyed Ben, wondering if he'd recover from the recent blows he'd suffered. He missed Susan and Jacques, that much was clear. Armand's refusal to speak to him added to his pain. She found the whole business tiresome. *Can't they just get over it? People die all the time, especially now.*

She was fond of Ben, and he'd always treated her well, but his losses had made him selfish. *He hardly ever speaks to me anymore, and when he does, it's just about them.*

As for Jacques, she'd never liked him. He'd always stood between her and Armand, not trusting her with his brother. *Good riddance.*

The problem was, Armand wouldn't speak to her either now. He was so caught up in grief over his stupid brother, he ignored her completely. When he wasn't mooning over Morgan, that was. Anger bubbled up inside. *What does he see in her?*

The hours passed as they worked to make the place habitable, and Angie was grateful when Elise called a halt. They were all hot, sweaty, and hungry. Gathering in the dining room of the old restaurant, everyone relaxed as Elise sent cans of cold drink and bottled water around.

Angie cracked open a Fanta Orange, grimacing at the sweet, sticky taste of the warm mixture, but she was thirsty, and it went down fast. Packets of chips and biscuits followed by a few cans of beans and viennas went around. Nobody seemed happy with the food, but without a working kitchen, it was the best they could get.

After their makeshift supper, the talk wound down as people sought their beds. Everyone was tired. Only the kids were hyper, and Angie blamed all the sugary food.

"Thanks," she murmured as Julianne gathered up the rubbish in a black bag.

"Are you okay?"

"I'm fine. It's just—" Meghan ran up and grabbed Julianne around the waist, giggling.

Little brat, Angie thought as Julianne scurried away. She scooped up her bedroll and lay down in a corner, hoping to sleep.

She struggled.

The sight of Armand's face drifted before her closed eyelids. She couldn't stop thinking about him. From the first moment she first saw him, she knew he was the one, but it was like she didn't exist at all. After everything they'd been through, she'd believed they shared a bond. They'd grown close over the weeks of running and hiding, fighting for their lives together, and now he was acting like a stranger, cold and distant.

After hours of obsessing, Angie finally fell asleep. The next morning, she rolled out of bed just as tired as when she turned in. An unappetizing breakfast was followed by more back-breaking labor. Today, there were no giggles, but by noon the building was spotless. After a brief break, they set to work on the bungalows.

A truck had arrived with a load of building material, and a team was engaged in building up the inner walls. All except Armand, who still worked on the solar system. Angie watched him from underneath her lashes. *He's so handsome.*

Sweat pearled on his forehead, and his blond hair stuck to his neck in the cutest way. She pictured his muscled arms cradling her at night. A giggle distracted her. Frowning, she noticed Liezel pointing at Armand and whispering to Rosa. *What the Hell?*

Angie calmed herself and flashed the two a dimpled smile when she noticed them staring at her in shocked surprise. She forced herself to turn away and return to work, but the rest of the day passed in a haze of red anger.

That night, supper was as dismal as the previous evening. Nobody talked to her, put off by her sullen mood. She felt lonely and rejected.

Once again she struggled to sleep and woke up exhausted. Washing her face, Angie stared at her reflection in the mirror, noting the dark circles under her eyes. She looked worn out, haggard.

She could feel something moving deep inside of her, like a worm burrowing into her heart. All the stress and strain, made bearable only by her love for Armand, was threatening to overwhelm her. Something had to give. Pressing her lips together, she marched outside to join the others.

"Angie!" Looking over, she saw Armand waving at her, and her stomach did a back-flip of delight.

Hurrying over, she flashed him a huge smile. "Hey, there. Looking for me?"

She cringed at the fawning note in her voice. *So much for acting cool.*

"Yeah, Morgan showed up with the truck. She wants us to join her on a scavenging trip."

Angie's heart dropped as she realized the excitement on his face wasn't because of her but rather the prospect of spending

215

time with Morgan.

"Sure. I'd love to." She gritted the words out between clenched teeth, her fingers curling into fists.

"Great. We're leaving now."

She followed Armand on legs that felt like lead. Her hands shook. Blinking back tears, she shoved her trembling hands into her pockets. Up ahead, she spotted the familiar figure of Morgan. A surge of jealousy suffused her mind. She shot a glance at Armand and saw the worship written there, moments before it turned to disappointment and anger. Looking back, she was treated to the sight of Morgan throwing herself into Logan's arms. They kissed with passion, not caring who saw.

Smirking, Angie stepped up and greeted the two lovebirds with a fake smile before jumping into the back of the truck. A forlorn Armand joined her and stewed in anger. The trip passed in loaded silence. *Men are so stupid.*

About fifteen minutes later, they pulled up to an Engen garage just outside of town and got out with caution. They surveyed the parking lot and determined it to be clear. The girls headed to the shop while the men siphoned gas from the underground tanks with a pump.

Inside the building, all was quiet. The place had been raided before, but there was still some stuff left. Picking through the rubbish, Angie shoved any useful items she found into her bag. Glancing at Morgan, she asked, "So, why did we come on this raid exactly? I thought we had enough supplies to last us a while."

"You know Max. He's always worried about not having enough, and besides, I thought a break from all that work would be nice. Have some fun instead."

"I think you're the only one who would consider this fun," Angie grumbled. "Are you sure you're not a psycho?"

Laughing, Morgan shook her head, "Nope. I just feel like this is my second chance, you know?"

Angie shook her head, mystified. "I'm not sure what you mean."

"I guess it would be hard to get. I mean, not everybody would see the apocalypse as a chance to live actually."

Angie frowned. Morgan was right. It was hard to get. Who on earth would choose to live like this? Before, life had been perfect. She'd had money, clothes, attention, anything she wanted. Now?

A shout resounded outside before she could reply. Running to the door, they saw Logan jump into the Nyala and start the engine.

Armand stood with one foot in the passenger door, clinging on while Logan raced closer. "We've got company. Get in!"

They slung their bags into the back and tumbled in, slamming the door shut as the first runners entered the parking lot. Angie clenched her hands into fists. "Why do those things have to be so damn fast? And why do some stay fresh for longer while others deteriorate in no time? And where do all the new ones come from? I thought we were the only survivors in the area? In fact, why did any of this have to happen?"

A note of hysteria had crept into her voice, and Morgan laid a soothing hand on her arm. "Hey, sweetie. Calm down. I don't have all the answers either, but we have to make the best of this."

Angie stared at Morgan's hand. Hatred boiled up inside. *Don't pretend to be nice. You're just a slut who parades around for all the men.*

Focusing on her rage, she calmed down enough to act normal. "I'm sorry. It's just so overwhelming, you know?"

"I know. Look on the bright side. At least, they're still stupid," Morgan replied. "Think how bad it would be if they were smart."

They drove around for a while before entering a quiet suburb on the outskirts of town. Stopping, the group got out and looked around.

"We haven't been here yet, and Max thought it might be a good place to look for supplies. The people here used to be well off," Logan said.

"So we go in together?" Armand asked, edging closer to Morgan.

A look of irritation flashed across Logan's faced, not missed by either Morgan or Angie.

"I think we should pair up. That way we can search more houses, and we each have a partner for backup," Morgan said.

"Sounds like a plan. Why don't you and Angie start over there? Morgan and I can go that way," Logan said.

Hope flared in Angie's chest at the thought of spending time alone with Armand but died when she saw the disappointment on his face. He gave a curt nod, slinging his rifle over his back and gripping his crowbar. "Fine. Come on, Angie. Let's go."

He marched to the nearest house, and Angie followed dragging her feet. She stared at the rigid muscles of his back and wondered where it all went wrong. She dashed at the tears forming in the corners of her eyes. *I don't know what to do anymore. Why can't he see me? I'm right here, I've always been right here.*

At the first house, they paused and listened for any sounds.

Angie pushed her feelings aside for the moment, concentrating instead on her surroundings. Inattention caused death. Inside, they checked the front of the house before moving to the back. All was quiet.

There weren't any cars in the driveway, and the garage doors stood open which they took as a good sign. Usually, that meant the occupants were gone. After a thorough search, this turned out to be true, so they turned their attention to supplies. Filling their packs with items, Angie tried to strike up a conversation. "Good thing we don't live in America."

Frowning, Armand asked, "Why's that?"

"Don't they all have basements and attics, like in the movies? That would be scary. Wouldn't you hate having to go into some dark and creepy basement with zombies waiting to ambush you?"

Laughing, he said, "Okay, I get your point."

After that, some of their old camaraderie was restored. For a time things went well. The next two houses both proved to be empty of life, and the raid progressed smoothly.

Angie wondered about the people who used to live there. Where were they now? Did they make it? Were they still alive? These questions milled through her head as she rifled through their belongings and stared at old photos.

Angie didn't know if her own family was still alive or not, didn't care really. She rarely gave them a thought. An only child, she had no siblings to worry about. As for her parents, she had nothing but contempt for them. Her father only cared about money, spending every waking hour at work while her mother was weak and easily manipulated.

As they approached the next house, the first sign of trouble revealed itself in the form of the family dog. Its carcass was stripped of flesh, and the desiccated remains were pathetic to behold. A car stood in the driveway with the boot open. It held suitcases and a few bottles of water.

They shared a look, readying themselves for a fight. Angie took the lead, her boots crunching on the gravel underfoot, followed by Armand's heavier tread. The kitchen door stood ajar, and dried blood smeared the handle. She pushed it open and winced when it creaked. Inside, the walls and counters were splashed with old blood.

Angie tried to steady her breathing and wiped her sweaty palms on her jeans. This was something she'd never get used to. The anticipation that something lurked around the corner, ready to pounce. She reassured herself that she had a backup in the form of Armand and a gun strapped to her hip.

They moved into the open-plan dining and living room, and it was evident a struggle had taken place. Furniture lay tossed about with more blood splashed across the walls in a horrid display. A doorway to a second living room beckoned. With a gesture to Armand to follow, she moved forward.

Angie rounded the corner and came face to face with a living nightmare. Inside stood at least a dozen zombies. They weren't doing much, swaying from side to side as they waited for someone like her to activate their hunting instincts. Angie's heart slammed against her rib cage so hard she was sure they'd feel the vibrations. So far they hadn't spotted her. She needed to move before they did.

Holding her breath, she backtracked and placed each foot with infinite care. Angie trusted in Armand's savvy, hoping she wouldn't bump into him. She kept moving, her eyes trained on the doorway the entire time. Each step felt like she was about to set off a landmine. She stretched out a hand and touched the walls to guide her.

Every instinct screamed at her to run, but she knew that'd be a mistake. Her head brushed past a picture frame. She swallowed as it scraped against the wall, dust trickling down. Her nerves were stretched to their limits.

Once back inside the kitchen, Angie turned around and motioned to Armand to go. He recognized the direness of their situation by the look of terror on her face and moved without hesitation.

The doorway loomed ahead. Safety beckoned. They stepped out into the midday sun, and Angie took a deep breath of oxygen. *Dear God, we made it out alive.*

"Go," she mouthed.

They jogged along the path and rounded the corner to the driveway. Without Angie noticing, Armand stopped abruptly. She slammed into his back with a thud, stifled a voluntary cry before she peered around him. In front of them stood another group of infected. Ice water flooded her veins. *We're trapped.*

In an instant, Angie realized they'd never be able to fight off the lot in front of them before the bunch in the house behind them were alerted. They'd be caught between the two groups and ground to mincemeat. *Or rather, chewed.*

Armand must have reached the same conclusion. Instead of fighting, he dropped his crowbar, gripped her by the waist and heaved her up to the roof of the carport. "Climb!"

Grabbing onto the edge of the zinc roof, she pulled with everything she had, motivated by the hunting cries of the infected. From the house, an answering roar rose. They had only a few precious seconds to get to safety. Levering herself up, Angie swung her legs over and turned, flinging out her hand.

Armand jumped, caught the edge with one hand and gripped her forearm with the other. Together, they inched him to safety. Small as she was, Angie possessed an iron grip. He got one elbow onto the roof and prepared to swing up his legs. Angie stared into his face, still holding his hand.

Without warning, a bubbling volcano of emotions erupted within her chest. Love, adoration, obsession, and despair, but most of all, hate. Pure and undiluted hate. *I could have given you everything. My heart, my soul, my entire existence. Yet, you chose her. Her!*

Angie gripped him by the collar of his shirt with her free hand. Instead of pulling, she leaned forward and whispered in his ear, "Goodbye love."

He stared at her in confusion. "What?"

She shoved him off the roof with all of her strength. Armand fell with a cry, landing with his left foot bent inwards. His ankle snapped with a loud crack. He stared at her, one hand stretched upwards in a futile gesture.

The first infected fell on him. They swarmed across his body like ants, ripping and tearing. His screams of agony rang out with awful clarity, every millisecond of suffering etched in unrelieved sound.

Angie leaned over the edge, and her pulse raced with excitement. Her dark hair hung down like a flag, reaching to him like black tendrils of death. She watched them render Armand into a shapeless, quivering mass of flesh. His blood spattered the stones.

The feelings that welled up inside her defied description, but one stood out above the rest. Power. The power of life and death over another.

Armand's voice grew fainter, gurgling through the fluid that filled his lungs. Silence fell. Disappointed it was over, Angie watched a little longer, prolonging the pleasure, before she assessed her situation. She was stuck on the roof of a carport with a crowd of zombies below. Not ideal.

Scooting over, she glanced at the Nyala. Beyond that, she spotted the figures of Morgan and Logan moving closer. They must have heard Armand's screams. Waving at them, she got an answering wave.

Working her way over to the other side, she cursed as the hot zinc roof burned her skin, raising blisters. Until now, she hadn't even noticed the heat. The opposite edge of the roof bordered the neighbor's yard. Checking that the zombies were still occupied with their meal, she lowered herself down and huddled behind the wall. From there, she made her way to the Nyala using what cover she could and giving the zombies a wide berth.

Logan and Morgan were there before her, faces pale, and Angie stumbled to a halt. Her breath staggered with raw, untapped panic. *Oh God, what if they know? What if they saw what happened?*

"What happened? We heard screams," Morgan said, her eyes winging in Armand's direction.

Angie slumped, relief coursing through her veins. *They don't know.*

Bursting into tears, she cried "Armand's dead."

Morgan gasped. "Oh, no!"

Logan stepped up and ushered them both into the Nyala. "I'm sorry girls, but we've got to go. Get in the truck."

They clambered into the vehicle with Angie sitting in the middle. She sobbed, blubbering her story while they drove. "I'm so sorry. I tried to pull him up, I did, but he was too heavy."

Morgan placed her arms around her shoulders, pulling her close. "It's all right. You're safe."

"It's all my fault. I let him die!"

"No, sweetie. It's not your fault. You did everything you could."

Angie pressed her face against Morgan's shoulder, hiding a smile. Her shoulders shook as the fake tears continued to flow. She allowed herself a moment's satisfaction at her ability to act. *If you only knew.*

The rest of the drive passed quickly with Angie huddled on the seat, allowing herself to be comforted. Basking in all the attention, she reflected that it had been an excellent day. Not only had she paid Armand back for his betrayal, but she could look forward to several days of pampering as the victim in this horrid tragedy. Of course, it wouldn't last, but that didn't matter. She was already planning her next murder.

Chapter 21 - Morgan

Morgan scrubbed the floor with ferocious intensity. The brush in her hand swept back and forth in a rhythmic manner, loosening the dirt ingrained into the dark tiles. The soap frothed around her chapped fingers, burning the torn cuticles. It was soothing, though. It helped calm her mind.

Ever since the disastrous raid during which they lost Armand, she felt...unsettled. Or maybe the real word she was looking for was guilty. *We shouldn't have split up. We should have stayed together.*

She hadn't planned on taking him along. It should have been just her and Logan. But Armand had been so eager, so insistent, that she hadn't been able to say no despite Logan's visible irritation.

Of course, Morgan'd been aware of Armand's crush. That's why she'd told him to bring Angie as well. She'd hoped the younger girl would distract him, which was why she'd suggested they split up. *It's my fault.*

She knew this despite Logan's reassurances. The sight of Angie's tearful face was bad enough, but Ben...that's what killed her. Every time she closed her eyes she could see the expression on his face when he got the news. Almost like he was expecting it, like the universe was out to get him, and he'd known it all along. *God, I'm so sorry, Ben.*

She hadn't seen him since. According to her mom, he was close to having a breakdown, but they were doing all they could to help him. Max had assigned him his own bungalow, and Joanna spent a lot of time with him. Suicide watch. Those were Julianne's exact words. Hannah even put him on anti-depressants.

Angie appeared to be coping, at least. She was a tough girl, and even though she mourned she still held her head high. Morgan shook her head, biting her lip. *We've lost so many. All of us. How do we keep going?*

She shifted back on her heels, flexing her cramped fingers. Her leg twinged, and she winced. It had healed well, without infection, and the stitches had been removed. Still, it hurt a little when she moved in a certain way. Not that she was about to complain. She was luckier than most.

She looked around, her eyes traveling over the whitewashed walls, the thatched roof, the double bed, and wooden drawers. Curtains fluttered at the small bay windows, and the scent of freshly cut grass drifted in on the breeze. It was theirs now, the cottage, assigned to her and Logan.

Our new home. Morgan relished the words on her tongue. It felt good, saying it. The previous place had never been anything more than a temporary base, but this could be home. *If we make it so.*

Her eyes fell on the lean figure of Logan, installing wiring through the roof. He balanced on a small ladder, his deft hands working to bring electricity into the bungalow from the solar panels on the ceiling. They'd never be able to turn back time, to watch television or surf the net again. But they'd be able to switch on a light at night or a fan in summer. Even listen to music or watch a DVD if they had enough power stored.

These thoughts faded away while she watched Logan work, noting the way his body stretched and moved. Her eyes fixed on his lips, and she smiled, remembering what those lips had done to her the previous night. Goosebumps rose on her skin, and warmth stirred in the pit of her stomach. She imagined him grabbing her and throwing her onto the bed, ripping her clothes off. He'd kiss her neck and slowly travel down to her—"

"Are you perving on me?" His amused voice tore her from her dirty fantasies.

She blushed. "Yeah, kinda."

He flashed her a look, tied off a wire, and climbed down the ladder. With slow steps, he closed the distance and reached out a hand. She stood up, her body sliding up against his. His hands snaked around her waist, warm fingers splaying across her back. One moved down, cupping her ass and grinding her hips against his.

A gasp escaped her lips, smothered when he kissed her, his tongue moving inside her mouth. Her nipples hardened, and the sensitive nubs brushed against his chest. Naked need built within her, and she longed for him to take her right there on the floor.

Logan broke off the kiss and pulled back. "Tonight."

"What?" Morgan groaned with frustration. "You can't be serious?"

"Oh, I am." He pressed a finger to her lips, stilling her protestations. "It'll be worth the wait, I promise."

She narrowed her eyes and gave him an evil stare. "It better be."

He laughed. "Let's go cool off, shall we?"

227

Morgan leaned back in his arms, puzzled. "How?"

"Let's go on a raid. It's still early. We've got plenty of time."

"Seriously? After what happened with..." Her voice trailed off, unable to finish the sentence.

"That's exactly why we should. It's been three weeks, love. Time to get back on the horse."

Morgan shook her head. "No, it's not that easy. I...I don't think I can."

"Yes, you can. Just you and me. No one else. That way you won't feel responsible for anyone. No guilt."

"I'm not...I'm fine!" Morgan pulled away, turning her back. "I don't feel guilty."

Logan sighed and placed his hands on her shoulders. "It's okay, love. I understand."

She closed her eyes, allowing herself to lean back against his chest. He enveloped her in a warm embrace. It was solid, comforting, and safe.

"I'm scared, Logan," she admitted.

The thought of leaving the relative safety of camp to face the undead terrified her, more than she was willing to accept. At night, when she closed her eyes, she visualized the infected tearing Armand to pieces. It invaded her sleep and gave her nightmares half the time.

"I know you're scared. That's why I think you should do this." He pressed a soft kiss to her neck. "You're not a coward, Morgan. You're a fighter. Face your fears."

Morgan took a shuddering breath. Logan was right. She couldn't allow this to drag her down. The words she'd said to Lisa on the wall echoed in her mind. "Don't let this beat you."

If Lisa could fight, could face her fears, then so could she. She turned to face Logan and met his eyes with a determined stare. "Fine. Let's go."

He smiled. "That's my girl."

***

They left camp in Logan's Landie. The interior was littered with empty cans and wrappers. Morgan pushed it aside with a twist of her lips. "When we get back, you're washing this car, babes."

He looked at her in mock horror. "What? Clean my Landie? Sacrilege!"

She laughed and reached into the cubby hole for a cigarette. She lit it despite the look he gave her, cracking the window half open to let the smoke escape. It was an argument they'd had before. He wanted her to quit, and she resisted. *It's not like I do it all the time.*

"So where are we going?" she asked in an attempt to distract him.

"I was thinking somewhere quiet. Maybe an outlying suburb."

Morgan shuddered. *Same as last time.* But she nodded and smiled. "Sounds good."

He looked at her, alerted by the strain in her voice. "It'll be okay, you'll see."

"I know." She sucked on the cigarette, letting the nicotine soothe her nerves.

Logan directed the car left at the turn-off to Riebeeckstad. They passed the garage they'd been to with Armand and Angie. Morgan averted her eyes.

The Landie turned left again, leaving the double lane highway and entering the suburbs. It was the other side of town, an odd mixture of wealthy and poor neighborhoods, old and new houses.

It had such a dilapidated feel already. The lawns and gardens had gone wild, nature taking back what once belonged to it. Potholes had grown into ditches, and now and then the stench of rotting sewage could be caught. Rats and pigeons abounded. Cats too. Dogs were a rarity, though. Most had been eaten during the first days of the outbreak. Now only the most feral still survived.

The streets were quiet with hardly any life to be seen. She felt her stomach do a slow flip at the thought of getting out of the truck. The idea of being exposed took her back to the first day it all began. *I was so scared. I hate being scared.*

Movement caught her eye, and she craned her neck. Infected. They congregated around a long low building with a zinc roof. It shared a yard with a house but had no windows, only a metal shutter set in the wall next to a single door. The zombies were clawing at the screen, their moans low and insistent.

Logan had seen it too and slowed. "They've got something trapped."

It was true. It had to be. There was only one reason the infected would be that desperate to get inside. Survivors.

"We have to help them," Morgan said. The words left her mouth before she considered the implications. There were a lot of them for two people. About half a dozen. Could she do it? Did she still have what it took?

Logan seemed to sense her uncertainty. "You don't have to do this. Not now."

"What do you mean?"

"We can come back with reinforcements."

Morgan hesitated. There was no judgment in Logan's eyes, no condemnation. Just endless love and patience. Whatever she might think or feel, he had faith in her, and that gave her the push she needed. She lifted her chin. "I can do this. Let's go."

The corners of his mouth lifted. "Time to kick some ass."

His words reawakened a spark of excitement within her, and she jumped out of the Landie with a sense of her old adventure. She was armed to the hilt with her gun on her hip, two knives strapped to her thighs, and a metal spear in her hands.

She twirled the metal spear like a baton, closing in on the nearest infected. It was a girl or used to be at least. Her braids clung to her scalp, the ends clicking when they moved as the colored plastic beads clacked together. It was the only pretty thing about her. With a snarl, she turned on Morgan, eyes feral.

For a second, Morgan froze, panic kicking in. Her breathing became shallow; spots danced in front of her eyes. She saw Logan stab one through the temple before whirling to stick another in the eye. Both fell.

The girl charged, snapping Morgan out of her funk. Instinct kicked in, and she dropped beneath the outstretched arms. Sticking one leg out, she tripped the infected girl and delivered a downward stab to the back of the head.

She turned, lunged forward and drove her shoulder into the next infected. It staggered backward and bowled over another. An upward thrust pushed the point of the spear through the soft tissue beneath the chin. It penetrated the brain and lodged in the top of the skull.

Morgan didn't bother trying to remove it. Instead, she spun

around and pulled out the two knives strapped to her legs. She fell on the next attacker, burying both weapons in its eye sockets. She looked up, panting for breath, in time to see Logan finishing off the last zombie. His head lifted, and their eyes met. Morgan nodded, conveying her silent gratitude. "Just like riding a bike."

He grinned and cocked his head at the door. "Shall we have a look?"

They knocked on the door, shouting. At first, nothing happened. Then the sound of a lock being turned alerted them. The steel door swung open to reveal a young couple.

They looked haggard with dark circles under their eyes. Hungry too. Both were painfully thin, their skin stretched taut over their bones. Morgan's gaze dropped, and she gasped. "Oh, my God. You're pregnant!"

The girl's slender hands cradled her protruding belly. It was all the more prominent because of her being so slim. A wedding band encircled her ring finger looking like it was about to fall off.

"Are you okay? No, of course, you're not," Morgan answered her own question. "We need to get you to our nurse."

"A nurse? You have a nurse?" Tears welled up, and the girl swayed. Her husband stepped closer and steadied her, concern lining his features. Morgan put his age at around twenty-two. He had sandy hair and wore glasses. The plastic square kind in a horrible orange color.

He blinked at her, the thick lenses making his eyes appear smaller. "I'm sorry. We've had a rough time of it. We've been trapped here for about a month, I think."

"A month?" Morgan looked over his shoulder into the dim interior of what appeared to be a shop. A run-from-home type of business. It stank, and so did the couple.

The girl must have realized because her pale cheeks colored, and she ran a self-conscious hand through her greasy auburn hair. Morgan immediately felt bad and reached out a tentative hand. "Don't worry, sweetie. You're safe now. We'll take care of you, won't we, Logan?"

"Of course," Logan agreed. "Let's get you guys out of here. You look like you could use some food."

"Thank you. We ran out a few days ago. Luckily we still had water or..." The boy didn't finish. He didn't have to. "Can I ask where you're taking us? We were actually on our way to the Riot control center."

"The Riot control headquarters?" Morgan asked, frowning. "On the edge of town?"

"Yes, we were told there were survivors there."

"Told?" Morgan asked, perplexed. "By whom?"

"This old guy. He saved our lives and told us to go there and ask for Max."

Excitement unfurled in Morgan's breast. "Old guy? Was his name Henri, perhaps?"

"Yes!" The boy's eyes widened. "How did you know?"

"He was my friend." Morgan reached out and gripped the boy's arm. "Where is he? Where's Henri now?"

He looked down, unwilling to meet her eyes, and shook his head. "I'm sorry. He didn't make it."

Disappointment rushed through Morgan, and she let go, stepping back. Blood rushed through her eardrums, and she hardly heard the boy's stuttered explanation.

Henri's dead? No. She didn't want to believe it.

Somehow, she'd always held on to the belief that he was okay. That he still lived on his farm, milking Lola and riding Pete.

She'd imagined that one day he'd show up on their doorstep, wearing his dusty khakis and battered hat. Now that hope was dashed. It was a fantasy, always had been, but a comforting one.

Logan grasped her shoulder with a gentle touch. "Come on, love. Let's go. They can tell us more on the way."

Morgan nodded, allowing Logan to steer them into the Landie. On the road, the couple's story emerged. Their names were Sean and Erica. High school sweethearts, they were devoted to each other and got married despite family objections.

During the outbreak, they tried as best they could to survive, managing to last several weeks on their own, but their luck ran out when infected discovered their hide-out. They ran until it seemed certain they would die. That was when Henri stepped in, saving the day. He found an overnight shelter for them but got bitten while clearing the house.

He left the two young ones with some supplies, a rifle, and a truck, telling them to go to Max. They never made it. The vehicle broke down, and they were forced to hide in the spaza shop. There they stayed until Logan and Morgan found them, living off bottled water, cold drinks, and packaged food.

Erica reached out a hand, laying it on Morgan's forearm. "We'd have died if you hadn't found us. So would our baby. Thank you."

Warmth filled Morgan's chest cavity. "It's nothing. I'm just glad we got here in time."

"You did. As for Henri, don't be sad. He wanted to go. He mentioned someone...his wife?"

"Yes, Hannelie." A tear pricked at the corner of Morgan's eye. "He loved her very much."

Morgan sniffed, thinking about the old couple who took them in all those weeks before. They embodied everything she held in high esteem. Honesty, generosity, and selflessness. *I can only hope we prove worthy of their sacrifice.*

Chapter 22 - Breytenbach

Breytenbach awoke to the sound of rain pattering on the canvas of his tent. For several seconds he just lay there, listening to the sound. Swinging his legs off the uncomfortable stretcher that served as his bed, he pushed himself upright, resting his elbows on his knees. Never had he felt this fatigued.

He'd seen terrible things in his life and lived through some hairy situations. Not least of them being the border war between South Africa and Angola. He'd slept on the ground, gone hungry, been shot a few times, and even got stung by a scorpion once.

Yet, he'd never experienced this level of quiet desperation before. Breytenbach wondered if it was because he was getting on in years. At fifty, he no longer had the resilience of youth. He hadn't even told anyone it was his birthday the day before.

Sighing, he pulled on his socks, grimacing at the smell. His right toe pushed through a hole, and he stared at it, wiggling it back and forth before he pulled on his boots. He slept fully dressed, only taking off his shoes when he went to bed. You never knew when the next attack would come.

He stepped out of his tent and waited for his eyes to adjust to the gloom. The camp stirred, and people stumbled about their dismal routine for the day, vague figures in the rain. One young woman came into focus as she trudged past him on her way to the large communal tent where meals were served. She carried a baby in her right arm and clutched a young boy with her left.

She looked the same way they all did. Pale, haggard, and starved. Without saying a word, Breytenbach fell in next to her and scooped up the little boy. "Let me help you. Going to the mess hall?"

She nodded and smiled. "Thank you, Captain Breytenbach."

"You know who I am?"

"Everyone knows who you are. You're the reason we're still alive."

He didn't say a word after that, surprised beyond measure. A structure came into view, obscured by the curtain of falling rain. They quickened their pace, eager to get out of the wet.

'Mess hall' was a grand word for the tent where volunteers cooked and served what little food the soldiers found. It was an impossible situation, and once more he cursed the idiotic politician who thought that this site would make a haven for survivors.

The people forced to stay there suffered under the constant threat of starvation or dehydration. For weeks, the summer sun scorched them with its relentless heat, making the situation worse until the rains came. For the first few days, it was bliss. People washed clothes and collected water in empty containers, enough to last awhile.

Tensions eased.

However, as the days passed and the rains continued, the situation worsened. The entire camp turned into a sea of mud. Clothes and blankets became moldy while shoes fell apart. The sewage trenches were the worst and became foul-smelling swamps. A stream of people overwhelmed the medical tent suffering from colds, flu, bronchitis, and fungal infections.

Breytenbach accompanied the woman to the long line of people waiting for breakfast and left her in the queue. He spotted Vicky, a volunteer, at the front of the line dishing out a small scoop of oatmeal to each person. The woman was a saint, working tirelessly for the betterment of others, and he held her in high esteem. "Hey, Vicky. How are things looking?"

Shooting him a glance, she shrugged, "You know how it is. We're almost out of everything. No supper tonight."

"I'm going out today. I'll see what I can do."

She smiled her thanks before turning back to her task, and Breytenbach left the tent with no food himself. He wouldn't be able to stomach it anyway with all those gaunt faces staring at him.

He realized why he felt so depressed. It wasn't his own situation that bothered him. He'd been through worse. It was the sight of all those sick and hungry women and children that sapped his strength.

"Captain Breytenbach! Wait up!" A familiar voice called out from behind him, signaling more bad news to come.

Turning around, he spotted Jonathan, the resident surgeon. Although Breytenbach liked and respected the man, he also felt his heart sink into his boots whenever he saw him. There was only one reason the doctor would single him out. "Yes, Doc. What can I do for you?"

"Are you and your men heading out today?"

"Yes, we are, and before you ask, I will look for medical supplies. I always do."

238

Jonathan flushed. "I know you do, Captain, and I appreciate it." He looked at Breytenbach, his eyes tired. "Could you also look for vitamins, please? I'm seeing the first cases of scurvy now."

Breytenbach reassured the doctor as well he could and hurried away. *Scurvy. That's just great.*

Then again, he'd expected something like that to happen. It was inevitable. Breytenbach reached the gates, squinting at the two soldiers stationed there. They looked miserable.

At the camp's vehicle convoy, Mike and Ronnie lounged against their truck, bouncing a cigarette. Spotting him, they straightened up and nodded a greeting.

"Where are the others?" he asked.

"Johan's on his way, and Lenka's over there," Ronnie answered.

Breytenbach turned his head and spotted Lenka questioning one of the patrols.

Stubbing his cigarette out with his boot, Ronnie blew out a stream of smoke through his nostrils. "Oh, and Kirstin's waiting inside the Mamba, cleaning that rifle of hers."

Breytenbach walked over to the military vehicle. It used to belong to the army, but he'd appropriated it for his use since they'd arrived. Nobody argued as long as they brought in the goods.

Going out on raids was dangerous for more reasons than just the infected. Several gangs had made themselves known in the past few weeks, and they were armed and dangerous. The Mamba offered protection from both gunfire and landmines and was suited to rough terrain, making it perfect for their use.

"Get everyone together, ASAP. We need to get going. We're

burning daylight here." He pulled himself into the driver seat and started the engine.

Mike jumped in, grinning. His green eyes glistened with excitement through a mop of reddish-brown curls. Slender, of average height, with a mischievous smile and pointed ears, he was formerly part of the Army Ranger Wing in Ireland. A first-rate fighter and helicopter pilot, he was also crazy in Breytenbach's opinion.

"Take your boots off my dashboard." Breytenbach shoved Mike's feet away.

Ignoring his Captain's ill humor, Mike twisted around in his seat and eyed Kirstin with a cheeky grin. "How about you and me go on a date tonight, love? I'll be sure to make it worth your while."

Kirstin stared at him for a long second. "How about I shoot your balls off instead?"

Laughing, Mike turned back and fiddled with the radio. It was an old dance between the two. No matter how many times she turned him down, Mike kept asking. Breytenbach couldn't figure out if he was genuinely interested or just trying to irritate the shit out of her.

Johan and Ronnie jumped into the back, grunting under the weight of their gear. Pure Afrikaner, they were large, brawny men with open faces and straightforward manners. They had both served with him in the bush war, and the three were like brothers. Lenka followed, an erstwhile member of the military police. A bear of a man, he bulged with muscle and towered over everyone.

Glancing back, Breytenbach met the icy blue eyes of Kirstin. She nodded a cold greeting before turning back to her high-powered Galil sniper rifle. Born in Norway, she was as Viking as they came with a tall, athletic body and stern features. Her platinum blond hair was smoothed back into a thick braid, and her skin was as flawless as marble. Beautiful but cold, she rebuffed all overtures of friendship. In all his life, Breytenbach had never met anyone who shot as accurately as her. *I couldn't ask for a better team.*

"So, where are we goin' this time, Captain?" Mike asked.

"You'll see."

The night before, Breytenbach had spent an hour pouring over maps trying to find a nearby place they hadn't raided yet. He'd decided on a small community thirty minutes from camp. It was a short drive, and as he pulled up to the little town, he hoped they would find what they needed there.

Strangely, the place seemed deserted—devoid of the usual signs of chaos and bloodshed. A few cars were parked along the main street, but no infected showed. It looked like any small town on a rainy Sunday afternoon.

Breytenbach spotted a shopping complex to the left and slowed to a halt in the parking lot. They surveyed the area, looking for signs of life, but it was deserted. Breytenbach shifted in his seat, uneasy with the lack of zombies.

"Right. Let's go," he decided. "Whatever's going on here, we need those supplies. You know the drill."

Kirsten pushed open the hatch in the roof and positioned herself with her sniper rifle. Putting her eye to the powerful scope, she examined the surrounding area before giving the all-clear.

They wasted no time, having performed the maneuver countless times. Mike and Lenka circled the perimeter, their knives at the ready. The other three followed behind, relying on them for safety.

Breytenbach could see the gleam of Mike's teeth in the gloom as he hummed the Jaws tune to himself. It was unnerving. Exasperating. The man was a basket case, but Breytenbach knew better than to rebuke him. It delivered nothing but trouble. He consoled himself with a muttered, "Idiot."

A brief scuffle broke out when Mike spotted an infected lurking by the cigarette counter. A few moments later, Lenka took out two more in the aisles.

"Clear," Lenka called, and Mike echoed him.

"Anything special?" Ronnie asked.

"You're on baby stuff," Breytenbach directed, "and you're on food, Johan."

They sprang into action, loading supplies into large bags while Mike and Lenka kept watch. In the beginning, Breytenbach had made the mistake of putting Mike on bag duty. Bored with the job, Mike loaded up with what he deemed to be a necessity: Whiskey. Bottle after bottle of whiskey. Premium stuff too.

Breytenbach had only found out once they got back to camp and nearly throttled him. Mike just shrugged it off and said they could all use a party. After that, Breytenbach carried his bags.

Today, he was surprised to find the shelves in the store fully stocked. Everything looked in order as if nothing had ever happened. The only discordant note in that little fantasy was the lack of electricity and the smell of rotting food.

Remembering what Jonathan had asked for earlier, Breytenbach headed to the medicine aisle and loaded up with remedies and vitamins. He stuffed the large bag until it was bursting. Once they each had a full load, they moved back to the Mamba, exchanging the full bags for empty ones.

Kirsten kept watch and once again gave the all-clear but only after sighting on Mike's crotch, face emotionless and cold. "Do you have a favorite?"

"Favorite?"

"Favorite ball. I'll let you keep one."

Mike paled, raising his hands. "Now, now, love. Don't be like that."

She smiled, canine tips showing and mimed pulling the trigger.

Wouldn't want to get on her bad side.

After three more trips, the bags were full, and they had several loads of rice and canned goods. Breytenbach signaled everybody back to the Mamba, satisfied for the moment.

"Let's scout around." Perhaps if the town was deserted, they could consider relocating everyone there. It would be much better than staying in that hellhole of a camp. Safer as well.

Breytenbach drove up the main street, scrutinizing the shops. Turning into the suburbs, he explored the rest of the town and came upon a few lone zombies, wandering around. But it was nowhere near as many as usual.

Deciding to head back, he turned down a small side street where he spotted a beautiful, ornate old church. Admiring the building, he felt a sudden lump form in his throat at the sight of the cross silhouetted against the sky. Never a religious man, he gave little thought to such things. Still, the cross seemed sad and forlorn now. A relic from a time when man ruled, not the dead, and God was revered, not forgotten.

So engrossed was he in his thoughts, Breytenbach didn't hear Kirstin speaking. "Captain, Sir."

"Huh? I mean, yes, Kirstin? What is it?"

243

"Look at all the cars, Sir." She pointed at a double row of cars parked along the street next to the church just as his gaze drew even with the doors. His mind scrambled to make the connection; then it hit him. The townspeople.

Spotting movement from the corner of his eye, he was in time to see the first infected push through the doors and run towards them. Its eyes locked on his, and it seemed to smile at him with demonic hunger. As if a dam wall broke inside the church, more infected flooded out. Abandoning all thoughts of exploration, Breytenbach raced away.

When the last figure disappeared from view, Lenka voiced what they were all thinking. "They sought refuge inside the church when the infection hit."

"Only to have that sanctuary turn into a tomb when some-body inside turned," Breytenbach confirmed, shuddering as he pictured the bloodbath that must have ensued. It took him back to the night at the kindergarten, full of dead and dying children. A night he would never forget.

In a sudden rage, Breytenbach slammed his hands against the steering wheel as his dream of an infection-free town flew out the window. *Damn it. This place would have been perfect.*

Silence fell inside the cabin, the atmosphere heavy. Mike shattered the somber mood. Propping his feet up on the dash, he sang a song, oblivious to everyone's stares.

"Take me to church; I'll worship like a dog at the...something, something. I'll tell you my sins, and you can sharpen your knife. Offer me that deathless death, woohoo..." He broke off and looked around, shrugging. "What? It's a great song."

After a moment of dead silence, Ronnie burst out laughing. "The singer, what was his name?"

"Hozier."

"That's right. He's probably dead now."

"More than likely."

"That's too bad."

"Who's Hozier?"

"Never heard of him."

Breytenbach burst out. "You're all a crazy bunch of fuckers, you know that?"

"Ah, but you love us all the same, don't you, Captain?" Mike fluttered his eyelashes, and Breytenbach tried to suppress a grin.

"Yeah, yeah," he muttered. "Now get your feet off my dashboard!"

It rained once more on the way back to camp. A damp, dreary drizzle that misted up the windows and turned everything into a monotonous gray canvas. Isolated inside his mind, Breytenbach tuned out the quiet talk of the team. He was tired. So tired. If only he could shake off the mind-numbing apathy that held him in its grip.

Up ahead, Breytenbach saw a figure stumbling along the side of the road. He slowed. Excitement gripped his heart when it became apparent that the person was a young girl. She was dressed in a pair of skinny jeans and a tank top, her head crowned with a wet and bedraggled looking ponytail.

Like a slow-motion scene in a movie, his window drew alongside, and he glimpsed her face. His heart dropped when he recognized the signs of infection. The blank eyes that stared ahead but turned hungry when they registered life, the thin lips that pulled back like a shark's, exposing her teeth, gray skin crinkling with decay.

Breytenbach sunk lower into his seat as he drove past, ignoring the girl who now stumbled after them with outstretched

245

arms. Just one more victim sacrificed to the plague. He felt like he'd swallowed a stone and wondered if he had the strength to make it through the day.

He pushed such thoughts aside as they neared the gates of the compound. It was mid-afternoon, and the weary soldiers on gaurd had been relieved with fresher ones. They looked no less miserable, though.

"Any luck today, Captain?" one of them shouted as he drove through. His pale complexion and hollow eyes reflected the same hunger and hopelessness they all suffered from.

"We'll eat tonight, soldier," Breytenbach called back, tossing them a box of smokes and two protein bars. It was a tradition. The soldiers looked forward to it as their only relief during a long day.

Parking the Mamba in its spot, they piled out, and each grabbed a bag of goods, preparing to drop it off at the supply depot. Walking through the crowds of people, dejected faces brightened up when they saw the bags. His weariness fell away at the relief and joy on the starving faces. *This is why I carry on, day after day.*

At the depot, they were greeted by a harassed-looking Lieutenant Nathan who ran around with a clipboard and a calculator. "What have you got for me today, Captain?"

"We got lucky, Lieutenant Nathan. We found a grocery store that's intact. I'm planning to go back tomorrow, but this should hold us for now."

"You're a lifesaver, Captain."

Turning to the team, Breytenbach said, "I'll help the Lieutenant here. See you at dinner."

Nodding, they disappeared to their various haunts. He spent the next hour unpacking as the Lieutenant arranged

246

the goods on the shelves and wrote everything down on his clipboard.

He was just about finished when Vicky showed up. "Hey, Captain. I heard you came back and brought goodies for us."

Waving to the full shelves, he couldn't help but smile. "That we did, Vicky. Help yourself."

"Oh, thank God! I was so worried there'd be nothing to feed the people tonight." Her freckled face shone as she sorted through the shelves, picking rice, salt, soup powder, and bully beef.

Boxes of cereal and long life milk rounded out her breakfast selection, and Lieutenant Nathan loaded everything onto the forklift. "I'll send someone over with the stuff. See you tonight."

Smiling, she said, "See you both at the mess hall, I hope."

"Will do, Vicky," Breytenbach promised.

Turning back to Lieutenant Nathan, he discussed the state of their supplies. They were in dire straits, with only enough to last two or three more days.

"I'll go back to that grocery store tomorrow. The town is untouched. I'm going to need help, though. We can't load enough supplies into one vehicle. Plus, we'll need backup now that the townspeople are out of the church."

"I'll arrange with the other teams to join you tomorrow. I'm expecting them back any moment."

"Have them meet me at the gates before dawn." Breytenbach gestured to two stuffed backpacks. "I'm taking this to Jonathan. He asked for meds and vitamins this morning. It sounds like things are going from bad to worse."

He trudged off in the direction of the medical tent, leaving the Lieutenant to his job. On the way, he stopped off at the orphanage. His heart quickened at the thought of seeing his little girl again. *That's what she's become. My daughter.*

Ducking through the entrance, he searched for Mannuru. She was the only remaining teacher of the three he'd saved at the kindergarten. Both Zelda and Linda had moved on, going their way. He wished them luck.

Mannuru took care of Sam when he wasn't around, and he relied on her to keep the baby healthy and happy. He spotted her head of dark bushy curls, the thick twirls brushing her shoulders when she moved.

She saw him and smiled, motioning him over to a playpen. Inside, Samantha sat upright, playing with colored blocks. She was plump and pink-cheeked, wisps of platinum blonde hair caressing her skin.

"There's my angel." He kneeled by the pen and reached out, brushing her cheek. She giggled, grabbing his calloused finger with both hands. Within seconds, she was chewing on it with spit drooling down her chin.

"Whoa, there, tiger. That's nasty. Chew on this instead." He reached inside his jacket and produced a small teddy bear for her amusement.

She squealed, reaching out two chubby fists to grab it and proceeded to smash its head into the bars. "You take after your mother, I see. A real fighter."

"She's doing well," Mannuru said.

"Thanks to you."

"And you," Mannuru protested.

Setting down the backpacks, he pulled out formula, vaseline, diapers, and baby wipes. "I know it's not enough, but I'm getting more tomorrow, I promise."

"It's all right. I know you try."

"Any special requests?"

"Yes. I ask that you get some rest, Captain. You look exhausted, and we all rely on you for our survival."

"I'll try."

With a soft touch, she left him alone with Sam. These times were precious to him, moments of peace snatched from the jaws of the beast. He watched her, smiling when she chewed on the teddy bear's ear and drooled all over it.

"You mean the world to me, little one. More than you'll ever know." He glanced upward. "Hope your mom's watching you. I'm sure she'd be proud to see you grow so big."

It was getting late. He took his leave of Sam, reluctant to leave her side, but duty called. *Time to get back to reality.*

He made his way over to the medical tent where the doctor tended to a long line of the sick and suffering.

"Captain. You made it, I see. Got anything for me?" Jonathan asked as he pulled off a pair of disposable gloves, tossing them into an overflowing bin.

"I got you vitamins and over-the-counter cold and flu meds. It's not much, but I should be able to get more tomorrow."

"Thank you."

Breytenbach eyed the doctor, recognizing the signs of burnout. He was young, barely out of med school—which was why he preferred being called Jonathan—and idealistic.

Reaching into his pocket, he pulled out two protein bars and handed it to Jonathan, ignoring his protests. "You need it more than I do. You're overworked and the only doctor we have. Eat."

Jonathan took the bars, promising to eat them later, but Breytenbach knew he'd likely give them to a sick patient or hungry child, instead. *Oh well. I tried.*

249

When Breytenbach reached the mess hall, dinner was being served. After queuing for fifteen minutes, he received a plate of rice with a generous portion of bully beef and curried vegetable stew from Vicky.

Sitting down on a plastic chair that groaned dangerously underneath his weight, he leaned his elbows on the rusty table and savored the food one bite at a time. Little by little, the ache in his stomach subsided, and the cramps eased.

Halfway through, he was joined by the rest of the team. They all ate their food in silence. They knew how little there was and enjoyed it to the full whenever they had it. Even Mike kept his mouth shut until his plate was empty. Afterward, they said their goodbyes, trudging off to their respective sleeping quarters. When he reached his tent, Breytenbach collapsed onto his stretcher.

He was passed out and snoring within seconds, even forgetting to take his boots off. He slept fitfully, tossing and turning until he awoke several hours later, confused and disoriented. *What the hell? Was that an explosion?*

Echoes of the blast rang in his ears and got him up in record time. He shoved his knives and sidearm into their holsters and grabbed his rifle, rushing outside. Another explosion rocked the night, and he pinpointed the direction. It was on the Western edge of camp, close to the gates. *Grenade. It must be another breach.*

All around him, people were waking up, screaming and panicking. The whole camp had erupted into chaos, with people running around like headless chickens. Pushing through the crowds of frightened people, Breytenbach made his way over to the blast area. A flare shot up, brightening the night sky. *What the fuck? Which idiot did that? Does he want to signal the entire zombie horde?*

Another flash lit the sky. "I'm going to kill that bastard."

Halfway to the fence, he was joined by Ronnie and Johan. Together they forced their way through. When they arrived, Breytenbach's heart dropped into his boots.

A whole section of the fence had been flattened. A horde of infected flooded the camp. Soldiers valiantly tried to stem the tide without success. *There are hundreds of them! No, thousands!*

With a scream of pain, one soldier disappeared beneath the onslaught but only after pulling the pin on his grenade. It exploded, and a shower of dirt and body parts erupted into the air.

Breytenbach grabbed a fleeing soldier. "Stand fast. We can't let them in." He turned to the breach, yelling at the faltering defense. "Hold them back. Hold!"

He took a position, flanked by Johan and Ronnie. They laid down suppressing fire on the horde pouring through the gap. "Somebody man the damn RPG's!"

His rifle clicked on empty. He tossed it aside, picking up another dropped by a fallen soldier. His eyes landed on the man's belt filled with grenades, and he fumbled for the buckle, pulling it off. With swift movements, he pulled the pin and tossed the entire string into the gap.

A series of booms erupted, rendering the scene in brilliant light. His ears rang. Lit by the explosions, Breytenbach saw the sheer amount of infected clamoring to push their way inside. *It's too late. Sam. Mannuru. The children. We have to get them out.*

He screamed at the soldiers, "Fall back. Evacuate now. Evacuate!"

To Johan and Ronnie, he said, "Spread the word and meet

251

me at the Mamba."

He turned and ran to get Samantha. Bursting through the tent flap, he was met by screaming children with the volunteers barely keeping order. "Get to the vehicles now. We're evacuating the camp!"

Screams of panic met his announcement, but the women acted quickly, scooping up toddlers and babies.

He pushed through the throng and found Mannuru. "Go! I'll get Sam."

Mannuru wasted no time, grabbing two children by the hand and dragging them to the exit. Breytenbach ran to Sam's crib and snatched her up. Clutching her to his chest with his left arm, he wielded his gun with his right.

"Follow me," he ordered, storming into the night. It was absolute chaos outside, but he forged ahead with single-minded determination.

An infected stumbled out of the darkness, leering. He shot it without pause. More people joined up, streaming toward the gate. Samantha screamed, but he ignored her, knowing that salvation lay in getting to the vehicles.

Pale faces flashed by, lit by occasional flares and explosions. It was hard to tell the difference between the dead and the living. To the side, one of the girls fell with a cry, disappearing into the black. He dared not stop.

His toe hooked on something, and he stumbled, nearly going to his knees. Hands grasped his jacket, and he wrenched free. Sam's voice rose to a shrill screech, ringing in his ears, threatening to burst an eardrum. The group of people around him thinned, falling victim to the dead. "Come on! We're almost there."

He snapped off another shot, but his gun clicked on empty.

"Fuck!"

Breytenbach dropped his shoulder and rammed into the oncoming infected, plowing through. He ducked through a gap, and the convoy came into view. He was relieved to see his team were all there, taking a stand. A handful of soldiers stood with them under the command of Lieutenant Nathan. "Faster, we're almost there!"

His team spotted them and laid down cover fire. Visibility was poor, but the floodlights positioned alongside the fence rendered the scene in gray. Reaching the Mamba, Breytenbach shouted at the women and kids. "Get in!" He turned to Johan. "Get them out!"

Johan fired up the engine, waiting until the last remaining woman, Mannuru, got in.

Breytenbach slammed the door shut, and watched as they drove off, followed by a steady stream of other vehicles. He watched them go with hope in his heart until he realized one important fact. He still held Samantha in his arms. "Fuck!"

More people pressed in around them, screaming for help. Behind them, the infected swarmed like locusts, devouring everything in their path. The panicking crowd pushed forward, savage in their all-consuming fear. Bellowing to be heard above the screams, Breytenbach shouted, "Fall back. Fall back!"

His team pulled together around him, forming an island of calm in the storm. Together they backed away from the tide of bodies. He aimed his 9mm with calm, taking down infected as they lunged out of the gloom. One appeared from the side. Unable to get his gun up in time, he shouldered it hard, bowling it off its feet. It fell with a hiss, clawing for his boots until a bullet from Kirstin finished it off.

Lieutenant Nathan closed the door on the last of the available trucks. It pulled away with seconds to spare as a large group of zombies swarmed him. The last Breytenbach saw of the lieutenant was a pale hand reaching out.

The realization that all the vehicles were gone hit him. He knew they'd never make it out on foot. Despair settled over his shoulders like a blanket, killing all hope. He didn't care so much about himself as Samantha.

He looked down at her tear-stained face. *I won't let them touch her.* Slowly, he raised the 9mm, heart hammering at the thought of what he was about to do.

"Captain. Captain!"

He looked around and saw Mike waving at him. "The chopper. Get to the helicopter."

The crushing weight lifted off his shoulders. He lowered the gun. "You heard him."

Retreating steadily, his little group made for the Puma helicopter. Mike jumped in and began the process of lift-off.

"Kirstin. Get in and cover us," Breytenbach ordered the Norse sniper. She obliged while the rest of them circled the chopper, keeping the zombies at bay.

As for the camp, it was finished. The infected had done their work, and most of the inhabitants were dead. From the interior, a low hum arose. Breytenbach froze, eyes searching for the source of the noise. At the edge of the light, his keen eyes picked out the first figure, running towards them with savage intent. "The camp's dead. They've turned."

"We've got runners!" Ronnie cried.

The figure dropped as Kirstin picked it off, but more surfaced from behind. Young and old, big and small, they came. The rotors picked up speed, and the air swirled, damp and cold with the threatening rain. Backing up until he felt the vibrating metal against his back, Breytenbach prepared to jump in.

A hoarse shout drew his attention. Jonathan emerged from the gloom, clutching a leather bag to his chest. Behind him was a figure in full pursuit. *Vicky.*

Her pale face shone in the poor light, and her frizzy red hair formed a halo around her head. She was running fast, with all the concentration of a predator. Jonathan would never make it.

Kirstin sighted on Vicky's face. Her trigger finger moved imperceptibly, and a neat little hole punched into Vicky's forehead. Her body jerked backward, halting her headlong rush. She plowed into the mud. Jonathan gained a small lead, but more took her place behind him.

"Run!" Breytenbach screamed. He jumped into the helicopter and took a knee, snapping off shots to make a path. Jonathan reached them with seconds to spare and dove in.

"Go, Mike!"

The Puma rose into the air, higher and higher until they were safe from the grasping hands of the infected. Thrusting Samantha into the arms of the red-faced Jonathan, Breytenbach leaned out to survey the camp as they gained altitude. Blood red streaked the sky to the East, bleeding into yellow and orange as it heralded the arrival of the sun.

Below him, thousands of fresh infected overran the camp, flushing out and killing anything that still lived. He spotted a group of people running for the gates, seeking to escape. Like the bloodhounds they were, the zombies followed, and a mass exodus from the camp ensued.

"God, I hope they make it," Ronnie said.

"Me too."

"What about the convoy?"

"They should be well on their way by now," Breytenbach replied. "We'll follow, find a safe place to hole up."

The Puma turned in a graceful arc, picking up speed as they flew over the snarling heads of the infected.

The small group racing to safety on foot raised their hands in despair, screaming. "Wait! Wait for us!"

Breytenbach swallowed, his heart heavy. There was no going back. The zombies caught up to the little group who fell to the tearing teeth. He choked on the words in his throat, "I'm sorry."

Seconds later, the infected moved on, following the convoy. Behind them, droplets of blood clung to the grass, glittering like rubies in the sun.

Chapter 23 - Breytenbach

Breytenbach gripped the metal sides of the chopper with numb fingers and leaned out into the cold wind. Strands of hair whipped across his eyes as he searched for the convoy, although such a motley assortment of vehicles could hardly qualify for the word.

Not that it mattered now. The only thing that mattered was the lives on board; the last remaining souls to escape the massacre. Mike dipped the chopper's nose and flew over the vehicles, heading for the front with Breytenbach squinting into the wind. A dark mass on the horizon alerted him to trouble.

"Mike!" Breytenbach pointed at it, and Mike flew towards it. As they neared the shapeless mass, individual forms became apparent.

Kirstin sucked in a breath. "Captain," she shouted over the rotors. "Infected."

"Oh, shit," Breytenbach swore as the truth sunk in. A horde was headed towards the convoy. Thousands and thousands strong. "We have to warn them. They've got to turn back."

"It's too late, Captain." Kirstin pointed to the lead car.

It bounced and rattled on the rough dirt track, careening around a corner as the wheels struggled to find grip in the slippery mud. The driver, seeing the mass of zombies ahead, slammed on the brakes.

The car slid across the road, seemed to hesitate for a moment before the balance tipped. It flipped through the air and rolled to a stop near the lead zombies. The windows had smashed in the crash, allowing them easy access. They plucked the hapless victims from the wreck like sardines from a can.

The second car was close behind the first. It too tried to stop, ending up in a ditch on the side of the road. The third followed, making a frantic turn only to plow into the fourth, showering the path with glass and twisted metal.

Breytenbach swallowed on the bile that rose in his mouth. "Mike. Find Johan. Now."

Mike complied, swinging the chopper low across the convoy. Towards the back, Breytenbach spotted the Mamba. "Radio Johan. Tell him to turn back."

Mike didn't bother with niceties or protocols. "Turn back. There's a horde up ahead. Turn back!"

"Roger," came the calm reply. The Mamba slowed to a crawl, performed a U-turn, then wound its way through the other cars to the back.

Breytenbach let out a nervous chuckle. "Johan. Always cool under fire."

"Captain. The infected from camp."

Breytenbach scrambled over, eyes widening as the first, fresh runners from field appeared. Johan and the rest would be caught between the two opposing forces, trapped in the middle. Breytenbach doubted even the Mamba could resist so many infected for long.

Mike jumped on the radio. "More infected coming your way!"

"Tell him to break to the left," Breytenbach ordered. The veldt was more open there, and maybe, just maybe, Johan could make it through. He didn't hold out much hope for the rest of the convoy. They were doomed. The Mamba turned, ramping over termite mounds and swerving to avoid trees. Hope rose in his chest. "Come on, come on."

Johan slammed on the brakes, coming to a stop.

"What's he doing?"

Breytenbach lifted his eyes. All hope left him. The zombie horde was too vast. They had encircled the area to the front and sides while the camp's infected cut off escape to the back. They streamed through the trees, stumbling over ditches and logs.

Hovering above the Mamba, Breytenbach tried to think of something, anything. The hatch in the roof popped open. Johan climbed out, followed by Mannuru. She clutched a child in her arms which she handed to Johan. He lifted the boy up into the air as high as possible. Breytenbach caught on.

"Mike, drop down as low as you can."

The Puma lowered, swaying above Johan's head. Reaching down, with Ronnie holding his belt, Breytenbach grabbed the boy. Mannuru reached down into the hatch and came up with a little girl.

The infected, seeing fresh meat so close at hand, sped up their efforts and closed in on the Mamba. Kirstin took up a position with her rifle. The shots mixed with the growls rising from the throats of thousands of infected and the whap, whap of the Puma's rotors.

Johan held up the little girl, and Breytenbach snatched her up. The infected were swarming faster than Kirstin could shoot, even with Lenka's help. They surged, reaching up to the roof with eager hands. The dead bodies of their fellows created a platform.

The first infected climbed onto the roof, followed by another. Johan and Mannuru coaxed another child out of the hatch while Kirstin shot down the encroaching zombies with crisp precision. It was no use.

"Too many," she cried.

Breytenbach pulled his gun and added his shots to the fray, opening his mouth to shout a warning. "Johan!"

An infected latched onto Johan's shoulder and sank its teeth deep into the muscle. Another grabbed his arm. Johan didn't go down. He roared in anger and bludgeoned them with his fists. He pushed Mannuru back inside the Mamba, reaching out to close the hatch.

Three more infected tackled him. He fell, his right hand scrabbling for the lid. Too late. Grinning grotesquely through ragged flaps of flesh, a zombie slithered down the hatch.

Even with all the noise, Breytenbach could hear the women and children inside scream as the monster fell into their midst. A pale hand thrust through the opening but disappeared when more zombies pushed their way inside.

On top of the roof, Johan fought. Great rips appeared in his flesh. He never gave an inch, roaring with rage. Whatever else he was, he was a fighter to the last. "Go!"

"No!" Breytenbach screamed in frustrated rage, preparing to jump out. Ronnie latched onto him, holding him back.

Johan went down, brought to his knees by sheer weight in numbers. They tore into him, and his blood coated the roof of the Mamba. Kirstin sighted down the barrel of her gun, the scope bringing Johan's face into sharp relief.

260

She steadied her aim and squeezed the trigger with the whispered words, "Hvil i fred." Johan slumped, face relaxing into the welcome arms of death. "Rest in peace, my friend."

Breytenbach would dream about that day for years to come. He would wake in a cold sweat as he relived his best friend's last moments, and listened to those innocent kids cry as they died in agony and torment. Hell had nothing on Earth at this point.

"Get us out of here, Mike," Ronnie said, still holding onto Breytenbach.

"No," Breytenbach cried even though he knew it was futile. The chopper rose, and the Mamba grew smaller. He stopped fighting and slumped to the floor, angry tears burning his eyes.

It was Samantha who roused him from his grief, her voice hoarse and shrill, stretched to its absolute breaking point. The strident peals penetrated his consciousness, and he took her from Jonathan. "Hush, Sam. Hush now."

Soothing her eased his pain. He leaned back, holding her close. The familiar smell of his jacket seemed to calm her, and she fell asleep from sheer exhaustion.

The boy and girl were terrified and shivering, but at least they weren't crying. Kirstin got them settled into their seats and buckled in. Breytenbach could imagine how they felt. He felt it too.

At some point, they found temporary shelter in a small town called Kroonstad. How they ended up there, he wasn't sure. Mike had headed for the least populated area on the map, and they were now somewhere in the Free State, a province he knew little about.

Mike landed the chopper on the roof of an office block.

261

Once they were sure it was clear, they ventured into the building itself. It proved empty of infected which Breytenbach was grateful for, but it also had nothing in the way of useful supplies.

Realizing that the children needed food and water, he looked at a shop across the road. It was small and manageable. Taking Ronnie and Lenka with him, he left Mike and Jonathan in charge of the kids. He was concerned about the doctor, though, who seemed catatonic.

"Jonathan," he said. "Doc." He snapped his fingers in front of Jonathan's face but got no response.

"He's in shock," Ronnie said.

"Just watch him, Mike. Make sure he doesn't do something stupid," Breytenbach ordered.

They crossed the road, their eyes peeled for trouble. Breytenbach pushed open the grimy, glass door and eased inside. A waft of warm air filled with the smell of death hit his nostrils, carrying the warning of infected. They each brandished a knife, preferring it for close-quarter combat.

Deeper inside the shop, a figure lurched towards them from the gloom. Lenka dispatched it with a swift thrust. It was a tiny shop carrying a little of everything, none of it quality, but he wasn't about to be picky. He filled a shopping bag with baby stuff and odds and ends.

Ronnie grabbed water and food while Lenka scrounged up a cheap pot, a packet of plastic forks and over-the-counter meds. As an afterthought, Breytenbach looked at the toy section. The selection was miserable, but he found a stuffed rabbit for the girl and a toy car for the boy.

Back on the roof, Sam's hysterical wails greeted his ears. "What's going on here?"

Mike jiggled her up and down. "I don't know. She won't shut up."

It would have been comical if the situation wasn't so dire. Sam's scrunched-up face was the color of beetroot, and her screams carried across town, calling every infected within earshot. The other two kids were also crying, huddled into little balls on the concrete.

"For the love of God, must I do everything?" Breytenbach shot a glare at the useless doctor and hapless Mike, grabbing Samantha. "Ronnie, give the kids food and water. Try to calm them down."

Breytenbach stripped off his jacket and lay Sam down. Undressing her, he changed her dirty nappy, smoothing bum cream over the rash that had developed. He cleaned her sticky body with the wipes and finished off with a sprinkling of baby powder.

Opening a jar of purity, he coaxed a spoonful into her mouth. Her rosebud lips sucked on the food, and her crying subsided to the occasional hiccup. "There. That should hold you."

It was hot, with no sign of the rain that had plagued them at their previous camp, so he didn't bother dressing her again. Instead, he rocked her gently, smiling when she burped. His team, meanwhile, watched him with various looks of amusement and glee. "What?"

"Never thought I'd see the day the Captain became a babysitter," Lenka said.

"Yeah, you're a real softy, Cap," Mike laughed.

Ronnie had a smirk on his face, and Kirstin was smiling.

"Oh, shut up, all of you!" He ignored the lot of them as they snickered and grinned but secretly he was pleased. It lightened the grim atmosphere.

He frowned, however, when he spotted Jonathan huddled in the same spot, still clutching his leather bag. The man hadn't moved a muscle since they landed over an hour ago. He opened a can of pears.

"Here, eat this." He forced the food into Jonathan's hands and pried the leather bag from his fingers. "It's going to be okay, doc. We'll be fine."

Jonathan gave a jerky nod and lowered his eyes to the can. Lifting it up, he drank the juice and fished out a piece with his fingers. Breytenbach gave his shoulder a squeeze. *At least, he's doing something.*

The kids had eaten and drunk, but both looked miserable. Hoping to cheer them up, he handed them each the candy bar and toy he'd scavenged. This rewarded him with faint smiles. After a moment the boy pushed his car around, making the appropriate vroom, vroom noises while the girl clutched the rabbit to her chest.

Squatting down on his haunches, Breytenbach opened up a can of meatballs and ate them one by one. He looked at his hands, weathered and worn from years of rough work. They were shaking. *Johan...Mannuru...I'm sorry.*

After finishing his meal, he grabbed a bottle of water and patrolled the rooftop, trying to clear his head. He had no idea what to do or where to go next. He was lost. To think that only yesterday he was responsible for three-thousand souls. Now they were down to nine.

"Captain!" Mike called, waving him over.

"What is it?"

"I raised someone on the radio, Sir. Other survivors."

"Where?" Breytenbach asked, a small flower of hope blooming in his chest.

"About sixty kilometers from here, Sir. Not far at all. Their leader's name is Max. He wants to speak to you."

Mike handed him the radio.

"This is Captain Breytenbach. Out."

"Pleasure to meet you, Captain. I'm Max. I hear you are in need of assistance. Out," a steady voice replied.

Breytenbach let out a deep breath. "We are. Our camp was overrun. Can you help us? Out."

"We can. We have a secure base, and if your intentions are good, you're welcome to join us. I've already given your pilot directions to the rendezvous point. Out."

"We aren't going directly to your camp? We have children and a baby with us. Out."

"No offense, Captain, but I don't know you, and I've learned not everybody can be trusted. Out."

"Fair enough. I will let you know when we reach the rendezvous. Out." Breytenbach replied. His respect for Max had increased by this point. At least, he knew better than to let just anybody into his camp.

"All right. You heard him. Get in the chopper."

"Do you think we can trust them, Captain?" Kirstin asked.

"I don't know, but with two kids and a baby, we need to find someplace safe. Fast. We don't have a choice."

"All right." She turned and hustled the two kids into the chopper, strapping them in. Breytenbach scooped up the sleeping Samantha and held her close during lift-off. Thanks to the medicine she slept throughout, not waking once.

After a while, he leaned back and closed his eyes. He was exhausted. Hell, they all were. His muscles relaxed, and his mind eased. Just like that, he nodded off. Mere minutes later, the sound of a grinding noise followed by a blaring alarm woke him with a start.

"What the..." Black smoke billowed out of the chopper. He coughed from the fumes of burning oil. *We're crashing.*

"Everybody hold on, we're going down!" Mike cried. He fought with the steering, trying to land them safely. Somehow, he gained control for a moment and took them further down.

If anybody can do this, Mike can. He could fly a sardine can if he had to.

A second grinding shriek reverberated through the air. They hung, suspended as if by a puppeteer's strings, then plummeted. Breytenbach's stomach clenched. He clutched Samantha to his chest, trying to shield her from the worst. The force of the crash slammed him forward. The kids screamed through the sound of shattering glass.

The seatbelt slammed into his sternum, and a deep rumble vibrated up and down his spine. Pain shot through his skull. The chopper was still moving, sliding across the ground before it came to an abrupt stop. Smoke and dust obscured his vision. In the distance, he heard Mike scream at everyone. "Get out! Get out now!"

Breytenbach fumbled with his seatbelt, unclipping it with numb fingers. Crawling through the wreckage with Sam clutched to his chest, he made it out. Hands lifted him to his feet. Lenka's soot-stained face peered down at him.

Shaking his head to clear the ringing, he looked down at Sam. She was awake, screaming but unharmed. A miracle. He looked around. Jonathan was unconscious, and blood trickled down his face. Ronnie dragged him further from the crash while Kirstin and Mike each carried a child.

"We need to get away, Captain. It might catch fire and explode." The urgency in Mike's tone brought Breytenbach back to his senses. He thrust Samantha into Lenka's arms.

"Go," he ordered, stumbling back to the crash.

"Captain, no!"

The smell of burning oil hung heavy in the air, searing his eyes and lungs. He ignored it and searched the wreckage until he found his backpack. Slinging it over his shoulder, he stumbled back. A muffled thump sounded. He was flung forward, ears ringing as he plowed into the ground.

"Captain." Ronnie and Lenka hoisted him up, dragging him further away for the raging inferno the Puma had become.

"The veldt is catching fire. We need to get out of here," Ronnie said.

Breytenbach looked around. Crimson flames, fueled by the crash, licked at the dry Acacia thorn trees, brush, and grass that surrounded them.

This place hasn't seen rain in a while, he realized. Fear coiled in his gut. He'd seen enough bushfires in his day to know the dangers.

"This way," Mike cried. "There's a dry riverbed. We might find water."

"Right. Everybody follow Mike." Breytenbach ordered. "Mike, are you armed?"

"Yes, Captain."

"Lead the way and watch for infected. They'll be drawn from miles to the crash."

"Will do, Captain."

"Lenka. Can you carry Jonathan?"

Lenka hoisted the unconscious doctor to his left shoulder, holding his knife in his right hand. "Ready, Captain."

"Kirstin, you take the girl. Ronnie, you carry the boy. I'll take Samantha." During this brief time, the flames had spread,

267

burning higher and hotter with each second. "Let's go."

The group stumbled off with Breytenbach taking the rear. Warm blood trickled from his left ear, and more ran down his right arm, dripping from his fingers.

Burst eardrum and who knows what else, he surmised. There was no time to stop, though. The infected would come, drawn to the crash. *We'd better not be here when they arrive.*

Chapter 24 - Max

Max handed the receiver back to Sean, excitement coiling in the pit of his stomach. They'd made contact with their first survivors, and it was all thanks to Sean. He beamed at the shy, young man. "You did it. You really did it."

A computer programmer in his previous life, Sean also knew a lot about broadcasting equipment and had set up a radio room. He fiddled with the various knobs, blinking every few seconds, a nervous tic Max had come to recognize. "I'm just glad I could help."

"I need to make arrangements for the rendezvous," Max said. "Call me if anything happens."

He left the cramped space and walked the short corridor to the common room. On the way, he strode past another small office. He couldn't help but smile at the sight of Meghan and Anne, doing sums under the tutelage of Michelle. A bright girl, Michelle loved kids and had volunteered to teach them. She shared that duty with Rosa. It was the ideal solution and kept the kids out of trouble.

It was lunchtime, and Max expected to find the cafeteria packed. To his surprise, it was a slow afternoon. Even Logan was missing. He did spot Ben, however, sitting in the corner. On the spur of the moment, he decided to ask him to join the team. The older man was slowly recovering from the loss of

Jacques and Armand, but it was still early days. Maybe some action and the prospect of other survivors would raise his spirits.

"Hey, Ben. We've raised a group of survivors on the radio. If they check out, we're bringing them in. Would you like to join us?"

Ben stared at his plate, chewing with care before swallowing. "Can they be trusted?"

Doubt underlined every word. Max knew it was because of what had happened to Jacques. While Armand's death was a tragic loss caused by the infected, Jacques was different. He died because of the evil of man. "I don't know yet. That's why I want you by my side."

Ben considered this. "Fine, I'll go."

"Thanks. Meet me in the parking lot in twenty minutes." Max stepped outside and headed for the walls, looking for Logan.

The place had changed in the time they'd lived there. So much so in fact that it didn't even look the same. A thick, stone wall about ten feet high encircled the buildings.

There were plans in place to make it even higher, with a walkway and guard towers at strategic points. Max knew this was essential to both their survival and their sense of security.

At least Joseph knew a lot about construction and had taken over the reins. Max was more than happy to leave it in his capable hands. Which was why he wouldn't be taking Joseph on this trip. That and the fact that Tumi was expecting again. The once shy, tearful woman had blossomed overnight with the news. She and Erica spent a lot of time together as new moms-to-be.

A quick jog around the walls proved fruitless, so he decided to go to the bungalows instead. There wasn't much in the way of grass anymore. Most of it had been trampled. He dodged a landmine courtesy of Buzz and made a mental note to get Peter and Thembiso on clean-up duty. "They wanted to keep the dog."

We should get walkways laid out in case it rains, or we'll all be slogging through rivers of mud. It will help with the dust. Maybe put in some concrete or paving. A park for the kids would be nice too.

The drone of a quad bike interrupted his thoughts, and he was relieved to see Logan driving with Morgan perched behind him. They dragged a small trailer with a Springbok carcass on top. Drops of blood beaded on its fur, congealing around a neat bullet hole behind the shoulder blade.

"What's up, Max?" Logan pulled to a stop and switched off the ignition.

"Can you two meet me at the gate? We've located a group of survivors."

"Okay, but let me deliver this to Elise first." Logan gestured to the buck.

"You went hunting?"

"Yeah, we're running low on meat, and Elise wants to do something special tonight." Logan shrugged. "Don't ask me why."

"Nice shot."

"Thanks," Logan replied. "Wind was in my favor."

Max mentally filed away the issue of the game reserve for the next meeting. It was protected by a sturdy fence, but he felt they needed to do more to safeguard the wildlife.

Morgan slid off the bike and flashed Max a cheeky grin. "Well, you know me. I'm in." She leaned down and planted a kiss on Logan's cheek. "I'll get our gear together."

"Try to find Angie as well, will you?" Max asked.

"Sure, no problem." She jogged off with a wave, ponytail swaying behind her.

Shaking his head, Max headed back. He had to admit he'd never seen his sister so happy in all his life. Even Logan was more relaxed. Less broody. All of which made Max happy for them but also a touch jealous.

Entering the common room, he cleared his throat. Not everybody was there but enough that the message would spread. In the expectant hush that followed, Max announced, "You should all know that we got into contact with a group of survivors."

An excited buzz filled the room.

"Survivors? Are they friendly?" Dave asked.

"Looks like it."

"Are you bringing them here?"

"If they check out, yes. They appear to be in need of assistance, and they've got kids with them. A baby too."

"A baby? When are you leaving?" Julianne asked.

"We're on our way there now."

"We'll make sure everything's ready for their arrival," Julianne assured him.

"Thanks, that would be great."

He readied to leave, but Sean appeared at his elbow, pulling him aside. "We've got a problem. The chopper crashed."

"What? Where? Are they still alive?" Max's heart sunk at the news.

"The pilot radioed in an approximate location as they went down and then nothing. I don't know if anyone's still alive."

"Right. That changes things. Hannah, can you come with

us, please? Bring a first aid kit. They might need medical attention, and you're the closest we've got to a doctor. Sean, you're with me."

Hannah jumped up to get her things, while Max and Sean hurried outside. Logan, Angie, Ben, and Morgan were already there, waiting for them. Hannah joined them soon after that, and they split into two groups with Max and Sean taking the lead.

It wasn't hard to find the crash site. A column of black smoke rose amidst a haze of charcoal gray. The veldt was on fire, and orange flames licked the horizon. Max canvassed the tar road until he found a dirt track leading closer.

"We better hoof it from here. We can't risk the Nyalas," Max ordered.

Everybody disembarked, and they set off across the blackened ground. The fire had swept through, radiating out from the crash site. With its dry underbrush and thorn trees, the veldt had provided an excellent feast for the inferno. It had burned hot and fast, leaving behind a circle of blasted vegetation. The smoke irritated his eyes, but with the brush gone, visibility had improved. "At least, we'll be able to see the zombies coming."

A few minutes later, they found the crashed chopper. Max was surprised to see it was a military helicopter. A Puma to be exact—or a burnt-out shell of one. What was even more surprising, was that it was empty. "They survived the crash."

"How do we find them?" Morgan asked.

Max was stumped. He turned around in all directions. "They probably had to get away from the fire and any infected drawn by the noise."

"Speak of the devil," Logan said.

Infected were making their way towards the crash site, hampered by the terrain. In a comical move, one of them face-planted onto the ground when it tripped over a bush. They did not look funny, though. The fire had burned away their skin, sloughing the flesh from the bone in places.

"Get rid of them," Logan said.

"Why? Let's just go. There's nobody here," Angie said.

"We need to know where they went. I used to be a Game Ranger. I can track them if you keep those things off me."

"Track them on this?" She pointed at the burnt ground, derision twisting her lips into a sneer.

Logan frowned and turned away, scouring the ground for clues. "Just keep them off me."

Angie pouted, and Max stared at her, perplexed. Always short-tempered and demanding, she'd grown even more touchy of late. Filing her behavior away as a problem for another day, he turned to the group. "Right, you heard him. Let's clear the area."

Killing the zombies was easy enough. The fire had done most of the work for them. It was a stomach-churning job, though. Max gagged as he hacked at one, its skull reduced to a grinning specter. The smell of cooked flesh clung to his nostrils and coated the inside of his mouth.

By the time the last one fell, Logan had picked up the trail. "Over here."

They followed a dried-out riverbed and walked across the cracked mud. It led away from the crash site in a north-easterly direction. The ground grew damp with occasional puddles of murky water. This became a trickle of water, and after slogging through ankle-deep mud, they were forced to leave the riverbed. Logan never said a word, forging ahead as he followed the trail.

Max kept a wary eye out for infected, ready for anything. It was hot and humid. Sweat trickled down his spine causing his shirt to chafe. A mosquito stung his neck, singing around his ears.

"We're getting closer. The trail is fresh," Logan said.

"God, I hope so. This is awful," Angie whined. Her face was flushed, and she looked anything but happy.

Max wished she'd shut up. Of them all, Hannah was the worst off, being older and not very fit, but she never complained.

They pushed on in silence until a cold feminine voice froze them in their tracks. "Stop. Do not come any closer."

Nobody moved. The only sound was the buzzing of insects. Max cleared his throat. "We're not looking for trouble."

"It wouldn't matter if you were," the smooth voice replied.

"Look, can I come closer? So we can talk?" Max raised his hands, holding them up in the air.

"I would not."

The voice held a tone that brooked no argument, a clear threat implicit in the timbre. Max had the feeling the owner of it wouldn't hesitate to kill him on the spot.

An uncomfortable silence fell, broken when Morgan bristled. "Hey, lady. You lot asked us for help. If you don't want it anymore, then say so, and we'll fuck off." She turned to Max. "Come on, bro. I've got better things to do than play games all day in this kind of heat."

Logan wore a look of mild amusement at Morgan's outburst while the rest were shocked, unsure of what to do.

Max shook his head, "Morgan, please. Calm down."

"I like her," the voice said, interrupting his pleas. "Captain."

A faint crackle of leaves sounded, and a rough-looking man appeared. His hair was graying at the temples, and he hadn't shaved in days. His clothes were torn and dirty, an odd assortment of army issue and khakis. Though exhaustion lined his face, there was nothing wrong with his steely eyes or the way he held a gun.

"You must excuse Kirstin. She's not the friendliest of my crew."

Max nodded, at a loss for words as a stunning woman stepped into view, carrying a rifle like it was an extension of her body. He swallowed, his mouth gone dry and unable to say a single thing.

Morgan flashed him an amused look and stepped forward, saving him from embarrassment. "You must be Captain Breytenbach?"

"Correct. And you are?"

"I'm Morgan. This is my brother, Max. You spoke on the radio."

Breytenbach's eyes never wavered. "That's right. So what happens now?"

"That depends on you." Morgan was not giving an inch, her face remote, eyes cold.

"We need a safe place to stay. At least, for a while."

"Can we trust you not to murder us in our beds?" she asked.

"You can," Breytenbach answered. "But how do we know we can trust you?"

"You said you needed help. We're here, aren't we? You've got children with you? A baby?"

Breytenbach nodded and gestured behind him. Max took that as acceptance and moved forward into a small clearing, followed by the rest of the group. Kirstin watched him, her face as smooth as marble. *She sure is something.*

This train of thought was interrupted when his eyes fell on a giant with coal black skin and a smooth head. His muscles bulged beneath his thin shirt, reminding Max of the Hulk and looking every bit as friendly. A wiry man with a wide smile grinned at them, leaning against a tree next to another guy with rusty hair and a full beard. They all looked dangerous.

"Max." Morgan nudged him and pointed to a little knot of shivering humanity, huddled on the ground.

A little girl clutching a stuffed rabbit stared at them from a tear-streaked face while a boy who couldn't have been more than eight, cried as he held his arm. Next to them crouched a young man, holding a mewling baby, and a scuffed leather bag. He looked out of it, eyes glazed and blood soaking a makeshift bandage on his head.

Max shook off his stupor. "I see a few of you need medical attention. Our nurse here will see to your injuries while I discuss things with my friends."

"Thank you," Breytenbach replied.

Max hustled the rest of the group off to one side. "So? Do we take them back to camp with us or not?"

"Yes," Morgan said. "We can't leave the kids out here. They wouldn't last the night."

"I agree. These people look like fighters. We could use them," Logan said.

"You're both crazy. We should leave them here. They're dangerous," Angie hissed.

"Ben? What do you think?" Max asked.

Ben took a while to answer, brow furrowed as he thought it over. "I believe we should take them for the children's sake but keep a close eye on them."

"It's decided."

Twenty minutes later, with the worst of the group's injuries taken care of, they were taken back to the trucks. A wary silence enveloped the two groups as they studied each other on the ride back. Nobody seemed ready to make the first overtures of friendship.

Darkness was falling by the time they reached the gates. As they drove through, Max wondered for the hundredth time if they were making a mistake. It was too late to turn back, however. He'd be watching them, though.

An armed Joseph waited to greet them at the parking lot. "They're waiting inside the common room."

"Who's they?" Max asked.

"Everybody."

Perplexed, Max set off, followed by the rest. Warm lights streamed from the windows of the main building, and the sound of laughter drifted from inside. Max grew more confused by the second. A wreath adorned the doors, bringing him up short. *Christmas?*

He stepped inside and blinked with surprise. Candles were scattered throughout the room, giving it a welcoming glow. Streamers decorated the walls, and people milled about with drinks and snacks. In the corner stood a Christmas tree with real wrapped presents underneath.

"Max! You're back," Julianne said, walking over with her arms spread. She looked elegant in black slacks, sandals, and a red silk shirt with her hair piled up. She embraced him, and he inhaled her familiar perfume of spice and orchids.

Max was stunned, mouth working as he searched for words. "Mom? What's going on?"

She flashed him a secretive smile. "I just thought I'd

welcome our new guests."

Breytenbach and his group filed into the room wearing uniform expressions of astonishment. Julianne smiled and extended her hand. "I'm so glad you're here. We don't often see other survivors and rarely children. I'm Julianne by the way."

Breytenbach shook her hand with a bemused look. "Er, pleased to meet you too. Captain Breytenbach."

"Let me take you to your rooms. We prepared them especially for your arrival."

Her charm washed over the group, rendering them defenseless. Max smirked. He'd seen his mother work a room before. None of them stood a chance.

"What about the children?" Breytenbach asked.

"They can stay with Meghan and Anne tonight if that's okay? You needn't worry. They'll be well looked after," Julianne replied.

"I'll take care of their injuries first," Hannah assured them. "And the young man too. Perhaps I can bring them to the infirmary?"

Breytenbach nodded, blinking at a rapid pace. "All right, but I'd like to check on them later. Keep an eye on them."

"Of course." Julianne smiled. "Please, let me take you to your quarters now. You can have a shower if you like. We saved some hot water for you." Her chatter faded away as she led them outside.

Breytenbach threw a questioning look at Max over his shoulder, who responded with a shrug, mouthing the words, "Beats me."

Morgan nudged him in the ribs, chuckling. "That's Mom for you."

"Yup. She's back," Max agreed.

"Think she'll run for office next year?"

"She might. Maybe Mayor."

Morgan snickered then fixed him with a teasing look. "And don't think I didn't see the way you looked at the Ice Queen earlier. Got a crush?"

Max felt a blush creep up his neck and scoffed, "Please."

Morgan snorted and saluted him with a beer. "Whatever you say, bro."

"Hey, where'd you get the beer?" Max asked. "And what's that smell?"

"Outside, in a cooler box. Better grab one quick before they're all gone." She clapped him on the back. "Don't you recognize the smell? Has it been that long?"

Max sniffed the air again, eyes wide. "You're joking. Beer and a braai?"

"It's Christmas, brother. We deserve it." She winked and flashed him a smile before disappearing into the crowd.

"Who'd have thought we'd live to see another Christmas, let alone celebrate one," Max marveled.

Maybe a party wasn't such a bad idea. It was the holidays, after all. Giving in to the spirit of things, he wandered off in search of a pint.

Chapter 25 - Julianne

Crickets sang in the background as Julianne walked across the grass with Captain Breytenbach and his team. Faint laughter and light from the party followed them through the night, but the newcomers were nervous and twitchy.

"Are you okay?" she asked. "I mean, considering."

The Captain nodded, then caught her elbow when she stepped into a hole, kitten heels sinking into the soft ground.

Flustered, she got her shoes unstuck, cheeks burning with embarrassment. "Thank you."

"No problem." He looked at her for a moment before waving a hand around. "How safe are we here?"

"You mean inside the camp?"

"Yes."

"Well, there's a wall surrounding the living area, and it's guarded twenty-four-seven." Removing her elbow from his grasp, she walked on. "Around the farm itself is another fence, and we're working on digging a trench around that."

"I see. Population figures of the towns around here?"

"We're out in the middle of nowhere here. The closest town is about twenty-five kilometers away, and that's a small one—about five-thousand. We've already swept the neighboring farms and houses. It's pretty clean."

He nodded. Julianne burned to ask a thousand questions,

but one look at his face told her now was not the time.

"You're armed?" she asked instead.

"With what we could salvage from the wreckage," he replied.

"That's good. We believe in being prepared here." Walls loomed in the darkness, and she waved a hand at the two cottages. "We've arranged these two for you. I hope that's enough for now?"

"It's fine," Breytenbach replied. "We'll share."

The oddball named Mike opened his mouth, but the Captain cut him off. "No Mike. Kirstin will not share with you."

Mike rolled his eyes while Kirstin smiled in that scary manner of hers. That set Ronnie and Lenka off, guffawing with genuine mirth.

Julianne watched the team interact, noting the ease of long familiarity. It made them seem a little less threatening. "Well, I'll leave you to sort yourselves out. When you're ready, please join us for the party. There'll be good food and company, I promise."

"Where can we wash?" Breytenbach asked.

"The ablution blocks are over there. Not all the cottages have bathrooms, sorry."

"That's all right. You've done more than enough."

"Do you need anything else?" Julianne asked. "If you're injured, I can take you to the infirmary."

"We're fine," he replied. "Your nurse did a good job earlier."

Julianne left the group to themselves and checked on the rest. The kids were in good hands for the night. The schoolroom had been converted into a den with colorful sleeping bags and toys. A TV and DVD player had been hooked up with kids movies playing on the screen. Meanwhile, Buzz and Princess wrestled on the floor.

Elise arrived with the two newcomers, Jenny and Mark, in tow. Both wore pajamas and had been bathed. Though shy, they were no longer frightened and sat with Meghan and Anne. Mark's broken arm had been set and put in a sling, and the girls were in awe of his war wound.

Michelle had volunteered to babysit for the night. Already she was passing around cold drinks and chips, inviting the kids to a sing-along.

Satisfied, Julianne paid a visit to the infirmary. It was no bigger than a broom closet. Already there was talk of building a separate clinic. Jonathan occupied the only bed. According to the Captain, he was a qualified doctor, but to Julianne, he looked like a terrified young man. At the moment, he huddled beneath the covers, curled in upon himself. "How is he?"

"Dehydrated, starved, and exhausted. I'd guess he's been running on guts alone for weeks, and the recent events served as the last straw," Hannah replied. "To top it off, he's got a concussion too."

"Poor boy. Is he going to be all right?"

"He'll be okay. He just needs time. Plenty of sleep, good food, a little kindness, and he'll be right as rain again."

"And the little one? How's she?"

"Oh, she's fine. Such a strong little thing and in good health." Hannah smiled at the sleeping baby in her arms.

"I'm surprised. A baby in a helicopter crash?"

"I know. Miracles never cease." Hannah cooed at Sam then fixed a stern look on Julianne. "Stop fussing and get back to your party. We'll be fine."

Julianne laughed. "Okay, I'll send you a plate of goodies."

Back in the cafeteria, she grabbed a cold cider and took an appreciative sip. It burned and bubbled down her throat. She sighed with pure enjoyment.

"A party, Mom? Really?" Max asked, joining her.

Folding her arms, she frowned, "It's Christmas, and I found this box filled with decorations in the storeroom, so I thought, why not? We all need to relax and have a little fun."

Max raised an eyebrow and gave her a small smile. "If you say so. Who am I to complain?"

"Do you think it's too much?"

"I don't know. Everyone could use a boost, and this is a great way but..."

"But?" she prodded.

"We don't know if we can trust them."

"The Captain and his team?"

"Exactly."

"Let's give them the benefit of the doubt at least."

"Don't have much of a choice, do we?"

He slipped back into the crowd, leaving her with mixed feelings. She watched as the people mingled, laughing and drinking. They looked relaxed. For once, they didn't have to be on their guard.

A deep voice from behind startled her out of her reverie. "Good evening, ma'am."

She whirled around and found herself facing the Captain. He was handsome in a rugged way. His hair gleamed from the shower, and his breath smelled minty. There was something in his eyes, though, something that pulled at her heartstrings. A hint of vulnerability.

"Captain Breytenbach," she said, plucking at her flimsy blouse. "How can I help you?"

"I wanted to thank you for all this."

"No need to thank me. It's much for our benefit as yours.

Something to keep morale up."

Smiling, he said, "Oh, I understand all about morale. And what you did here tonight was genius."

Blushing, she felt awkward and self-conscious, exposed beneath the intense regard of his eyes. He offered her his arm with a smile, and she relaxed a little.

"Since you are our hostess tonight, would you care to tell me more about yourselves? You are well organized here."

"Organized?"

"You have running water, electricity, and more than enough food. Even medicine."

"Oh, that. We've been lucky, I guess," Julianne replied.

"I'm willing to wager my piece it had nothing to do with luck."

She grabbed another cider and took to the floor, introducing him to everyone. She noticed Max standing off to the side with Kirstin. The two were deep in conversation, and Julianne watched with interest. She was as yet unsure of the Nordic sniper.

"Where's the tall gentleman?" she asked. "The big one?"

"Patrolling. He joined your man Joseph up on the walls."

"That's sweet of him."

"He's not one for partying." Breytenbach shrugged. "To be honest, I don't think he trusts your defenses and wants to check it out for himself."

She laughed. "That's fine. I'd do the same in a strange place."

An hour later, they were clapping hands along with the rest as Mike did a drunken Irish jig, feet a blur. He keeled over after a few minutes, and Ronnie helped him up, the two staggering off to find more beer.

Deciding it was time Julianne signaled to Elise, and the

children were fetched from the school room. They filed in, and Michelle settled them down on cushions in a half circle around the Christmas tree.

They giggled with excitement, and Julianne winked at Meghan which earned her a toothy grin. Peter, Elise's boy, entered in a Santa suit. He looked ridiculous. The clothes were far too large, and the beard kept falling off. None of that mattered to the children.

Peter made it to a chair without losing his belly and sat down. One by one he doled out the presents, booming out their names in a jolly voice. It hadn't been easy, but they'd scoured their supplies for suitable gifts earlier. Each child got something, including the baby.

Watching the happy scene unfold, Julianne felt tears pricking her eyelids, and she swallowed hard on the knot in her throat. The past three months had been brutal—filled with the loss of loved ones. Watching those happy faces shining with joy reminded her why they couldn't give up. Why they all had to keep fighting for a future.

With the presents gone, the children returned to the schoolroom, clutching their new toys. Santa departed amidst loud cheers, tripping once when his fake stomach fell out.

"All right, people. Food's ready!" Elise announced. A mini-stampede followed with Logan first in line, as usual.

"We'd better dish up before there's nothing left," Julianne said.

"Agreed," Breytenbach replied when Mike staggered past with a plate loaded to the brim. "That man eats like a horse."

"You haven't seen Logan in action yet," Julianne snorted.

The food looked amazing. The table groaned beneath the weight of the dishes displayed—honeyed carrots, fresh garden salad, and beans. The Springbok took the place of pride in the center. Enterprising as ever, Elise had used every single bit of the buck. The ribs and chops were marinated and barbecued, the legs slow roasted in the coals and a mouthwatering stew made with the rest. A huge jug of gravy and big bowls of rice rounded out the spread.

"You people don't joke around when you feast," Breytenbach said.

"Elise never does. She comes from good old-fashioned Boer stock. But don't think we eat like this every day."

"The simple fact that you have food to spare is a miracle."

"You can thank Max, Logan, and Elise for that. In the early days, they scavenged freezers from people's houses and froze everything they could get their hands on." Julianne laughed. "Either that or preserved it."

"Clever."

"Hi, mom. Enjoying the party?" Morgan asked, joining them at the back of the queue.

"I guess."

"You guess? Then you haven't had enough to drink yet," Morgan said, raising a beer in a mocking salute.

"I could never keep up with you youngsters."

They reached the front of the queue and Julianne dished up a generous amount of honeyed carrots, her favorite.

Morgan, as usual, dished up nothing but meat and pudding as she eschewed vegetables of any kind. This was ironic considering the career path she'd chosen in her old life.

"If you don't mind, I'll eat with my team," Breytenbach said, excusing himself. Julianne watched him go, a little sad at the empty space his departure caused.

"Come on, Mom." Morgan found them seats at a nearby

287

table. Logan joined them, already on his second plate.

Julianne watched with disapproval as Morgan downed her beer in one gulp before tucking into her food with gusto. "Slow down. You'll make yourself sick."

Morgan groaned and rolled her eyes. "Relax. Live a little." She punctuated her advice with a forkful of roast and gravy.

Logan joined in on the fun. "Listen to your mom. You'll get fat," he joked, poking her in the ribs.

"What? Don't you dare call me fat." Morgan shoved another forkful into her mouth. She chewed with relish before swallowing it with another swig of beer. Logan's beer.

"Hey, get your own," Logan said.

Julianne sighed, watching them. Kids. They never grew up, and a mother never stopped trying to teach them manners. She noticed Morgan go pale. First pale, then green as a light sheen of sweat broke out on her forehead. "Morgan? Are you okay?"

Mumbling something incoherent, Morgan clapped a hand over her mouth and ran from the table. A startled Logan followed her, only to return a few minutes later.

"Don't worry. She's just nauseous. Too much booze." He sat down and scraped the food from Morgan's dish into his own, and dug in with pleasure stamped all over his face.

Shaking her head in amusement, Julianne said, "I warned her. But she's incredibly stubborn."

"Tell me about it."

After dinner, Julianne decided to have a last drink before retiring for the night. She grabbed a cider and walked outside, hoping for fresh air. The breeze was pleasant against her hot skin, raising goosebumps.

A boot scraped against gravel, and Julianne realized she

wasn't alone. A few feet away, Breytenbach sat on a wooden bench, looking at something in his hands. She walked over, not sure if her presence was wanted.

"Can I sit?" she asked.

"Sure."

Julianne perched on the edge of the bench in silence, not sure what to say. The minutes passed, and neither said a word. She shifted, playing with the bottle in her hands, picking at the label.

"I still think of that night," Breytenbach said. The words were low, rough in timbre. "It haunts my dreams."

She looked at him and waited, knowing if he wanted to say more he would.

"I was on a mission but got sidetracked. They were trapped in a pre-school. The women and children. We tried to save them, but we were too late. So many of them died that night. Torn apart. I still hear their screams in my head."

She swallowed, trying not to imagine what it must have been like. "Did you manage to save any?"

"We saved a few, even evacuated them to a camp where we fought for weeks to keep them alive. They're all dead now. Except for Sam."

"Sam?"

"The baby, Samantha. I took her from her mother that night. She gave her life so her daughter could live, shielding her with her own body. Her little boy was dead by the time I found them. I never want to see such a thing again as long as I live."

Breytenbach was silent while he relived the horrors of that night. Julianne did nothing, lending her quiet support while trying not to imagine all those children dying in such a horrid manner.

After a while, he continued. "She made me promise to look after Sam, and I will keep that promise with my last dying breath. That little girl means the world to me."

He looked at a worn photo in his hands. "I found this among the woman's belongings. Sam will want something of theirs one day. Something of her own."

"Can I see?" Julianne asked.

She took the photo he handed her and looked at the family smiling at the camera, oblivious to the impending tragedy. Her hands shook, breath hitching in her throat. Her vision narrowed until all she could see were their smiling faces.

"What's wrong? Are you okay?"

Julianne hardly heard him through the buzzing in her ears. Tears welled up, and she sobbed, one uncontrollable spasm after the other. "That's my daughter. Her husband. Their children. Sam!"

Next moment, her feet were flying, skimming over the ground to the infirmary. She burst through the door and scared a dozing Hannah out of her chair. In a makeshift crib made from an empty box, Samantha slept, one chubby fist jammed into her mouth. Curls so blond they were almost white, framed her face. Julianne reached out trembling fingers, brushing her cheek. *She's grown so much.*

She registered Breytenbach's presence behind her, followed by Max and Morgan. She assumed he'd told them the news but couldn't bear to look away from Sam.

The full force of Lilian and Michael's death hit her once more. She gasped, doubling over. The pain coiled and burned through her body like fire.

It eased when Max and Morgan stood by, lending their silent support and sympathy. At least, she still had them, and

Samantha. Meghan too. Perhaps, instead of mourning, she should be celebrating. *If only life were that easy.*

Chapter 26 - Morgan

Morgan woke by slow degrees, her lids fluttering open with reluctance. The mattress was soft beneath her hips, and Logan's warmth cradled her limbs. Early morning sunlight spilled through the curtains, and she could hear the soft cooing of doves outside the window.

With a sigh of contentment, she stretched out her arms and legs, reveling in the strength and health of her body. She felt supremely happy but supposed it was hard to be unhappy when you were young and in love. Even the zombies couldn't take that away from her.

Easing out from underneath Logan's arm, she made her way to the bathroom. Padding over the tiles, she washed her face and brushed her teeth. Halfway through, her stomach roiled. Spitting out the toothpaste, Morgan waited for it to subside.

Her muscles contracted, and cold sweat beaded her forehead. Clutching her mouth, she rushed to the toilet. After several minutes, she was reduced to dry heaving, tears streaming down her face. *God, what's wrong with me?*

Ever since the Christmas party, she'd felt peaky and nauseated. At first, she'd put it down to a hangover but after three days was forced to admit it might be something more.

"Are you okay, love?" Logan asked.

Mumbling something incoherent, Morgan threw up once

more, clutching the bowl with both hands. Logan pressed a cool cloth to her forehead and brushed the hair away from her face. After a few more heaves, the nausea subsided, and she stood up on shaky legs. She brushed her teeth again and splashed cold water on her face.

"Feeling better now?"

"A little. The worst is over, I think."

"I think you should talk to Hannah. Maybe she can give you something."

"I'll see her after breakfast."

Logan had already readied the shower for her, so Morgan stripped off her pajamas and stepped in. The water flowed over her body. It relaxed her muscles and smoothed away the tension.

It was pure luck that today was their turn to shower. The borehole and solar panels only provided so much hot water, and a roster had been drawn up providing everyone with a five-minute shower twice a week. She and Logan combined theirs half the time.

Logan's hands slid over her stomach, and she leaned back onto his chest. He nuzzled her neck, nibbling her earlobe as his hands explored her breasts, awakening a raging fire within. He teased her nipples, sending electric currents through her nervous system. She tilted her head back, gasping when his hand slipped between her thighs. His fingers massaged her sex and circled around the sensitive nub.

She shivered, legs growing weaker as the pleasure built. He looped one arm around her waist, holding her up. Within seconds, she was reduced to a quivering puddle of desire as the force of her orgasm crashed over her.

With a growl, he slammed her up against the tiles. Her legs

293

wrapped around his waist, and he thrust inside her. She cried out, clutching his shoulders with her fingers. The rhythm built, becoming faster and more intense. Morgan clung to him, eyes closed as she rode the wave.

Logan groaned, a deep shudder wracking his frame. He gripped her tightly to him, her wet hair covering his back with long tendrils. His warmth filled her, mirrored by the flow of hot water over their bodies. He slowed, hips bucking then stopped, breathing raw and ragged. His lips pressed against her ear. "You'll be the death of me yet."

She grinned, a throaty chuckle escaping her lips. "Perhaps. Do I detect a complaint?"

He smiled, letting her down. "Never."

They finished what was left of their shower, and got out. Morgan slipped on a pair of panties and a bra, followed by her trademark shorts, tank top, and boots. With smooth glides, she combed her long hair, watching while Logan dressed.

He glanced at her. "Breakfast?"

"Sure. I'm feeling better now."

"Good. I need to build my strength after that little workout."

"Grandpa," she teased.

He smacked her on the ass. "No need to get cheeky."

Still laughing, they shut the door behind them and headed to the dining room. The low murmur of voices greeted her along with the smell of coffee and eggs. Her stomach flopped like a dead bunny. "Oh, no."

Sitting down, she breathed through her mouth and tried to ignore the smells. She flashed a weak smile at Julianne who walked past with Samantha on her hip. Though the loss of Lilian and the rest of her family still hurt, the baby was a great comfort to them all. Meghan, of course, was ecstatic to discover she now had a little sister to cuddle.

"Hungry?" Logan asked.

"Not really. Just coffee for me, thanks."

Logan ambled off to get breakfast, and Morgan amused herself by watching the people around her. Peter and Thembiso were bickering about something. Fast friends, they were joined at the hip and did everything together these days.

Meghan, Anne, Mark, and Jenny sat at the kiddies table. They messed around more than they ate, a fact that would not go over well with Elise if she noticed.

"Good morning," Joanna greeted as she passed.

"Morning," Morgan replied.

She watched as Joanna took a seat next to Ben. Despite her age, seventy-something as far as Morgan knew, she looked good. Ben looked good too, more relaxed, at least. Sitting with them were Hannah and Dave. The four got along well together.

Logan returned with a full plate and coffee. She sipped on the warm brew, wondering what to do next. This question was answered when she turned in time to see Logan squish his bread into his runny egg yolk. While she loved soft eggs, today the sight was too much. She rushed off to the nearest bathroom, retching.

After another exhausting session, she turned to find Hannah in the doorway. "Are you all right, dear?"

"Not really." Morgan washed her face with cold water. "I'm feeling off these past few days, and I was hoping you could help."

"Why don't you see Jonathan? He's in the infirmary."

"Is he up to it? I thought he was sick." Morgan said, surprised.

295

"He's much better now. Besides, I think he needs to feel useful."

"Oh, okay. Thanks." Morgan followed the corridor to the infirmary and found a bored-looking Jonathan slumped in a chair, doodling with a pen and a piece of paper.

"Keeping busy, I see."

Surprised, Jonathan sat up with an embarrassed cough. "Not much to do."

"Well, you could always come on a supply run with me."

Jonathan blanched, all color draining from his face. "Yeah, uh, I'd rather not."

Morgan could have kicked herself for that thoughtless remark. The man had been to hell and back in a matter of days, losing all of his friends and patients, everyone he knew. The thought of facing zombies again must be a scary prospect.

"Kidding, kidding. We'd never risk the life of our only doctor." Morgan flashed him a dazzling smile, hoping to cover her gaffe. "Besides, I'm sure you'll have plenty of sick people to pamper soon."

"Is that why you're here?" he asked, responding with a half-smile.

"As it happens, I am." She sat down on the bed, rubbing the back of her neck. "I don't know what's wrong with me."

Jonathan assumed a brisk mien. "Start at the beginning."

"Ever since the Christmas party, I've been nauseous all the time. I can't keep my food down or even handle the smell of it."

"Nothing at all?"

"Maybe some coffee and juice. A little cereal or toast." She shrugged. "That's about it."

"Any other symptoms?"

"Now that you mention it, I'm tired and achy. Do you think I might have the flu?"

"Why don't you lie down, and I'll take a look?"

Several minutes later, Jonathan finished the exam. Pursing his lips, he hesitated. "I'm not sure if this is something you'll want to hear or not."

"What?" Morgan asked, swinging her legs to and fro on the edge of the bed in agitation. "Tell me."

"You're pregnant."

For once, Morgan was shocked to silence. She stared at Jonathan for several seconds. "Pregnant? Are you serious?"

"Perfectly. All the signs are there. I need you to do a test, though, to be sure."

"How is that possible?" she asked.

"Well...you and Logan?"

She waved a hand in the air, dismissing his words. "Of course, but we use protection."

"Nothing's foolproof."

"A baby. I can't have a baby," she cried, wrapping her arms around her middle.

Jonathan rummaged in a drawer and handed over a home pregnancy test. "Do the test first thing tomorrow morning and report back." He patted her on the back. "It's not so bad. You have a lot of support from what I've seen. Julianne, Logan, Max."

She took the test with numb fingers and tucked it into her pocket. "Thanks, Doc. I guess I'll see you tomorrow then?"

"I'll be waiting."

"Um, can we keep this between us for now?"

"Of course. Oh, and Morgan? It'll be fine, you'll see." His manner was warm and reassuring, giving the impression he'd look after her. For the first time, she got a glimpse of the real Jonathan.

She walked out of the infirmary and returned to Logan. "So? Are you all right? Did you see Hannah?"

"I saw Jonathan. He said I'm fine. It's just a bug. Nothing serious." The words felt wooden, falling heavy and stilted from her lips.

"Well, that's a relief. Here, have some coffee," Logan replied.

It killed her, sitting there and pretending nothing was different even though it burned a hole through her chest. In a single moment, her whole world had changed. Everything she expected, wanted, wished for, would now have to be set aside to make way for something new. *A baby. I can't believe it. During the apocalypse? The end of the world?*

These thoughts milled through her head the entire time they talked, making it hard to keep up the pretense. When she had the opportunity to escape with a reasonable excuse, she grabbed it, relieved not to have to fake a smile anymore.

Logan went off to help Joseph with the construction of the wall, while she headed out to the vegetable plots. The morning passed in a blur, her hands occupied with planting, weeding, and pruning. This left her mind free to roam.

She'd never planned on having children. The more she thought about it, the more excited she became. Would it be so bad after all? Erica was pregnant. So was Tumi. They had a doctor and a nurse. Even a pharmacist. They could scavenge for the supplies needed. *How will Logan feel about it? Will he be happy? Angry?*

"Are you okay, sweetie?" Julianne asked when she brought her a glass of water.

Morgan straightened up, easing the crick in her back. "I'm

fine, Mom."

"Are you sure?" Julianne's eyes scanned Morgan's body, her expression shrewd. "Something's different about you."

"I'm feeling peaky, that's all."

"Have you seen Jonathan about it?"

"I have, and it's just a bug. Seriously, Mom." Morgan downed the water in one gulp. "I'm not a kid."

Julianne shook her head, face wan. "You'll always be my kids. All of you." She looked down at Sam on her hip and gave a half-smile. "I can't lose any more of you."

"I'm sorry, Mom. I didn't mean it like that." Morgan hugged Julianne. "I miss Lilian too."

"I think about her and Michael every day. Ronald too." They stood in silence until Julianne gave herself a visible shake. "I've still got all of you, though, and that's enough for me."

Morgan watched her walk away and hoped she'd never have to live with losing a child. Now that a tiny person might be relying on her, she felt fear dry up the saliva in her mouth. *Can I raise a child like this?*

A few hours later, she had finished weeding the last of the green beans when Logan rode up on a quad bike, balancing a covered basket in front of him. "Feel like taking a break?"

"Uh, sure. What's that?"

"A surprise. Hop on."

Morgan climbed onto the back and wrapped her arms around his waist, taking comfort in the feel of his strong back. She closed her eyes and savored the feeling. After a while, he slowed to a stop. She opened her eyes to find he'd taken them to a remote spot between a clump of willows. The trees created the illusion of privacy, and the grass was soft, springy to the touch. A light breeze whispered through the leaves, cool and fresh. "What's going on?"

Logan opened the basket and pulled out a blanket. He threw it down on the grass, then bowed, flourishing one hand."Have a seat, M'lady."

"Why certainly, good Sir." A giggle welled up, but she played along. Keeping a straight face, she sat down with prim composure.

He whipped out a bottle of champagne and two glasses. "A toast," he proposed, "to the woman I love."

"Uh, okay," she answered, watching his grandiose gestures with dubious interest. "No champagne for me, thanks."

He deflated. "What? Why not?"

She thought fast. "I'm not supposed to drink alcohol with a stomach bug."

"Are you sure?" he asked, thrown off his game. "Can you at least eat?"

"Sure. I'm starving." And indeed, she was. No breakfast followed by hours of hard labor had given her a healthy appetite. In hindsight, she now recognized her nausea for what it was—morning sickness.

Happy that his surprise picnic was back on track, Logan pulled out an array of food from the basket to tempt her.

"Wow. Thanks, babe. This looks great."

Morgan eyed the spread. It looked delicious, and her tummy rumbled. She popped an olive into her mouth, savoring the bitter taste. A handful of fresh cherry tomatoes followed. She'd picked them herself that morning, and they tasted like sunshine.

It was too bad that Logan stared at her with unwavering intensity, like a hawk watching a mouse. She shifted beneath his scrutiny, growing uncomfortable. *Does he know?*

Morgan wracked her brain for something to say. Nothing presented itself, and she stuffed a boiled egg into her mouth instead. Jamming the whole thing in wasn't the best idea, and her eyes teared up as she struggled to chew.

With the worst sense of timing, Logan leaned forward while she was in mid-chew. "Morgan, I'm not very good at this sort of thing, so I'm just gonna come out and say it."

"Mmm?" she mumbled.

He pushed himself up onto one knee and slipped a small black box out of his pocket.

Morgan's eyes bugged.

"Morgan." He held out the box, snapping open the lid. "Will you marry me?" Inside lay a ring of white gold and sapphires. It glittered and sparkled, beguiling with its promise of love and fidelity.

A sudden intake of breath proved to be her undoing, and she choked on a lump of egg. Coughing and spluttering, she hacked like a cat with a hairball.

Logan was up in a flash, pounding her back and shoving a bottle of water into her face. After a deep swallow, she heaved oxygen into her lungs, fighting for a semblance of dignity. "You want to marry me?"

"That's the plan," he replied, sitting back.

"The plan?"

"I mean, I want to marry you. I love you, and I want to be with you, and..." He stopped abruptly and ran a hand through his hair. "I'm rambling. This is much harder than I thought it would be."

"Where'd you get the ring?"

"I picked it out at a jeweler during a raid last week. Why? Don't you like it?" Sudden anxiety washed over his face. "I can get you something else."

"No!" She shook her head. "I love it. It's gorgeous."

"Is that a yes then?"

With the force of a bolt of lightning, it hit her. Logan wanted to marry her. Elation sizzled through her veins. "Yes! Of course, I'll marry you."

With a look of intense relief, he swooped in for a kiss that left her breathless then slid the ring onto her finger. It was a perfect fit.

"How did you manage that?" she asked.

"I asked your mother for help."

"You asked my mom? Seriously?"

"Who do you think packed the basket? Or told me you like sapphires?"

An hour later, they lay side by side, staring up at the clouds. Morgan felt replete. Like her body was filled to the brim with every good emotion that existed. She gazed up at his face. "I love you."

He gazed at her with the kind of devotion you only read about in stories. "And I love you."

She shivered as he trailed his fingers up her arm, raising goosebumps. "I wish this moment could last forever."

He kissed the top of her head then her lips, hands cupping her face. "It will."

***

The next morning, Morgan got up as quietly as she could in the pre-dawn hours, trying not to disturb Logan's sleep. Sneaking to the bathroom, she took out the pregnancy test. The moment of truth awaited. She fumbled with the packaging and peed on the stick.

Her foot tapped on the tiles as she waited, impatience and nerves making her jittery. After several tense seconds, the first line appeared. She chewed her lip. Maybe she wasn't pregnant. Then, it showed, becoming brighter with each passing moment. The second line. *I'm pregnant.*

"Oh, shit." Her hands trembled. An indescribable feeling welled up inside. Joy? Fear? It was hard to tell.

After tossing the test into the bin, Morgan slipped back in bed and nestled up against Logan, hoping his presence would soothe her. It did not. Her mind was in turmoil.

For an hour she tossed and turned, unable to sleep. Finally, she couldn't take it anymore. "I'm going for a run, babes."

He mumbled something and turned over, snoring. After their engagement yesterday, there had been a celebration party, and Logan went overboard. He was not the only one. There would be quite a few headaches today, she was willing to bet. Strangely enough, she felt fine this morning. The nausea was there but subdued, manageable.

Perhaps it's the dry crackers and ginger tea I had before bed. A little tip from Jonathan whispered into her ear.

It was a beautiful morning for exercise. Crisp and clear. Easing into a slow jog at first, she did a circuit of the buildings. She was preparing to do another when a familiar voice called out.

"Hey, Morgan. Wait up." Angie jogged over the dew-laden grass, looking girly in a hot pink tracksuit. "Can I join you?"

"Sure. Let's go."

"Why don't we run down to the far end? Follow the fence?"

"Sounds good. We can make it count as a patrol."

They set off and fell into the rhythm of running, their

feet forming a steady beat. Morgan felt good, her breathing smooth and even. She kept thinking of her pregnancy, getting more and more excited. *I'm having a baby!*

A spontaneous grin broke onto her face, and she placed a hand over her taut belly, wondering at the life growing there. *I'm telling Logan as soon as I'm done here. In fact, I'm turning back now.*

She slowed. "I'm going back, Angie. I need to tell Logan something important."

"What?" An undefined emotion crossed the younger girl's face. She stuttered a reply. "Are you sure you don't want to go a little further?"

They'd left the buildings behind but were not out of sight yet. The fence was still a distance off. Morgan shook her head. "No, I'm sure. I need to see him right away."

"Okay. I'll go with you," Angie replied. Her dark eyes were hooded, but Morgan hardly noticed.

They turned back the way they came, and she thought she'd burst out of her skin with excitement. *I'm going to be a mom! I can't wait to tell Logan. I'm sure he'll be happy. Just as happy as I am.*

They'd gone only a few paces when Angie cried out, doubling over in pain. Morgan stopped. "Are you okay?"

Angie gasped, clutching her side. "I think I've got a cramp."

"Take it easy. It should pass soon."

"Just give me a minute," Angie said.

Her face was twisted with pain, and Morgan moved closer to offer support. "Here, let me help you."

"Thanks, I'm sure it will go away any moment."

Impatience prompted Morgan to glance over her shoulder. In the distance, she spotted Logan's tall figure striding toward her. A smile grew on her face, her heart swelling with joy. She looked back at Angie to spur the girl along. "Can you walk—"

Angie's hand flashed to her waist. A glint of silver showed. Her body twisted, and the object swung towards Morgan's unprotected stomach.

Alarm flared in Morgan's mind. Instinct kicked in. She pulled back but not far enough. Pain exploded in her abdomen. She gasped, trying to catch a breath with lungs gone empty. She gripped Angie's wrist, trying to remove the stinging agony. "What are you doing?"

"I've been waiting for this moment for ages." Angie grabbed Morgan's shoulder. Her fingers dug into the muscle, pulling herself closer. The knife cut deeper.

With a cry, Morgan wrenched at Angie's arm. Her other hand lashed out, a fist catching the girl on the cheekbone. She broke free, pressing against the bleeding wound. Blood pumped out between her fingers, thick and warm. *My baby!*

She gazed at Angie's triumphant face with confusion. "Why?"

"Why? You want to know why?" Angie lunged, the knife stabbing at the air. Morgan staggered to the side, narrowly avoiding it. "Because you took Armand away from me."

"No...I didn't..." Morgan's brain scrambled, unable to form a coherent thought. *She's crazy. I have to get away from her. I have to...Logan!*

She looked over her shoulder, spotting him running toward them, but he was still so far away. Too far. "Lo—"

Angie sprang forward and used the moment to her advantage. Morgan dodged, but she wasn't fast enough. The knife slid into the flesh beneath her sternum. It bit deep, sinking to the hilt.With a brutal cutting move, Angie sawed upward.

The girl shrieked in anger. "He was mine!"

The pain morphed into a hellish trail of fire, burning up into Morgan's chest. She screamed, her body set alight. Clawing at Angie's face, she broke free. A river of blood pushed up her throat. She choked, the crimson fluid gushing over her lips. Her knees buckled, and she fell, the world moving past her eyes in slow motion. Angie's face hovered above hers for a second, gloating. Morgan blinked, tears fogging her vision. "Please."

A hoarse shout sounded, and Angie was plucked away. Logan appeared in her stead, his face contorted. "Morgan. Hold on, baby. I'm here."

She tried to speak but coughed. The words gurgled in her throat. She was drowning in her own blood. Logan grabbed her by the shoulders. He pulled her upright, holding her against him. Her head lolled forwards, and the fluid dribbled out onto his chest. It allowed her to breathe, and she sucked in a lungful of air. "Logan."

"Don't speak, my love. Save your strength. I'm going get help, okay? Just hold on."

"Don't leave me. Please."

"I won't. I promise."

The world dipped and swayed around her. Her muscles were weak, the strength leeching from them on the tide of her breath. She lay against Logan's chest. His scent enveloped her, warm and safe. His voice whispered to her, the words near and yet so far.

I'm here. I'll never leave you. I promise.

Stay with me.

Stay.

Chapter 27 - Logan

"Don't leave me. Please."

"I won't. I promise." Logan slid his arms beneath Morgan and stood. He set off at a run, heading for the infirmary. She lay against his breast like a broken bird, her blood soaking the front of his shirt.

"I'm here. I'll never leave you. I promise."

"Stay with me."

"Stay."

He murmured the words over and over, hoping to keep her awake. The distance seemed to stretch forever. Her rasping breaths were terrible to hear, but even worse was the sudden silence.

Logan stumbled to a stop and looked down. Her eyes were closed, her skin paper white. Laying her down on the ground, he pressed his ear to her chest and felt for a pulse. Nothing. No heartbeat.

"No. Don't die." He grabbed her face with both hands, tapping her cheeks. "You can't die."

No response.

He leaned forward, breathing into her mouth. Her chest rose and fell. He repeated the procedure, punctuating it with chest compresses. "Come on, baby. Fight!"

Morgan lay lifeless, her blood soaking into the ground.

After a few minutes, he was forced to acknowledge the truth. She was dead.

He brushed his thumbs over her mouth, leaving crimson smears on her cheeks. "I saw the test. I know."

His hands curled into fists, and he choked back a bitter sob. Deep inside, something broke. Something that died years ago at his father's hands only to come alive again at her touch. Fury welled up inside. A cold, unforgiving hatred that pushed out any thoughts of mercy or kindness. *Angie.*

Logan strode back to where he'd left her. His mind flashed back to the moment he saw her attack Morgan, his desperate run to intervene, the despair when he was too late, his anger...no his rage at her perfidy. He'd ripped her away from Morgan, his fist connecting with her jaw and knocking her unconscious.

An ugly bruise had formed on the side of her face, and her lip was split and bleeding. He grabbed her by the arms, lifted her up and threw her over his shoulder.

At the main building, people were gathering for breakfast. He headed there and dumped Angie on the ground, prodding her with his boot. She stirred, moaning.

"What the hell is going on?" Max asked, striding over.

"This bitch killed your sister."

"What?" Max stopped short, floundering.

"She killed Morgan."

"What do you mean killed? Morgan's dead?" Disbelief flashed across Max's features.

Angie sat up, shaking her head. She groaned, rubbing her swollen jaw. Blood trickled from her lip. She opened her mouth to speak, but Ben interrupted. "Angie? Oh, my God, Angie! What happened?"

He pushed through the crowd and reached down to help her to her feet. She leaned against him and pointed a trembling finger at Logan. "He hit me. Logan hit me."

"You son of a bitch. How dare you touch her? I'll break your neck, you little whelp!"

Angie clung to Ben, staring at everyone with huge eyes. She looked fragile, doll-like. Not a person there could believe her capable of murder. Angry glares turned on Logan. Silent condemnation spread from one to the other.

"Logan? What's going on?" Max asked. His voice held a pleading note, begging him to tell them it was all a joke, a misunderstanding. "Where's my sister?"

"I told you. She's dead." Logan looked at Angie. "Angie killed her."

"You're crazy. Angie would never hurt anyone." Ben's face grew purple with fury, puffing up like an angry bullfrog's. He placed a supportive arm around her shoulders and looked at Max. "You can't honestly believe what he's saying?"

The crowd gathered closer, forming a half circle. A ripple spread through their ranks, whispers buzzing in the air.

"I saw her do it," Logan said. "She betrayed us, betrayed Morgan."

"He's lying. He's the one who did it. I tried to stop him, and he hit me."

All eyes turned on Logan, evaluating, considering. He stood stock still, face a blank, but his hands were covered in blood. The bruise on Angie's face likewise accused him.

"Logan?" Max asked.

"I didn't do it, Max. I loved her. You know that. She was my whole world."

A disturbance interrupted them. Elise had summoned

309

Julianne who pushed through the crowd, crying out, "Where's my daughter?"

Logan turned to her, and his face softened. For a split second, he allowed his pain to shine through. "She's over there."

She rushed in the direction he showed, followed by Max. Breytenbach and his group had shifted to the side, watching the scene unfold with grim expressions, neither participants nor bystanders.

Lisa too had drifted apart. She stared at Angie, and a strange emotion washed across her face, almost accusatory. Logan knew that she'd been friends with Morgan and now hoped she was on his side.

Elise ushered the kids and Michelle away from the spectacle, dragging a protesting Thembiso by the arm. The crowd thinned.

Logan turned back to Angie. His face hardened, becoming a mask of stone. "Tell the truth. There's no point in lying, and it won't save you. That I promise."

"You're crazy." She backed away, looking like a hunted doe. "You need help, Logan. The only killer here is you."

"Last chance."

"Leave her alone," Ben said, shielding her with his body. He looked like he had before. Strong, determined, and protective. The air of fragility that had hovered about him for weeks disappeared.

"Stay out of this, Ben. She's manipulating you," Logan replied.

Ben didn't answer, but neither did he move. Angie retreated further behind him, her eyes glittering. To Logan, she looked wicked, like a malignant tumor that clung to Ben's side. *Why*

310

can't they see it?

"Don't listen to him. He's trying to blame me for what he did," she said. A sneer twisted her lips. "You killed her in a jealous rage, didn't you Logan? Who did she screw this time?"

Logan felt violent anger twist inside him. He itched to wrap his hands around her neck and squeeze the life from her. With an effort, he remained calm. His next words dropped into the atmosphere like a stone. "Did you know she was pregnant when you stabbed her? Did you know you were killing a baby?"

Confused emotion flitted across Angie's face. She stuttered. "No...I'm not...it wasn't me."

"She was pregnant? Why didn't she tell me?" The choked words alerted them to Julianne's presence. She stood next to Max who carried Morgan in his arms. She looked like a broken doll, her head cradled against his chest, arms and legs limp.

"Yes, she was." Logan tried not to look at the lifeless body of his beloved lest he break down. "I'm sorry, Julianne. I'm sure she would have wanted you to know, but she only took the test this morning."

"This is insane! My daughter is dead, and...and..." She grabbed Max's arm for support, swaying. "Just tell me. Which one of you did it?"

"I already told you. She did." Impatience turned Logan's tone brusque. Despite his pity for Julianne, he felt angered that people were so ready to turn against him. "This is a waste of time. You all know me. I've been here from the start, helping you, all of you, to survive. Why would I kill Morgan?"

The crowd shifted, uncertain whom to believe. Breytenbach stepped forward, looking first at Logan and Angie facing off, then at Max. "Examine their knives. Whoever stabbed her will have blood on the blade."

His words fell into the tense atmosphere, causing a ripple of speculation. Max nodded. "Good idea. Logan? Will you show us your knife?"

"Here," Logan replied, pulling his from the sheath. He held it up. The steel edge glittered in the sun. It was spotless.

Calculating eyes turned toward Angie. She paled, taking a step back. "This is ridiculous. I don't even have a knife on me."

"She dropped it on the grass," Logan said.

"I'll get it," Breytenbach said, slipping away.

While he was gone, the tension grew. Each second ticked by slowly. Angie fidgeted, her head swiveled as if looking for an escape route. Breytenbach returned, holding up a bloody dagger. It was long and slim, pearl handled. He turned to her and asked, "Is this yours?"

"No. No, it's not," she replied, but her eyes had gone wide.

Ben stared at the knife for several seconds. He paled. "Angie? What did you do?"

"Nothing. It's not mine."

Ben backed away from her, shaking his head. "I gave you that knife."

"But...I...it's not mine, I swear. It's a different one." Her lips quivered. She reached out to Ben, grasping at air and pleaded, "Please. You must believe me."

Ben shook his head. He did not take her hands.

Naked rage flared in her eyes. Her hands clenched into fists, and she stamped her foot. "Stupid old man. You're supposed to be on my side."

"But...Morgan. Why? Why kill her?"

"Why not?" she said. Her dark eyes glowed. "She deserved it."

Ben looked stricken. His mouth worked soundlessly, and she laughed.

"Armand got what he deserved too, running after her like a stupid little puppy dog." She pounded a fist on her breast. "He could have had me! But no, he only wanted her!"

"Armand? You killed Armand too?" Max asked.

Angie smirked, folding her arms. "I'll never forget the look on his face when I shoved him off that roof. The betrayal. Now he knows what it feels like." Her smile grew wider. "He screamed like a girl while they ate him."

A collective gasp went up, and people retreated from her like a wave from the shore. She turned in a circle, glaring. Her face had sharpened, lips drawing back to expose the canines. She looked like a demonic child.

"Oh, I see. You're all staring at me like I'm crazy. You know what? I don't care. You're all just a bunch of cowards, hiding behind your walls, pretending to be civilized. Civilization is gone, people. Only the strong can survive now."

A subtle shift occurred, a ripple through the crowd. The strongest members of the camp stepped up, closing in on Angie while the rest retreated. Too late, she realized what she'd done. She was surrounded.

"No, wait. I didn't mean it." She tried to retreat. "I was confused."

"Shut up, Angie. We all heard you. It's over," Max said. "You're guilty by your own admission."

"No, please."

"Do what you want with her, Logan," Julianne said. Her face was white, her eyes like chips of glass. "No one will interfere."

Angie tried to run. Logan grabbed her by the wrist, and she screamed. He locked his hand over her mouth, picking her up off the ground. She wriggled like a worm on a hook and kicked her legs. He ignored her struggles, dragging her to the Landie. With a length of rope, he tied her arms behind her back and tossed her into the back. She never stopped screaming.

"Logan, please." Ben approached him, wringing his hands. "I know what Angie did was unforgivable, but don't kill her. She's still...she's like a daughter to me. I couldn't bear it if she died."

Logan stared at him and struggled to control his anger. "She killed Morgan. She murdered our unborn child."

"I know, but..." Ben broke down in tears, his large shoulders shaking. Joanna led him away, whispering words of comfort in his ear. Logan felt a twinge of sympathy for the man. It was not enough to prevent him from doing what he planned to, however.

Logan slid behind the wheel and drove, never registering the scenery flashing by. To him, it was all just a blur of nothingness. In the back, Angie struggled against her bonds, but she wasn't going anywhere. He knew how to tie a knot. She cried out until her throat became raw, pleading for him to let her live. He hardly heard it.

Morgan is gone. She's dead. His grief knotted inside his chest in a ball of pain. It had to wait, though. He had a job to do. Koppie Alleen loomed in the distance. The lone hill towered above the flat landscape like a beacon and heralded the entrance to Riebeeckstad. Hence its name—which roughly translated to Lonely Hill. A white cross adorned the top, mocking him with its promise of eternal love and forgiveness.

There's no forgiveness for what I'm about to do.

He drove through the abandoned streets of the small town until he reached its center. A heart that was now as dead as the body, no longer pumping with life and commerce. Parking the Land Rover in front of the nearest shop, he climbed out and opened the back.

A terrified Angie scooted away from him, eyes wide with fear. Her face was streaked with tears and snot. He grabbed her ankle and pulled her out onto the pavement. She fell hard, unable to brace herself. Closing the door, he bent down and pulled out his hunting knife. Logan stared at it for a few seconds, contemplating all the things he could do.

She watched him, naked fear flickering across her features. "Please don't."

Logan was surprised to find he felt nothing. No pleasure, no satisfaction, nothing at all. He lowered the knife. She flinched. He cut the ropes binding her.

Angie stared at him in shocked surprise. "You're letting me go?"

"I'm leaving you here."

"Really?" She pushed herself upright, blubbering. "You'll never see me again, I promise."

"No, I won't." In one smooth motion, he unslung his rifle from his shoulder and shot her in the knee. At such close range, the high caliber bullet packed a brutal punch. Her knee exploded in a shower of blood, flesh, and bone. She uttered an inhuman cry, unlike anything he'd ever heard before.

Angie collapsed in a crumpled heap, alternating between wailing and sobbing. She clutched at her leg, trying to stop the bleeding. It pushed out between her fingers in a dark crimson stream.

315

Logan walked away and climbed into his truck. The first shambling corpse appeared in the rearview mirror. Others joined it, the shot drawing them in. They closed in around her and cut off all escape. She crawled, dragging the shattered leg and leaving a trail of blood behind her.

The first corpse fell upon her, sinking its rotting teeth into her open wound. Its fingers hooked into the splintered bones like claws, ripping the joint apart. Sinew and muscles tore. Raw animal cries issued from her throat.

Logan watched. Still, he felt nothing as they feasted on her flesh. Once Angie ceased to exist as a human being, he drove away. Halfway back to camp, he pulled over. For a long time, he sat, staring at nothing.

Unmoving.

Empty.

Hollow.

He turned his head and looked at the cubby hole, popping it open. The cigarettes Morgan had indulged in, lay there. He took them and got out, the Land Rover's door creaking. He put one of her smokes between his lips and lit it. The acrid smoke filled his lungs, a hit of nicotine entering his blood vessels.

He used to nag Morgan to stop smoking. An ex-smoker himself, he knew what a bad habit it was. She'd never quite managed. Now, it didn't matter anymore. She was gone. He'd never see her again.

The empty feeling inside him built and built, growing until he couldn't contain it. He crumpled the cigarette in his hand, burning his fingers. A tightness built up in his throat, demanding release. A howl of fury tore loose. Rage infused his mind. "Why? Why her?"

He screamed until his voice broke then slumped to his knees. His rifle rested in the dust next to him, and for a moment...but no. He couldn't. He wasn't a quitter.

A shambling figure on the road got him to his feet, and he climbed back inside the Land Rover. He drove past the zombie, not paying it any heed. As the camp drew closer, his heart grew heavier. He didn't know if he could face the questions, the sympathy, the attention. In the end, it didn't matter.

He didn't plan on staying long, anyway.

Epilogue - Breytenbach

Julianne looked both beautiful and frail in a black dress; her hair was done in an elegant twist that exposed her slender neck. She stared at Morgan's grave without a tear in sight, grieving silently for the daughter she'd lost and the grandchild that would never be born.

In the few days he'd known her, Breytenbach had come to admire her. She had a quiet strength, a grace that appealed to him. He had not shown Julianne how he felt, though. Not yet. It was too soon. For now, he would just be there when she needed him.

At her side stood a tearful Meghan, clinging to her mother's leg. Her eyes were wide as she stared at the grave. To her, death was still a mystery. A frightening specter that took people away forever, just like her daddy.

Max stood beside them, likewise grieving for the sister that had been so close to him, almost like a twin. His eyes were dry, but the tension in his shoulders and mouth betrayed his emotions.

Breytenbach shook his head, remembering the insanity reflected in Angie's eyes when she spat out her hatred like bile. The depths of the human psyche never failed to amaze him. *What a senseless tragedy.*

Then he looked at Samantha squirming in his arms and

reflected that even though they had all lost so much, they still had each other. He had found his family at last, and he knew he'd protect them with his dying breath.

The rhythmic thud of dirt hitting Morgan's shroud sounded loud in the late afternoon air. Sunlight bathed the clearing in a golden haze, reflecting off the circle of grim faces gathered together. The whole world was quiet, as though it too attended her funeral.

Big Ben was the worst off, perhaps. His eyes were lost, swiveling around without focus while his mouth worked soundlessly. The once great stature he'd possessed was gone, his body crumbling in on itself like an ancient statue. Joanna stood next to him offering silent support, but he hardly seemed to notice her.

The quiet drone of Dave's voice filled the air as he recited Psalm 23 from the battered Bible he always carried in his pocket. It had been Morgan's favorite, chosen by Julianne for the service.

'The Lord is my shepherd; I shall not want.

He maketh me to lie down in green pastures: he leadeth me beside the still waters.

He restoreth my soul: he leadeth me in the paths of righteousness for his name's sake.

Yea, though I walk through the valley of the shadow of death, I will fear no evil: for thou art with me; thy rod and thy staff they comfort me.

Thou preparest a table before me in the presence of mine enemies: thou anointest my head with oil; my cup runneth over.

Surely goodness and mercy shall follow me all the days of my life: and I will dwell in the house of the Lord forever.'

The words offered hope and absolution to all except Logan.

Since his return, he had not said a word nor looked at anyone. Nobody dared ask what had happened to Angie. Her fate was apparent to all, etched into the grooves that lined his features.

There had been no mercy for her, Breytenbach knew. He also knew the deed would change Logan forever. A man cannot kill with such cold-blooded cruelty and not have it stain his soul with the act. No matter how justified.

The old Logan was gone. He looked like a man fashioned of steel. No emotion was reflected in those hard gray eyes, and Breytenbach wondered what he would do next. For a man to have nothing, only to find everything then lose it again was a hard, hard thing.

When the last shovelful of dirt covered the grave, Logan turned and walked away. Breytenbach watched as he climbed into his rusted Land Rover and pulled away with a roar of the engine. He left only a cloud of dust in his wake; a void echoed in the hearts of many.

The service was over. One by one, people drifted away, their murmured condolences humming around Julianne. She thanked each with a stiff nod, her hands clutching Meghan's shoulders in silent despair.

Max hugged her close before leaving to take up his shift at the wall. Even now, the infected could not be forgotten. They had to remain vigilant.

Breytenbach turned his attention to Julianne, leading her and Meghan away. What they needed the most now was privacy. That and time to process their loss.

Sam was the only one who seemed oblivious to the atmosphere. A monarch butterfly flitted past her face, brushing across her baby-soft skin. She giggled, swinging pudgy fists through the air. Her laughter prompted smiles from Julianne and Meghan while her innocence promised hope for the future.

The sun dropped toward the horizon in a slow descent, streaking the sky in a splendid display of cosmic glamor. As the day drew to a close, Breytenbach felt sure there would be another. Days filled with sorrow, perhaps, but also joy and happiness. *We will last another day.*

***

I sincerely hope you enjoyed reading this book as much as I enjoyed writing it. If you did, I would much appreciate a short review on Amazon or your favorite book website. It would mean the world to me and enable me to keep doing what I do best. Write.

If you'd like to find out what happens next then read further for a sneak preview of the sequel and more apocalyptic fun!

Author's Note

So we've reached the end of Last Another Day but not the end of the adventure. Would you like to find out what happens next to Logan, Breytenbach, and the rest? Then turn the page for a sneak peek at Fear Another Day, the sequel to Last Another Day. And in case you missed it, there's also a prequel called Survive Another Day which contains bonus material and short stories.

Survive Another Day - Available Here
https://www.amazon.com/dp/B01N7RVLEW
Fear Another Day - Available Here
https://www.amazon.com/dp/B071J2D2DN

If you'd like to learn more about my books in general, see upcoming projects, and get clued in on new releases, check out my website. Plus you'll get your very own FREE starter library just for subscribing!

My Website - www.baileighhiggins.com

OR you can choose to follow me on Amazon and receive an email from them whenever I publish a new book. Convenient, huh?

My Amazon Page - www.amazon.com/author/baileighhiggins

Last, but not least, you can like my Facebook page for a daily dose of apocalyptic fun. I love chatting with my readers and posting awful zombie jokes to cheer up your day! Not to mention the competitions, giveaways, teasers, updates and more. Need I go on?

My Facebook Page - www.facebook.com/BaileighHiggins

OR you could just send me a good old-fashioned email to fiction@baileighhiggins.com

Thanks for reading and never stop being a survivor!

Sneak Preview

This is a preview of Fear Another Day, the sequel to Last Another Day.

Available Here
https://www.amazon.com/dp/B071J2D2DN

Chapter 1 – Nadia

The sun threw its last dying light across the horizon creating a brilliant tapestry of color. A few rays filtered down through a tiny window into the wine cellar below and painted the air the color of diluted blood. Nadia stirred beneath the sheet that covered her thin frame, staring at the window. *Time to get up.*

It was almost nightfall. She shrugged off the material and stretched her limbs, joints cracking from being locked in a fetal position for hours on end.

A sheen of sweat covered her skin, beading on her upper lip and forehead. Autumn rated barely a blip on the radar in this region, the only sign of its coming being the chill that descended at night.

During the day, the thermometer hovered around a scorching forty degrees Celsius, made worse by the enclosed atmosphere of the cellar. It was the safest place she could find, though, and safety was the only thing that counted anymore.

Nadia pushed herself upright with a sigh. Every day it was harder to get up than the last. One day, she wouldn't get up at all. That knowledge frightened her less with each passing week. *What's the point of living if you're all alone?*

She folded up the mattress, sheet, and pillow, placing it on the bottom rack of a shelf against the wall. With a handful of wet wipes, she cleansed her skin, ridding it of the accumulated sweat before slipping on leopard print underwear. They were the most expensive knickers she'd ever owned, pilfered from the closet of a dead rich lady.

A pair of skinny jeans, combat boots that reached to mid-calf, a see-through vest, and a leather jacket followed. She ran her fingers through her spiky black hair then applied a thick layer of black eyeshadow and liner. "If I'm going to die, I might as well look good."

It was silly. She knew that. Holding onto your vanity when it was the end of the world, was stupid. She couldn't help it. Vanity was all she had left. It was the last thing connecting her to her old life and the teenager she used to be.

An array of rings went onto her fingers, chunky stones and silver skulls gleaming in the fading light. A cross as long as her hand hung from a thick chain around her neck, followed by several studs and earrings.

After zipping up the short jacket, she slung a belt over her hips containing a variety of odd implements: a screwdriver, bolt cutter, knife, hammer, and scissors. In her pockets, she carried a lighter, nail file, hairpins, and paper clips.

Armed and ready to face whatever the outside might throw at her, Nadia strode to the door and pressed her ear to it. In the thick silence, not a sound could be heard. She rapped her knuckles on the wood and waited for any telltale moans. Still nothing.

With a heave, she pushed the heavy metal box that barricaded the door away and dropped down on all fours to peer through the gap beneath it. No movement. All was quiet.

Nadia pulled the hammer from her belt and held it ready as she opened the door. Her heart thumped while it creaked open. No matter how many times she did this, it never grew easier.

The short passage leading to the stairs was empty, the door at the top of the stairs still closed. Nothing had entered during the day. Her hideout remained undiscovered. For now.

She fumbled for a flashlight and shone it upwards, placing each foot with care as she walked up the stairs. Some of them were creaky, and she stepped accordingly.

When she reached the top, she repeated the procedure from earlier before stepping out into the kitchen. It was pitch black as all the windows had been boarded up, and she swept the beam of her torch up and down, assuring herself it was empty.

A quick check of the house proved it was undisturbed. Nothing had entered, either dead or living. She couldn't decide if that was a good or a bad thing. Some days she wished a horde would find her and put her out of her misery. Other days she hoped survivors would stumble upon her.

Then she'd remember what happened to the last group she was with and a lead weight would settle in her stomach. *I'm better off alone.*

Dusk was nearly over by the time she was ready to leave the house. A full moon had risen, casting ample light over the darkening streets. She did a quick circuit of the yard, noting the weather, before sidling up to the gate. After a careful look around, she scrambled over.

Fifteen minutes later, she was hiding behind a dumpster, waiting for a trio of infected to shuffle out of sight around a corner. Avoidance always trumped confrontation. A lesson learned early on during the outbreak.

Once they were out of sight, she continued in the opposite direction. Her methods were simple. She carried a hammer in the right and a screwdriver in the left. Both were efficient at caving in rotten skulls.

She went out at night, on days when the weather was clear and the moon bright. Moving silently, she stuck to the shadows, pausing in strategic places to ensure the route was clear. It was a tactic that had kept her alive thus far. Whether her luck would hold or not, was a different story. Not that she had much choice. A girl had to eat.

The small supermarket where she got her supplies, loomed at the end of the block. She crouched behind a low wall, surveying the street. It looked clear. Her stomach growled. She was starving. Scurrying across the street, she sprinted along the wall of an apartment block, abandoning caution in her haste. *Nearly there.*

A few meters from the shop, a hand reached out from an alley, grabbing the collar of her jacket. Her feet flew out from underneath her as she was jerked to a sudden stop. The air left her lungs in a whoosh. Nadia gasped for breath, fingers scrabbling on the concrete for grip.

A diseased face loomed above her, leaning in for the kill. She reacted on instinct, punching it hard in the teeth. Its head snapped back, granting her a split second. She grasped the cross lying on her chest and stabbed upward, aiming for its eye. The cross slid in as neatly as a dagger, the long point sharpened by hours of honing on a concrete floor.

The zombie stiffened, putrid fluid spraying from the punctured eyeball. Nadia gagged, turning her face away. She heaved the corpse off her chest, searching on the ground for her fallen weapons. Her fingers closed on the hilt of the hammer. She jumped up, crouching on the balls of her feet. She was ready in case the zom had friends, but a quick whirl assured her it had been a loner. She relaxed.

"Gross!" She shuddered as she wiped at the putrid stuff running down her face, heaving when the smell hit her nose. "This sucks."

She gave up trying to clean herself and instead ran the last few steps to the shop. The keys to the padlock were hidden beneath a brick, and she struggled with the chain, fingers trembling from the adrenaline.

Once inside the shop, she leaned back against the wall, closing her eyes. Her heartbeat slowed, and the rush of the close call she'd had faded from her veins. It got easier with time. Killing was something that came naturally now.

"Well, let's get this over with." Her voice echoed through the empty shop, reminding her once more how alone she was. Tears pricked at the corners of her eyes. "Why do I even bother?"

For a moment, she considered giving up. Her mind envisioned swallowing handfuls of pills from the drug store. "It would be like falling asleep. It'd be easy."

Brandon's face hovered in the background, his dimpled smile making her heart beat faster. They could be together again, in heaven. She snorted. "There's no such thing. Heaven doesn't exist."

It's your fault he's dead. It's your fault all of them are dead.

A tear ran down her cheek, and she wiped it away. Even if heaven did exist it wasn't meant for the likes of her. She deserved to suffer here on earth, deserved every second of her miserable existence.

With a shrug, she pulled out her torch and trudged to the nearest fridge. Grabbing a bottle of lukewarm water, she swallowed it in one gulp. Once her thirst was sated, she hunted for cloth and soap, washing the zombie gunk off her face and clothes.

"That's better." Her voice had evened out, numbing calm taking the place of the desperation from before. She was okay now, the crushing guilt pushed back into its little box in the recesses of her mind.

She picked a backpack from a shelf and filled it with various items. Enough to last a few days. Bottled water, nuts, dried fruit, protein bars, juice, and toiletries. She shoved a book, socks, and painkillers on top and zipped it up. Her stomach cramped again, growling at her. "Yeah, yeah. Hold your horses."

In the kitchen aisle, she found a can opener and fork, using it to scoff two cans of spaghetti and meatballs. She missed real food and longed for a hot meal but had no idea how to go about it. The power was off, and she didn't know how to rig up a generator or how to get the fuel to run it. Besides, the noise would draw infected.

Her shoulders slumped as she faced the truth. She was on a slippery slope to nowhere. She'd either starve, die of disease or thirst, or get eaten. Alone.

Nadia shook her head. "Not today. Today we have a good old-fashioned pig-out."

She grabbed a packet of chips, juice, and a huge slab of

chocolate, sitting down on the floor next to the magazine rack. There wasn't much she hadn't read yet, but it was better than nothing. No way was she going back to that dismal cellar right away.

A stubby candle provided light, the flickering flame throwing shadows across the pages. Weeks before, she'd stuck old newspapers across the glass doors to prevent any infected from seeing inside or spotting the light. Secure in the familiarity of her surroundings, she settled down to read.

A corner of the newspaper, old and yellowed, sprang loose from the brittle glue with barely a whisper of sound. The end drooped, a triangle of glass becoming exposed.

An hour passed, broken only by the rustling of packets and pages as Nadia gorged herself on chocolate and chips while leafing through magazines. So engrossed was she in this activity, that she never noticed the shadow flitting past the glass doors. Followed by another, and another.

A loud bang startled Nadia, and she shrieked. Dropping the book on her lap, she scrambled to her feet. The glass doors shivered and creaked under the onslaught of several bodies, cracks working its way up the center.

"Shit," she gasped, backing away.

Her head swiveled, looking for an escape route, but she knew there was none. The only other exit was locked with metal shutters, and there were no windows to crawl through. Nowhere to hide either. She had no other option but to make a run for it.

They'll pull me down like wolves.

Her eyes fell on a large cardboard display.

Not if they can't see me.

She grabbed the backpack and shrugged it on, gripped the

screwdriver in her right and grasped the display with her left. The glass wouldn't last much longer.

She rushed forward, stopping close to the doors but off to the side. Nadia squatted down and planted the display in front of her, hiding her scrawny body behind it. A few more bangs and the front of the shop exploded in a shower of glass. Her heart hammered in her throat, and she squeezed her eyes shut for a brief second.

The infected pushed through the opening and rushed into the shop, growling and snapping at the air. She waited for the bulk of them to run past her. The moment she spotted an opening, she darted forward.

Time slowed to a crawl; it felt like her body pushed through water. She slipped around the nearest infected, pushed through a gap between two more and ducked beneath the grasping arms of another. The cold air of the night beckoned. Fingers brushed through the back of her hair, one hooking on an earring. A flash of pain flared as it tore out of her earlobe, throwing her off balance.

Nadia stumbled, falling onto her hands and knees. Jagged glass cut into her hands. She cried out, but fear kept her moving forward, and she crawled right between the legs of a zombie. It bent down to grab her, but the backpack stymied its efforts, and it toppled over.

Snarls echoed from behind her as she shot to her feet, sprinting across the street and heading for an alley between two buildings. Her breath came in ragged gasps, and her hands were on fire. She didn't care. A grin spread across her face as she tore down the alley and turned a corner. *I got out. I can't believe it.*

She risked a quick glance over her shoulder, and cold fear

wormed its way into her stomach. "Fuck!"

Two infected.

Fresh.

Fast.

The worst kind.

A young woman trailed behind a beefy man dressed in khaki. He looked like a farmer. *Locals. Survivors like me turned recently.*

Nadia ran faster, pumping her arms and legs with furious effort. *I can't let them catch me. Not after everything.*

She raced through street after street trying to lose them but failed. They were too fast, too determined, and didn't get tired. Unlike her. Her lungs were burning. A stitch stabbed into her side. She couldn't stop. Fighting two fresh infected was impossible.

She ran all the way through the town center until faced by rows of houses. Slow infected, rotted and aged, shuffled on sidewalks and lawns. They uttered creaky moans at the sight of her. Nadia never slowed, ducking in and around them with the agility of the young and desperate.

With a fresh burst of speed, she turned a corner and headed for a low fence. Zombies weren't good climbers. Behind her, one of the infected fell over something judging by the frustrated snarls and crashing sounds. A quick glance over her shoulder confirmed it. The woman was gone.

Hope lent her strength, and she vaulted over the upcoming fence, using one hand for support. She screamed as the glass shards ground deeper into the flesh of her palm. Then she was over the wall.

Nadia dashed across the overgrown lawn, hoping she wouldn't trip. A low hedge appeared, and she crashed over it. Another headlong sprint and she smashed into the next barrier, a concrete border. Her fingers gripped the edge, and she pulled herself, falling to the ground with a graceless thump.

The remaining zom was now well out of sight, trying to climb over walls and fences his uncoordinated brain wasn't meant for. Nadia hurried across the lawn, hissing when she stepped into a hole and twisted her ankle.

She pushed on, waddling on her sore leg like a penguin. Only when she was sure it was safe did she stop to crouch behind a bush, gasping for breath. As her heartbeat slowed and the fear receded, the precariousness of her position hit her.

She was lost in a strange neighborhood far from her safe house. Her hands were injured. Even now as the adrenaline wore off, fiery pain shot through her arms, screaming up her nerve-endings. *The blood will draw more. I need to hide.*

A rustle of leaves to the left alerted her. Nadia scrambled to her feet, holding the hammer. In the pale light of the moon, two eyes shined yellow, staring at her with unblinking intensity.

She swallowed, primal fear flooding her veins as every nerve screamed at her to run. Run from the monsters, hiding in the night, waiting to devour her soul. Her feet remained rooted to the spot. Running wouldn't help her now.

Nadia tensed her muscles, gripping the hammer in her right hand despite the pain it caused. The eerie eyes never left her, following every move she made with predatory intensity. A cloud moved in front of the moon, drenching her in darkness and the glowing orbs disappeared.

Seconds ticked by, and the tension grew until the moon

reappeared. Snarls sounded nearby, and the yellow eyes blinked, a lithe figure jumping up onto the pre-con wall and disappearing into the night. All this time she'd been facing off against a cat, wasting time and allowing the zom to catch up.

"Fuck," she muttered under her breath, head whipping about as she looked for an escape route.

Her eyes fell on the house whose yard she stood in, but she dismissed it. Too dangerous. She had no idea what waited inside, and the zom would follow. Doors didn't mean much to fresh infected. They were freakishly strong.

Up.

Go up.

Nadia looked around cataloging and dismissing each option as it came.

A minibus in the street; too low.

The top of a garden shed; too flimsy.

The rooftop of the nearest house; no way to reach it.

The growls were coming closer, and Nadia knew she'd be spotted soon.

Her heart thrummed in her chest, adrenaline rushing through her veins as her body tensed, gearing up for its fight or flight response. Unable to find a place to climb up, she jogged across the yard and promptly tripped over something in the dark. The fall alerted her pursuer.

The snarls increased in volume.

It was after her.

Nadia went faster, pushing her body into a sprint, but she knew she'd never last as her muscles burned with fatigue. Then her eyes fell on the carport. *The roof!*

Her eyes flicked about, landing on a small boundary wall next to it. She grabbed the top and dragged her body up onto it, right boot searching for secure footing. She got up, balancing precariously on the top with her arms windmilling for balance.

Straightening, she gripped the edge of the tin roof and pulled, ignoring the tearing pain shredding her hands. Her arms screamed in protest, and the muscles quivered with the strain. She'd never been the most athletic girl and now regretted it. The approaching sounds of the infected spurred her on, however. *I'm not on the menu tonight.*

With a shuffle, Nadia edged sideways until she was next to the nearest pole. With a determined leap, she pushed off and got her elbows over the edge. Her feet scrabbled against the pole for purchase until she was up and over. Just in time too as the zombie's fingers brushed the tip of her boot.

She collapsed onto her back, chest heaving, eyes fixed on the stars above but not seeing them. Below, the infected scratched at the pillar and screeched its anger and frustration. Not long after, a second infected showed up. Then a third. She was attracting a crowd.

Her immediate problem lay with her hands, though. It was too dark to see clearly, but she saw enough by the silvery moonlight to tell the damage was bad.

Nadia slid the rucksack from her back and rummaged inside. She rinsed both hands with a bottle of water and spent the next twenty minutes picking out shards of glass. It hurt like a bitch, and she couldn't get all of it out, especially the splinters. She bandaged the wounds with a pair of socks and swallowed a handful of painkillers. "Shit. This is an infection waiting to happen."

She lay back, using her pack as a pillow and waited for the pain to abate. Her mind whirled as she tried to think of a way out of her predicament. The roof was not the ideal place to spend the day. What she needed to treat her hands with, lay in her cellar. Besides, the sun would cook her until she resembled boiled beetroot.

The pain in her hands did not lessen. It grew worse. "I know I shouldn't do this, but…" She swallowed more pills and wrapped another pair of socks over each palm. Exhaustion dragged at her eyelids, the strain of the chase and the massive dose of medicine taking its toll.

With a sigh, Nadia curled up into a little ball. Her breath evened out, sleep claiming her tired body. Morning found her still asleep and perched precariously close to the edge of the roof.

One arm dangled down. Blood dripped down her fingers, each ruby red droplet sliding down to the tip where it swelled. It grew fat before it plopped down onto the face of the zombie below. He growled, licking up the blood as he eyed her fingers. She was so close.

Available Here
https://www.amazon.com/dp/B071J2D2DN

About the Author

South African writer and coffee addict, Baileigh Higgins, lives in the Free State with hubby and best friend Brendan and loves nothing more than lazing on the couch with pizza and a bad horror movie. Her unhealthy obsession with the end of the world has led to numerous books on the subject and a secret bunker only she knows the location of. **Visit her website to sign up for updates, freebies, and more!**

WEBSITE - **www.baileighhiggins.com**

95197802R00207

Made in the USA
Lexington, KY
05 August 2018